By

Linda P. Kozar

* * * * *

PUBLISHED BY:
Linda P. Kozar

Cover design- RomCon
Cover photo- © *konradbak - Fotolia.com*

Alligator Pear
Copyright © 2013 by Linda P. Kozar

*****

To my tireless critique partners, Joanne Hillman and Louise Looney, thank you for the many hours you invested in me. I so appreciate your encouraging words, patience and enthusiasm for this story.

To my family—we are rooted in Christ and the Crescent City. No storm can wash away our spirit and determination, nor dilute our joy.
Le Bon Temps Roulet!

To my Abba Father, I dedicate this novel to you. May it bring glory to your name!

April 1932
New Orleans, Louisiana

Prologue

Tiny feet tippy-tapped on a patch of wood floor edged by lush Persian carpet. The little girl edged her way closer to the sitting room window. Her blonde hair, tamed into fussy coils, sprang up and down with every strike. Finally, she lifted the white lace curtains and sighed.

"Philomene? Where could they be? I've been waiting for over an hour."

The housekeeper smiled back at her young charge from a wingback chair. Sleek black hair pulled into a neat chignon at the base of her neck, Philomene laid aside the doily and tatting needle and stood, smoothing her crisp grey dress and white organza apron. "Chile' be patient. Your mama and papa are drivin' from Mississip' Dat's quite a spell away from what I hear."

"If I hadn't caught the *chickenpops*, I would've gone too." She lifted a hand to scratch at a blister on her neck.

"Stop dat! You know what I tol' you 'bout scratchin' 'em. Baby, you still recoverin'. You don' need to be worryin' yoursef and gettin' all overheated."

"But I miss them." Fleur D'Hemecourt crumpled her China doll features into a dour frown as she dug the toe of her leather shoe into the thick pile of the carpet. The only child of Rene' and Eleanor D'Hemecourt, indulged and coddled according to some, her behavior often confirmed the lack of propriety and patience expected of the family name.

Philomene rested one elbow on an arm of the brocade-covered chair. "*Mon cheri,* you as impatient as the wind. I never seen a chile' so full o' bumble bees. An' please don't muss the carpet wit your shoes. It's mighty 'spensive you know. Your papa paid a pretty penny for it."

Fleur stomped her foot, exasperated. "Oh, how I hate waiting."

Philomene joined her at the window, staring out the expanse of green in front of the house. "Don' we all? Why, I had to wait mos of mah life fo' things. Waitin' in line while other folks cut's ahead--waitin' fo' buses that's too full, waitin' fo' checks to come in de mail. Now you know." She weighed her head from side to side. "Ummm Ummm. Ummm. Check's is always late, but bills always come on time. Dear heart, if I was to add up all de time I spen waitin', I'd be rich as de Queen o' Sheba."

Her blue eyes intent, Fleur shook her head. "Well I hate it."

She corrected, "Say dislike, chile' Hate is not a word for propa young ladies to speak."

Fleur crossed her arms. "I'm not a lady. I'm a little girl and that's what I aim on staying."

Philomene pulled a crisp handkerchief from her pocket and dabbed her temples, an obvious attempt to hide the smile brewing on her face. "Since you set on bein' a chile' fo' eva, look outside." She swept aside the lace curtains.

A broad swathe of bright green lawn stretched half a block long ahead of the house. The property, edged by mighty oaks, fragrant jasmine hedges, and azalea bushes laden with pink, red and white blossoms greeted the eye with an explosion of color.

"It's God's good day." She shot a backwards glance. "How kin you ignore a day like dat? Sun and birds and a blessed breeze! You should be chasin' afer butterflies or skippin' true de rose garden out back. Or sittin' in dat Chin-palace."

Fleur laughed. "Chinoiserrie, silly. You never could pronounce it right."

Philomene rested her hands on her hips, her lids narrowed together.

Recognizing the look that the family housekeeper had just about enough of her insolence, Fleur reached for Philomene's hand and brought it close to her cheek. With the prospect of her parent's upcoming travel plans this summer, it wouldn't do to have Philomene upset with her.

She purposed a slow blink of the eyes to offer a humble apology. "I'm sorry. You're right about me. I like that place. I could sit there for hours just staring at all the pretty things."

The housekeeper's face softened into a smile. "Now that's better Miz Fleur, but not because you waving them cornflower blues at me. I 'jus like it when you're propa an respectful the way a young lady should be." She reached up to brush away a few stray strands of hair from the girl's face. "Why don' you go on outside an' enjoy dis sweet sunshine? The time'll pass by fasta an' befo' you know it, you mama and papa will be home."

Fleur let out a drawn-out sigh, far longer than the first one. "Oh, all right. I'll go." But instead of moving, she pressed her lips together.

"What's wrong?"

Head lowered, the child reached into her pocket and pulled out a jumble of gold and silver necklaces. "I'll be needing Papa to untangle these for me the way he always does."

Philomene bent down to take a closer look and gasped. "Oh my. No wonder you want your papa's help. If your mama sees what you done to her jewry, she gonna spit nails. Din' he untangle those fo' you a couple weeks ago?"

Face solemn, Fleur nodded.

A ray of sun filtered through the lace curtains glinted off the glittering necklaces, settling on one in particular. The image of a silver tree, a gold cross running up the middle. She scooped the pendant and held it in the palm of her hand for a moment. "Dat one's ya mamas favorite."

"The family tree." Fleur whispered.

"The maid shook her head. "Dose' chains is so tiny. I don' know how you papa has de patience to untangle dem. I would just trow mah hands up in de air an' give up."

"But he never does." Fleur's lips curled into a tiny smile. "And Mama never stays mad. Not for long."

Philomene slipped an arm around Fleur's shoulders. "Dat's because she love you so much." She lifted the child's chin with the tips of her fingers. "But you need to promise me you gonna stay outta your mama's jew'ry box from now on."

Eyes down, the child nodded. "I promise."

Philomene smiled her approval. "Good. Now off you go."

Poised at the door, her body half in louvered shade, half in the brilliant light of day, Fleur implored. "If you see the car coming before I do or they ring you at the house, call for me, promise?"

Philomene chuckled as she picked up her doily. "A watched pot neva boils, you know." After a long pause, she looked up, eyes all a twinkle. "I promise."

Halfway across the lawn, Fleur looked first to the gnarly oak tree with her wooden swing. She loved to swing high and launch off into the soft grass. Then she looked over at the Chinoiserie, its shaded pagoda cool and inviting.

But from there, part of the driveway was hidden by a stand of huge Camellia bushes laden with deep red blossoms. And she wanted a clear view of the driveway. So she decided to head for a patch of bright clover nearer to the house. She pulled a small quilt from the clothesline, pausing a moment to draw it to her nose. Philomene told her once that clothes dried in the sweet sunshine took in all the fragrance of the day. After drawing a deep breath, Fleur decided Philomene was right. She enjoyed the scent of fresh-cut grass and gardenias and the pure, fresh smell of the sun.

She spread the quilt out on the grass, and eased back into a soft crush of green clover and closed her eyes. She imagined the silken light illuminated her eyelids into Chinese lampshades, radiating golden warmth throughout her body. Fleur cracked one eye open for a moment at the rustle and snap of the white bed sheets billowing in a sudden breeze on the line. Content in the cool shade, she turned on her side.

The smell of spring seasoned the air with the clean scent of grasses and open buds and new rain. In between the lazy whir of mosquito hawks with each rise and fall of the wind, she heard the rusty squeak of a wheelbarrow as the gardeners moved mountains of moist earth to new beds.

Fleur caught a whiff of something musty and moldering too, the scent of rotting leaves, tree bark and mosses. The gardeners liked to fill the beds with a concoction of the stuff. From snippets of conversation she'd heard around the house for the past week, the cuttings and young sprigs would go in tomorrow. The gardeners had big plans for the estate this year. That's what they'd said.

Then, faint at first, she heard the sound of a car, wheels crunching the graveled drive as it approached.

At last! She arched up on her elbows for a look.

A different car? Probably her aunt and uncle come to call again. Images immediately came to mind. Aunt Florrie, clownish hoops of red rouge on each cheek, the horrid way she prated on about herself or her sourpuss cousin Piper, but most of all that annoying titter of a laugh. Fleur's father always found a way to excuse himself from the room whenever Aunt Florrie began to laugh.

Then there was Uncle Bernard. Certainly more on the quiet side, at least some of the time—he always insisted she sit on his lap. But there was nothing comfortable about sitting so near to him. Not the warm, cheerful way she felt near papa. Thinking of her father again made her long for her parents even more. A hot tear rose and skidded down her cheek.

As more tears fell, she began to sink back into the clover, but stopped as she noticed the color of the vehicle approaching. Not her parent's sedan. Not her aunt and uncle's either. This one had a little red hat on top the hood. Fleur recognized it at once. A police car!

She recognized her aunt and uncle's sedan following the police car up the drive. Both vehicles stopped close to the house. Two officers emerged from the squad car and Uncle Bernard, Aunt Florrie and her cousin Piper from the other vehicle. Aunt Florrie's face was puffy, her eyes rimmed in red. All were silent. Fleur stood.

Though she longed to run from the side of the house to the front door, instinct kept her feet planted where she was. A dreadful shiver ran down her spine.

July 1947
New Orleans, Louisiana

Chapter One
Fever Pulse

Family and friends of the deceased gathered like black clouds before a storm. Near the gilded ironwork cross at the entrance to Saint Louis Number One, they whispered prayers, consoling one another. But discreet voices faded to reverent silence as the priest approached, followed by a young acolyte bearing a crucifix.

Breathless and flustered, Fleur D'Hemecourt paused to smooth her dress and hair, tousled from the hurry-scurry carriage dash. Young and attractive, her honey-hued curls bounced along the curve of her elegant shoulders as she inched ahead to take her place with the immediate family. But all heads turned in response to the sudden arrival of the hearse, its roof festooned with a pleasing array of saffron-colored lilies, red roses and fragrant jasmine.

Men removed their hats as the hearse came to a stop. Some flicked lit cigarettes to the ground and shuffled them out. But one man, face half-hidden under a gray hat, took a few lingered puffs before snuffing his out against the iron fence, showering red ash on the grass below. When he removed his hat, she noticed a mat of thin hair Brill-creamed to a high gloss. His eyes, small and black, focused on hers, but she turned to avert his gaze, focusing her attention on the hearse instead. No need to encourage the man.

Six pallbearers drew near. The hearse driver in a black suit and cap stepped out and patted the ebony hood. "It's a Eureka three-way loader. Just acquired it." Pulling a handkerchief from his breast pocket he polished the spot he'd just touched. "We can unload from either side or the back."

The funeral director emerged solemn-faced from the passenger door, shot a frosty glance toward the driver and motioned to the pallbearers. "Gentlemen, if you would approach the right side of the car please." At that, the driver snapped to attention. With the flick of a lever, the right side of it rose up, revealing the dark mahogany casket within. The pallbearers clasped the handles, lifted and took a few asynchronous steps before repositioning the load at the funeral director's instruction.

Then, with spider-like unison, their faces barely masking the strain, the six men bearing the casket stood behind the priest. The immediate family fell in behind—Florrie's husband, Uncle Bernard and Piper, her cousin, who caught Fleur's eye and motioned for her to join them. The priest opened a small prayer book and began to recite in Latin, the cloud of mourners followed as he led the way forward, some in pairs leaning in grief upon one another, others alone.

"Domine Iesu, dimitte nobis debita nostra, salva nos ab igne inferiori . . . "

Fleur started forward, but to her surprise walked out of her right shoe. In the time it took to slip it back on, dozens of people had already joined the procession. She waited for an opening and blended into the line. She tried to work her way through the crowd and managed to fall in behind her Aunt Babette, but it was no use. There were too many people in front of her and the narrow path between tombs made it next to impossible to forge ahead.

After a few hapless attempts, she lifted a dainty arm to shield her eyes, blinded by the brightness of the noonday sun. She caught a glimpse of Piper's hat.

But for the exquisite ceiling frescoes in the St. Louis Cathedral, she would have been on time. When the service concluded, she'd lingered behind to admire the artistry and as usual, lost all track of time.

" . . . perduc in caelum omnes animas, praesertim eas, quae misericordiae tuae maxime indigent."

Though Latin was not her strong suit, she listened intently to the priest as he read and managed to remember a rough translation from childhood prayers. "Jesus, forgive our sins, save us from the fires of hell: lead all souls to heaven, especially those who are most in need of your mercy." Prayers for Aunt Florrie--could there be any doubt as to her destination?

Sheathed in a simple black dress, she tugged at both sides of the flared collar to widen it, glad that polished muslin breathed well in the humidity. Years of living in a cold climate had done little to help reacclimate her for the semi-tropical heat. She even felt a twinge of pity for all the men in wool suits, especially the pallbearers.

She began to follow the sad solemn line of family and friends with her gaze, connecting names with faces and faces with memories. But her vision soon settled on the vibrant brilliance of the priest's garments. As the procession veered to the right, she had a better view of his ornate robes. Clothed in fine linens embroidered with gilded gospel images—a cross, a chalice, a tree--his measured steps trailed the way to the family tomb.

The images of the tree and the cross somehow brought to mind her mother's favorite pendant. Fleur reached up to clutch the chain at her neck. Cast in gold, it depicted the tree of life, its trunk fashioned into a small cross. Her mother, a skilled artisan, had designed it herself. She would be proud to see Fleur wearing the cross, but disappointed at the lack of faith it inspired in her. How had mama said it? "Remember my dear ma *fifille*, our family tree is rooted in Christ."

But so far her interest in God was limited to the masterful artistry she found in churches--stained glass masterpieces, sculptures in marble or cast in bronze, ceiling frescoes, altar crosses.

Attracted by movement in the corner of her eye, she spotted the iridescent gleam of mosquito hawks hovering low to the ground, diaphanous wings emitting the faintest whir. Outside of New Orleans people called them dragonflies.

A whiff of cologne sailed through the air, likely patchouli, cheap, plentiful and vile. In the middle of a sudden sneeze, she missed a step on the uneven brick path and her right foot sank to the base of her best pair of shoes, her Greenbelts, no less, in a mire of clay.

Yet another shoe catastrophe! With a flick of her ankle, she shook free. One side of her heel now caked in mud, or rather clay. She let out a sigh, frustrated at the recent turn of events in her life. As if to make matters worse, the smell of the horrid cologne lingered in the hot, humid air.

Insufferable southern summers! She'd planned to move back to New Orleans after graduating, but not until autumn, and only on a temporary basis. She'd receive a small inheritance within the year—as soon as she turned twenty-one. Finishing the season in

New York would have suited her just fine, but after receiving the telegram about Aunt Florrie's unstable condition, her plans had changed.

Tiny rivulets of perspiration began to trickle from her temples down her neck. She dabbed at the moisture with the small linen handkerchief in her hand and turned her attention to the surroundings--anything to take her mind off the heat, the cologne, death and dying. She dreaded seeing her parent's tomb. Memories of that day still shadowed her.

Before her, rows of aboveground tombs plastered white, gleamed in the brightness of the day. The yawning silence broken by brief sighs of grief muffled by lace handkerchiefs or stoic coughs. Little white houses, all in a pretty row . . .

Fresh flowers cascaded from stone vases in front of some—tiger lilies, fern fronds, red roses, bright orange hibiscus, fragrant gardenias and pale pink camellias; wilted petals rolling together in cigar shapes, perfuming the still air. And the stark silhouettes of withered, utterly desiccated blooms in others.

But native blossoms paid respect as well. Morning glories curlicued slithering vines from tree to tomb, violet blooms dotting the slender stalks. Angel's trumpets twined arches between tombs, heralding visitors, and brilliant yellow railroad daisies peeked from cracks and chinks in the plastered walls—even on the flat roofs. A tropical jungle, creeping, covering, reclaiming . . .

The sight of crude graffiti on a certain tomb sent an icy shiver up her spine. Crossmarks in threes scrawled across the door in red, the color of dried blood. Voodoo. Petitions to Marie Laveau for vengeance, riches, love.

Shards of red brick below the tomb door revealed the source material. Red brick dust. A sigh of relief escaped her lips. But as she walked on, she noticed other tombs further vandalized, gaped open, the brownish bones of the dead visible to all who passed.

Ahead, Uncle Bernard's younger sister Babette, stout as a railroad trestle, made the sign of the cross as they passed the desecrated tombs, her left hand clenched around the garnet rosary she carried. Her mumbled petitions dissipated at once in the heaviness of afternoon heat--the distant prayers of the priest, now a mere echo of sound.

Sister to her late father and present guardian, Uncle Bernard, Babette spent most of her time in church and chapel, lighting candles, her prayers and petitions a means of making herself useful. A spinster, doomed to a solitary life. Fleur had heard the story time and again. While still in her teens, Babette aspired to be a nun but was refused permission to enter the convent by her father. No matter. She seemed to have chosen the austere life, albeit in a roundabout way.

Fleur strained to hear the prayers of the priest beyond a sound in her head—a strange whir, joined by the pound of her heart. Her legs began to wobble and give way. The stink of cologne mixed with the cloying scent of floral decay. She blinked, trying to steady, to focus on tombs now gone opaque. Dizzy. The sights and scenes washed in white. Her legs refused to move. She followed the procession with her ears--footsteps, sobs.

She wilted, hand over knee. By force of will, she struggled to rise to her feet only to collapse in a dazed heap, eyes wide open. At once, a pair of strong hands grasped her waist and shoulder. Raised to a seated position, her back supported by strong arms, she gazed wide-eyed into a somewhat familiar face.

"I saw you fall. Are you all right? Should I send for an ambulance?" A face, strangely familiar, hovered above hers but soon blurred into a pool of watercolors.

She shook her head, but felt as if she were doing so in slow motion.

" . . . didn't eat today."

"I see. You must be quite distraught. But in this heat, it's not advisable to pass on a meal." His eyes came into focus, eyes filled with sincere concern, yet they illuminated recognition.

"You're Fleur D'Hemecourt, aren't you?" A smile widened across his jaw line. "Why, it's been years since I've seen you. In fact, you were just a child the last time we met. Are you all right?"

"Fleur, how are you dear?" Aunt Babette's round rosy face intruded, the garnet rosary beads cascading from her wrist.

She tried to nod. But she wasn't sure how to respond. The procession, now in complete disorder, every eye strained to see what had happened. She closed her eyes and wished she were invisible. Muted voices and whispers hemmed in on her.

"Miss D'Hemecourt?" he asked.

"I-I'm fine." Though she still felt a bit faint, she managed to look up and meet his gaze. Louis Russo. A face from her childhood memories, the object of her one and only childhood crush, forever etched in her mind. Her first sight of him was from the vantage point of her swing under the wide oak tree. He'd arrived at the house with his parents for a summer picnic.

Wearing a short-sleeved green and white-checkered shirt with gray pants and a matching jacket, though he carried it on his arm in deference to the heat. Tall for his age, she remembered his dark hair and dashing looks. Thereafter, her heart beat faster at the sight of him, at the very mention of his name. Though the two had never spoken a word to one another, she'd imagined many a conversation with him.

She swallowed hard. "I remember you well." She corrected herself. "As well."

Soon surrounded by a small crowd, she repeated that assurance over and again, hoping they would move on so she could breathe. "Please." She latched onto her aunt's hand, surprised at the softness of her skin. "Please send them on. I don't want to be the cause of any interruption."

The man nodded, "Don't worry, I'll take care of her."

Her jaw set in a determined square Aunt Babette tilted her head forward and stood up straight. She noticed her aunt pull at a few sleeves. "Hurry along everyone. Fleur is fine."

Fleur watched as he waved the stragglers away with patient determination, then helped her stand. "Are you all right now?" An expression of concern washed across his face.

Her lips quivered, though she tried to smile. "I'm fine, I believe. Thank you ever so—so much." She looked around, longed for an open space, away from the wag of tongues and judgment, far from whispers and hushed conspiratorial tones. To her relief, concern and curiosity sated for the moment or perhaps by the influence of the two, the line of mourners began to move again.

"…she's always been an odd one. . ."

A hot sting rose to her eyes, but she forced her emotions back. His strong arms circled and led her a short distance away from the other mourners where he lowered her to a seat on the stoop of a large tomb. Squatted next to her, brows in a cozy frown, he examined her for injuries.

She followed his stare and noticed two small streams of blood rolling down her shins.

"May I?" He looked up for permission to lift the hem of her dress. "I know a bit about first aid. Every soldier does. . .did." He reached in his suit pocket, then pant's pockets as if searching for something.

"You fought in the war?"

He nodded, but his expression changed for a moment. She watched his lips move as if to speak. "I remember now. I gave my handkerchief to a woman. She was crying and had forgotten to bring one."

She smiled. "I seem to have forgotten mine as well."

"Hmmm, you've done a job of it. Knees skinned, wrists slightly scraped, and your nylons are ripped to shreds. Other than that, Miss D'Hemecourt, how do you feel?"

The realization hit her as he spoke. "Oh no."

"What is it?"

"My nylons." Though the war was over, nylons were still hard to come by. It took her six months and far too much money to finally find a decent pair—now in shreds.

"Pardon me? All that hubbub about nylons?" He shook his head. "You had me worried."

"If you knew how I'd scrimped and saved . . . "

Before she could finish, an elderly woman in a dark grey dress with a lace collar approached and stretched out a thin hand to the young man. "Here son, I don't need it, and take this too."

He reached for the linen handkerchief and a small bottle of orange water cologne. Fleur caught a glimpse of the monogram "AE" before she pressed it into his palm.

"Are you certain, Ma'am?" he asked unscrewing the small cap on the bottle and sniffing its contents.

She smiled, revealing an accordion of rice paper skin under the shade of a wide-brimmed black hat. "I've cried my share of tears in this world. No need for more. Besides, it's the least I can do." Frayed silk hair, white as milkweed escaped from the confines of her hat, faint wisps loose about her ears. Gray eyes, surely striking in her youth, now sunken and rheumy, widened.

The woman gestured toward the family mausoleum ahead. Fleur dreaded seeing her parent's names carved in the rose granite.

"Rene' D'Hemecourt, Eleanor D'Hemecourt—died April 21, 1932."

The woman continued. "You probably don't remember me, but your aunt and I were dear friends. I knew your parents as well. Lovely couple. I was sad to see them taken so soon from this world."

Fleur blinked, trying hard to remember, thoughts and memories boiling madly. "Your face is familiar to me. Maybe I've seen you in photographs."

"Bless you, child. I do hope you feel better soon." She cast a sorrowful glance, and turned to rejoin the others, leaving a pleasant resonance of orange water as she passed. Better than the awful cologne she's been subjected to earlier.

A sudden memory of the orange water fragrance filtered through her mind--a flash of two women talking, or was it arguing? The woman and Aunt Florrie! She followed her sleight shape as she walked away. Why would they argue? And what were they arguing about? What was her name?

As if he'd read her thoughts, Louis called out to the elderly woman. "Oh, Ma'am, I didn't get your name."

The woman held her head up straight when she answered. "Miss Elliot. Adelaide Elliot. And yours, young man?" She motioned toward her head. "My memory . . . "

"Louis Russo." He waved at her and smiled, as he soaked the handkerchief with cologne and began dabbing at Fleur's wounds. Bright red splotches soon dotted the pure white of the linen.

"This handkerchief looks expensive. I hate to use it, but I'll have it cleaned and pressed and return it to her." He smiled. "This stuff isn't exactly rubbing alcohol, but it has enough in it to do a decent job of disinfecting your wounds. And your knees aren't as bad as they look, you know. Though I'm guessing they will be sore for a few days at least."

Thoughts of the past vanished in his presence. Her knees began to sting as he applied the cologne, but she hardly noticed. Her heart pounded. He's just a man, the mere object of a childish crush. Louis Russo, at my side? She flinched at the thought and decided to focus on a clutch of wisteria wrapped around the tomb, branches intertwined like a woven basket. The fragrant blossoms reminded her of purple grapes. She pressed a cluster in her hands. Soft as velvet. *Am I dreaming?*

"Sorry, I know this hurts. Do you know the woman?"

She shook her curls and stared back at him as if for the first time. "I'm not certain. I was trying to recall if I'd seen her before." Fleur stole a glance his way again--dark, chocolat-y waves of hair, eyes sincere and brown, lashes feathery. *Darling, truly darling.*

"Doing all right?" he asked, concern in his eyes.

"I'm fine. Only a bit overheated and undernourished, thank you." She fanned herself with her hand. "Is it particularly warm today, or am I the only one who thinks so?"

He glanced up at the sky and loosened the dark patterned silk tie around his neck. "The heat and humidity are most likely why you fainted. It's always hottest before a summer storm. See those clouds?" He drew closer and pointed over her head. The presence of him so near made her breathless. But she lingered on his eyes, and turned to see where he pointed. Billowing mountains from the west, gloomy and full, traveled the speed of pachyderms--or seemed to.

"A bad one, do you think?"

Louis nodded. "Not so bad. Just your garden variety storm."

She shrugged. "Will it rain soon?"

He glanced off to the left, then back to her. "Oh, in about an hour I guess; maybe less. Probably just enough time for us to finish paying our respects."

He paused, face flushed. "How callous of me! I honestly didn't mean for it to come out that way. She's your aunt, isn't she?"

"Don't be embarrassed. You didn't offend me. Aunt Florrie was ill for quite a long time. To tell you the truth, it was more of a relief for the family—an end to her suffering. Is that awful for me to say?"

Silence hung between them until he spoke, crashing into it with a strong voice. "Not in my opinion. I've seen a lot of suffering. Too much." His brows came together for a moment, as if dredging unpleasant thoughts.

He stood. "Do you feel up to walking now Miss D'Hemecourt? The last person in line passed us. We should catch up." He tucked the handkerchief into his breast pocket.

"Yes, I think so." She flashed him a reassuring smile.

Louis fastened his grip on her arm and shoulder and placed the other around her waist. She felt she would swoon at his touch, but managed to keep what was left of her composure. This is a funeral procession, not a USO dance.

As they made their way slowly along the uneven path, Fleur caught his eye. "Mr. Russo, thank you for helping me. Frankly, I don't know what I'd do if you hadn't come to my rescue."

"It's all in a days work for a knight-in-shining-armor."

A smile crept across her face. Louis had a way about him, an easy charm. The man was even better than she'd imagined he would be.

By the time they caught up, the priest was almost done. He made the sign of the cross and the cemetery attendants lifted the polished mahogany coffin above their heads. A deep guttural wailing began--her uncle, the loudest of all.

A short, squatty man with receding hair dyed an unnatural black, and watery brown eyes even under normal circumstances, he paused to stare at Fleur, then covered his face in his hands. His only daughter, Piper stood by his side. But the only expression on her face was the disapproval she glared at Fleur.

Surrounded by cousins, in-laws and friends, Bernard sank to a tomb step, head bowed, an agony of bereavement across his face.

A few tears rose without warning, and in spite of her resistance, brimmed from her eyes and down her cheeks. Surely he must have loved her. Wasn't there a bit of sorrow--a shred of grief? She studied her uncle's features between sobs. To the best of her recollection, she'd never seen him cry. She thought back to her parents' funeral. Were there tears then?

She was five-years-old when it happened and the tears flowed easily, but in the years since, emotions rationed out of her in stingy portions. Fleur blinked back the mounting sea, and leaned against the corner of a smaller tomb, her hand clasping the corner of the rough-hewn stone. She took a deep, lingering breath.

Focus on anything other than this. She began to read the words chiseled on the tomb her body was pressed against.

Beatrice Anne Robichaux 1792-1792
"Sweet Child of Heaven."

She brushed her fingertips over the inscription. A newborn. Probably died of yellow fever. A lonely echo of grief filled her heart. She'd buried her own parents. How much harder must it have been for parents to bury a child!

Louis's hand quietly brushed across the inscription and touched hers, returning her startled expression with a look of earnest concern. He must have seen the anguish on her face.

Grim faced attendants began sliding the coffin into the tomb, accompanied by the sounds of wood and stone, scraping against one another. Aunt Florrie, home at last. Her bones at rest with those of Fleur's parents, now surely reduced to dust and mere fragments.

The monotone voice of the priest repeated the words he knew so well, "…ashes to ashes, dust to dust." The last words as he sprinkled a handful, but just as he did, a sudden gust of wind caught and scattered the earth to the air. Leaves in the ornamental trees began to flutter like flags in a used car lot. Aunt Babette's black cloche' hat lifted and blew off and rolled like a square tire down the corridor of tombs before the funeral director caught it, a triumphant grin on an otherwise dour face.

In spite of the wind, the square alabaster door was hoisted up and fitted into place, and sealed. The inscription carved in anticipation of her death, added to the previous names. Aunt Florrie had been sick for a very long time indeed. Time enough to prepare. Time enough to wait. Time enough to die.

Chapter Two
Alabaster Doors

Though Fleur was clearly able to stand on her own, he slipped an arm around her waist. "I should see you to your car. You may feel faint again or your knees might give way." He braced himself against the wind. "Besides, the storm . . ."

Fleur placed her hand across his tie. "Mr. Russo, I don't have a car."

"And thank you, but I don't want to leave just yet."

An ache rose in her throat. Not that she'd miss her aunt much. The funeral stirred up the silt of painful memories, thoughts of her parents, of her childhood of . . .

She turned to wipe a tear away.

"I'd offer you a handkerchief, but I'm afraid this one is soiled. I neglected to bring one of my own today." She caught a glimpse of it balled up in his hand. The scent of orange water drifted out.

A deep sob prevented her from answering.

The sunshine sifted in and out, as clouds positioned above and gusts of wind whistled between the tombs. She noticed distant relatives and family friends—women wailing and men swiping at tears with their sleeves.

Some women gathered to arrange flowers in the urn vase. Petunias. Aunt Florrie's favorite. Mrs. Elliott, her aunt's mysterious friend, added a small bouquet of pink camellia's, another, one perfect Magnolia, still another, a pink Peony. Each adding one perfect blossom as was the D'Hemecourt custom—a bouquet garni of honor for the deceased.

A little boy of about four approached, a bouquet caught in the stranglehold of his tiny fist, Sweet Peas and Railroad Daisies. He offered the wilted stems.

Cousin Collette's son! Fleur barely recognized Rusty with his hair combed back. They lived in the Quarter in a tiny apartment near her low rent artist's flat on Royal Street. The few times she'd seen him since her unexpected move back to New Orleans, the freckle-faced boy had been dressed in overalls or ragtag outfits, covered head to toe in dirt—a boy through and through.

Though still a bit shaky, she kneeled down to his level. "Hiya Rusty."

The boy smiled back, revealing gaps.

"Goodness, I see you've lost some of your teeth."

The boy nodded, blue eyes lackluster.

"Did you put them under your pillow for the tooth fairy?"

His bright eyes glazed. The child looked away for a moment.

"What's wrong? Didn't the tooth fairy bring you something?"

He shook his head, wiping away a tear. "Mama says I'm a bad boy 'an the tooth fairy ain't bringing me nothin'."

Instantly, Louis was next to her. "Rusty, hello, my name is Mister Russo and I'm an attorney. I regret to inform you that the tooth fairy's wings got tangled up in a willow tree on the way to your house. She authorized me to give you this. He held out a crisp dollar bill.

The boy's eyes lit up. "Wow." He reached out to grasp the money and held it in his hands, staring. "Can I keep it?"

"Sure you can." Louis smiled. "And do you know what else the tooth fairy told me to tell you?"

"No." he said, eyes wide. He swallowed hard.

"She told me to say you're a good boy." Louis winked. "At least some of the time."Collette approached, her voice smoke-ravaged, raspy. She walked past Rusty and focused her attention on Fleur, who stretched to her feet with difficulty.

"I saw you fall. Are you okay?" Before she could answer, the woman continued. "My, your pretty, even with bloody, skinned knees. I never took you for a tomboy."

"You noticed my fall?" She stared down at her knees draped by the hem of her dress but for the wind, then looked toward Louis. "Mr. Russo, this is Collete LeBlanc. We're cousins. Second cousins."

"I'm serious.' Collette went on, "Your skin is so dreamy and that hair…" She reached out to 'pet' Fleur's head. Where did you ever get all those curls?"

Fleur stiffened at the woman's touch.

Collette ignored her reaction and turned to Louis, her manner coquetish. "You look familiar."

He smiled. "You've probably seen me at the D'Hemecourt house on occasion. My parents used to visit sometimes when I was younger—before we moved to Baton Rouge."

She snapped her fingers. "Dat's where I've seen you, at the house. Dat's it. " She brushed a hand as if to touch his chin. "So handsome."

Collette then turned to Fleur. "What a lucky girl to have a man who looks like dat. Why, if my old man had looked like him, I'da kep him around longer, in spite o' all the other skirts he chases."

"An' such a beauty. Turned some heads even den. When we was little I was always envious of her natural curls and those Cupid's bow lips o' hers." She puckered her lips into an exaggerated imitation. "She never had to put her hair up in pin curls like the rest of us. My hair was always stick-straight and my lips thin as an old coat. Some gals have all the luck."

Collette took a step forward and tapped Louis on the chest with her index finger, "So-o-o, what brings you to the funeral? You with Fleur or paying your respects?"

He shook his head. "As intriguing as that thought is," he winked, "I'm actually here both as a friend of the family and for professional reasons."

"Professional reasons? You dey lawyer?" she asked wide-eyed.

"Pardon me?"

She pointed at him. "You dey attorney?"

"No, I'm with the firm that represents the family."

"That's nice. But listen, maybe since you work wit dem other pencil heads, you know what's in da will," she cut in.

Taken aback by her directness, Louis swallowed hard. "Pardon me?"

Collette tapped his chest again and he responded by stepping backwards. "You know what's in Florrie's will. She had a new one made before she died. Der's a rumor going round dat we all supposed to get somethin'."

Louis crossed his hands over his chest. "Madam, the contents of a will is privileged information and, with all due respect. . ."

"C'mon." Eyes open wide, Collette grasped his wrist, "I won't tell noone. I really need to know."

He stiffened and stood straight. "Madam, I would not reveal so much as a comma or period to you or anyone else out of turn."

Surprised at a man willing to uphold his integrity in the face of such a bully, her heart warmed even more towards him. But she knew Collette wasn't one to give up on things.

Her cousin stepped forward further still, until she was just inches away from Louis. Her face, a maudlin attempt at sophistication—with lipstick smeared above and under her thin lips and powder caked over every inch of her weathered complexion.

"Tell me what you know." Her eyes narrowed to deep slits. "C'mon. Like I said, I won't tell nobody. I-I just need to know cause I-we could really use the money. My old man, don't send us money when he's supposed to. Truth is--he's a real deadbeat."

Louis's face softened, but he remained firm. "I'm sorry for your situation, but I can not and will not compromise on this issue."

The wind whipped with renewed vigor between the tombs, stronger than before. A shiver rippled through Fleur, a result of the cloud-imposed shade. She drew her arms to her shoulders. "Mr. Russo, I really should put something on my knees. They're starting to—to tighten up."

The relief in his face evident, he turned away from the persistent woman. "Of course." He reached for her arm. "Will you excuse us, Mrs. LeBlanc? It was a pleasure, uh, meeting you."

They managed to maneuver past her stony gaze. With their backs to her, the woman uttered a shrill whistle. Louis and Fleur looked back. Hands on her ample hips, Collette threatened. "I'm not done with you yet, Mist'a."

They glanced at each other, then back to her. Leaves, sticks and dust stirred by the wind, began to rustle in circles and gusts. Collette swiveled and stomped over the uneven path to retrieve her son and hasten back to the limousine with the others.

"We should put some pep in our step in case she makes good on that threat. Collette's a real pill," Fleur added.

"Thanks for the warning." He clutched her arm closer and winked. "Are your knees really starting to stiffen up? If you aren't keen on riding in the limosine with your cousin, I don't mind driving you home. That's where people are going afterward, isn't it?"

Her knees were in truth, beginning to feel weak, but it had nothing to do with her injury. Still, she summoned the boldness to speak. "I came by carriage from the cathedral."

"Really?"

She paused. The words seemed to stumble out. "I fell behind and couldn't hail a taxi for the life of me. To be honest, my knees only sting a little, but I'd be a fool to turn down a ride in this weather."

He responded by squeezing her hand. "Good."

Relieved, she added, "We could sit in the Chinoiserie and talk—that is, if the rain holds off."

"I doubt it will," his comment nearly drowned out as a menacing jolt of thunder rolled across the sky. A veil of ominous darkness fell over the cemetery as people scrambled to vehicles. Fleur and Louis quickened their steps as he led the way.

He raised his voice in competition with another roll of thunder. "Miss D'Hemecourt, would you consider dining with me at Antoine's some time?"

"Well I . . . " She strained to hear as another jolt of thunder vibrated. She sidestepped a loose brick on the path. Stray Wisteria blossoms surfed past them on the rising wind.

Passing by a large tomb, the noise shielded for the moment, he apologized. "I don't know what I was thinking—asking you out. I'm losing all sense of propriety."

"I can't hear . . . " A sense of urgency in the air, she looked about. Tiny pinpricks up her spine warned her of something more ominous. She felt as if they were being watched. The wind whipped fearsome gusts forward, shaking ornamental trees, chasing blossoms and twigs down the uneven cobbles.

He raised his voice. "I'll give you a ride. Perhaps you can freshen up at the house, maybe even put some Mercurochrome on those sad knees of yours."

They reached the car before she answered. Pitching her voice louder she responded. "Mr. Russo, I accept your gracious offer to dine at Antoine's some time in the future. And, I'm not sure my sad knees need Mercurochrome. A skilled medic took care of me. Gifted, even."

His eyes twinkled in response. As Louis unlocked the black sedan, a flash of lightening seared the sky, revealing a dark silhouette, frozen for a moment against a gray tomb. But with the next flash of lightening, the shadow was gone.

She drew her arms up round her shoulders, a tremble tingling through her body. Her mind playing tricks, that's all.

A few tentative drops began to dot the ground. He opened the passenger door for her and clanked it shut, then sprinted round the front of the car. As he climbed into the driver's seat, the rain began to pour down in shear curtains. She drew her arms close around as a shiver ran through her body.

When the sedan was halfway down Basin Street, Fleur looked in the rearview mirror and noticed steam rising from the crooked brick pavers, ghost-dancing off the rooftops of the living and the little white houses of the dead. And she wondered--about doors that open in life. And those better left closed.

Chapter Three
The Chinoiserie

    The home on St. Charles Avenue near Audubon Park, a sprawling Louisiana manse, encompassed the property along its borders as well. Over a hundred years old, built of sturdy cedar wood tempered in the damp muck of swamp and marsh, there were ample windows on all sides. Verandas on both the first and second floors coiled round the structure and a huge attic suite with a widow's walk on top. In fact, the home was three stories if one counted the attic, which boasted four enormous dormer windows on the north, south, east and west to take full advantage of the cross winds. When all the drapes were drawn on the lower floors in the evening and the lights on in the attic suite, visitors often commented that the home resembled an owl—much to the chagrin of Bernard and Florrie D'Hemecourt.
    The rooms, grand and generous, featured high ceilings, wooden floors that creaked in certain spots, marble fireplaces throughout and a brand new modern kitchen, as Fleur discovered the day she returned.
    The original kitchen had been in a separate building in back of the house for safety from the threat of fire, and because it kept the main house cooler in the savage heat of summer. The servants, accustomed to numerous trips bearing silver trays of steaming food to the dining room in the main house for all family meals, happily adjusted to the shorter trek from indoor kitchen to dining room.
    In addition to the installation of a modern kitchen, Bernard and Florence had commissioned an ornate remodel on the Chinoiserie—a gazebo and elaborate guesthouse designed by Rene' and Eleanor. The guesthouse skirted the very edge of the property, a beautiful spot bordering the park, yet hidden from the street by a thick wall of bamboo, bushes and a canopy of wisteria. The gardeners revitalized the ornamental rose garden around the gazebo as well. Though gazebo hardly described the architectural oddity, the topic of many a whispered conversation over the years.
    The burial concluded, people began to arrive for the private reception, though the thunderstorm hovered dark and dense over the Vieux Carre'. Beyond the bounds of the Quarter, prongs of intense sunlight dappled the streets through dense cloud cover. .

Louis drove along the winding driveway and parked to the side. It was obvious the rain hadn't touched this part of town yet. However, a rumble of deep thunder threatened to make good on that possibility.

As Louis and Fleur walked to the main house, the brick-lined path flanked by irises and tiger lilies, he stopped to admire the rose garden until his eyes set on the structure behind it. His hand reached for hers and grasped. His other hand found the small of her back.

His touch caused a curious flutter in her heart but she followed his lead towards the structure.

"Is that what you were talking about?" He pointed. "Do you mind?"

She shook her head and swallowed hard. He helped her hop over several miniature gardenia bushes and an expanse of lush lawn to reach the red brick path leading up to it. From there was a clear view of the elaborate pavilion.

Louis gasped.

"Well, what do you think of it—I mean, of the Chinoiserie?" she asked.

He pressed his palms to his temples in disbelief. "I've heard of it. I'm not sure what a Chin-whatever it is—is, but I believe I like it so far. Could we see more?"

"Shin-wuh-sir-eee. And, of course we can see more. I find it hard to believe that you've never seen it though. You've been to the house before."

As they approached the rose garden, the fragrance of tea roses ended their conversation for the moment. He took a deep breath, the perfume of so many petals overwhelming intoxicating. He stopped and grasped her other hand as well, pausing to admire her beauty, skin pale and smooth as a rose petal, light blue eyes, a bob of honeyed curls.

"I-I did hear of it," he waved at the gazebo-like structure, "but never had the opportunity while visiting your aunt and uncle's home."

She interrupted. "Actually—well—it's my home. The estate belonged to my parents and when they died my aunt and uncle became my guardians."

He paused, eyes frozen on hers. "You must be nearing the age of twenty-one?"

Fleur's eyes opened wide. "My, my, Mr. Russo. Guessing a girl's age? You *are* losing all sense of propriety."

Sheepish, his face flushed. "The attorney in me spoke out of turn. I seem to be batting a thousand today. Please forgive me."

She smiled. "Consider yourself forgiven."

"Thank you."

He clasped his hands together. "Now, as I was saying, before I put my foot in my mouth, that is, I've been to," he extended an arm, "your home on more than one occasion through the years. However, I invariably tagged along with my father who spent the bulk of those visits enveloped in a cloud of cigar smoke in the study. Which is where I learned to talk politics with stuffy old men."

"I hope I'm better company than a room full of stuffy old men."

He leaned in closer. "My dear Fleur," he bowed, "I would be more than glad to trade them all in for but a glimpse of you, skinned knees and all."

She wagged her finger. "Shame on you for making light of my poor knees. They're going to be stiff for a full week at least, and I'll certainly look a sight longer than that."

Fleur took a step toward the gazebo. "I suppose you'll want to know what a Chinoiserie is."

"That would be helpful. Enlighten me, please."

"Well then, she made a sweeping gesture. "Let's have a look inside."

Constructed in the shape of an outdoor pagoda, the open frame in fragrant cedar wood, the interior was hand painted in whimsical style. Mandarins carrying flower parasols crossed cobweb bridges in lush mountain climes. Monkeys hung askew from fairyland borders, and fanciful vegetation flourished around delicate pleasure pavilions in bamboo.

Eyes wide, he strolled, examining texture and shape with his hands, brushing fingers along walls and lacquered furniture. "How delightful Miss D'Hem. . .may I be so forward as to call you by your first name, Fleur?"

"Of course, Louis." Warmth ran up her cheeks as she said his name.

He circled the room taking in the details. "Extraordinary."

"This is one instance where my degree in art comes in handy." She sank into a black lacquered chair cushioned in embroidered silk and brushed a stray curl away from her face. "A picayune explanation, just for you." She smiled. "The Chinoiserie came from an artistic style that originated in Europe. It's rather nice, don't you think?"

Eyes focused on her, he nodded.

"It reached its peak around the middle of the eighteenth century and from there, found it's way to Rococo.'

"Rococo? Is that some sort of chocolate beverage like Ovaltine? Sounds delicious."

She decided to ignore his remark and continue. "...a style heavily influenced by the Chinese, but not a realistic depiction of the country or culture. It borrows a fanciful imagery of an--of an imaginary China."

He held up a dish to examine it and frowned. "Is this real or imaginary?"

She smirked.

"No really, is this metal?"

A merry laugh escaped as she answered. "You look funny when you frown. And the answer is, yes and no."

"Well, you look funny when you make faces. What kind of answer is that? Yes and no?"

Fleur stifled a smile. "That piece is an example of faience, fine tin-glazed earthenware. The potter adds oxide of tin to the slip of a lead glaze. I don't want to bore you with more details. But it is beautiful."

He nodded and carefully placed the dish back on the small table where he had found it. "This place is like a museum."

"A pleasure pavilion."

"Sounds sinful," he smirked.

"Hardly--it's a place to loll about, a cool place to withdraw from the summer heat and have a spot of tea and conversation. I've always loved it."

He smiled and sat into a chair opposite her, spreading an arm comfortably to the side. "I can see why." Louis leaned forward and motioned for her to do so as well.

Her stomach felt as if a hundred hummingbirds were zipping about.

"Tell me," he asked, "has anyone ever been married here? All the roses and latticework remind me of a bridal bower." He stared straight into her eyes. She looked away, heart beating fast in response.

"No, not that I can recall." She found it hard to swallow.

"Did I hear something about marriage?" Piper D'Hemecourt stood at the archway.

Startled by her sudden entrance, they turned. Uncle Bernard's daughter stood, a chic' silhouette against the rising clouds behind, still as a Grecian statue. Sleek black hair smoothed into a tight bun, she wore a charcoal gray stockinet dress with a small black lace collar at the neck. An old maid, at the age of twenty-six, she presented quite an enigma in social circles. A beauty from a young age, she turned away suitor after suitor until they stopped beating a path to the house. Her skin was a shade pale and drawn today however, and her light green eyes betrayed a rind of grief. "I thought I saw you two head this way."

"Oh, hello Piper. How are you?"

With a graceful stride, Piper leaned to embrace Fleur.

"You look beautiful as always my dear, but. . ." she glanced at Fleur's knees made visible from her repose on the settee. "Whatever happened? My, you're a sight."

Fleur glanced down. "I fell. . ."

"More like collapsed." Louis finished. "She collapsed from the heat because she hadn't eaten anything for breakfast."

Piper rocked her index finger. "You need to take better care of yourself, Little Miss." She craned her neck over Fleur's shoulder to speak to Louis. "I noticed the two of you today."

"Piper, I'm so sorry. I tried to catch up with you and uncle, but my shoe caught in the mud and then I fainted. Mr. Russo, came to my rescue and we became reacquainted."

Fleur and Louis exchanged glances.

"I see. How fortunate for you that Louis was there." Piper nodded towards the man. "Keep your eye on this one, my dear. He'll steal your heart away."

Fleur lowered her eyes, a flush rising to her cheeks.

He squinted, the sting of her remark visible on his face.

Piper reached for Fleur's hand. "Oh, by the way, Father's been asking for you. I hate to break this little reunion up, but would you mind? He's in such a state with mother's passing."

The approach of the storm, heralded by a waltz of dead leaves across the grass, rumbled with ominous intent.

"Oh?" Fleur paused. "What does he want to talk to me about? Do you know?"

"I'm sure it has to do with mother's wishes, but I can't say more."

Fleur swallowed, her throat constricted. "Yes, of course. I'll go right away." As she stepped down onto the soft grass, her eyes shifted to Louis. "If you'll excuse me?"

"That's perfectly all right. Don't worry, I'll catch up with you later." He stood and edged near the step. Unless you want me to accompany with you--I don't mind."

She lifted her palm in response as she backed down the steps. "No, stay here for awhile and enjoy the breeze. I'm sure Piper won't mind keeping you company." With that, she turned and strode away, offering a backward glance at the two while she thought better of going alone. In fact, as soon as the words escaped her lips, she regretted saying them.

Philomene used to warn her about Piper. "Trust is free da first time, Fleur, but once broken, it's got to be earned back." Yet she persisted in trusting her cousin. On the way to the house, she checked her watch, clenched and unclenched her fists and quickened her steps. I should have let him walk me to the house. I should have.

With Piper there was no way of knowing. No assurance. Her loyalties shifted with the wind.

And the wind was beginning to blow in a new direction.

Chapter Four
Crying Uncle

After a glimpse of all the people milling around, Fleur decided to avoid the front door entrance. She veered away keeping to the veranda. There weren't as many people on the alternate route, though she did offer polite exchanges with the few she encountered.

Past a clutch of vines hugging the ornate wooden balustrades, she admired the bright orange Angel's Trumpets, as she made her way to the back door--like the ones in the cemetery.

"Where you going, *Cherie*"?

She stopped short. Alcide stepped out from behind a hibiscus bush and stood before her. He snuffed out a cigarette underfoot, and released the cache of smoke from his mouth. Since arriving back in town, she'd managed to avoid seeing him. Over the years, her uncle had sometimes brought the child around, an unkempt boy with dirty hair and no manners. Yet here he stood, grown to manhood.

From an artist's point of view, she had to admire his bone structure. The sandy hair, now sleeked to the side, his short frame swallowed by a dark suit a few sizes too large, Alcide looked the part of the illegitimate son of Bernard, and Sally Mae, a woman of coarse background. Besides all that, he had a reputation for skirting the law.

"Why, hello."

He stepped forward to greet her with a kiss on each cheek but she stiffened at his touch.

"You act like you ain' glad to see me." He stared at her, a wry smile on his face.

She backed away. "Of course I am." Fleur looked toward the kitchen door.

He stroked a chisled cheek. She noticed dirt under his nails. His knuckles were red as well, with small fresh gashes.

"Ain't you gonna ask what I'm doin' here?"

She folded her arms. "Very well then, why are you here?"

"I'm working fa ya uncle now."

"What?"

"That's right." Alcide smiled. "He took me on, seeing as we're blood'n all. Not that I'm s'possed to tell nobody. But you already know 'bout dat." His gaze traveled up and down her frame, eyes lingering.

She bit her lip. "What sort of work are you doing for him?"

He shuffled his foot in the grass. "Oh, dis 'n dat."

"I see." Likely her uncle had hired him for unsavory dealings. "Well, congratulations. I suppose I'll be seeing you around here then?"

"I 'spec so." He met her eyes, a raw longing in them.

Her heart began to thump. "I should be going." She rushed past him. "Uncle wants to see me."

Alcide called after her. "I'll be seeing you, *Cherie'*."

As she approached the kitchen door, she turned. He stood in the same spot, staring after her. He waved.

A clap of thunder startled her, followed by a zigzag of lightening in the trees beyond. Unfazed, he stood staring back at her, hands lost in his pockets.

A shortcut through the kitchen would bring her right to the study, only a tiny distance down a servant's hallway. The top half of the Dutch-split kitchen door was wide open to allow the heat to escape, though flies buzzed in and out freely. She turned the knob and entered a room hot as an oven.

The steamy kitchen bustled with activity. Servers in starched white cotton jackets and black bow ties carried trays of steaming food, appetizers and drinks, beads of sweat rising off dark foreheads. She knew some of them, but today most were strangers hired and brought in to assist in the event. Those who knew her nodded an acknowledgment as she entered or flashed a quick smile. As Fleur walked through the kitchen she took a deep breath of creole cookery, the intoxicating aromas of steamed rice, bell peppers, chopped onion and fragrant bay leaf sautéed in olive oil. Cooks chopped at cutting boards. She recognized one man cooking and waved. Reuben, hair now iced with grey, flashed a wide smile.

She continued. Fires blazed on the stovetop as cooks ignited dark red wine in rich sauces of butter, herbs and pungent garlic. A wafting of Sassafras leaf floated in the air. The clang and clash of pots and silverware, somehow comforting, slowed her walk. But as she passed a small kitchen office, she heard a familiar voice call her name.

"Fleur? Dat you?"

She paused and turned back, poking her head through the open door. Philomene had supervised the D'Hemecourt household as long as Fleur could remember, and many years before. Her dark, sleek hair tinged with silver was, as usual smoothed away from her face in a tidy chignon. But this time, a strand of hair hung loose. Perspiration glittered her brow.

Fleur wrapped her arms around the dear woman who raised her. "Mama Phil." She drew away, but clasped the woman's hands in her own. "I was disappointed when I didn't see you at the funeral, but I figured you couldn't come."

"You right 'bout dat chile', I had to make sure things was ready for all da folks back here. I wanted to pay Miz Florrie respects, but I 'spec I'll have to go later."

Kind brown eyes met hers and drifted down to the young woman's skirt. "Miz Fleur', what happened?" She lifted Fleur's hem, took one look at her knees and sighed.

"I took a fall in the cemetery."

She folded her arms. "You eatin' child'? If I tol' you once, I tol' you a thousand times . . . " But she stopped herself in mid-sentence. Instead, Philomene motioned to a plain wooden chair next to the small desk she was sitting at. "Sit 'yousef down and let Mama Phil take a look at dat."

"But I have to meet Uncl--"

"No es-cuses. Sit." She walked out the door and returned a minute later with a white porcelain bowl of water. Before closing the door behind her, she looked to the right and left down the hall.

Fleur knew it was no use arguing. Mama Phil clucked over her like a mother hen and had always done so--taking pity on her when Aunt Florrie, often absent from the house and distant when present, never quite offered the maternal nurturing she needed.

Philomene returned to her wooden chair. Out of a bottom desk drawer, she pulled out large cotton balls and disinfectant, an amber bottle of Mercurochrome, gauze and white medical tape. She cleaned the scrapes first with Wright's Coal Tar soap and the bowl of warm water.

The warm soap water felt good on her skin, but for the pungeant odor. She turned her face to the side.

Philomene smiled. "You don't take to dat smell, huh? Well, it's good 'nuf to do the job."

Fleur reached for her hand. "Philomene, when did Alcide come to work for uncle?"

She shrugged, her face registered distaste. "Bout two mon' ago."

"What does he do around here?"

Head still down, her eyeballs focused upward briefly. "Whatever your uncle needs him doin' I s'pose."

Fleur nodded, knowing full well what that meant. Her uncle had a reputation of his own.

"You'd best stay away from that grifter, ya hear?"

She patted the scrapes dry with a clean white rag and reached for the Mercurochrome, painting swatches of the red antiseptic liquid across her knees. "How 'bout I do what I used to do when you was little?"

"What?" Fleur, wide-eyed stared back.

"Don' you remember what I used to do when you was a lil sprout?"

Fleur swallowed hard. "I'm afraid to ask."

"Seems like you were always skinning those knees of yours. Running everywhere. You didn't care 'bout walking nowhere. You was in too much of a hurry."

"What was it you used to do, Philomene?" Intrigued, she listened with intent.

Philomene looked down. "This." She painted appendages out from the circles of red."

"Why it's a ladybug." Fleur threw her head back and laughed as Philomene joined in. They laughed together until their eyes watered.

Philomene pat her knees. "Oh it's so nice to have you back here honey bun. This is your house you know. You belong here. Things is come full circle now."

She reached for the old woman's wrist. "Thank you Mama Phil--you've always been good to me."

The older woman dimpled in response, her apple butter cheeks gleaming. But her expression turned serious. "Why you goin' to see your uncle?"

Fleur shrugged. "Piper told me to. She said he wanted to talk to me about something."

She pursed her lips. "Hmmph, dat girl is always up to sumpthin' of her own." She cut out squares of gauze with a pair of silver scissors and placed them over Fleur's knees, then cut strips of medical tape and secured the gauze in place.

Fleur looked at the watch on her wrist and stood, pulling her dress down, at first tentatively, staring down at the tape over her knees. "I have to go."

"I know."

Their eyes met.

Philomene clasped her hands around Fleur's and looked up at her. "Chile' member what I used to tell you when you was discouraged? I used ta say you was like de alligator pear, tough on de outside an' soft on de inside."

A surge of raw emotion kept her from answering right away. "I had to be tough."

"Mama Philo knows, *mon cheri*."

She brushed away tears. "It's funny, but in New York I once asked a waiter if there were alligator pears in the salad and he looked at me as if I'd lost my mind."

Philomene smiled. "Dey jus' goin' hafta learn de right way ta say it from us here in da Crescent City."

Fleur laughed. "I'll see you later." She stood and walked towards the door.

"God go with you, honey. I'm praying for you. Always have."

She offered a profile of a slight smile in response. Her thoughts ill-matched to Philomene's however. What had God ever done on her behalf?

Fleur walked out the door and into the hallway. The study, only a short distance away, reeked of the acrid smell of cigar smoke. Philomene's words followed her down the hall. "I'm praying for you. . ."

The mahogany doors to the study were not the double doors she remembered from early childhood, but a find, spirited by her uncle from an old abandoned plantation house one night. Her uncle, never keen on the formalities of social propriety, salvaged a few more items from the country estate as well, a stained glass window from a family chapel depicting the nativity, a small breakfast buffet and of all things, a family Bible, somehow left behind in the vine-covered shell of the sitting room. As a teen, she remembered sneaking into the study when no one was around to open the hinged leather covers and read. The pages, lush with color fascinated, but the words perplexed, and often vexed her.

She swallowed hard and offered a tentative knock. All she could hear was a cacophony of voices, muffled into nonsense by the solid door and thick panels of mahogany lining the walls. Judging from the aromas of sweet pipe smoke and cigars lingering in the hallway, the inner room was likely full of stuffy old men and cigar smoke, as Louis had described it earlier. She turned to go, but as she did, the door sprang open, the sound of voices loud and boisterous, even merry. Her uncle stood, a dark form against the light behind, his meaty mouth revealed long, sallow teeth clenched about the smolder of a cigar.

"Fleur!" He grabbed her shoulder and pulled her back toward him.

The sickening smell of horrid cologne filled her lungs. No doubt, Bernard was the source of the offending odor she'd experienced earlier at the funeral procession. She turned her head and held her breath as he embraced her.

"Just who I wanted to see. I sent Piper to look for you."

"She told me you wanted to see me."

"That, I do." He pulled away and slipped his head back through the door for a moment to make an announcement to the rowdy bunch of men.

"I'll be back in a few minutes. Daniel will take care of your drinks." He nodded to the white-jacketed bartender and closed the door.

A sinking feeling coursed through her veins. She resisted the urge to run. His arm slithered around her waist.

He drew back and stood face to face with her, his voice lower than usual. "I was on my way back to the reception." He lowered his voice to a whisper. "I know it's not the time for revelry, but the boys and I were celebrating. You haven't been around. The new king and court were chosen. It's a secret of course, but," he winked, "the king of carnival may be closer than you think."

She tilted her head. "You?"

"Yes." He winked.

"Well con-congratulations uncle. I'm glad to hear of it." But a thought nagged at her. How could her uncle afford to pay such an exorbitant amount of money? Besides the initial cost of the royal position, the king, above all others on the court, was expected to fund many of the extravagant events, and elaborate costumes.

Bernard held an index finger to his mouth. "Shhh. No one must know. Don't tell Piper, but I'm going to ask her to be my queen."

"How wonderful." She mirrored his action. "My lips are sealed, uncle."

He coiled his arm around her again. "I haven't seen enough of you since you moved back my dear. Things have been rough lately. But you mustn't be a stranger." He squeezed her waist tighter. "After all, we're family."

"Y-yes of course. I-I'm sorry. I've been busy."

The smell of liquor, heavy on his breath, he spoke close to her ear. That, blended with the cologne was almost more than she could bear.

"My dear, let's go up the back stairs and talk in your old room. It'll be more private that way. The house is crawling with people. I don't know how we'll ever get them all to leave."

Her heart pumped so fast she felt faint, yet her legs followed him up the steps. Her ears tuned in to the clunk of footsteps clomping up the stairwell, so ordinary, so familiar. Yet the sound of it somehow chilled her to the bone. He turned the knob and the door creaked open revealing a room infused with light from four angles--the head of the owl.

Every window opened wide, the sheer white curtains adorning them billowed in the wind like ship's sails. The servants must have opened them to help cool down the house. The cleansing scent of rain filled the room. Thankfully, the oversized dormer windows would keep most of the water out.

A large oriental rug covered the length of the room, leaving narrow strips of pine wood floors uncovered. The rug stopped short of her easel and dressing table, situated by the south window.

The dressing table was just as she left it, a crystal bottle of Shalimar, a silver brush and comb resting on a small mirror plate. She shut the window next to it and the curtains fell silent as feathers.

Placed in diagonal form, two club chairs in a pleasant red and white floral print faced each other. The chairs and a small scalloped-edged pie plate table in between occupied the space by the west window, which she closed, and a chest of drawers, a small cedar chest at the east, and her old brass bed at the north. When she moved into the room as a teen, the servants had painted white enamel over the elaborate railing to match the airy feel of the room. She closed the remaining windows and the room fell silent.

Very quickly, the scent of the rain still was soon overpowered by the unpleasant odor of her uncle's cologne. She thought the better of her action and reopened the north window and the curtains, reanimated by the wind, unfurled, cheerily snapping to and fro. Lingering at the window, she inhaled fresh air, while suppressing a feeling of dread. Being back in her old room again stirred unpleasant feelings.

She turned and took a step toward a club chair.

"No, here." He sat down on the bed and patted the white Cheneille spread. "Sit here. I want to be comfortable."

Fleur hesitated, her heart pounding an urgent tune. He patted the bedspread again. "Don't be afraid. I won't bite." A wide smile broke through fleshy jowls, as if to reassure her.

She lowered herself to the bed, a discreet distance away. "I'm sorry for your loss Uncle. I saw how you cried at the funer--"

He interrupted with surprising vigor. "I don't want to talk about it any more. I'm done with the stench of illness in this house." Bernard motioned to the top of his head. "Had it up to here with that." He leaned toward her. "I'm having the rooms cleaned and fumigated tomorrow so I don't have to be reminded of what I went through. Every bottle, every bedpan will be gone." He snapped his fingers. "Like that."

Shocked by his tone, she fumbled to respond. "I-I know it's been difficult for you."

"Do you? You've been away for four years. Didn't even come home for the holidays or summers. No Fleur for Thanksgiving or

Christmas. You came back right before. . ." He shook his head, ". . . before she died. How would you know how hard it's been?"

Moved by his expression of grief, she reached over to lay a hand on his shoulder, but he turned and grabbed her close. Tears fell. The weight of him hard on her shoulder, he mumbled. "What am I going to do now? Help me Fleur. I'm undone. No one cares about me."

He raised his head, his face close to hers. For all his wails, she noticed there were few tears. Perhaps being back in the atmosphere of her childhood room brought up the memory, but dots and dashes of a song she used to sing as a child came to mind, repeating over in her head like a scratched record:

"She sailed away on a happy summer's day on the back of a crocodile. . .The croc winked his eye as she bade them all goodbye wearing a happy smile. . ."

The blur of two raised black moles on Bernard's right cheek stood out against his ruddy complexion. A roadmap of broken blood vessels stretched across his bulbous nose. His breath, hot and putrid with alcohol sickened her. She began to squirm, hoping to free herself from his grip. The light-headed feeling she'd experienced earlier that day began to creep back. Fleur struggled to think. A variety of polite, but firm excuses to leave ran through her head.

"Do you care, Fleur?" He licked his lips. "Do you?"

A loud knock on the door gave her the opportunity she needed. Seizing it, she broke away and stood, knees knocking together. She further backed away toward the club chairs and sat stiff and upright on the edge.

"Who's that" he called, voice gruff and clearly annoyed at the interruption.

The door opened and Philomene poked her head in, her eye searching the room for Fleur. Mister Bernard, I sorry but theys some people ready to leave and theys lookin' fo' you ta tell you goodbye."

Dear Philomene. Fleur relaxed at the sound of her voice. Now she had an excuse to leave, rather than be pawed by the drunken fool.

Chest heaving, he ran his huge hands through his hair, a grimace on his face. "All right. Tell them I'm on my way." He looked at Fleur. "What I wanted to tell you is that . . ." He turned and narrowed his eyes at Philomene. "Do you mind?"

"Oh, I sorry Mister Bernard. Sorry." Philomene locked eyes with Fleur and winked, before she withdrew, closing the door behind her.

Don't leave me. Fleur's left eye began to twitch.

Chest still heaving with anger, he shifted position on the bed to face her. "That woman gets my goat. I don't know why I keep her around." He huffed. "Guess I'm a sentimental old fool."

Bernard brought his palms together. "Here's what I wanted to discuss with you." He cleared his throat. "My brother, Rene' was very good at making money. I, on the other hand, was always better at spending it. Not long before they passed away, Florrie and I volunteered to be guardians for you and the estate should anything untoward ever happen."

He sighed. "And it's a very good thing they accepted. The accident was a terrible tragedy and that's how we, my dear child, came to live with you."

"Uncle, I'm well aware. . ."

"Just listen. Indulge your old uncle for a minute, please."

She nodded.

He twiddled his thumbs. As I said, I've always been better at spending money than making it."

Her eye stopped twitching. "And?"

"Well, allow me to be frank. Besides what we spent on your university tuition and living expenses, you've no doubt noticed some changes around here. Your aunt and I used some of your inheritance to make renovations and improvements to the house and grounds, as much as we were allowed to spend from the estate."

"Yes, I know. I noticed right away."

"There's still a lot more to do, of course, but we did as much as we could, given the monetary restrictions. You do know there are limits as to how much of your money we are allowed to use as guardians? The laws are written to protect heirs from those without benefit of scruples."

She moved her lips to speak, but he continued.

"Of course that doesn't apply to our family. You know your aunt and I always had, rather, have your best interests at heart."

"And you spent my inheritance on home renovations? Why, I thought you'd spent all my parent's money years ago."

"I'm flabbergasted. How could you think such a thing about us?"

She was about to respond when he raised his index finger. "Some of it. We only spent some of it. Believe me, there's still a lot of simoleons left for you to spend--a comfortable fortune. Allow me to remind you of the fact that this is your home and as your guardians, it was incumbent upon us to see after your property. An estate this size must be kept well on the inside and out."

Fleur's mouth came unhinged. A gasp escaped.

He continued. "Of course, you are well aware my dear, that you are entitled to receive your inheritance on your twenty-first birthday."

Bernard fashioned another smile, but the expression on his lips ill-suited the one reflected in his eyes.

Fleur sat back in the chair. "I'm to come into a fortune?" Through the years, she'd wondered. Florrie and Bernard lived the extravagant life. She assumed they'd spent whatever she might have inherited from her parents, but her father, God rest his soul, had planned well. The news was more than she'd hoped for. She'd only dreamed of inheriting enough to make a modest new life for her self from whatever dregs were left of her parent's estate.

She slid from the arm of the chair to a seated position. "I've been living on tins of meat and beans."

"Ah, the austere life of an artist. No more, my dear." He swept one arm outward. "I don't know why you chose to stay in that dingy old flat in the Quarter instead of coming home. You could live quite comfortably here, you know. Three square meals, maid service, everything you need."

"I need my privacy."

He clasped his hands together. "Well why don't you settle into your favorite place for now, that is until you become the beautiful, young heiress of the estate?" He winked. "The Chinoiserie will serve as your temporary quarters. You'll be with your family, yet retain your privacy and save money. Whatever it is you're paying for that 'sumptuous' flat I've heard about, is too much."

"The light, the atmosphere is perfect where I am. There are some finishing touches I need to do on a few paintings, but yes, I'll do it."

She thought of her feelings earlier in the day, the annoyance of ruining her only good pair of shoes in the mud that morning, the ripped nylons too. Now she would soon be able to afford to live without forever pinching pennies. Her life, her circumstances would soon change for the better.

He offered a hopeful smile. "Florrie and I didn't think you'd mind helping us out a bit financially. After all, we sacrificed everything to raise you as our own daughter."

Thoughts spun round her head like cotton candy. She found herself responding. "Of course, I'm grateful."

Grateful for the cold, empty life her aunt and uncle had provided her growing up. Giving and going to lavish parties, keeping up the façade of the perfect family. And always a reminder to her and polite society about what a stupendous sacrifice they had made.

She swallowed hard, wondering how much they'd squandered over the years. Calculating the cost of renovating the ornate guesthouse, the exotic pavilion and the new expensive furniture throughout the house, she imagined they had spent quite a lot of her money. A new thought propelled her mouth. "I can't imagine what the kitchen must have cost."

He looked down for a moment. A sly smile peeled his mouth open. "Well, it was necessary you know. The kitchen is part of the house we brought into the twentieth century. You remember how our kitchen used to be outside in back of the house? It was a necessity, an absolute necessity for us to build a modern kitchen. I know it sounds hard to believe, but we did it for you, dear one. It was all for you. As good stewards of your estate, we were, ah, compelled to do so for your benefit."

She folded her arms. I have one other question, Uncle." Though shaky, she managed to fix her eyes on his. "We both know that serving as the King of Carnival bears a heavy financial burden, the costumes, the receptions, the gifts. How do you plan on paying for all that?"

He folded his arms. "Why do you want to know? Don't you think I have some money of my own? Am I not a grown man, free to do with my money as I please?"

Fleur remained silent, hoping her lack of response would encourage him to continue speaking.

Finally, he acquiesced. "I have friends fronting me part of the money."

"Loans?"

"Yes, loans." His voice rose in anger. "I've won twice that amount in one day in the casino."

"And lost."

He snapped his fingers. "A good businessman always has a contingency plan. Don't worry your lovely head about these matters, my girl. Your uncle's problems are not your problems. I'm not going to ask for your help. You've done more than enough. Besides, no matter what you think, I'm well able to make my way in the world."

"I hope so."

Bernard scowled. "Look girl, I've come clean with you on everything." He cleared his throat, perhaps thinking the better of his outburst.

"The entire estate belongs to you—well almost. You'll inherit it on your twenty-first birthday." He accented the sentence with a playful wag of his finger.

Fleur nodded.

His face relaxed. "I thought that news would please you. We'll take care of all the paperwork later." He held up his fingers. "Your birthday is less than a year from now. There's plenty of time." Her uncle rose from the bed and turned to go.

"What is to become of you and Piper?"

He paused for a moment. "That, my dear, is up to you."

Her chest rose and fell at the thought. Growing up under the relentless control of her aunt and uncle, two adults so unlike her own parents, she had often thought what it would be like to gain the upper hand. And now that the power was hers, Fleur felt nothing, aside from pity.

"Uncle there will always be a place at my table for the two of you. You are, after all, family."

"You mean you wouldn't put us out on the street with tin cups? How generous of you, little flower." A laugh rose, his great barrel-chest heaving with amusement. He snapped his fingers. "We'll be refugees, orphans under your charge."

"I'm glad you find such merriment in the situation. Some people might find it unsettling to find themselves in the decline of years without means of employment or resource."

"How astute of you to point that out." He stared at her, as if for the first time, as if seeing her with new eyes.

Bernard stepped forward and stretched his arms toward her. "I really should go before Philomene starts hounding me again. How about a nice hug for your favorite uncle?"

He wrapped his arms around her and lingered in the embrace, stroking her back. Uncomfortable with the extended closeness of their proximity, she pushed him away.

"Your guests are waiting." She managed a smile.

He lifted her chin with his finger and kissed her forehead. "Such a lovely face. I'll enjoy having you live close to me again." Bernard started toward the door. "Oh, one more thing. You might want to be discreet about coming into so much money. Otherwise you'll be mobbed by suitors all vying for your attention, young men who'd give their right arm for a chance at a beautiful heiress."

She watched as he opened the door. After it shut behind him, she threw herself on the bed, shaking. She made a vow to herself to go away somewhere the moment she came into the inheritance, as far away, as soon as possible. Perhaps return to New York or an extended stay in Paris to study art. Or Milan.

But her heart reminded her of someone. Louis.

Chapter Five
The Piper Plays

Piper motioned to a lacquered settee. "Louis, darling, let's visit for a while."

An ominous rumbling thundered overhead, the sun now blotted out by the steady approach of dank clouds. A dank chill rose in the air.

He turned his face to her voice with deliberate slowness, his eyes focused to the last second on Fleur as she neared the house.

They sat down together and he spread one arm along the settee back. He dreaded situations like these, but decided to muster his social skills. "Piper, how are you? I'm so sorry about your mother. Her passing must be a terrible thing for you to endure."

Her eyes void of tears, she replied. "Yes, it was difficult to lose her, but truth be told, mother's been on the brink of death for many years now. One comes to expect it. However, when the day arrives, no amount of preparation can ready one for it."

"I'm truly sorry for your loss."

She pressed an index finger to her lips and tapped them, the prolonged silence deliberate.

He coughed. "Is there, something on your mind?"

She stared into his eyes, squinting emotion. "What are you up to?"

"What do you mean?"

"Are you after her money? Lest you forget, you work for the law firm that represents us and thereby know exactly what Fleur is coming into. Besides, it's no secret your family has come into financial difficulties since your father passed."

When she narrowed her eyes, he noted her eyes glinted green as emeralds in the waning light. Another man might have found her attractive, but he wondered how he had ever thought her a beauty.

"There's no denying you're an up-and-coming attorney in this town, handsome as well. There are other young women who would bring you finer dowries. Why ever would you be interested in her?"

Anger at her insinuations produced bitter bile within him. "Nothing of the sort. I wouldn't, couldn't behave in such a disingenuous manner."

She stared. "I know you, Louis. It's quite obvious you're infatuated with her."

Louis took a deep controlled breath to calm his anger. "I'm enamored, it's true, but after all, we've only just met."

"Oh really? Last year as I recall, you were crazy about me."

"So it's come to this."

If Piper was ready to have it out with him, he resolved to sit and take the assault like a gentleman. He straightened against the settee.

"Look Piper, you and I dated for a few months and then . . . "

" . . . and then you stopped calling on me." She sniffed, the tone of her voice indignant.

He continued. "I knew sooner or later we'd have to discuss the matter."

Eyelids narrowed together, she spoke. "I want to know why. Tell me Louis, why did your feelings for me change?"

"Do you want a frivolous excuse that caters to your vanity, or the absolute truth?

"The truth, of course."

"Very well then." He positioned himself with her, eye-to-eye. "Your jealousy drove me away."

Piper's mouth hung open. She pulled a dainty handkerchief from her pocket and drew it close, as if waiting for the waterworks. Instead, a silence churned between them, heavy with malevolence.

He opened his mouth to speak, but thought the better of it. The woman was not ready to hear the truth about herself--how she'd behaved like a lunatic, ringing him on the telephone at all hours, not to mention all the accusatory telegrams and notes through the post he'd received. The admiration he had felt for her in the beginning turned to disdain when he realized the depth of her possessiveness and insecurity.

She lifted a tear-streaked face to him. "Aren't you worried that I'm going to tell Fleur about the horrid way you treated me, how you tossed me aside like a rag doll?" She stared down into her handkerchief, threading it between her fingers.

Voice smooth, even-keeled, he answered. "You know I don't want you to do that."

Piper's eyes etched a message that chilled him. "She has no idea. Fleur was away at an art college in New York, you know."

"So you didn't write or tell her in conversation?"

Inside, his heart raced. *She hates me. She would tell Fleur out of spite and ruin everything.*

She paused, a smile on her lips. "No, I didn't."

Her smug smile brought a look of concern he couldn't keep off his face.

"Piper, please don't, that is, if you still care at all about me in the least. I-I would like the opportunity to tell her myself. We've only just met, or rather, become reacquainted."

She crossed her legs towards him. "My, my, you're smitten, aren't you?"

He looked up at the carved slats in the open cedar wood roof. *Think hard about every word you say to the woman.* "There's something special about Fleur. I can't explain it."

Piper cleared her throat. "I expect you want me to tell you more about her."

"Please."

"Why should I?"

"Very well then." Louis stood as if to go.

"Louis, sit down. I'll tell you whatever you want to know."

He sat back down.

"We've been here with her since she was five. That's when her parents—my Aunt Eleanor and Uncle Rene' died in an automobile crash on their way back from Mississippi.

"Yes, you've told me that before. I remember hearing about that years ago."

She nodded. "It was a terrible tragedy for our family. We came to live with her. Even though I was a bit older, we got along well. In fact, we shared a room for a year, until father gave Fleur her own room in the attic. He had it remodeled just for her." She tapped her fingers on the settee. "I used to resent sharing the attention, but mother and father reminded me about all the girl had been through. And to tell the truth, the attic rather frightened me. I was somewhat of a scaredy-cat back then."

Piper pulled a pink climbing rose close to sniff it. "Fleur's always been quiet." She reached for another rose on the stem and gently pulled it down toward her. The smell of rain permeated the swirl of air about them.

He laughed. "Are you trying to dissuade me from seeing her with that description? A beautiful, quiet woman--what man could resist that kind of girl?"

"All right, then. She's strange, a real oddball. Do you like those qualities in a woman too? Fleur is beautiful, but is that enough?"

"What are you insinuating?"

"You'll see."

Thunder cracked, reverberating across the sky. His heart punched the inside of his chest.

A flash of lightening in the distance confirmed the scent of approaching rain. He closed his eyes for a moment, fingers on his temples. The crack and rumble, the flashes brought back memories—memories of battles he hoped would fade.

He jumped to his feet. "Perhaps we should walk to the house, Piper."

She ignored him and instead plucked a rose from the bush, twirling it with idle fancy between her fingers. "These climbing roses are so beautiful to look at, but they aren't very fragrant" As if to send a message of casual nonchalance, she brushed the rose against his hand. "I suppose you're right about that. I should have known better. Men seem to like women who don't speak their minds. Or for that matter, speak at all."

"Piper, did you hear?"

"Is that why you don't like me any more?" She leaned in closer. "Is that really why you ended our relationship, because I'm so outspoken?"

"Piper, I've explained why."

She continued, as if she hadn't heard. "Or don't you find me attractive?" Her body stiffened. "Am I too old?" She pursed her lips. "You know I'm considered an old maid by some. And Fleur is so much younger."

"What do you mean?" he shook his head. "Piper, you're breathtaking and you know it."

She closed her eyes, tears rolling out the corners.

"Today of all days, with the acute loss of your mother, the service, the interment and all the people here, all that can't help but heighten your emotions."

She reached over to stroke his arm, slender fingers in a slow crawl.

Swallowing a mounting sense of urgency, he stole a glance toward the house before he replied. "Piper, I'm sorry." He straightened up and pulling his arm away. "But the time for us has passed."

Lightening crackled through the atmosphere, closer now. The hair on his arms stood up. But she continued, oblivious.

"I've had so many opportunities before, all young men from good families. Now most are married. Some even have children." She drew her arms close in an embrace. "Do you ever get the feeling that life has forgotten you?"

The threat of the storm crackled the air with dark urgency. He grasped her hands in his. "Dear Piper, as I said, you have waxed emotional today, with good reason. But rest assured, you are beautiful and full of feminine charm. You could still have your pick among the finest families if you showed the slightest interest. Life hasn't passed you by." He smiled. "Not yet, anyway. It can only pass you by if you allow it to do so. "

He put his hands in his pockets and walked to the steps. "Rejoin society. How long has it been since you attended a garden party or a christening, a birthday, carnival ball or even a wedding? I've heard people speak of you. You've been a social hermit. Everyone knows it."

She gripped the arm of the settee. "I'm not a hermit. I-I'm seeing someone."

"Seeing someone? I'm confused. Then why did you argue with me?"

She buried her face in her palms. "I wanted to know—that's all. You have to believe me. I-I was hurt."

He waited until she composed herself. "Who are you seeing? Do I know him?"

She shook her head. "Papa doesn't approve. His name is Jack Holcombe. I met him at a dance a year or so before the war ended, and after the war he took a job back in North Carolina."

If he's there, then how?"

He's in sales. New Orleans is part of his territory so he makes his way to this part of the country once a month."

"Why doesn't your father approve of him?"

"He's never met him. My guess is father's disapproval is based on Jack's monetary situation. Jack came out of the Air Force without a sou. He sent all his money back home to help support his family. His father was injured in a munitions plant and can't work."

"I should like to meet him."

"Why?"

"He sounds like a nice fellow. And I want to make sure he knows what a great girl he has on his arm." Louis stood. "Who knows, if things work out with Fleur, maybe we'll go on a double date."

Eyes on her hands cupped in her lap, voice barely above a whisper, she answered. "Very well then. Perhaps the next time he's in town."

Louis looked towards the house and back to her, this time with authority. "Piper, no arguments this time. The sky is dark and about to pour. Time to go."

"You're anxious to see her. I understand. Perhaps Fleur is visiting with people who haven't seen her in a long time. The house is positively overflowing."

He offered his arm. "Funny you should mention that. There's a crowd headed this way, though with the sky ready to open up I can't understand why.

She slipped her arm into his "They're probably three sheets to the wind."

They strode fast across the lawn, avoiding the oncoming crowd.

"Louis, your eyes were trained on the house the entire time we talked."

"And I thought I was being discreet." He squeezed her arm.

"Go on, ask me more about Fleur."

They crunched through the short-cropped grass at a brisk pace. Lightening zig-zagged near a stand of trees.

They hurried along. "Piper, when did Fleur develop an interest in art?"

"The art? Sometime after she moved into her own room. Drawing at first, then pastels and watercolors. Oils too." She clasped her hands."

"I would love to see some of it."

"You should. It's quite different—dark, even dreary. I don't understand it at all. The meaning of modern art, any kind of art, eludes me. We were told she was highly acclaimed at her art school in New York and at some gallery showings too. Mother and Father had to hear the news from her instructors however. Fleur never informed us. She didn't visit us during those years and even requested we refrain from visiting her."

"I wonder why."

Piper shrugged. "As I told you before, Fleur is different. Unlike most people, she's quite comfortable alone with her canvases."

"Did she tell you about the upcoming gallery showing? When one of the gallery owners heard she'd moved back, he scheduled a showing. He absolutely raves about her work."

They paused at the front door, the muffled sounds of voices, and savory waftings of food beyond. The door was draped in mourning crepe and further adorned with a black wreath, the exterior presented a contrary façade to the merry sounds within.

A peal of thunder followed by a stab of lightening turned the crowd of people they'd passed, back toward the house. Squealing at the tentative drops of rain, the women ran before the men, barreling towards them.

"Do you think they'll make it?" she asked.

He laughed. "They might be a little soggy by the time they get here. Is there a side door?"

"Yes." She took the lead along the right side of the porch, following the length of it until they reached the side entrance.

Her lips counted the days. "And as to the gallery showing. Hmmm. Two months from now? No three. Well, it's at that funny little gallery in the French Quarter, on Royal Street. You know the one, with that odd statue in the window."

"I know the one." As he reached for the knob, a distinct sound rose and fell with a burst of wind. "Did you hear that?" He tilted his head.

"Why yes, I do hear something." Piper followed Louis as he followed the sound. Crouched against the wall, behind some Adirondack chairs on the veranda, a young black man sobbed and whimpered. Collapsed in a heap, his shirt torn, his body shook.

Louis reached down to touch his shoulder. Startled, he jumped to his feet. "Don' hurt me Mista."

A tender tone to his voice, Louis answered. "Did someone strike you? Tell me."

Before the young man could answer, Piper interrupted. "Tadpole, what are you doing here? You belong in the kitchen. Get back there, now."

Shivering, the young man did a couple of half bows. "S-sorry Miz P-Piper. I din mean nuthin. Don' be mad." Tears ran down his cheeks.

Hand on the young man's shoulder Louis spoke to him in a calm voice. "No one's going to hurt you. Please tell me what happened."

"Don't bother yourself with him." She sniffed. "He's a moron. My father pays the idiot to sweep up around here and he can't even do that right."

Louis took a good look in the man's eyes. The man was not as young as he'd supposed. He guessed him to be near the age of thirty or so. The stare the man returned was like that of a child—a child who feared something or someone. Ignoring her remark, he introduced himself. "Hello Tadpole, Glad to meet you." He held out his hand. Cautious, the man held his out and they shook hands. "Who hurt you?"

The man's eyes shifted to the left and to the right. "The bad m-m-man." He pointed to the left side of his face. The beginnings of a fresh bruise colored his cheek. Then, in between sobs, he pointed to his shoulder. "Hurts."

Impatient, Piper interrupted again. "Let's go. Why are you bothering with him?"

Louis examined his cheek and shoulder. "Looks like a strong cuff on your face and a pretty good one on your shoulder. Did the man hit or push you?"

His head jerked up and down.

"Why did he hurt you? And who hurt you? What's his name?"

"Dunno. He mean."

"Send him back to the kitchen."

Annoyed by her lack of compassion, Louis looked at her. "If you don't want to listen, by all means, go."

"Oh Louis, really?"

A figure came flying out from the back yard. "Tadpole. Tadpole." Frantic, searching, the woman called out his name.

"Here." Tears ran down the man's face as the woman ran up the steps and onto the veranda.

"Praise Jesus! I found you! I din' know, din' know where. Oh thank the precious Lord I. . ." Philomene looked from him to Louis to a smirking Piper.

"Sorry, please Miz Piper. So sorry."

"Man hurt Tadpole."

"Shhh."

Louis helped him to his feet and the young man leaned on her, the echo of soft cries into her shoulder.

"Take him back to the kitchen before anyone else see's him," Piper ordered.

"Yes'm." Philomene, head down, nodded.

"Let me help you." Louis reached out.

"No thank you Mista Louis." Eyes wide, she held her hand up. "That's kind o' you to offa', but I got him okay."

"Let's go." Piper summoned.

Louis watched as the two hobbled off towards the back of the house. Only then did he turn to face Piper.

She mocked. "Well, well. I never figured you were so softhearted. Really Louis, the boy's a blithering idiot who didn't understand a thing you said."

He paused, taking in the sting of her remarks.

"Maybe, but he understands kindness. You know what kindness is, don't you?"

She didn't answer.

With that, he walked past her to the door. Hand on the knob, he glanced at her.

Piper stiffened her back. "Look, I-I'm sorry about all that mess back there. It won't happen again. I promise." She offered a half smile. "And just to show you I mean business, I won't tell Fleur about the two of us. It will be our little secret."

He opened the door, a sinking feeling in his chest.

Chapter Six
Ghosts in Cedar

The side door opened into a hallway, which led to the parlor. All eyes were upon them. An opaque cloud of cigarette smoke hovered above. People everywhere, in big groups, small groups, all speaking at once. Not in low hushed voices as one would expect, but in loud, boisterous voices, as if at a party, not a funeral reception. Such was the laissez-faire attitude.

People occupied every square of space downstairs, spilling out of the parlor and great room and into the foyer. They sat on the steps of the winding staircase, lounged against walls and even one another. A few even filed past them to perch on chairs on the front porch. A soggy couple arrived about the same time and followed them in.

"Dear Piper, I was so very sorry to hear about your mother." A heavy-set woman in a ridiculous feathered hat pulled her to the left toward the parlor. A sideways glance told Louis that Piper was caught in a current she could not escape.

Louis raised a brow. "It seems as if you will be rejoining society today, whether you like it or not."

He veered away from her, to the right and into the great room, a large open, high-ceilinged space with pale frescoes of half-clothed figures on the ceiling and plush oriental carpets atop polished mahogany floors that groaned and creaked at the weight of the crowd. Black crepe draped across the grand mirror, a tradition many no longer followed. But some families, including his own, adhered to some of the old ways of mourning.

"Louis Russo?" An attractive young blonde snared him by the arm.

He blinked recognition. "Luanne? Is that you? I hardly . . . "

"Yes, it's me." She bellowed a deep, gutteral laugh that made him wince.

"Well, that's the girl I grew up with." He offered a polite smile. Now I recognize you, my dear, by your charming laugh. I could never forget that."

Luanne, the skinny, freckle-faced-girl with the most bothersome laugh in all creation--how could he possibly forget her?

"Louis, you're quite awful to me. Do you think I've forgotten how you used to tease me in elementary school?"

He laughed. "No, no you're mistaken. It couldn't have been you. The girl I teased had buck teeth, freckles and she . . . "

She barred his lips with two fingers for a moment. "That's quite enough."

"But in all seriousness, you look wonderful, Luanne. All grown up, and not a buck tooth in sight."

She raised her arms to her hips and frowned. He flinched in mock horror. "I'd better take my leave before you truly lose your temper. You know, hell hath no fury as a woman scorned." "Or teased," he added. Before she could offer a reply, he turned, using the occasion to make a quick exit. Gone pecan.

He wove through the length of the room, scanning for signs of Fleur, then moved to the parlor. Piper, surrounded by a galaxy of women, shot a doleful expression his way. But he turned and walked in the opposite direction.

From the kitchen to the study, library, downstairs bedrooms and wraparound veranda, Fleur was nowhere to be found, at least downstairs. So he ushered past people clustered at the foot of the oriental carpeted stairs, gingerly stepping past ashtrays and drink glasses.

As he climbed the curve of the staircase, he gasped on the landing when he caught sight of her, a reaction that surprised him. Her profile took his breath away. No woman had ever evoked such an emotion in him. He approached, perplexed at her view. Her stare seemed directed at a narrower set of stairs, what he assumed might be the attic he'd heard about.

"Fleur? Fleur? The sound his voice seemed to startle her. She blinked at him.

"Louis?"

"What are you doing up here? I've looked all over for you."

"Remembering . . . " She turned away to face him. " . . . my childhood years."

"I thought you were going to talk to your uncle."

A flush bloomed across her face. "I did."

Her expression both puzzled and worried him.

"It seems I'm to receive quite an extraordinary birthday gift this year."

"Let me guess--your inheritance?" He lifted his brows in mock surprise, but her expression told him she was not amused. Louis reached for her hands and clasped them in his own. "Fleur, I hope you don't think that I would ever."

"Shhh." She held a finger to her mouth. "For now, at least until May 10th, I'm just like any other woman my age struggling to make ends meet."

He nodded, a look of relief on his face.

"But," she added, "I'll be moving to the Chinoiserie after my lease is up next week at the flat. I only rent month-to-month. That will give me time to put the finishing touches on a couple of canvases." Her voice trailed off.

"Piper told me you're an artist. I'd like to see your work some time."

"All right." She blew out a breath in frustration.

"What's wrong?"

"Uncle told me they used some of my inheritance to live off as well as to remodel the Chinoiserie and modernize the kitchen.

"He let go of her hand and wandered a few steps. "I suppose there are some ways to finagle those monies within the boundaries of guardianship, especially if those home improvements were of benefit to the upkeep and value of your property. You were not informed, I take it?"

She shook her head. "Until today I had no idea there even was an inheritance. I assumed they'd taken whatever belonged to my parent's estate just as they'd taken over the house, my mother's jewels, everything. No one ever discussed any of this with me."

"And you are reasonably sure your aunt and uncle appropriated part of your fortune?"

"I'm certain of it. To my knowledge, uncle has never held down a job, yet he and my aunt traveled with and seemed to live in top-drawer style most of their lives. You travel in the same circles. Haven't you heard? My uncle has quite a reputation."

He stroked his chin. Yes, I must admit that I have heard more than a few stories."

"Isn't it probable they've been living at my expense all these years?"

They locked eyes.

"Fleur, I'm not familiar with your estate. Normally, when there is a trust established in a child's name, guardians are unable to access the inheritance for personal use. You should set up an appointment to meet with the attorney assigned to the trust."

She crossed her arms. "Yes, I will do that right away. Regardless of anything untoward having occured, uncle assured me I would receive a substantial amount. I hope so." Fleur glanced around. "And I suppose I should be glad they kept up my home, especially the Chinoiserie."

"This is quite a lot to take in, isn't it?"

Her head moved in slow motion. "I'm amazed to find out I'm to come into money. Then to discover my guardians may have used my inheritance over the years, albeit part of it, to fund personal extravagances . . . "

"Fleur, I'm certain everything will work out well."

She tugged at his shirtsleeve. "C'mon, Louis, let me show you around. I'll bet you've never seen the rest of the house."

"I can't say that I have. Just the downstairs." He clutched at her shoulder. "Are you sure you're all right?"

"Yes, just a little thirsty. Now stop fretting and let me show you around."

"Thirsty? Let me run downstairs and fetch you some water."

She twined her arm in his. "I'm fine for now. We can get something to eat when we go downstairs." She motioned. "Follow me."

They peeked into sitting rooms and bedrooms, even closets. But when they reached Piper's room, Fleur hesitated near the door for a moment and took a step forward. Spotting a crystal canister by the bed, she poured a glass of water and drank.

He followed her in. "Want some?"

"No thanks."

Pointing to the ornate four-poster bed, her voice caught as she spoke, as if on the verge of a sob. "There's just one bed in her room now, but she and I used to share little twin beds. When she first arrived here." She turned to him. "You've no doubt heard the whole story of how they came to live here? Piper so loves to tell it."

Fleur stroked the fringe on the soft green floral curtains. "She's done a lovely job of decorating the room, don't you think so?"

He shifted from foot to foot, clearly uncomfortable in a lady's boudoir, especially Piper's. "I suppose."

"We used to tell each other stories late at night." She sat on the edge of the bed and winced when she tried to cross her legs; skinned knees painted bright orange-red.

A wide smile moved across his face. "You've gotten hold of some Mercurochrome, I see."

"Yes, I did. Philomene took care of me." She tugged her dress down and lay on her side. "There was one particular story Piper loved to tell. One that always frightened me, a family legend about a ghost in a cedar chest."

Louis leaned against a cedar robe but pulled away to point. "Sounds intriguing. Is this the one?"

She shook her head, spilling curls against her face. "No, I heard that long ago, before the attic renovation, there used to be a large chest stored there. Family and servants claimed they could hear noises from inside, but I've never seen or heard anything. Normally, stories like that don't frighten me."

His arms uncrossed. "What did it sound like?"

"Well, when the chest appears . . . "

"Appears? Does it materialize from thin air?" He laughed. "What kind of sound does it make?"

"Scratching. Crying. Knocks. Moans. There's a story, and mind you, I don't know how much truth there is to it. Supposed to have happened right before the Civil War. A young slave woman resisted the advances of one of our ancestors, the master of the house, so he locked her in the cedar chest to 'teach her a lesson.'"

He leaned forward. "What happened?"

"The man assumed the old chest had enough air for her to breathe until he came back for her, but when he came back for her and lifted the lid she was dead--asphyxiated."

"Horrible." He shook his head. "I've never heard that tale, and I thought I'd heard most. You should know this about me. I'm rather fanatical in my interest regarding local stories and folklore."

Fleur winked. "I'll be certain to remember that little fact about you. It might come in handy one day."

"Please go on."

His interest piqued, she continued. "They say the ghost of that poor woman now haunts this house and whenever the cedar chest appears, someone in the family line of her feckless master is about to die."

"Like the legend of the banshee, eh?" He chuckled. "Nice story."

She shrugged. "As I said, the chest was originally stored in the attic. But Uncle Bernard built a room for me there, and I've never seen the chest. Though you might be interested to know the servants claim it appeared in Aunt Florrie's room the night before she died. Thankfully, I visited that day and was able to talk to my aunt before she passed, but Piper was alone with her that evening."

He froze. "Do you think it's true, the chest made a death bed appearance?"

"You might want to ask Piper. Knowing her as well as I do, I'm not at all certain."

Louis rotated an exaggerated shiver. "You must have been terrified growing up in this place."

She lifted her palms up. "No, it's my home. There's a lot more to fear from reality. As to the supernatural occurrences here, I try to convince myself it was all just a childhood fairy tale or maybe if there was a ghost, it went away to haunt another house."

Louis glanced up at the ceiling as if he half-expected a ghost to appear. "Your room was in the attic, eh? Wasn't it hot up there?" he asked. "Attics are usually insufferable."

"It's not a true attic. It was simply a third floor great room that was not in use until I occupied it. A big room used as a place for storage. With four dormer windows and plenty of air and light. I took up painting and needed lots of light."

She hopped off the bed. "I'll show you the room, but there are a few left on this floor we haven't seen. Let's move on. I must admit all this reminiscing is making me feel a bit melancholy." She smoothed the pale green and white Chenille bedspread before they exited.

Relieved to move on, he followed her to the first door on the left and opened it. A wash of sunset flooded the room with a rose and golden glow. A youth bed in a butternut wood dominated the room. Shelves lined with toys and books stretched across one wall and an ornate rocking horse occupied a corner.

"This was the nursery, my room when I was a small child." The rainstorm, intense, but short in duration, had passed and the afternoon sun's golden glow reflected off the polished wood floor. "I've always liked this room."

"I can see why," he said. "It's pleasant--lots of cheery light. What child wouldn't enjoy a room like this?"

He pointed to the toys. "I'll bet the dolls were your favorite."

Fleur shook her head. "I loved my dollies, but guess again."

He glanced over the room again and spotted an easel and drawing tablets on the shelf. A smiled dawned on his face.

"Bravo, Louis." She clasped his arm. "You're a fast study."

The stairs creaked from behind. Collette approached, panting from the climb. "Dat's Rusty's room now."

"What do you mean?" Fleur asked, looking to Louis and then back to her cousin.

Collette parted part them, the staleness of cigarette smoke on her breath. "You know my marriage ain't goin' so good. I tol' ya'll a little about that. Well, my husband's not paying the rent on our flat in the quarters no more, so now we gotta move. Rusty and I, we needed a place to stay and Uncle Bernard said we could live right here wit' him. He's such a good man, a real saint. And he's taken a real liking to Rusty too.

Fleur's mouth fell open. "You mean that you and Rusty will be staying here? Here?" Fleur's lips parted. She shook her head. "No, no you can't. It's not a good idea. You can stay with me instead."

Collette laughed out loud and threw herself against Louis's shoulder in exaggerated laughter. "In your small apartment? It's no bigga dan a closet. An artist's flat. This place is big." She spread her arms out.

"No, I'm moving into the Chinoiserie. You and Rusty can live with me."

Collette's squinted. "So you got the guest house and that fancy gazebo thing? Did your uncle get the house for taking care of you all those years?"

Fleur lowered her head. "No, the home belongs to me. I will inherit it from my parents."

She looked toward Louis and smirked. "Well, that's very good news for you. Now she's beautiful and rich, quite a nice catch now, ain't she?"

"Collette, I . . ."

But the woman's jaw was already set in defiance. "Thanks for the offer honey, but we're staying here. Florrie's gone. Bernard and Piper are the only ones living here besides the servants, and now you. All these rooms is going to waste. We're family and we'll be comfortable. Cozy, even." She ran her index finger along the chest of drawers. "Besides, Rusty could use a father figure in his life."

Fleur grasped at the air in front of her. "No."

"Why not?" Collette shrugged. "What could you possibly have against your uncle? The man just handed over a fancy schmancy house to you and this is the thanks he gets? He's a saint I tell you, a real saint."

Chapter Seven
That VooDoo You Do

  Philomene walked through the parlor and into the grand entryway frowning at the stench left behind by the herd of yesterday's folk. The morning light revealed all the spots and wrinkles of excess. Spilled drinks left stain splotches on the carpets and floors, the ashtrays overflowed with small volcanoes of ash, dirty glasses, and stacks of plates, cups and saucers occupied every surface both high and low. Busy at work from the first wink of light, the household staff clinked and clattered dishes back to the kitchen on large serving platters. But above all the noise, the sound of a simple broom brushing across the marble floor near the threshhold drew her.
  His arms and legs, lanky and long seemed out of proportion with the rest of his body. He'd lost weight in spite of her best efforts. She looked him over. Nothing but skin 'n bones and bruises from the beating he took. "How's my Tadpole t'day?"
  The smell of the corn fibers released to the air helped to dull the other scents in the room. Her brother looked up, a joyful grin on his swollen face. "Tadpole happy."
  She answered with smile and an affectionate squeeze to his arm. "You be sure ta go'n git you some breakfas' in the kitch'n. Reuben'll fix you up, ya hear?"
  "Yes'm." His mouth in a wide-open grin, she noticed how his fine white rows of teeth seemed bigger against the smallness of his body.
  "Go on now," she ordered.
  In a flash, the broom cracked against the floor. She started to call after him, but thought better of it. Leaning down, she lifted the willow broom handle and set it against the wall.
  A smile cracked through the apprehension holding her face in a vise. No use putting it off any longer. Philomene took slow, deliberate steps down the hall to Mister Bernard's study. Summoned by Cecelia, her heart sank as it always did, when called into his presence. No telling what the man would say or do.
  How many times had she made her way down that long hallway since then? Her thoughts went back to the first day, to the first summons she'd received.

***

The next morning the staff gathered around the kitchen table preparing for the ardous task of polishing the silverware, a household tradition. Usually the gathering was an opportunity to have a little breakfast and chitchat. But this time the group assembled around the table was a solemn one. The sudden loss of Rene' and Eleanor D'Hemecourt had left a veil of sorrow and uncertainty in the air. Today they pursued the time-consuming job in silence.

Fleur was upstairs, still asleep, so Philomene stole away for coffee and a quick breakfast. Normally, Philomene would have had the child up and about and tending to her studies, but her parents weren't there to teach her. She was going to need a tutor now, like the Schoenfield children on the other side of the avenue. Just as she began to pour a cup of dark coffee, she received a note from Florrie via the downstairs maid. The rest of the staff stopped what they were doing and looked to her.

Rueben, the cook put down his knife in mid chop to ask. "What they want?"

She shook her head. "Dese is uncertain days here at dis house. Best put owa bes' foot forward, y'hear? I been called to go an see de new folks in charge. Things is goin' be different 'round here. Dat Mista Ben'nad's nuthin' like his fine brotha Rene'. He couldn' hold a candle to Mr. Rene'. Dey as diff'nt as Cain 'n Able."

The new upstairs maid, Lottie asked. "What 'bout the Misses? What's she like?"

"She a clown." Cecelia answered.

Muffled laughter and merriment filled the kitchen with the warmth of camaraderie, but Philomene shushed them. "Let dere be no mo' of dis." She pointed towards the other side of the house. "Like I said, things is diff'nt now. Keep serious. No buffoonin'."

She took a quick sip. The rich, mellow taste of the coffee calmed her. Philomene put the cup back in the saucer and straightened her dress. She took a step to go, but turned instead, reaching for the cup again, downing its dark contents in one swallow.

Reuben smiled, rows of perfect white teeth against his dark skin. He called after her. "Coffee 'n chicory. 'Black as de debbil, strong as death, sweet as love, an' hot as hell.'"

The walk down two hallways, through the drawing room, past the sunroom to the door of the bedroom seemed to take forever but she couldn't help smiling for a bit at what Rueben said.

The closer she got to the bedroom, the more her legs felt like sledgehammers. She paused outside the door because she thought she heard an unfamiliar noise inside. Resolved to get the visit over and done with, she rapped firmly on the door.

"Come on in."

She pushed open the door. Florrie, her doughy flesh stuffed into a sheer pink negligee, sat at the dressing table admiring her reflection in the mirror. She held a piece of Eleanor's jewelry to her chest, one of several important pieces that had escaped Fleur's notice--the diamond and sapphire necklace Rene' gave his wife on her birthday. "Isn't it delicious?"

She closed the door behind her and approached the dressing table, but made sure to keep a respectable distance between them. Though her mouth longed to fall open at the sight of this vulture going through Eleanor's things, she resolved to cement her lips together for the duration of the meeting.

"Doesn't it bring out my eyes?" Florrie turned her head demurely from side to side, admiring every sparkle.

Bernard emerged from a door to the side garden just in time to answer. Wearing a black suit, starched white shirt and tie, he paused, locking eyes with the visitor in the room. But despite the eye contact, he ignored her when he moved.

And how he moved. Philomene couldn't help but notice. Like velvet. Confidant. Smooth. He loomed behind Florrie's dressing chair and rested his chin on her shoulder. "Yes it does my dear. Might I say, you're a beauty in those rocks."

"Oh Bernie . . . " Her face flushed as she reached for the glass of champagne on her dressing table.

As if noticing her for the first time, Bernard turned around and stood straight up. "You're Philomene, aren't you?"

"Yes sir."

He circled around her, inspecting, observing every detail. Anger began to rise within. Like scalded milk. These two were nothing more than flimflammers preying on the child and her estate.

"I've heard good things about you. Some very good things." He walked to the door. "Follow me to my—ah—the study, will you. You and I need to talk." He tipped an imaginary hat to Florrie, who giggled, sipping the rest of her champagne as she did.

Heart pounding, Philomene followed him down the dark hall to the room he now called "his" study. Why, he'd already taken possession of the home as if it were his own. And that detestable woman! Modelling Eleanor's jewelry and she not dead in the grave more than a week. Scandalous. Besides, the house, the jewelry and everything belonged to Fleur. Those two were nothing more than . . .

He opened the door, studying her face as she returned the gaze. "Penny for your thoughts?" Smiling, he held the door open for her, but instead of moving aside to let her pass, he stayed where he was, forcing her to brush past him. Bernard eased into the Oxblood leather chair behind Rene's massive mahogany desk. He pointed to a chair in front of the desk. "Please be seated."

"Yes sir." Philomene walked to the chair and sat on the edge, her back erect, formal.

He leaned backwards, the chair springs squeaking as he did. Arms behind his neck, he looked at her. "You're name is Philomene St. James. You're one of six children but you live on Terpsichore Street with your mother and a younger brother. Much younger."

"Yes suh, I do." She tried her best to swallow, but her throat felt as if it were collapsing on itself. *Stay solid, Philomene.* She tried to keep her eyes down, focusing on her shoes but inside, her heart raced.

He fiddled with his hand, as if engrossed with a fingernail. "Tell me, what's it like to have a melonhead in the family?"

In spite of all her attempts at self-control, she gasped. "What?"

But the man stayed cool as a cucumber. "Your mama gave birth to a retarded baby, a stupid moron. What's it like having a loon in the house?"

She stood, body vibrating with emotion held back by the thinnest excuse.

He motioned with his hand. "Sit back down."

When she did not comply right away, he barked another command. "NOW."

Philomene collapsed into the chair this time, angry tears rising.

"Before you get your liver all in a quiver over what I said, hear me out." He stood and walked over to the window, pulling open the curtains. The mild light of early morning filtered in, almost softening his hard features. "You call him Tadpole, right?"

She nodded, face quivering.

He focused on something outside the window. Voice mocking, he continued. "Because he likes to play with tadpoles. Always did. From what I hear, that's pretty much all the boy does. How old is he?"

Bernard turned from the window and focused his gaze on her. "That's all right. You don't have to answer that. I already know." He approached her and stood to the side of her chair looking down. "He's twenty and never held a job."

She shook her head, tears streaming.

"Well how would you like him to have one? Why, I'd be happy to keep your little melonhead in my employ. That's right. Just to show you what a nice guy I am, I'm gonna give the little fella a job here on the estate."

She mustered the boldness to ask. "D-doing w-hat?"

"I dunno. Sweeping maybe. He can sweep, can't he? Even morons can do that."

She stared straight ahead, holding her tongue and her anger back.

"Well then, whaddya know? He has himself a job, his very first job." He grabbed her by the arm. "Well, aren't you going to say anything?"

Startled, Philomene drew back, but his grip stayed tight until she answered, then released. Stay cool. Stay cool. "Why, t-thank you Mister D'Hemecourt."

His eyes shifted across her face, lingering as he spoke, face drawing closer.

"She walks in beauty like the night. Of cloudless climes and starry skies. And all
 that's best of dark and bright."

With that, Bernard kissed her, pressing his lips hard on hers.

She fell back against the chair, eyes wide with horror.

Then he shuffled back to the desk and shrugged. "Lord Byron. What can I say? I have an ear for good poetry. And beautiful women."

"Mister D'Hemecourt. P-please may I—may I go now?"

At the bar, he filled a glass. "Care for something? A little Bourbon and branch water, maybe? Or do you think it's too early? It isn't for Florrie. Nor for me either, it seems. Oh well."

Bernard tipped the glass back. 'You might be asking yourself, why is this wonderful man doing such a benevolent thing for me? And what do I have to do in return?"

Chest heaving, she slid to the edge of her chair, ready to make a run for the door.

He waved the hand holding the drink. "Relax, although I think you are luscious, quite frankly I am attracted to younger women. "No, I'm thinking about other kinds of favors you might do for me from time to time. I take care of you. You take care of me and everybody's happy, including Tadpole. You got it?"

Philomene stood to her feet, stretching out her backbone as she did. "Tadpole don't need no job. I take care of him."

"That's true . . . but what if . . ." He stroked his chin. "What if you lost your job? Then what would happen?"

"You'd sack me?" She closed her eyes.

"I'm not saying that, but let's face it, something like that could happen. You never know about these things. And of course, when word like that gets out, other people wouldn't want to hire you. Why, you'd be blacklisted around this town." He laughed. "Hey, that's kinda funny. Blacklisted an all."

Mind racing, she recognized the truth in his veiled threat. He could fix her good. Fix it so she would never get another job in New Orleans again. She'd have to move far away from her family to find another decent job. "Mister D'Hemecourt, what do you want from me?"

Bernard put his drink down and walked towards her. She watched his every move. Inside, part of her shrank back, afraid that he would try to mash his mouth against hers again or worse. She stood her ground though. But instead of trying anything, he stood facing her, the dark circles around his eyes mesmerizing.

"Good, I like your directness. Okay, here's the deal. I want to hire your brother to work for me and I want you to thank me by doing some innocent favors for me from time to time. I need someone to deliver messages and to work on special projects here and there. Someone who can keep quiet and not ask too many questions."

The part about innocent favors relaxed her a mite, though she weighed the lesser of two evils, not liking the thought of either. "Maybe."

He studied her. "I still don't think you're too keen on it, but I will accept your affirmation, my dear. And there's more. You'll benefit financially. I reward my people. You know why? Because I value loyal service."

"May I go?"

He opened his desk drawer. "Certainly, but before you leave, I want you to take a look at something."

Heart in her throat, she stood, her body shaking under her and walked to the desk. Her eyes traveled down to a small black pistol. In one swift motion, he pushed the drawer shut.

"Like I said, I value and reward loyalty. Remember that and you'll do okay."

As she bolted for the door, he called after her. "Have the boy start tomorrow."

The very second the door was shut she looked both ways down the hall wondering which way to run, where to go, what to tell folks. She needed to think, to sit and think--the linen closet! A fast dash and she was in.

Surrounded by floor to ceiling shelves of clean, pressed sheets and towels, folded and starched to military precision, sprinkled with rose water. The room smelled fresh, clean and inviting, but more than that, safe. She pulled up an old stepstool and sank to it.

Every instinct told her the man was of the devil, evil through and through. His kiss disgusted her. She rubbed the hem of her apron over and around her mouth, spitting into it to remove all traces of his bile and bad spirit.

No way she was gonna tell the staff about this. There was danger in that. What could he want from her? Philomene grabbed a fragrant towel and buried her head in it. She began to weep in silent dismay, her sobs shaking the uneven stool from side to side. In her heart of hearts, she knew Tadpole was in danger and so was she. And somehow, she knew sweet Fleur would be next. Those two were after the fortune Rene' and Eleanor had left to her. And Fleur stood in the way of it.

His words circled in her head until suddenly a thought came to her like a bolt of lightening. The horror of it left her cold. "Lord no." Fleur was supposed to be on that trip with them, but she got sick and couldn't. The trip, a guided tour of plantation homes, was a birthday gift to Rene' from his brother and sister-in-law. In fact, Bernard and Florrie had arranged everything. What if? Could it be?

From that moment on, a resolution filled her soul. Her own life, be forfeit if she did not live it to prove their guilt and somehow, some way protect Fleur's life. She fell to her knees in prayer. "Please help her Jesus. And Lord help us all."

***

She knocked on the door and it opened at once. Alcide held the doorknob and waved his hand for her to enter. Philomene resisted the wave of anger that rose hot up her neck. At the sight of him, an odious sickness filled her stomach.

"Come in Phil. Please." Bernard sat in front of his desk, not at it this time. Nestled in a wingback chair by the window, the sunlight revealed every broken capillary on his nose and chin. He looked older and unhealthy, a fresh crop of gray at his hairline.

He held a paper in front of him and took his eyes off to view her.

"Yes Mista Bernard."

He continued reading. "One moment. I'm almost done." He held up the paper. "Alcide, take this letter to Piper. I want this typed up. Bring it to me as soon as she's done. I'm going to send Philo to deliver it to Dr. Duplessis."

Bernard scrubbed his hands together. "Phil, did I mention to you that I'm to be the next King? Pierre LeBouissiere had to back out suddenly for health reasons and of course, I expressed an interest--anyway, they voted me in as his replacement."

"Congrat'lations Mista Bernard."

"Piper is to be my Queen. Lucky for me, the former king was similar in size. The costumes are already made, but need to be fitted. You're to arrange for Piper's fittings." He handed her a card. "Here's the number to call. The first is tomorrow and the seamstresses will have to move fast. They have to alter the dress intended for a bigger boned girl, though I suppose the task is easier trimming a dress down."

She cast her eyes down, afraid to see the look in his eyes. "Yes sir, Mista Bernard."

"And one more thing." He sighed. "That letter I'm sending you to deliver is to a psychiatrist friend of mine. He's going to send a messenger with it."

Her mind raced at the mention of that name. Duplessis. Gerard's last name. His father? "Suh? Are you. . ."

He shook his head. "No I'm not sick, Phil." A sardonic smile eclipsed his face. "But thanks for your genuine concern."

Her lips stuck together, throat dry as a bone.

"Look at me."

She forced her head up.

"I want you to prepare a draught."

An inward shiver rolled through her, heart thumping hard in response.

"You remember how, don't you? Just like you used to prepare for my dear wife when she was having trouble sleeping."

He stood. Back to her, he stared out the window. She caught a glimpse of his line of vision. Rusty bounced a red ball back and forth with Tadpole on the lawn. Sun shining, his hair a brilliant red, the child laughed as Tadpole chased after the wayward ball, his large feet kicking the ball further away.

"You didn't answer."

She swallowed and somehow found her voice. "I do."

"As soon as the medicine arrives, I want you to let me know. Then I will let you know when to prepare it and for whom. Do you understand?"

Shaking, she answered. "Yes suh."

He turned around. "Don't you want to know who the draught is for, Phil?" He circled her. "Aren't you the least bit curious?"

"No suh."

Settling behind her, he placed his hands on her shoulders and whispered into her ear.

God forbid. A lone tear ran down her cheek, the first of many to come, though not now. She would not cry in front of this man. Would not give him the satisfaction of seeing her weep.

Oh, and one more thing. I want Florrie's room cleaned out. Have all the furniture removed and burn all the linens. A decorator is coming in next month. Dispose of all her clothing too. I want the closet clean as a whistle."

Get rid of all of Florrie's things? So soon? What was the man up to? "Yes suh Mista Bernard."

"May I go now?" She stood as still as she could.

He sat back in the chair and waved her away. "You're free to go, but," her pointed, "inform me right away when the medicine arrives. I mean it."

"Yes suh, Mista Bernard."

She shut the doors behind her in slow motion and retreated to a familiar place. The linen closet had changed little during the years. Still a place of peace and refuge from his tyrannical outbursts, she sat in the new stool. Made of metal, it felt hard on her rear end, so she found a towel, pressed in a neat square on the shelf and slipped it under her.

Philomene hugged her arms around her shoulders and rocked back and forth. "God bless Fleur." She looked up. "Jesus, I need you. Lord Jesus please come an' hep us. Nobody's safe from him, not nobody."

***

Piper gazed out the second floor window of the Chinoiserie at the same outdoor scene. Rusty and Tadpole tossing the ball to one another. Her mouth puckered up in distaste.

"Look at them. Two children at play. Honest, I don't know why father keeps either one of them around. And the child's mother is awful. I hate Collette. I'm ashamed we're related. She's so common, and her accent grates on me."

"Come back to bed."

"I want to leave this place. Travel around." She continued her stare out the window, but looked up at the blue of the sky instead. "Do you realize I've never been anywhere at all? Not to Paris or London or Rome. I haven't even been to New York. Most girls my age have been everywhere."

"I'm lonely." She heard him patting the mattress.

Piper clutched at the window frame. "Father says he'll make up for it though. He says I'll have the best of everything; he'll see to it. Do you believe him? Should I?"

She turned, clutching the thin robe about her coyly. The man, muscular arm propped on a pillow, smiled. "I'll take your mind off your problems."

Piper strode to the bed and stood, eyes locked on his. With deliberate slowness, she let the robe fall, and slid under the sheets.

Chapter Eight
Chameleon

Collette's question rang through her head like a broken record, the needle digging a groove ever deeper. Why don't I want them to move in? There's no logical reason. And yet, an ominous sense of dread gripped her inside when she thought of it.

Running late for an unexpected surprise, a luncheon date with Piper, she'd splurged on a cab. Somehow, knowing that she was to come into money did little to assuage her present condition. But she managed.

Piper said she needed to talk. Perhaps grieving over her mother's passing, the pain still acute. Mourning. Well, if her cousin needed to talk, Fleur would be there to listen. After all, the two of them used to be quite close--like sisters. In latter years however, they'd grown apart. Going away to school didn't help matters. She and Piper wrote letters of course and there was the occasional phone call, but no visits. And since her return to New Orleans, they'd spoken to one another but few and far between.

A scant two months had passed since the funeral. Fleur balanced her time between two things, painting and Louis. He'd taken her dancing, dining, to the opera house, the cinema and even a romantic picnic or two in City Park. In fact, they'd been almost inseparable since he rescued her. Fleur's heart swelled at the mere thought of him. An odd feeling, one she'd never felt for any other man before.

***

A practiced line of smoke rings paused together in the air above Bernard D'Hemecourt. Settled in his favorite chair, he held a Cuban cigar in one hand and a cocktail in the other.

"So you believe you can carry out this--this venture? You really do?" His eyes widened.

"Piece of cake."

Bernard sat forward, triggering the inevitable squeak of the chair springs. "Gerard, is there something you haven't told me? You tell me, 'it's a piece of cake' as if you've done this sort of thing before. Have you?"

Gerard Duplessis looked and behaved the part of a wealthy young man. The matte black suit and tie he wore contrasted with his fair features. But beneath the surface of a privileged exterior, his heart stirred a darker roux. He and Bernard shared a similar mindset and from time to time, he used the lad for a few special jobs. Not that the young dandy cared about the money. No, there was something more in it for him. He wondered if there were limits to what the man would do.

As if ignoring the question, Gerard went on. "There are legends in the swamp, stories of people disappearing. The Will-O'-the-Wisp for instance."

Bernard put his drink down and stretched back, eyes narrowing. Tendrils of cigar smoke coiled ever higher above his head. "I've heard a few of those myself. What's with the fairy tales? He pointed the cigar at him. "What I want to know is--do you have the guts for it? Alcide thought he had the know-how for it, but he failed miserably. In my opinion, I think the boy's sweet on Fleur. Maybe he didn't really want to get rid of her." He raised his glass. "Who can blame him though? She's a rare and beautiful creature."

"He's weak, a two-bit hustler." Gerard snapped his fingers. "I'll have her eating out of my hand. Fast as you can blink, she'll be gone. I swear it with my life."

The whites of his eyes gleaming against dark pupils, Bernard locked eyes with him. "Then the stakes are high indeed. You have an interesting perspective, young man. And I do appreciate that. However, the point is, our boy from the parish tried to do away with her in some very creative ways that would have looked like accidents, and still he failed. You call him weak. What makes you so strong? How do I know you have the stomach for it?"

"He's got what it takes, Father." Piper rested her hands on Gerard's shoulders. "He's colder than an ice house. Aren't you, darling?" She leaned in close to him, eye to eye.

Gerard stared at her. "You make me sound like a monster."

She cupped his chin in her hand, charm bracelet jingling. "My dear Gerard, a monster is exactly what we need."

Piper checked her watch. We'd better get a move on. She'll be arriving any minute."

Bernard put on his reading glasses and called out to them as they reached the mahogany doors. "Time's running out, you know.

Our little foundling has to go away before her twenty-first birthday or we won't have a pot to . . . "

"Wait." Gerard stayed the door. "There's something I want to know."

Bernard slid his glasses low on his nose. "Yes?"

"Why didn't you get rid of her before? You had ample opportunities."

But Bernard seemed intent on straightening the papers on his desk. Without looking up, he answered. "Mind your own beeswax and do your job."

***

Fleur stepped out of the taxi and paid the driver. Tadpole, on the far side of the veranda, stopped his sweeping and flapped his hands in greeting--a wide, white smile accompanying his welcome.

She waved back, amused at his childlike enthusiasm. "Hello Tadpole."

As she approached the house, she heard laughter coming from the direction of the Chinoiserie and noticed the figure of a man, partially obscured by camellia bushes.. She continued to the front door. A mystery guest? Could it be the boyfriend Piper had told Louis about?

Flery rang the bell. Cecelia opened the door and gave a little curtsy. Streaks of gray in her hair were the only hints she'd aged. Skin clear and unlined, her hourglass figure had remained the same over the years.

"Welcome home, Miz Fleur."

"Thank you Cecelia. It's a pleasure to be here again." The moment she said the words, she wondered at their veracity. Did she really feel at home here in this house?

I'll take you to Miz Piper. Lunch is almost ready. As Cecelia turned to go, Fleur stopped her and pointed. "Wait a minute. Who's the man out at the Chinoiserie?"

"Oh, that's Mister Duplessis."

"What's his first name?" she asked.

"Mista' Gerard."

"Who is he? A friend of Piper or Uncle?"

She drew closer to Fleur and looked around. "Both of 'em, I think. They's together a lot. He in biznus wit Mista Bernard." She whispered. "He propa rich an' come from a well-to-do family."

She nodded wondering why Cecelia, who hardly ever said anything was so talkative. "Thank you." Fleur wet her lips with her tongue. "Don't worry about announcing me. Just take me to her."

Cecelia winked "Lunch at da Chin-wah-sheree. Follow me."

"Where's uncle. What about Collette and Rusty?"

"Oh, dey all at de zoo. Rusty cute as a June bug! He wanna see de elefons so dey took him."

"That's nice." A sense of disappointment filled her though. "Seeing the youngster always cheered her mood."

The woman led her through the house, rooms shuttered to the noonday sun, but halfway to the door, Fleur stopped.

"Miz Fleur?"

Cecelia, I want to say hello to Philomene for a moment."

She frowned. "Philomene love to see you any time. You shore right now is when you wants to visit wit her? Miz Piper's waitin'. Mebbe you could go afta."

Fighting the annoyance to her suggestion, Fleur replied. "No, I'm going to see her now."

She drew her hands together in front of her apron. "Awright den, Miz Fleur. Please follow me. She in the kitchen office."

"Thank you Cecelia, but I know the way."

"Yes ma'am."

Cecelia followed behind Fleur. The woman took out her aggravation on the floor with hard deliberate steps.

Head in her hands, Philomene looked up and sat straight when they entered the room.

"Fleur? I'da thought a herd o' elefons was runnin' trew da house. Thought mebbe Rusty brought sum back from de zoo."

The young woman hugged her neck and brushed a kiss on her cheek. "Philo. I don't know why, but I had the strongest feeling that I needed to see you." She glanced back toward the door. "That'll be all for now Cecelia."

"Yes ma'am." She closed the door.

"Oh chile'," Philomene latched onto her hand, tears welling her eyes, "we always did have a heart string connecting us."

"Is anything wrong?"

The older woman sighed, leaning back in her chair. "Somebody hurt Tadpole."

"Oh no." Fleur gasped. "When? Is he all right? I saw him a few minutes ago."

"I think so. But he was banged up good. It was the day of Miz Florrie's funeral. Mista Louis, he tried to hep him an'all, but that Miz Piper spit venom out her lips. She got a black heart that one. Black as her fath--" She caught her breath in mid-sentence.

"Anyways, I dress his wounds 'n, fed him a 'lil sumpthin' an put him in mah bed." She shook her head. "Jus' cause he simple, don't mean folks kin pick on him. I never undastan why anyone would do sumpthin' like dat to him."

"That's horrible. Do you know who did it?"

"I has my suspicions. An' Lord help Alcide if I fine out fo sho' in da state I'm in right now."

With the promise to help Philomene look into the matter, Fleur followed Cecelia to the side door, which led to the garden path to the Chinoiserie, the very door she'd walked through the day her parents died.

Memories of the day floated through her mind as she stepped from the darkened interior into the bright sunshine. She squinted before stepping out to follow Cecelia down the brick path across the green lawn. The voices grew louder—and the laughter. Piper's voice clear and melodic pierced through, a voice better than Florrie's, more pleasant to be sure. But today, her voice had an extraordinary lilt.

When Cecelia climbed the steps to announce her arrival, a man in a dark suit turned to face her. His features lovely, endearing--Fleur delighted in the strands of sunstreaked hair around the man's face, and the way it accented the translucent blue of his eyes. As she stepped up to the pavilion, he bowed low before her. "Miss D'Hemecourt." He rose to full stature. "Gerard T. Duplessis, at your service. I am delighted to make your acquaintance Mademoiselle, though I must admit, I've heard so very much about you, I feel as if we are old friends."

She held out her hand. "Fleur D'. . ." But the shake she'd expected became a kiss. And another surprise, her skin tingled at the touch of his lips. She noticed a subtle accent in his voice, curiously enough, an Acadian lilt.

"Fleur." Piper joined them, embracing her, with a kiss on the cheek. Her shiny black hair, waved into a fashionable shoulder-length style suited her more than the severe styles she wore while in mourning. Her eyes sparkled when she spoke. She seemed more youthful, happier.

"So glad you could come today. I know you're busy finishing up for the gallery showing." She turned to Gerard. "Just as I told you. She's an artiste' of rare and extraordinary talent. I'm so excited about her show. I've invited everyone who's anyone in this town to come. You'll have quite a troop come through those doors. I hope your little gallery friend is prepared for the invasion."

She smiled. "Yes, I do believe he is. I'm afraid the onus is on me to finish the work."

Piper patted her back. "You'll do it. Shame on you for doubting yourself." She turned to Gerard. "My cousin is quite talented you know, though she'd never admit it."

She pointed towards a table set in the middle of the pavilion, beneath a canopy of blooming wisteria, and motioned towards Gerard as well. "Let's do sit. I'm famished." Gerard pulled their chairs and the three were seated.

Piper snapped the napkin in one quick motion and laid it to rest on her lap. "Now then, Fleur I know this little luncheon was to be for the two of us, but when I found out our Mr. Duplessis was to be here at the house all day instead of being called away on business as is usually the case, why I thought we could handle an uneven number for the noonday meal. Besides, it's high time the two of you met. He's been staying in your guesthouse for the past couple of weeks you know. I hope you don't mind, my dear." She cupped her hand in conspiratorial mirth. "It's Fleur's favorite place."

"Really?" Fleur looked into his eyes. The indirect sunlight revealed golden flecks of color floating in the midst of pale blue.

"Why yes, a most unusual place. It has been a pleasure to stay there, but had I known it was a place special to you Miss Fleur, I would have treasured it all the more." He smiled.

Cecelia returned from the main house, carrying a small tray with linen napkins and little bowls of clear water, a thin slice of lemon floating in the center of each. She held the tray first in front of Fleur, who cleaned her hands and dried them on the small towel. Piper came next, and Gerard followed suit.

Piper lifted a crystal pitcher and began to pour minted tea into tall frosted glasses. The sight of the frosted glasses brought on a sudden thirst and Fleur indulged in a few extended sips from her glass before the others even raised theirs. Sweet tea infused with fresh garden mint and honey, a delight.

Two new servants Fleur recognized from the kitchen the day of the funeral emerged from the house, food on lidded silver trays. The servants placed the trays on a wide etarge', lifted the lids and began to serve. Chilled bowls of salad topped with lump crabmeat, followed by cucumber soup, crusty French bread and a lemon parfait for dessert.

As they began to eat, Gerard started off the conversation. "So you're an artist. What sort of mediums do you paint? Bowls of fruit?"

She held a hand to her mouth to laugh, as did Piper.

"Hardly."

An amused expression on his face, he held his fork in mid-air. "Then what do you paint?"

Piper answered. "Her work is different. How should I best describe it? Hmmm." She looked to Fleur.

"Her paintings are darker, different from what one would expect. The painted images tell a story."

"A story?" He asked.

"Yes," Fleur spoke up, "a story." She pointed to the wall above the etarge'. "Notice the characters on that wall. They're all hand-painted from traditional Chinese folk tales. The girl for instance."

"The girl?" He leaned in closer as if to follow the direction of her eyes. She swallowed. "Y-yes, the girl with the parasol. Do you see her?"

"Why yes, I do." Piper joined in. "She appears to be running."

"Yes, she does. She's looking over her shoulder I think," he added.

Fleur nodded. "Very observant. In fact, she is.

Her name is Meng Chiang-nu. Her husband was forced into service to build the Great Wall by the Chinese emperor. Seasons passed and he did not return. There is a song she would sing to pass the days:

In March the peach is blossom-dressed;

Swallows, mating, build their nest.
Two by two they gaily fly....
Left all alone, how sad am I!

So she sewed her dear husband some warm clothing and set out to find him. She traveled over a great distance. However, when she reached the Wall and inquired of the other thin and suffering workers, she found that he had died some time ago. She cried with bitter grief for him, her mourning so great that two hundred miles of the wall crumbled. When the emperor came out to see for himself what sort of person she was who could do this, he saw that she was as beautiful as a fairy and asked her to become his concubine."

"And did she?" Gerard asked.

Fleur blinked. "She agreed on three conditions."

Piper rested her elbows on the table. "What conditions were those?"

"That the body of her husband buried unceremoniously under the Great Wall, be dug up and placed in a golden coffin, that the emperor's ministers and generals go into mourning for her husband and follow the coffin and that the emperor himself would mourn and follow the coffin to the tomb. The emperor agreed because he was quite taken with her beauty."

She continued. "On the day of the funeral, the emperor, his ministers and generals followed the golden coffin containing the remains of Meng Chiang-nu's husband. She watched as he was given a proper burial and then threw herself into the river that flowed nearby."

"The woman took her own life?" Piper asked. "How sad."

"Yes and the emperor, infuriated, commanded his attendants to pull her body from the river. But before they did, she had turned into a beautiful silver fish that looped gracefully into the blue green water and was never seen again."

"What a beautiful, terrible story." Piper rested her head in her hands. "I don't know whether to laugh or cry."

Gerard nodded, attentive to her words. "I like it." He pointed to the wall. "I would never have spotted that just from looking at the walls here. I've stared at them all the days I been here and never once thought there might be a story attached to the pictures."

"Well," Fleur smiled, "now you do." A sudden gust of wind sent a stray curl over one eye. In an instant, eyes locked upon hers, he lifted his hand. With a gentle touch, he brushed it away from her face. Fleur's heart quickened, her chest rose and fell. Proximity to such a man seemed to evoke high voltage electricity. She coughed, a ruse to break the silent connection between them.

"And now I really want to see what masterpieces this famous artist has painted." He raised his head, focusing his wondrous eyes upon her. "I'm intrigued at the stories she has to tell."

She stared back, amazed, mesmerized. But thoughts of Louis stilled her rampant emotions and she was able to collect her voice enough to answer. "This place with its curious artwork and artifacts, inspired me to pursue my dream of becoming an artist, to tell a story on canvas instead of in a book, with a paintbrush instead of a pen."

He cleared his throat. "When may I see them?"

"At the gallery showing."

Piper joined in. "Don't feel bad. She never lets us see her work before it's done."

He scoffed. "I will convince her."

"Perhaps you will, Gerard. Perhaps you will." Piper sat back, a smile on her face.

Gathering boldness, Fleur asked him. "Where are you from, if you don't mind my asking?"

He seemed surprised at first by her question, but answered at once. "Why from here, of course. But if you're referring to my accent, I spent a lot of time in the bayou country where my parents have a fishing camp. We went there quite a lot when I was growing up. I'm afraid I'm quite the sportsman."

"Yes," Piper added. "That's how we met. Our camp, Coeur de l'eau is about five miles from his and curious though it is, in all these years of going to our camp and fishing, the two of us never crossed paths, until late last year that is. My father adores him, just adores our dear Gerard."

Alerted by a sound, Fleur noticed her taxicab rolling down the long graveled drive. "I see my transportation has arrived." Fleur removed her napkin and stood, followed by the two of them. She embraced her cousin, "My dear, thank you for a delightful afternoon. Both the luncheon and company were superb."

She turned to shake Gerard's hand, but again he brought her hand to his mouth, his eyes locked to hers seemed amused by her discomfort.

"What a pleasure it was to meet you Mr. Duplessis."

"Gerard. Please call me Gerard Perhaps we will meet again soon. I must see those paintings of yours."

She drew back her hand. "We shall see." Fleur gathered her purse and her gloves and set off through the yard toward the taxi.

***

Piper drew near to Gerard. "I told you she was beautiful, didn't I?"

"You did," he smiled. "But most people exaggerate beauty. I hardly expected her to be quite so handsome in person."

She wrapped an arm around his waist. "Do you think she likes you? From my vantage point, it seemed so."

Unfazed by Piper's conversation or touch, Gerard watched the vehicle turn and head out toward the street. "Indeed I do."

Piper fastened her eyes on him. "I hope so." She pulled a slip of paper from her pocket and handed it to him. "Here's her address. Call on her soon. Like father said, time is running out."

Chapter Nine
A House Divided

Fleur plopped her paintbrush into a murky jar of mineral spirits and folded her arms. She backed up to get a different perspective of her latest work, a rendering of the house on St Charles Avenue. Hmmm. Aunt Florrie would have been pleased with the moonlit aspect, and perhaps Uncle Bernard as well.

But there was something not quite right about it. The haze of evening surrounding the home certainly had the ethereal quality she'd purposed. Eyes in a steadied squint, she considered solutions, perhaps more shadowing in the foliage surrounding the veranda, or additional highlighting on the side of the house to reflect the luminous light of the full moon. Hmmm.

A knock on the door interrupted her musings. She snapped her wrist forward and gasped at the hour on her wristwatch. Oh no, the time. When she stood in front of a canvas, the world and everything in it ceased. Pick up a paintbrush and minutes turned to hours and hours to days and days to nights. Meals were forgotten, appointments lost. But these were the times she came closest to understanding the concept her mother taught her of God as Creator--each life a blank canvas to stroke with feathered prisms of color, with brightness, shadow, life.

She pulled off her artist's smock and began a frantic rush to wipe enough oil paint off her hands so she could answer the door. In her hurry, she forgot her cardinal rule as an artist—to cover the canvas. "Coming. Is that you, Louis?"

"Yes, it's me." came the muffled reply.

Hands still sticky with paint, Fleur grabbed a rag and used it to turn the doorknob. The sight of him took her breath away. Wearing a dark, fitted suit in grey pinstripe and matching grey silk tie, Louis Russo cut a handsome silhouette.

The smock slipping from her hands, she gulped.

A slight bow forward, a charming smile on his tanned face, Louis spoke up. "Well, aren't you going to invite me in?"

"Oh, please excuse me, Louis. Come in." She got a grip on the smock and held her arm out to show him into the apartment. Fleur followed, closing the door as she did.

He stopped in the middle of the room to look around. A mountain of wall-to-wall boxes surrounded them.

"I can't tell if you're moving in or out."

She smiled, aware of an awkward shyness in his presence. "Both."

His gaze settled on her skirt and blouse. She held her breath. Though his face registered confusion, he rallied.

"You're even more beautiful when you smile." Louis stepped close reaching out to clasp her hands, but she took a step back. "What's this?" he asked. "We're still dining at Antoine's, aren't we?"

"Why of course. I-I. . ." A flood of pink rushed to her cheeks as she held up her hands to reveal the viscid smudges of oil paint adhered to her palms.

"Ahhh, you've been busy I see."

Fleur rushed to grab a rag, opened the cap on a tin of Turpentine, turned it over and swished some into the cloth. She joined him still standing by the door.

"What is that concoction?" His nose accordianed distaste. "It smells awful."

"Paint thinner." Fleur smiled as she pressed the saturated cloth hard against her skin. She cast a look down at her shabby clothing, smeared with old dabs of paint, torn at the hem, a missing button at her collar. "Louis, I'm so sorry. I wear this old outfit when I paint. I was working and lost track of time."

Fleur put down the rag and sprinted to the door of her bedroom. "I'll just be a minute if you don't mind waiting. Why don't you have a seat?" She pointed to the grey wingback chair and tried not to bite her lip, a vexing habit. Would her suggestion keep him from gravitating to the opposite side of the room toward the canvas she'd neglected to cover? She always insisted they meet in the courtyard below, until today that is. With the state of her flat, Louis would surely consider her a lazybones.

He grinned. "I don't mind. I'll just make myself at home here in this forest of boxes."

A hesitant glance, she scurried into the bedroom, closed the door behind her and leaned against it, eyes shut in relief. *Louis Russo, why oh why am I forever flustered in your presence?* She'd returned to New Orleans only months ago and they'd become quite an item, the serious attorney and the eccentric artist. Though pleased that he had come to court her, Fleur had reservations concerning the fast pace of their relationship and her life--the art degree, the move from New York back to the Crescent City, Aunt Florrie's passing . . .

She thought of the yellow checker taxicabs in New York, meters ticking away, driving round and round the city. Their relationship up to this point had been as hurried and frenetic. But a thought nagged at her—that it would only a matter of time before he found fault with her. No matter how promising previous relationships started out, they all ended the same—in heartbreak.

Her eyes fluttered open. She wiped away beginning tears.

Clothing layed out on the bed, she lauded her earlier efforts at preparation for their dinner date. Smart thinking. She'd also taken a bath in lavender salts earlier, washed and pinned her hair, pressed her clothing with rose water, and set out her shoes and nylons as well. Contrary to her cousin Collette's belief that Fleur had naturally perfect hair, Fleur pin curled her honey-colored locks every other day.

At the bathroom sink she lathered a bar of Ivory on her hands and forearms to clean all traces of turpentine. She ran a comb with care through small sections of her hair and swept the curls away from her face to each side, fastening her locks with small mother of pearl combs, a perfect match to the petite pearl earrings she wore. A careful application of China red lipstick followed by a blot on a piece of salvaged tissue paper and she was ready. Almost. She pinched her cheeks and was about to open the door when she spotted the bottle of perfume. Perhaps a dab of Shalimar on her wrists, and maybe on her neck as well. She tipped the crystal decanter sideways to her fingertips and applied the fragrance, savoring wisps of vanilla, lemon, jasmine, rose. She felt a blush rise at the thought of Louis's tender lips on her neck.

In a scant few minutes, she emerged from her room to find him standing in front of her work. "Oh no, you mustn't see it. Not yet." Heart racing, she reached for a sheet to cover the canvas, but a gentle movement of his hand folded over her wrist.

"No, please don't." She watched, astounded as he brushed a tear away. "This is your uncle's house as I've never before seen it before. Nor imagined it to be."

She snapped the sheet out. "I'm rather particular about showing my work to anyone before it's complete."

He peeked over his shoulder at her. "Not even me? Surely you'll make an exception for the new president of your fan club, as of right now at least." He winked. "Your picture is remarkable. I'm quite amazed."

"Really?" Fleur took a few steps to stand beside him. "It's not finished. You really like it?"

Louis shook his head. "I don't like it. I adore it." He grasped her shoulders. "I am truly impressed with your talent and . . . " he stepped back to look at her, " . . .and with you." He exhaled. "That's some dress."

"Thank you."

Beyond her, his eyes settled on something. "Is that clock right?"

She followed his gaze. "It's ten minutes fast."

Louis stroked his chin. "Let me guess. It helps keep you on time." He laughed. "Except when you're painting."

She reached for the sheet. "May I? A cover over the canvas keeps it from drying too fast."

"And the cover prevents curious people from seeing it as well." He laughed and helped her arrange the sheet over the canvas. "Say, don't you have a gallery showing on the calendar?" He gestured toward the painting. Is this one going to be in it?"

She shook her head. "I-I don't know yet."

"Well I'm no expert," he drew close, "but I think this one should be included."

Though her skin tingled at such an intimate distance, she maintained her composure enough to comment. "By the way Louis, just so you know, it's a painting, not a picture.

He kissed her hand. Face-to-face, he whispered. "It's a work of art, like you."

When he spoke, her heart fluttered ten thousand feet above and plummeted to the depths of the sea. At least she imagined so. She tried to answer and realized she'd stopped breathing. Her mouth finally opened enough to suck in some air. "We should go."

Louis held out his arm. "I'm ready if you are Madamoiselle."

He stopped to sniff the air. "I much prefer the perfume you're wearing to that eau 'd paint thinner." Louis smiled and held out his arm. "May I escort you?"

Fleur smiled in response. "Yes, you may. And if I look wonderful, it's only because you were so patient to wait for me. Sorry to be such a fuss and bother."

He gave her arm a little squeeze. "You're no bother, but even if you were, you'd be worth the wait."

She glanced down at the outfit she'd scrimped and saved to buy in New York. The navy blue narrow skirt and floral halter topped by a light wool suit coat fit her to a tee. What an irony to have had good taste, but no budget to indulge an appetite for fashion.

Descending the stairs from her second floor flat, they set out through the pleasant shade of the courtyard. Fountain bubbling, large green banana leaves soaring above they started out on the short walk to the restaurant, arm-in arm.

Chapter Ten
Intuition

The familiar façade of Antoine's in view, a smile bloomed across her face. Fond memories of dining there with her parents embraced her heart. The restaurant was part of a grand family tradition in New Orleans, offering a treasury of French Creole food to generations. In the golden light of late afternoon, the couple arrived at the entrance, the name shaded under the ornate black ironwork balustrade above. A bank of windows across the entrance affected a charming glow, the ethereal meld of sunset and gas-lit splendor. Martin, Louis's personal waiter met them in the foyer. Those who frequented Antoine's often, or were generational customers, as was the case with Louis's family and her own, had their favorite waiters-- a step above the hoi polloi. The men in the family carried "the card" in their billfolds as a sign of status. Martin had an intuitive skill when it came to suggesting their favorite cocktails and dishes and in fact, often brought them to the table without being asked. And Fleur decided to enjoy being pampered for a change. After living off what she could heat up on a hot plate, the prospect of another elegant dinner here with Louis excited her palate.

They followed Martin through the grand room, past cypress windows, plastered walls, and elegant chandeliers stabbing crystalline light in geometric patterns throughout the room. The passed the famed carnival rooms—Rex, Proteus, Twelfth Night, the 1840 room, which once served as a French Quarter jail according to Martin. He escorted them past a vast dining room of set with fine silver and crisp white tablecloths, down a narrow hall decorated with a checkerboard of black-framed pictures against a bold red wall.

"Where are we going, Louis?"

He patted her hand. "Martin, why don't you tell her?

The waiter tipped his head to the side. "As you wish, Monsieur Louis."

An older man, she guessed perhaps in his early sixties, grey hair gleamed with silver streaks, his face was of an amazing smoothness for what she supposed his age to be.

"Mademoiselle D'Hemecourt, we are on our way to The Mystery Room."

She cast a sideways glance at Louis, mouth open. "Why…I'm intrigued."

All of a sudden, they stopped before a powder room. She slipped her arm from Louis.

"Is this some kind of joke?"

Louis laughed but Martin maintained his composure. "You'll see."

Martin produced a set of dangling brass keys and unlocked the door. He motioned for them to enter.

"But it's a…"

"A powder room," Louis finished. "One that has obviously not been in use for quite some time."

"That it is." added Martin, squeezing a conspiratorial wink.

She stood her place, refusing to budge an inch. "Not just any powder room—a Lady's powder room."

Louis offered his arm and smiled, suppressing a laugh. "Trust me, Fleur."

Something about his look convinced her, or perhaps a knowing nod from Martin, but she slipped her arm back into his and closed her eyes.

"Why are your eyes closed?"

"I trust you, Louis, but I don't think I should see this."

This time he laughed out loud. "Open your eyes dear, and your ears for that matter. Martin?"

Eyes squinted together, fluttered open. Martin led them through an ornate dressing room in pale pink and green marble, the walls papered in a trellis of silk roses. They followed him to a wall with a painting of a 1920's flapper reclining in a red chair—a lovely woman in a silver beaded sheath dress, her dark eyes haunting, beautiful. Martin reached up to touch an ironwork candle sconce next to the painting. And at once, her eyes came alive. No longer brilliant blue, but brown…and they moved, as did the wall.

The painting, the sconce, and the wall all swiveled to the side, held open by a slim brown-eyed waiter. Martin motioned for them to follow. Louis grinned and led her into a red-walled room. A similar grid of black-framed photos hung on the walls, but she could see, even at a distance, that these held the likenesses of people both famous and infamous.

"This," said Martin, mystique in his tone, "is the Mystery Room."

Her mouth repeated the words in disbelief. "The Mystery Room."

Martin led them around the room to show off the pictures, autographed and framed, on the walls of the oblong room. Souvenirs of famous people were displayed throughout the room as well.

She pointed to a beret. "And who belonged to that if I might ask."

"Why Groucho Marx of course."

Breathless, she sighed, "No."

"Oh yes Mademoiselle Fleur. Oh yes."

She threw her arms around Louis's neck. "Louis, this place is wonderful, a true delight. And to think, I've eaten at Antoine's countless times before, but never in my dreams guessed that a room like this even existed. Thank you so much for bringing me here." She kissed his cheek.

Martin pulled a serving cloth from a buffet drawer and draped it over one arm.

"This room was set up during Prohibition and was closed up in 1933. Those were thrilling days if you don't mind me saying so." Martin moved his head from side to side. "A time of revelry and Le Bon Temp Roulet."

Louis and Fleur looked at each other and laughed. "No, we don't mind you saying so. In fact, we'd love it if you would tell us more," Louis answered.

"Yes, please do," Fleur added.

He pointed to the secret door from which they had just entered the room. "During those years, people would go through a door in the lady's powder room and leave with a coffee cup of booze." Martin smiled. "The Mystery Room got its name from the secret words that had to be spoken to get in."

He showed them to a table set in white linen and dishes rimmed in gold acanthus leaves and they were seated. "People would ask where they could buy alcohol and the waiters would shake their heads and say, "Sir, or Madame, you know that the sale of alcohol is in strict violation of the 18th Amendment to the Constitution of the United States. No, we do not serve alcohol.'" He held up his index finger and wagged it back and forth. "But those who were in the know, knew what to say.

Elbows on the table, Fleur cradled her chin in her hands and asked, "And what did they say? What?"

"They said, 'It's a mystery to me.'"

She threw up her hands. "That's it?"

"Yes, they said, 'It's a mystery to me,' and then they were shown to the secret entrance."

He struck a match and with theatrical flair, lit a tea candle in the center of their table, ringed by tiny white tea roses, then handed Louis a wine menu.

"And now," Martin looked down, his merry face glowing in the incandescence, "may I ask, what beverage you wish to begin the meal with Monsieur Louis?"

Fleur and Louis, eyes wide, looked at each other and in the same instant repeated, "It's a mystery to me." Then erupted into laughter.

Martin nodded with a knowing smile. "Very good Monsieur. Mademoiselle. He snapped a crisp napkin open and let it fall in graceful descent to Fleur's lap, then did the same for Louis.

"The usual, Martin."

"Very good Mr. Russo." He bowed. "I'll return shortly." He turned and exited through another secret door behind a bookcase.

Fleur leaned in closer. "And the usual is?"

Louis pressed his fingertips together into an arch, his dark eyes twinkling a joyful mood. "Oysters Rockefeller, Filet de Truitte Amandine, Petite Filet Marchand de Vin And Champignons, Pommes do Terre Soufllees, Omelette Alaska Antoine. Do you approve?"

She sat back in her chair. "Ummm, most definitely." Fleur paused, "And the meal sounds good too."

Martin soon returned with the entrant. The sight of one of her favorite appetizers reminded her that she had not eaten all day. Fleur clenched her stomach to quench a rising growl. How dreadful--how embarrassing an errant growl would be!

Oysters Rockefeller on a bed of coarse rock salt. On the half shell, cooked in butter with spinach, onion, herbs, hot sauce and a hint of Herbsaint, the scent of the rich sauce set her mouth watering.

Fleur smiled. "I can't wait to. . ."

"Shall we say grace?" he asked.

The sight of the tantalizing oysters had caused her to forget for a single moment, that Louis said grace before every meal. "Of course." She bowed her head and clasped her hands together on the table. Why would anyone place such an emphasis on offering homage to an invisible being? But like her parents, Louis seemed to think a lot of the act of prayer, and if praying made him happy, why not?

"Father, we thank you for this food we are to consume. We thank You for Your gracious hand which provides the food on this table and for our every need. And I most humbly thank You for my beautiful Fleur, the most beautiful flower of the south. She has ravished my heart with one look of her eyes…"

He reached across the table and clasped her hand in his.

Fleur smiled back at him. "So poetic."

"Poetry? His mouth crinkled upward. "In a way. It's from the Song of Solomon, Chapter Four, Verse Nine."

She stared back at him, puzzled.

Realizing her confusion, he added, "The Bible. It's from the Bible."

"Oh, well, I didn't realize, I mean, recognize it. How very beautiful." She looked down at the table. "My mother used to read to me from it."

He squeezed her hand for a brief moment. "You have truly ravished my heart Fleur."

She felt a blush fever her face as the two picked up their forks. Martin delivered each course with subtle flourish. They continued their meal with Filet de Truitte Amandine, Petite Filet Marchand de Vin And Champignons, and Pommes do Terre Soufllees.

Martin's assistant scraped the crumbs from the table with a silver crumb comb and removed the dishes. He returned with small bowls of lemon water for them to cleanse their hands, and stood to the side in unobtrusive attention.

Fleur dabbed with dainty effort at the corners of her mouth. "The meal was lovely. Delicious. Magnificent. We've dined at

Antoine's together before, but never like this. Louis, you've outdone yourself."

"Your very welcome, my dear. But Fleur, your presence here is what made the meal all the more special." He cleared his throat. "I wanted to bring you here for dinner because Antoine's is where we had our first date."

"I remember . . ." Fleur's heart beat faster.

"Let me remind you however, our meal isn't over yet. There is still the matter of dessert." As if on cue, Martin emerged from a side door bearing a Baked Alaska, a sparkler in the middle of it.

"Oh my." Fleur gasped. "Is that our dessert?"

Louis chuckled. "Yes, I believe it is."

Martin set the platter down in the middle of the table. "May I present to you Monsieur, Madammoiselle, Omelette Alaska Antoine."

The reflection in his eyes seemed to sparkle in time with the fireworks on the dessert.

"It's so festive, Louis." She clapped. "How did you know? Baked Alaska is my absolute favorite."

Martin extinguished the flame and put the stick to the side. A silver blade in hand, he cut through the middle and set the first slice on a plate for Fleur. As he placed it before her, she noticed a gleam from the side. She looked up. Both Louis and Martin were staring at her with curious intensity. She picked up her fork and coaxed at the gleam with the prongs. A ring? A diamond ring!

Martin picked the ring up with the prong of a fork, dipped it in lemon water and dried the ring on fresh linen before passing it to Louis.

Fleur pushed back from the table, her mouth unhinged. "What?" *Am I dreaming?*

Louis sank to one knee, ring between his thumb and forefinger. "Fleur D'Hemecourt, I fell in love with you the day I saw you fall." He smiled. "We haven't dated very long, but you are the girl of my dreams. Would you do me the great honor of becoming my wife?"

Eye to eye, they shared a wordless communication. She admired the earnest gaze of a man so adoring and sincere in his love for her. The kind of look her parents had for one another. The look she'd dreamt of seeing in the eyes of her own husband, all her life. Tears ran down her cheeks. "Yes my darling. Oh yes."

Fleur hardly remembered the walk back to her apartment, nor the tender kiss at her door. As if she'd walked on clouds, not cobblestones. She stared down at the engagement ring on her finger. One beautiful pear-shaped diamond set in platinum surrounded by petite diamonds on either side. She held the band up to the light--an extraordinary stone. It seemed to catch the light at every angle.

But back in her apartment, reality cut an angry swathe through her joy. She wandered through her tiny front room, a mountain range of boxes around. Heart pounding, she grasped the back of a wingback chair.

I said yes to the man I love, but what have I done? Do I deserve a man like Louis? And why do feel this way? Fleur buried her head in her hands as if to cry, but there were none.

She strode to her canvas and ripped the sheet off.

The manse on St. Charles! Windows aglow, as if on fire, darkness all around! She stared at the painting, hoping as she always did, that the image of the house would yield its secrets.

A resolve began to form in her heart. The key to her past, to her moods, to the lapses in memory were somehow linked to that house, perhaps even back to that fateful day she lost her parents.

I must move back now. Light or no light, she would finish painting her canvases and preparing for the show on St. Charles instead of the Vieux Carre.

Fleur resumed her work, shading the night sky around the house, painting for hours until she reached a state of utter exhaustion. At dawn, she backed away from the canvas and covered it. She set the brushes to soak, removed her smock and curled into a ball on the divan where she fell into a deep sleep.

Chapter Eleven
Changeling

A scream slit through the air. The gardeners jerked away from their shovels. A dog barked. Philomene. Feet somehow uprooted, Fleur ran skidding across the grass to the front porch, past her aunt and uncle and cousin, past the officers. On her knees sobbing, Philomene's eyes met hers Face tortured by sudden grief, she reached out her arms. From the other side of the porch, her aunt began to cry anew.

"Mama? Papa? Where are they? What happened? Why aren't they here?"

Philomene's head wobbled. Arms circled Fleur, her voice ragged and intermittent, she told her. "Dey wit de Lord, chile'. Dey gone home."

Her words filled the air about them, wet and weighty like clothing hung out to dry. She forced her mind to squeeze, to wring the meaning from the unthinkable sounds.

"But this is home. Where are they?"

"In h-heav'n chile'. In heav'n . . . "

From deep within her belly, a continuous wail began to sound, exiting Fleur with rage, with shock, with rage--screams that would not be stopped for all the comfort afforded her.

"I know. I know. I know chile'."

An officer carried Fleur into the house and laid her on a divan. The house filled with activity. People talking, running about, shouting for this or that—panicked at the shuddersome news. Wails of lamentation, and sorrow. For hours she howled in pain, her loss too great to bear--a heaviness of emotion.

"M-m-mama ddddead. Gone. My p-p-papa too? No-no-no-no-no. No." Cutting words stuttered out in short bursts. "I want mama and papa, Liars. Go get them. N-n-not true. N-n-not true."

Philomene tried her best to soothe her with embraces and shushes and cool cloths across her forehead. Clothes soaked with perspiration, Fleur fought the weariness that began to overwhelm her. Time moved at a different pace. She noticed the approach of twilight, a thin sliver of moon through the lace curtains. But she continued until late evening, when tucked into her own bed that she fell exhausted into a fitful sleep. A sleep like twilight, caught at some point between night and day.

Some time during the night, her eyes fluttered open to a blinding light, brighter and more intense than any light she had ever seen. As if the sun had come to earth.

She tried to blink the sleep out her eyes. The room around her was shrouded in darkness. The source of the light came from above. Fleur looked up. There, to her amazement, her mother and father, borne up at the shoulders by angels looked down upon her, their faces serene, joyful. The sight of her parents took her breath away. Fleur wanted to call out to them, but her mouth wouldn't move. Neither did the figures in the vision speak.

Shaking, she shifted her gaze to the faces of the angels. There were two of them--tall, wings tapered and ethereal, clothed with beams of pure light, their eyes terrible, wonderful. Her mouth finally began to move, her arms lifted high. "Mama! Papa!" she shrieked. In an instant, they were gone, the angels and her parents with them. Darkness swallowed the room in one bite.

Fleur sat straight up and looked around the room. Nothing. A shroud of darkness covered the still air. But a resonance of something remained, of sweetness, and of light. "Come back," escaped her mouth in a whisper. But there was no answer.

For an hour she laid awake, heart pounding, thoughts racing. A dream—only a dream, or a horrible nightmare! But Mama always came to her whenever she had a nightmare. Came to her bed to comfort and sing her a lullaby until the fear left, and her eyes grew heavy again. But she knew in her heart, Mama would never come back and her Papa would never bounce her upon his knee again.

Could the dream be real? If so, Mama and Papa were truly in heaven, borne by angels to the eternal reward mama always talked about. She closed her eyes and prayed. "God, take me too. I want my r'ward. I want to be with them wherever they go. Let me go with them. Amen."

Her eyes filled again. Weak from spent emotion, she closed her lids, sending the salty well coursing down her cheeks. Sleep alone would take the pain away. Dark, blank, soothing, sleep. And maybe if she closed her eyes and prayed with great diligence, she would wake up in heaven.

The next morning, she opened her eyes confused and disoriented in her own bed. Cheerful rays of sun streamed over the chenille bedspread. Her China dolls dressed in tea party finery sat at her table, favorite book open on the chair next to the window, her drawings spread over the floor. A slight breeze stirred the curtains. Everything seemed so normal, so familiar. A hopeful idea grasped her thoughts as she blinked the sleep from her eyes. Was it all a dream? A nightmare about . . .the car crash? A sudden panic gripped her heart as she looked around the room. Philomene was asleep on a cot next to her bed, her face streaked with dried tears.

Fleur bolted upright at the sight, unable to speak, to voice or express her pain. She pushed back towards the headboard. Finally able to moan, she gripped the wooden frame, nails to wood. She called out at the ceiling. "Why didn't you take me? I want to go too. What can't I go too?"

Philomene woke startled and in one swift movement had her arms around the child.

When the sobs waned, and finally ceased, Fleur regained the use of her voice. Though scratchy, she stammered out her about the vision the night before. "Phil-phil-phil-omene, do-do-do you think it's-it's r-real? Did I see-ee them?"

Philomene cradled the child in her arms, and didn't answer right away. She stroked Fleur's hair, silent in her thoughts. She extended her arm over Fleur to the bedside table, opened the drawer and pulled out a Bible.

Fleur asked. "W-what are you doing?"

"I thought mebbe I read sumthin' 'bout angels bearing you home." She leafed through the leather-bound book, her fingers familiar with its pages and soon found what she was looking for. "Here it is, in Luke chapta sixteen, verse twenty-two." She smiled wide. "It's in the story of Lazrus' and the rich man. Lazrus' was sick and po' an he sat at the gate of the rich man's house, beggin' fo' crums from his table. One day he died and was carry by de angels to Ab'ram's bosom." She stuck her finger to the page. "Here it is."

Fleur looked up. "Maybe I did see what I saw."

"Or might've been a bad dream is all chile'. But who know fo' sho? Only de Laud. Don matter none. If I was to s'ppose on who was fit to go to the Promised Land though, it would be your mama and papa. Two of the most God-fearing folks I ever know'd. If they ain't in heaven, then ain't none of us fit to go there. That's fa true."

***

A week after the funeral, Fleur's spirits were no better. She moped around her room, using sleep to avoid reality. She liked the room dark during the day and Philomene allowed her to keep the curtains closed. Bless her for that. She looked up at the housekeeper who sat near to her, crocheting in silence, the rocking chair falling forward and back. Philomene knew her better than anyone else, with the exception of her parents. She stayed close, but let Fleur work things through on her own. In a week's time, she hadn't said much to anyone, and didn't intend to for as long as she could get away with it.

She wondered in her grief, how the rest of the world could go on as if nothing had happened. People smiled. People laughed. The sun still came up every morning, and the moon at night. Flowers still bloomed. Dogs barked outside. The gardeners proceeded with their big plans for the beds. But nothing felt the same to her. Life was just a shattered thing. A broken remnant of what it was just a week ago today.

A knock on the door sounded. Cecelia, the downstairs maid wearing a black dress, under a gossamer white apron, came with a whispered message to Philomene, and backed out the door, shutting it behind her.

"Chile', let's get you in the bath and get dressed." She walked to the chiffarobe and pulled out a black dress, ironed and starched to crisp pleats. "This one. And the bow you wore with it yesterday."

"Why do I have to get dressed?" Fleur curled back under the covers. "I don't want to get dressed. I don't want to do anything."

Philomene leaned over with a tender kiss on the cheek. "I know, dear heart. I know. . .I wish I could let you do dat. If wishes was riches I'd be richer den. . ." Her voice trailed off.

Half an hour later, hand in hand, Fleur and Philomene walked down the stairs, their steps slow and deliberate. As they descended, Fleur heard voices in the parlor. They exchanged glances. Her aunt's voice trumpeted over the others.

Fleur took a deep breath at the last step. The two walked into the parlor. High-ceilings painted with a mural of some gardens in France—the Versailles—that's what mama called them. She kept her eyes on the pretty scene when she entered but her uncle addressed her right away.

"Ah, there's our girl." Uncle Bernard, dressed in an ill-fitting black suit, rose from the divan to greet her. He mashed out a cigarette into a rose patterned saucer, part of her mother's favorite tea service. "Fah-leur. My, but you're pale." He grasped her free hand and pulled her toward the divan, next to him.

A short man with thinning coppery hair and ruddy cheeks, his most prevalent feature was most uncomplimentary. Though only a couple of years older than his brother, Bernard had deep circles under his eyes that made him look tired, owlish. He drew closer, his breath foul, teeth uneven, yellowed with tobacco. "And how are you, my pet?"

Aunt Florrie, in a svelte black dress, hair swept away from her face in impossible waves, joined in. "Yes dear." She planted a sloppy kiss on the child's cheek. Philomene stepped forward with a handkerchief and wiped away the red smear left behind. Florrie motioned her away, as if annoyed someone had seen fit to remove her mark.

Fleur turned her face away from her aunt and stared down at the patterned carpet. The sight of the cigarette butt in her mother's dish made her ill. "Child. Child, for goodness sake, please look at me when I speak."

She obeyed, moving her gaze from the carpet to her aunt's garish face.

Florrie smiled, a line of lipstick on her teeth. "Thank you, dear. Now dear, we know this is a horrid time for you, but we asked Philomene to bring you here for a very important reason. Didn't we darling?"

"Yes," Bernard continued. "We want you to know that you are not alone, my dear niece. You don't ever have to worry about going to a foundling's home." He stood and walked, pacing his steps to the fireplace mantle, jingling the change in his pocket as he walked.

"No, you'll not have to go anywhere." His eyes widened. He pointed to the floor. "You can stay right here in your own home with us looking after you."

Puzzled, Fleur shot a glance to Philomene, who stood tall and serene in her place. But her eyes told her a different story. She didn't trust them, didn't like them. Fleur could tell.

A smile devouring her face, Florrie spoke. "Dear heart, we are going to be your guardians. Isn't that wonderful?" She clapped her gloved hands together, but the muffled sound, left less than an exclamation to her announcement.

Bernard leaned on the mantle. "Your parents had something called a "Will." It's a paper that tells folks what to do with your things when you're gone." His mouth opened into a reassuring grin.

"Or loved ones left behind, darling," Florrie added, a quick glance to her husband who scowled back.

"My brother left instructions that your aunt and I were to become your guardians in the event of the early demise, ah, er, death of either parent." He coughed. "We will guard you until you're all grown up. That's why we're called guardians, you see. And we will see to your care until you reach the age of twenty-one, when you are grown up enough to assume control of the estate, which means your property. You'll inherit it, or rather, claim it then. Do you understand what I'm telling you, child?"

Fleur nodded, though she didn't understand or care.

With that, Florrie began to chatter. "Won't it be wonderful to have a playmate? You and Piper will get on together like two peas in a pod. I can see it now. Even though she's a bit older, I know you two will get along famously. She's outside somewhere right now." She craned her neck as if to spot her. "Where ever could she be? I called for her to come to the parlor. Oh well, you'll see her. You'll have plenty of time together." Raising the teacup to her mouth for an instant, she paused to take a sip. "Of course, I hope it won't bother you if we take your parent's bedroom downstairs."

"Darling . . . " Bernard interrupted, deep creases between his brows.

"Such a grand room and I adore the floor-to-ceiling French windows. It troubles my sciatica to go up and down stairs all the time and I do like to take an afternoon nap and a second bath during the day so it would be all the more convenient for me."

"Darling, stop babbling so. I'm sure the girl has other things on her mind right now." Bernard interrupted. He sank to the divan, one hand curling about Fleur's arm.

"Fleur, your aunt and I can't possibly take the place of your parents. We know you're missing them." He placed her hand over his heart. "My heart is hurting too, child. After all, I've lost my beloved brother and sister-in-law. What a tragedy, a terrible tragedy."

He tick-tocked his head from side to side. But all Fleur could feel was his heart pounding fast at the touch of her hand against his heart. She pulled it away and stuck both hands in the pockets of her dress.

Florrie tilted her head to the side, a sorrowful expression on her clownish face. "But we're so thankful you weren't on the trip with them. We might have lost you too, my dear, and that would have been awful, just awful." She raised the teacup again, motioning to the steward to refill it.

Bernard lifted a strand of Fleur's hair, twirled it with his finger and whispered. "It would have been a tragic loss."

Florrie added, "Then it's decided. We'll move in tomorrow." She held up her teacup, as if in a toast.

"Tomorrow, it is." Bernard looked over at Philomene.

She took a breath. "Yes suh."

Chapter Twelve
Day and Night

Fleur awoke to a shaft of light across her face and looked around the room, half expecting to see her childhood bedroom. Childhood memories had come unbidden, flooding from her mind's depths.

She slid from the divan to the floor, head cradled in her hands. The sobs that wracked her body that day seemed as fresh, as real to her today. Her body ached from head to toe with the pain of loss.

And the vision. Even with the passage of years, the memory of that vision stayed fresh in her mind. Fleur looked up as if God or heaven were on the ceiling or the blush of sky beyond. The sound of her own voice startled her. "Mother, Father, are you there?"

But no vision came, and no answer. The sky refused to part. She pushed up from the edge of the divan and stood. The one beam soon joined by other sunbeams, specks of dust dancing in the light. The light seemed to beckon her to the balcony for closer inspection. She pulled back the drapes, bathing the room in the soft glow of early morning. Her eyes settled past the rooftops and trees to the lace of clouds in the distance bearing the first rouge of day.

Fleur stepped on to the balcony and moved to the wooden rail. She leaned forward to rest on it. The moment she did, the telephone rang and as she pulled away, the rail collapsed from the posts and crashed to the courtyard below.

She jumped back at the movement. Gasping, she gathered the courage to step to the edge and look down. Several residents peered out of their windows. A man stood in the courtyard in a state of half dress. Busy pulling his suspenders over a white sleeveless undershirt, he hitched up his pants from hip to waist. Mr. Clements, the manager stared up at her. A cigarette forever leaning on his lip, he called. "You okay girl?

"Yes, I-I'm so sorry. I tried to rest on the rail and it fell apart."

"Good thing you caught yourself." He laughed, "But the ground woulda broke your fall."

She took a deep breath.

"I'm kidding, missy."

"I know. You. You're right."

He waved his arm. "Look, it ain't nothing. You're okay. Nobody down here got bonked in the head. I'll have the thing fixed up in no time."

"Thank you Mr. Clements. I—I. . ."

"Don't mention it." Before she could respond, he turned and walked back into his flat.

Fleur backed into her apartment, shut the balcony door behind her and took a deep breath to calm her nerves.

The telephone began to ring again. She lunged for it. "Hello?"

"Fleur? It's me. I called a minute ago and there was no answer. I'm sorry to call so early. I hope I didn't wake you."

"Louis." Her heart warmed at his voice. "No, you didn't wake me. The sun did."

"He laughed. "Oh, so the sun beat me to it, eh? Well, I don't feel like such a bad fellow then."

"Louis, I almost tumbled off the balcony."

"What? What do you mean? Are you all right? You're not hurt, are you?"

"I walked out to look at the sky and leaned on the rail. The telephone rang and I turned away. Right then, the balcony rail gave way. Your call saved my life. Louis, you saved my life."

Silence sliced through their conversation for a moment.

"Fleur, I don't know what to say. Forget what I said a moment ago. I've never been more happy to make a telephone call."

"I'm fine, just a bit shaken up. What was it you were calling about?"

His sigh drifted through the receiver. "I called to invite you to have coffee and beignets with me at the Café du Monde before I go to work, that is. But if you're too shook up, we can go some other time."

She glanced at the wall clock, then at the delicate watch on her wrist; ten minutes difference between them. "As I said, I'm fine, just fine. Of course I'll meet you. What girl would refuse a chance to meet with her fiancé?"

"Wonderful, Can you be there in fifteen?"

"Yes."

She set the receiver into the cradle and made a mad dash to the bedroom. Five minutes to wash up--another five to dress, and another five to walk. A brisk walk, yes, but she'd make it. Fresh out of school, she knew how to make herself presentable in a scant amount of time.

After donning a white cap-sleeved shirt, she slipped into a beige raw silk skirt. She cinched a thin belt around her waist and tucked her curls under a petite beige hat. Flats on her feet, gloves in hand, she sprinted out the door and down the stairs.

The dog days of summer upon the city, the early hour would be the only relief during the day. Vieux Carre' shopkeepers aimed hoses at the front stoops and banquette to clean the vagaries of the night before. The smell of bacon, of fry cakes, of coffee in the air, she quickened her step, keeping an eye to the uneven cobbles underneath. She glanced down Pirates Alley, soon passing in front of St. Louis Cathedral, the deep bells pealing out the hour. Past Jackson Square, pearls of dew still rolling off banana leaves, she spotted him standing under the awning of the Café du Monde. Newspaper tucked under an arm, hands in his pockets, she smiled at the sight of him. And he smiled back.

"Darling, I'm so glad you could come," Louis greeted.

They embraced and entered the outdoor café and sat. An awning shaded the interior and though the sights and sounds of the city intruded, both seemed unaware of anything or anyone but each another. The small table and chairs enabled them to sit close to one another, encouraging a tender and prolonged kiss. A streetcar clanked past just as Fleur came up for air and whispered the words.

He cupped a hand and held it to his ear. "What?"

Fleur giggled. "I said I love you, Mr. Russo."

Louis reached for her hand and kissed it. "And I love you soon-to-be, Mrs. Louis Russo."

"Have you told anyone yet?"

"No," he answered, "not yet." He cleared his throat. "Well, my maybe my mother when I returned home last night."

"Was she happy?"

"Well I don't know. She was too busy bouncing off the ceiling." He kissed her hand again. "Of course she was happy. She's elated."

"I suppose I should tell uncle and Piper." She bit the side of her lip. "They invited me to dinner tomorrow night. Perhaps I could ask to bring you along. We'll surprise them with the news."

"All right then. That sounds like a good plan to me. Let's do it."

Dressed in a white shirt and pants, waiter apron and hat, the waiter approached, a sly smile on his face. Fleur flushed when she realized the man had witnessed the kiss. Louis must have recognized the look as well for he addressed it in an offhand way when he spoke.

"What's your name?"

"Bob."

"Well Bob," he placed his arm around Fleur's shoulders, "we're celebrating our engagement today. I've asked this beautiful young lady to be my wife."

The man tipped his waiter hat. "Congrats. What you want?"

Louis released her shoulders. "Two orders of beignets."

"Oh no, Louis," Fleur protested, "there are three to an order and all I ever have is one. You can have the other two."

"Make that one order of beignets and, darling, how do you like your coffee? Black or au lait?"

"Au lait."

"And two caffe au laits, please."

The man nodded and walked off.

Louis shifted his eyes from the waiter to Fleur. "That fellow didn't have much to say, did he? I hope your family has more enthusiasm when we announce our engagement."

"They will. I've no doubt about it." She smiled.

The coffee and beignets soon arrived with an unceremonial plonk on the table. The man of few words turned at once to take an order at the table next to them. Fleur measured two spoons from the sugar shaker and stirred them into her coffee.

Louis watched her, a smile on his face. "Ma'am, would you mind passing the sugar?"

"Of course." She handed the shaker to him.

"For the record, I take two as well." He winked.

The coffee and chicory, rich and dark, warmed her throat. She eyed the plate of beignets, square fried cakes lavished with an abundance of powdered sugar. They each took one, sugar tippling off the sides, toasted one another and took their first bite.

"Ummm." She wiped sugar from the sides of her mouth with a paper napkin. The dough, steaming hot from the fryer, melted in her mouth.

"You can say that again." Louis finished his first beignet in three quick bites, and looked down in dismay. "Why oh why do I always seem to wear a dark suit when I eat these things?"

She laughed. The lapel of his dark suit was sprinkled with white powdered sugar. "You should have followed my lead and tucked a napkin into your collar." She glanced down. The paper napkin was covered with sugar. "See?"

"True, but you're wearing a white blouse. A smart move on your behalf, young lady. Even if you did get some sugar on your blouse, not a soul would suspect."

She pulled a handful of napkins from the table dispenser and began to wipe his lapel. "Never mind. You'll be right as rain in a second."

"What would I do without you?"

She glanced up at him and in that moment, as if a cloud had passed, a darkness seemed to cover the brightness of his eyes.

"Fleur. . ."

"What?" She continued to clean his lapel until he took her hand in his.

"There's something I have to tell you."

Her heart began to pound. "What is it?"

"There's something I've been meaning to tell you from the beginning. Something I should have told you sooner, but was afraid to."

"Why?" She felt a scarcity of air.

"I didn't want to lose you."

She leaned back in her chair as if to brace herself. "Tell me."

"Well, long before I met you." He paused. "I-I don't know how to say this."

"Go on."

"For a brief time, I dated your cousin. Piper."

The words stung her heart. *I wonder why Piper never mentioned it.*

"I see." She wrapped her fingers around the side of the coffee cup.

"But it ended long before I met you, well, became reacquainted with you anyway. And there was never anything serious between us. I thought you should know."

She sat in silence, trying to understand why it bothered her.

"Please," He leaned forward. "Say something, Fleur."

"Does she care for you?"

He looked down. "I don't know if you would call it that."

"What do you mean?"

"The way she behaved wasn't normal. She was jealous and accusatory, utterly relentless. I knew at that point, could no longer continue our relationship."

He continued. "The day of your Aunt Florrie's funeral, Piper and I spoke about it. That's when she told me about the man she's dating."

"What's his name? There was a man at the house when Piper and I had lunch. I didn't expect another guest. The two seemed quite cozy."

"A fellow by the name of Jack Holcombe."

"Hmmm. No, the man's name was Gerard Duplessis. She's never mentioned the other name to me."

Louis shrugged. "She said she's seen him on and off since before the war was over. He's in sales now and whenever he's in town, they see one another."

Fleur took a slow sip of her coffee. Perhaps Philo would know more about him.

He continued. "I even suggested we all go on a double date." Louis shook his head. "I don't know why I said that. I guess I was just relieved she'd found someone else."

Fleur put her cup down and looked him in the eye. "So you never had feelings for Piper?"

"No, not ever."

"And you stopped seeing her because she was jealous?"

He looked away. "I don't know if I should tell you."

She cupped his chin in her hand and pulled his face toward her. "Louis Russo, nothing you could tell me about my cousin would shock me. Nothing."

"I still don't understand it, but her behavior was strange, erratic. She would ring me on the telephone dozens of times a day, send telegrams, messengers asking me where I'd been, what I was doing."

"Really?"

"She would show up wherever I happened to be. At first I thought it might be a coincidence. But time and again, she would make an appearance at business lunches, private family functions, and I began to realize that her arrivals were orchestrated."

"Piper followed you." Fleur shook her head. "How odd."

"Yes."

"Oh Louis, what did you think? What did you do?"

His fingers clenched and unclenched. "I wasn't sure what to do, but I had to get away from her. I-I ended it."

The clamor of a streetcar interrupted.

"And what did she do? How did she take it?"

"Not well. She showed up at my mother's door."

"Louis," she wrapped her arms around his neck. "I'm sorry. Thank you for telling me. I so admire your character. It's only one more reason to . . . " She stifled a tear.

"To what?" He stared back at her.

"To love you."

Chapter Thirteen
Dinner With The D'Hemecourts

The couple stood on the broad veranda of her home on St. Charles, facing the massive front door. Carved from one ancient cypress, the front door was a rustic work of inferior artistry depicting Louisiana wildlife; deer, nutria, alligators, ducks, pelicans, and fish. The carved door stood out like a sore thumb against the rest of the architecture. Fleur wondered how much the monstrosity cost.

Louis looked to Fleur. "Are you ready?"

She nodded. "Are you?"

He reached for her hand and brought it to his lips. "Yes, of course."

Louis sighed. "I-I'm just glad you're all right. That close call with the streetcar. . ."

"I'm fine. The man who caught me was more rattled than I."

"I owe him a debt of gratitude I can never repay. I should never have agreed to have you meet me here. I should have picked you up or rode the streetcar with you."

"You had a late meeting, darling. There was no other way." She smiled. "Besides, I got here in one piece."

With that, he rapped on the door. A resolute rap, confidant.

"Louis. . ."

He glanced over at her.

"There's a doorbell." She pointed.

He stood back to survey it. "Oh, I see. New door, and new doorbell."

"Louis, you're being so polite about it. Don't we know one another better than that now?" She gave him a quick peck on the cheek. His face flushed in response.

"If that's what happens when a fellow is polite, I think I'll be polite more often."

Fleur laughed. "I don't know where he found the thing, but in my opinion, it's hideous."

"Well," he pointed, "I do like the cypress. It's a fine wood. Lasts forever."

"How wonderful," she commented, "an absolutely hideous door that will last forever." She pointed to the elaborate brass rectangle with a circle of ivory in the middle. "Now how about pressing the doorbell?" Fleur smiled.

But he shrugged as the sound of footsteps approached. No need for the doorbell after all. The heavy door opened without a creak.

Philomene appeared, a wide smile on her face.

"Mr. Louis, Miz Fleur. How delightful to see you two this evening. Won't you follow me to the parlor? The rest of the family is waiting for you there."

"Of course," Louis answered, casting a glance at Fleur, pulling at his collar as if in a sweat.

She smiled at his antics. Since their engagement, their relationship had become richer, and much more comfortable, as if the air were cleared somehow. The formal side of Louis had given way to this playful side, and she'd found herself delighting in it. With the ring on her finger, her thoughts had turned to memories of her parents and how they'd interacted. They'd always seemed at ease with one another, laughing often, conducting spirited discussions and conversation on a variety of topics, at the dinner table.

Small snippets of things she remembered about them began to surface. The way her father always untangled her mother's necklaces, for instance. Fleur couldn't keep her hands off them for long. In fact, when her aunt and uncle came to live with her, she still had a tangle of costly chains and gems in her dress pocket. Philomene had decided to hide them away in a safe place instead of handing them over to Florrie and Bernard. All but one, the tree of life pendant remained hidden away.

Over the years, the two had moved the cache of jeweled necklaces to different spots so her aunt wouldn't get her hands on them. Florrie had carte blanche with the rest of Eleanor's jewelry box, and as far as Fleur could tell, had no intention of passing it on to the rightful heir. Over the years, she'd seen familiar pieces hanging on Piper's lovely neck.

Fleur made a mental note to ask Philomene about her mother's jewelry, especially in lieu of the wedding. Wearing a piece of her mother's jewelry after all these years, particularly the sapphire, would be a nice touch--something old, something blue.

"Fleur?' He squeezed her hand. "Are you daydreaming again?"

"Oh, sorry." She clutched his arm. "I was."

He kissed two fingers and touched her forehead. "As long as I'm in your daydreams, I don't mind."

As they followed, she noted how Philo walked slower today, without the usual spring in her step.

"And here we are." She slid open the pocket doors to the parlor. Bernard stood by the mantle, holding a cocktail in one hand, a cigar in the other. Piper sat on a nearby divan. Dressed in an attractive kelly green frock, accented by the sapphire necklace, one Aunt Florrie used to wear often.

Piper looked the part of a fashion plate. Lovely to look, at and beautiful to see. Fleur dug her fingernails into her thighs. The very nerve!

Their conversation halted as the couple entered the room. She noticed an unfamiliar butler stood in the corner by a tray of glasses and liquors. Philomene stole a glance at Fleur before she slid the doors shut behind her and departed. But the glance disturbed her, a look of desperation in her eyes.

"There's my beautiful girl." Bernard left his glass on the mantle and deposited his cigar in an ashtray produced by the butler in one swift movement. He strode forward and wrapped his arms about her, depositing a kiss on either cheek, and clasped her ring hand for a closer view.

"Louis, my boy." A hearty handshake followed. "If that rock on my niece's finger is any indication of your prosperity, she'll be in good hands."

Dismayed by Bernard's usurping their surprise, Louis spoke. "Sir I. . ."

Piper rose to hug Fleur, then wrapped her arms about Louis as he spoke. "Congratulations are in order for the two of you." She circled back to her place on the divan and sat down.

Fleur looked to Louis, then back at them. "How did you?"

"Word gets around." Bernard emptied his glass and held it up to be refreshed.

"Well, there goes our surprise." Louis laughed. "Since you are her uncle, and guardian, Bernard, it was my intention to ask you. . ."

"Nonsense," he answered. "These are modern times and those are stuffy old-fashioned formalities. But, if it pleases you, know that you have my permission—after Fleur is twenty-one of course."

"Thank you sir. I do appreciate that. I don't believe my mother would forgive me such a lapse in formality." He looked to Fleur. "And are you agreeable with that, darling?"

Fleur gazed into his dark eyes, marveling at Louis's sweet temperament, and resolving to match it with every effort. "Of course I am. Why, I'm walking on cloud nine, as it is."

A bell rang. The double doors opened. Philomene declared dinner to be ready.

The table, set with pure white linen, was starched to a sheen, and decorated with the best in china and silver. Fleur knew that the staff was behind such a move. The finest silver candelabras, china vases brimming with lilies, magnolias, hyacinths and gardenias decorated the surface, including the fine serving utensils, the best of the silverware, everything done to a tee.

The moment Fleur saw it she smiled at Philomene. A subtle smile returned. But it spoke volumes to her. Tears welled in Fleur's eyes.

She spoke. "It's beautiful. So charming."

Though as surprised as the couple, Bernard answered, surveying the room. "Yes, we spared no expense when we heard. The very idea of giving away our little Fleur in holy matrimony deserves a royal celebration. Indeed."

Though the dining room table could accommodate twenty in relative comfort, their chairs were arranged together at the far end. Servants pulled their chairs and when seated, then launched them with a gentle push toward the table. Fleur and Louis sat next to each other across from Piper and Bernard.

The servants began with Fleur, ladling a creamy velvet soup from a large tureen embellished with a bas-relief of crustaceans, into a pristine white bowl. "Corn and crabmeat soup? My favorite."

Piper answered. "Yes, my dear." She glared back at the servants. "For your engagement dinner, we—we've apparently spared no expense."

Louis seemed pleased as well. "Darling, I didn't know that was your favorite. It's mine as well. When I was a boy, I used to beg mother to have it on the menu once a week."

A wide smile on her face, she replied. "Yet another thing we have in common. Another reason to adore you, my Louis." She paused to admire his profile--the taper of his cheeks, the masculine chin shaved smooth and fragrant even at a distance, with the scent of Bay Rum. Her heart stirred at the deepness of his voice, the familiar sound of his step, at the very mention of his name.

"Harumph." Bernard cleared his throat. "Say, I hope you two aren't planning to elope." He wagged a finger at them. "Though I'm not keen on formalities, I won't stand for anything like that. We won't, we can't be cheated out of a proper marriage ceremony."

Fleur spoke first. "The Summer. We plan to be married in the summer—June to be precise."

Piper's lips parted at her words. "But that's only a little more than six months, hardly enough time to put together a proper trousseau. Not to mention a wedding."

"On the date, we are most decided, dear Piper." Louis put his arm around Fleur's chair. "Fleur wants a June wedding, and if not this June, we would have to wait another year."

Piper sniffed her disapproval. "There's nothing wrong with a long engagement, you know. Many couples wait two years to marry."

"Not us." Fleur replied. "I've found the love of my life in Louis."

"And I . . ." Louis kissed her hand.

"This is unheard of." Piper dabbed at the corners of her mouth and pushed her bowl forward. A servant hurried to remove it.

All the while, Bernard dipped his spoon and ate, answering after his final spoonful. "Now, now girl. Don't get your liver in a quiver." He waved his napkin. "These two lovebirds don't want to wait that long. What's it to you? Let them marry and be done with it." A servant removed his dish. "June you say? Then June it is."

"But."

He brought two fingers to his mouth. "Not another word. I have spoken. Am I the patriarch of this family or not?"

Fleur lifted her napkin and placed it on the table, judging this to be the right time to duck out for a few minutes and talk to Philomene. "Won't you excuse me, please? She looked to Louis first, then to the others.

The servants opened the doors and shut them behind her. Philomene would be waiting in her office. She knew the look on her face earlier and the message had stamped itself on her heart. Trouble.

The top of the door was of textured glass, a rippled pattern, the bottom panel made of wood painted a fresh white. She could see two forms in the room. Fleur knocked before turning the knob.

"I don't have much time."

"Fleur." Philomene reached to embrace her. "Thank you, chile'." She dabbed at her eyes.

"Flower." Tadpole, a dark bruise ringing his eye, smiled. Tall and lanky, his physique at first glance seemed normal. But one look at his face gave away his mental state. A vacuous expression revealed his capacity for higher thought. The choppy words and slur in his speech cinched it.

She hugged him. "How's my Tadpole?"

He pointed to his face. "Tadpole hurt."

"I can see that." She turned to Philomene.

"It happen'd again. He say a blond hair man done it . Now I know Alcide's the one been using Tadpole like a punchin' bag. When I tol' your uncle, he din' care! He laugh."

"No."

Philomene buried her face in her apron. "I gotta git Tadpole out here or dey gonna wind up killin' him."

Fleur paced back and forth. My uncle, for whatever reason, condones this behavior. If Alcide has his approval, it won't stop. After all, the goon works for him. But what possible reason could he have for having Alcide pick on a retarded boy?

A flutter of sobs flooded out when Philo began to speak. "I know'd they would be trouble when I seen dat boy come 'roun here."

"I'll figure something out. I promise. We'll get him out of harm's way. Right now, I've got to get back to dinner, but I'll be in touch."

"Thank you, baby." Philomene turned to comfort her brother.

Piper gave Fleur the eye when she returned to the table. "We missed you, dear."

Fleur let out a melodic laugh, "My, my, I wasn't gone that long, was I?"

Louis laughed as well. "Even a few seconds without you seems an eternity."

"Thank you my sweet."

But Piper continued to stare at her, off and on through the remainder of the meal. Somehow, she knew Fleur hadn't visited the powder room. Piper knew her well enough to figure out where she'd been.

Fleur hoped her cousin wouldn't try to interfere with her plans to rescue Tadpole. If she did, there would be trouble of another kind.

***

After dinner and a champagne toast in the parlor, Fleur and Louis departed.

As Piper and Bernard stood on the veranda, waving goodbye, she spoke. "Could you please explain yourself?"

"Why, whatever do you mean?"

Fuming, she grabbed his shirt collar. "Why did you oppose me?"

Eyes twinkling with mirth, he answered. "Oppose you? Why, I'm on your side, dear daughter. What does it matter when those two decide to marry? You and I both know they won't ever get the chance. She won't live long enough to walk down the aisle."

Her grimace relaxed at his words. "Oh Father. It's just that I. . ."

"Now its 'Oh Father,' eh?" He gave her arm a sympathetic pat. "Relax, I know how you feel. In due time, you shall have the handsome and eligible Mr. Russo for yourself." He piled her hands together and placed his on top.

Tears rolling, she squeaked out the words. "I don't know what to say."

"Why are you crying?"

She rested her head on his shoulder, and mumbled from the crook of his arm. "Don't you ever feel bad about--about Fleur?"

He lifted her chin with his index finger. "You're not going soft on me, are you?"

"No, far from it. Now and then, memories from our childhood come up."

"Keep your focus on the brass ring, child. Don't allow emotions to deter you from achieving your goals in life. Focus on lofty goals. That's what I do. You and I are cut of the same cloth. Remember that."

Arm around her, he led her through the door and back into the house.

***

As the door shut behind them, a slender figure stepped away from the side veranda, pausing for a moment. Black as cast iron against the light of a full moon, he hastened away.

Chapter Fourteen
Blue Ribbons

A sharp rap on Fleur's door interrupted the tedious addition of tiny leaves and flowers to her latest canvas. She opened the door a crack. Gerard? A sense of trepidation on her heart, she opened it.

"Miss Fleur, good morning." Tall, lanky and muscular, he filled the doorway. A lock of sunstreaked hair out of place, he looked as if he'd stepped off the silver screen.

"Good morning, Gerard. May I ask what brings you to my flat?"

"I've come to coax you out of your cave and into the sunshine."

"How did you?"

He peered over her shoulder. "Piper knows you well. She told me you would be working."

Throat tight, she answered. "What a surprise. However, as you can see, I'm quite busy."

"Too busy for a new friend? Piper told me you would say no, but I didn't believe her."

"It's not that. Let me be frank with you. I am at work both day and night to prepare for the showing. And aside from that, well. . ." She held up her hand, the diamond sparkling in the brilliant sunshine.

"You are. . .spoken for? Engaged I see. And so soon? Congratulations my dear Fleur. Who is the lucky man?"

"Louis Russo."

"The attorney?"

"Yes."

"A very good one from what I hear. Isn't he with the firm representing your uncle?"

"Why, yes."

"Hmmm, doesn't that present a little conflict of interest?"

"Well, I . . ."

"Never mind. I'm not here to talk about legal issues." He rested a tanned arm on the doorjamb above his head.

She continued. "As I was saying, it's not a good idea for me. . ."

"Nonsense. I most certainly respect your status as an engaged woman. This trip is no more than an outing between friends. New friends. I would be honored, as your friend, if you would accompany me today. I should like to go canoeing. Or are you no longer allowed to do as you please now that you're spoken for?"

She paused. "Of course I can do as I please, and it would please me immensely to get back to painting."

He laughed, pushing past her into the house, heading straight for her canvas. "Ahhh." He stepped back to admire it. "This is Coeur de l'eau, is it not?" He folded his arms and stared. "I do like it, but you seem to be missing some details. Mind you, only a trained eye would notice."

"Details? Please elaborate."

"There is far too little of the Spanish moss in the trees. And where is the wildlife? You and I know you cannot go two feet without a bird, a reptile, the splash of a fish."

She stood in silence for a moment, eyes scrutinizing the canvas. "You're right. I do need to add more details."

"I don't mean to offend. After all, as Piper says, you are a 'true artiste'."

Fleur shook her head. "It's been years since I was there."

He snapped his fingers. "Then this outing would be perfect for you. Take your sketchbook."

Mind running in a thousand directions, she glanced over at him. "Gerard, you are a gentleman I am not well-acquainted with. I don't think my fiance' would approve."

"I'm a close friend of the family. Your uncle and cousin will vouch for me. Why don't you call them?"

"No, no, I'd rather not do that."

He leaned in. "Listen to me. You'll be back before he misses you." Gerard lifted her chin with his fingers. "Although if you were mine, I should miss you every second you were not in my arms."

She stepped back, surprised by his candor.

However, the lure of his words had already begun to stir something in her. After making arrangements to spirit Tadpole from the house to work for Louis's family short-term, she'd retreated to her artist's den to complete the collection. Since then, she'd been cooped up in the flat for days, up till all hours of the night, losing track of time, not eating or caring about anything but her work.

Louis, understanding her intensity, telephoned her once a day with tender encouragements, and vowed to see her on the weekend to help her move. She'd been alone with her work. Yet tomorrow she would move to St. Charles and there was still a great deal of packing to do. A day in the sunshine, on the open water might do her good.

She walked back to the front door and he followed. Instead of answering him, she pulled at the hem of her smock. Muggy with fatique, her thoughts slow, the words drifted out.

"I don't know."

A splash of color caught her eye. The door to the courtyard was wide open and there, past the banquette, out on the street, a red canoe stood out like a sore thumb, strapped to the roof of his car.

He touched her shoulder. "Artists and their angst. You must remove yourself from your work and come and do something different."

Those eyes.

She heard herself saying, "Yes," though she knew she should stay put. After a quick change into dungarees and sneakers, she packed a small satchel of personal items, including her sketchpad. As she picked up her keys to lock the door to her flat however, she had a thought. Disappearing inside for a moment, she reappeared with her Brownie camera. A "must" for some of her art classes in college, it proved invaluable for capturing images she could later draw, and far more practical than trying to sketch in a moving canoe.

After a two-hour drive, they carried the canoe above their heads to the water's edge. She followed his feet. Maybe he was more eager than she was to explore the Honey Island Swamp, but their awkward push-me/pull-me movement almost toppled them onto the muddy bank. Shoes hopelessly slimed, they laughed, squishing into the canoe one at a time and launched out with their oars.

The murky waters glistened like polished onyx and every creeping vine seemed laden with parasol buds, waiting to unfold a spectrum of exotic colors. Tiny alligators surfaced in the midst of plate-sized lily pads, each serving up a peach-hued blossom. Their eyes, shiny black beads, observed the canoe's passing, both with caution and curiosity. The couple edged their canoe close to one of them for a better look. The tiny creature waited watching them, seemingly immobile until they drew near enough to reach down and stroke his rugged back. However, to her disappointment, the baby reptile whisked out of sight with a tinkly splash and a delicate ring of waves to accent his departure.

They reached a bend in the waters and decided to follow a slight opening through some cypress trees. A steep cavern of branches encased them high above. She aimed her camera at the crux of branches and the target of blue sky in the midst. Gray moss hung in curled clumps from the massive limbs. And the stillness of the place seemed to resonate, as if silence were a sound of its own.

Eerie speckles of sunlight ribboned through the branches, spotlighting certain features of the leafy cavern. Cypress knees, like gnome-shaped periscopes, poked above the water's surface. She touched one. Curious...brown and smooth but dense and weighty, more like a rock than a living thing.

The water dipped low in the knot-shaped cavern.

This time she aimed the lens at him.

"Watch this," an air of mystery in his voice. He plunged his paddle into the rotting mulch beneath the dark water to provoke a cauldron of boiling bubbles. "Pretty keen, huh? It's methane gas-- the legend behind the Will-O'-the-Wisp."

Interest piqued, she asked, "You mean, the evil swamp spirit they talk about? Whenever we vacationed at my uncles's camp, Piper and I would stay up late with Philomene, and she would tell us the most remarkable ghost stories."

His voice low and laden with mystery, they drifted as he told the story, "In the past, green-glowing mists of the gas, hovering, mysterious, in the dark night were the basis for those who told tales of malevolent spirits, 'faery fire,' and wandering souls neither welcome in heaven or hell. But Malva Toussaint knew better. One night, she set out to find the Will-O'-The-Wisp." He paused to catch his breath.

"You're some storyteller. Well," she asked impatient to hear the rest, "what about Malva Toussaint?"

His eyes widened. "She never returned."

That's it?" she demanded.

"It is supposed to be a true story. My aunt told me of it. They never found her… Malva, that is."

"That's about the most ridiculous stor-."

Without warning, the canoe slammed into the soft earth of the embankment. He caught her in his arms as she bounded forward, the bulky camera between them. She pushed away at once, or almost at once. But the few seconds it took to part from his muscular frame, lingered longer than it should have.

They pushed off the embankment with their paddles and continued on, but a silence followed. Her heart thumped against her chest so hard, she wondered if he could hear it. She decided to concentrate on the scenery to take her mind off of him.

Cypress tree limbs clothed with honeysuckle dripped perfume on their heads as they glided past. Saw Palmettos winnowed insects, both common and exotic. Animals trilled, rattling through leaves large as elephant ears. Bubbles and pops resurrected from the murk of the water. A still, stealthy feeling, like a shadow followed them.

Was it the story? How laughable. More the breath of imagination than methane; conjecture more than conjure. She found herself shivering nonetheless. All of a sudden, she wanted to leave this tomb of plants and animals long dead, as if lingering too long would absorb her as well. Even as they paddled out of the darkness, she shuddered away an inward urge to escape, as if casting off…what?

"Thirsty?" he asked rooting through a small metal cooler.

"Huh?" she asked, still in meandering thought.

He touched her arm. "Something to drink?"

She dabbed at her neck with a bandana, "Oh, I'd love something. What do you have?"

"Coca Cola?"

He produced a bottle opener and lifted the cap.

She reached for the bottle. "Yes, thank you."

She rolled the small bottle across her forehead before opening it, savoring the fizzy coolness before gulping the contents.

They emptied their bottles together, finishing at almost the same moment.

He rattled a bag, "Potato chips?" He removed a small metal canister of Charles Chips.

She snatched it from his hands, "My favorite. Oh I loved these in college." She mashed a handful into her mouth.

He dipped into the bag as well, but she noticed he managed to eat in a more civilized way.

Her lips curled into a small smile, "Thanks. I haven't been eating much lately."

"They're just potato chips."

"No, I mean thanks for dragging me out of my flat today. It's so beautiful here and…"

"Fleur, you're having a good time with me, aren't you?" "You see," he added, "it's possible."

She glanced away for a moment, her thoughts on Louis. Why was she here with this stranger, this other man? Why did her heart pound so around him? "Maybe we should get going."

He shrugged, disappointment in his shoulders, and picked up the oars.

"I'm not sure where we are right now. We're going to have to drift a bit so I can get my bearings, okay?" He turned to look at her.

"Okay."

His face registered a look of surprise at the sight of her and he pointed to her head, eyes full of wonder. Fragile, yellow butterflies hovered and began to touch, alighting in her hair, perhaps attracted to the lavender shampoo she used. She could feel the faint touch of their spindly legs and the flap of their wings, faint as baby's breath.

But the rest of the insect world began to intrude as well. She did her best to ignore the swamp's lesser inhabitants and to search with keen intensity for a trail a large sign at the launch point had instructed. It stated that a particular trail marked by blue ribbons was host to a delightful assortment of bird hatchlings in the lower branches of dwarf magnolias and wild shrubs.

She closed her eyes.

Please God, if you're real, help us find the way. I need to get home. I shouldn't have come here with this man.

She remembered something her father told her so many years ago, words that began to echo in her head. "In a swamp, look beyond the surface. Things are often not what they appear to be."

When she scanned the lush growth surrounding them, she noticed a thick brown branch on the opposite bank, its surface thick and slimy. A four-foot Water Moccassin lay half-coiled upon it, soaking the warmth of the sun into its cold form. Quiet, even content, it never moved but for a flick of its tongue. She noticed that the markings and coloration of the snake perfectly matched the shades and perforations in the wood.

Further down the narrow corridor of water they traveled, perhaps twenty-five to thirty feet away, she saw the peaks of an alligator three feet larger than the one they had encountered earlier. It half-crested the solemn waters in silence, observing their canoe with impassive grace. Its cuplike eyes, halved by eyelids seemed ready for sleep. Beyond the gator, she spotted the first blue ribbon tied to a cypress tree on the edge of the bank.

Thank you, Lord. Perhaps Louis was right about prayer.

Encouraged by this sight, their paddles dipped with renewed vigor as they coasted into the watery trail. Tall, reedy grasses fringed them, effective at blocking out the soft breezes of the open waters. Deeper in, the way became muggy, the water a mass of muck. A veil of perspiration sealed clothing to skin. Breathing became a laborious task.

In each instance, she was the one who noticed the markings on the trail. Though experienced, Gerard could never seem to find the familiar blue ribbons tied at irregular intervals in the tall grasses, or in the low branches of miniature trees. Each time it seemed they were lost in the strength-sapping heat; she would look up and find the ribbon.

After a time of meandering in the dusky grasses, she wondered if the trail was indeed worth the insect stings and panting heat.

Then, they came upon the nests.

There were rows and rows of dwarf trees and larger shrubs ornamented with brown straw nests, some as large as soup saucers, others more compact–the size of halved coconuts. They took turns standing up in the canoe to view the nurseries. Adorable little hatchlings peep-peeped in response to their looming faces. The bird mothers circled overhead, squawking reassurance to their offspring. But they took care not to touch either baby or nest.

As she stood, the canoe wobbled precariously. He reached for her arm to help her stand in order to gain a closer look. In spite of mental resistance, her skin tingled at his touch. Considering the view worth the risk, she planted her feet on the floor of the canoe and tried to balance.

She concentrated on the nests. Delicate bodies in downy feathers, the baby birds made adorable music, amidst the remnants of blue eggshell around them. Fleur listened in rapturous pose, as if at an opera or concert featuring a famed virtuoso.

She looked to Gerard and tried to speak, to say something but there were no words. He lowered her back down to the canoe as it tipped side-to-side, muscular arm cradling her. Filled with wonder at the sight of the hatchlings, their lips found each other in a long passionate kiss. With his lips on hers, she seemed to drift in and out of reality.

Feeling weak as his kisses traveled down the nape of her neck, she regained her senses and pushed him away. I've dreamed of Louis's kisses on my neck, not this man.

Instead of drawing back however, he pulled her closer and brushed his lips behind her ears with more intensity.

"Stop, you musn't." She tried to shove him away, the canoe tipping precariously. Eyes wide open staring back at his, Fleur stiffened in his grasp . "I'm engaged, remember?"

He voice tattered and rough, he let go of his grip on her shoulders. "Of course. I-I'm sorry." He pulled a kerchief out and wiped the back of his head. "I suppose I got carried away." A smile grew on his muscular face "It's just that you're so. . ."

She let out the breath she'd been holding in. "Perhaps we should get going."

"I'm sorry. My behavior is inexecusable." He paused, "But aside from that, I wish I had met you before your fiancé did. Who knows—maybe you'd be wearing my engagement ring on your finger." Gerard took her hand and kissed it. "If you ever change your mind, madammoiselle," he looked her up and down, "I could make you forget him."

"Stop!"

"I'd be honored to take you dancing. There's a little Cajun place I know. There's a fais do-do every . . ."

"I won't be seeing you again. I shouldn't have come here with you. It was a mistake in judgement on my part."

His jaw tensed at her rejection. A cold hardness in his tone, he replied. "As you wish."

To her chagrin, instead of moving further back in the canoe, he stayed where he was, much too close. She balked at his lack of politeness and the fact that he'd made inappropriate moves, but thought it best to remain silent for the moment.

They took up their oars and moved past, leaving the nests, the tiny blue-speckled eggs and the hatchlings in pristine condition.

Thankfully, the waters were low in the section of trail ahead. It became necessary to push and pull the canoe at certain intervals, a painful reminder of the state of her emotions. A battle raged within—between her love for Louis and desire for Gerard. The passionate crawl of his lips upon her neck . . .

All of a sudden, she felt clammy and hemmed-in. She decided to avoid looking at him and instead, kept her eyes on the course, always looking for the next trail marker. She regretted coming. The man was nothing more than a masher, far from the gentleman he claimed to be.

From the corner of her eye, she thought she could see little furred creatures skipping across the dense brush close to the water's edge. Nutria? Or swamp rats. She squinted, lingering in gaze and thought, as the canoe slowed to a halt. Gerard lifted the oar out of the water.

"Let me show you something." He set the oar in a western direction and nodded for her to do likewise.

Though reluctant to do so, she lifted her oar as well and paddled. She stole a glance back. His skin gleaming from the work of the oar, shirt collar unbuttoned, he exuded masculinity and strength. Her heart thumped against her better judgment. *Stay your thoughts on Louis.*

"There's an ancient Cypress just around that bend to the left. If you make a wish there, it's supposed to come true."

"No," she stopped paddling and shook her head, "we have to return." She swallowed. "Besides, my wishes have already come true."

He cast a sideways glance, frightening in its intensity. "Ah, *Cherie*, but sadly, mine have not."

But she remained still. Without paddles to propel, the canoe swished in a circlular pattern.

"We've come so far, Fleur," her entreated. He reached over and circled her arm with one hand."

"No, no. We've gone far enough." She shook him off.

"It won't take but an extra ten minutes. And I promise to leave you alone—for good."

She took a deep breath.

He held his right hand over his heart. "I, Gerard Duplessis, do solemnly swear to leave you, Fleur D'Hemecourt, alone."

"Promise?"

"I promise."

She paused, calculating what time she would return home. What could it hurt to see the tree? "Oh all right then, but no more than ten minutes."

He smiled, dipping the oar from side to side with renewed purpose and strength. A scant few minutes away, she spotted the cypress, lording over a patch of ground no bigger than a swimming pool.

A monster in height and width, the tree spouted hundreds of knees through the waters surrounding it. She snapped a photo of the mighty cypress, surreal against the draping of mosses and the shadows of trees holding court around it.

She snapped a photo of Gerard paddling toward it as well, preferring to let him finish the paddling.

He slowed, maneuvering the canoe through the knees until it came to rest next to the little patch of land. He stepped up on the bank, pulled the edge of the canoe up onto the land, and held out his hand for her.

But when he helped her up, he pulled the engagement ring off her finger and shoved her to the ground.

"What? Why did you push me? As she struggled to get up, she had a better view of the massive cypress and gasped. Moving ropes coiling and uncoiling. Snakes. She turned, panic setting in. Gerard, now back in the canoe, was launching out from the bank.

Without her!

"What are you doing?" She stomped the soft earth with her foot. "Come back here this instant!"

Moving with surprising rapidity, he glided past the cypress knees and turned the canoe to her.

"Sorry my dear. I'm afraid I won't be coming back for you."

"Why not?"

"I promised to leave you alone, didn't I?" A wicked grin contorted his face.

"In March the peach is blossom-dressed;
Swallows, mating, build their nest.
Two by two they gaily fly....
Left all alone, how sad am I."

"What? Have you lost your mind?"

His laugh startled some birds from nearby trees and they flapped away, squawking.

"On the contrary. I've never been more lucid."

"Look back at the tree, Fleur."

She did a slow turn, fear rising in her chest. There, in a hollow of the tree, a large snake twined and slithered. Choked by fear, she moved to the very edge of the water and implored Gerard, who threw his head back and laughed. "Cottonmouths to be exact. Underneath this tree is their den, the place they come to mate each year." He looked around. "They are quite partial to the cypress knees as well. So many places to hide."

"Why, why would you do this?"

He held up an oar. "Do what? Leave you to be bitten by hundreds of venomous water moccasins and die an agonizing death alone in the swamp?" He pursed his lips as if in thought. "Or to be eaten by an alligator? Let us not forget that possibility. If one or more of the snakes don't get to you first, my love, the alligators most certainly will."

Tears ran hot down her face. "Please don't do this. Come back and-and we'll pretend this never happened."

"I assure you Miss D'Hemecourt, this is no prank. I would be happy to take your advice and pretend this never happened." He pointed. "Look down at your feet. Go on, look. . ."

Awh, there's a baby. Isn't he precious? Of course he probably doesn't have much venom yet. Before night falls, you'll be praying one of them bites you so you can put an end to the terror."

"Nooooo. Please don't." She froze at the site of the small snake squirming near her canvas shoe, it's tiny tongue flickering out. To her relief, it slithered away in the opposite direction.

Dipping his paddle, his voice jolly, Gerard shouted to her. "Who knows? Perhaps like the story goes, you'll turn into a beautiful fish. *Au revoir madamoiselle.*"

No, don't. Please." She screamed after him, but Gerard paddled away and never once looked back, though she followed him with longing eyes until his disappeared at the bend.

Hours passed, hours of tears, of shouts--but to no avail. The long, lazy shadows of afternoon crept in as she swatted at insects. Alone in the swamp, Fleur began to listen to the chatter and call of birds, imagining herself one of them, high in the sky, viewing the solitary figure below. Rustlings and movements in the brush on other patches of land across the water had her feeling more and more uneasy. Daring not to look much at her own island prison, she tried to focus on the blue of the sky or the intricacies of the Spanish moss curling on the trees.

The sun blazed down hot on her head and neck. Fatique soon set in as well, and though her lower back ached, she dared not sit or lean against a bush or small tree. She began to notice small, subtle movements all around her, tiny bubblings at the water's edge, curls in the green glass of fluid. Her breaths shallow, terror deep within, she felt as if she would faint, but what then? Would she awake to the sudden pierce of fangs on her face or hand?

Oh Louis, what have I done? Why did I go with this man, this stranger? What possessed me to trust him? And why did he take the ring? Would he leave her to die all for the sake of robbery? Surely the man knew about what she stood to inherit. Gerard worked for her uncle. He and Piper seemed on familiar terms as well.

She wiped her forehead with the back of her hand and thought of Piper. If she only knew what kind of man he was. Could she be in danger? Or was Piper part of the family betrayal?

Perspiration flowed down her temples. Surrounded by water, yet none to drink. Drinking swamp water would make her ill, but she decided to quench her thirst. If I die, I won't die of thirst . . .

She took a small step and eased down with great care, to the water's edge. But as she bent down, hand cupped, she noticed a rift in the water about twenty feet away and caught a glimpse of the unmistakeable scales, greenish gray in color. Elegance of motion lashing forward, efficient, with purpose--an alligator. She stood straight, screaming till the back of her throat hurt. Undeterred, the beast continued its forward motion. She froze at the sight, unable to utter another sound.

It was then that a tiny voice inside her heart began to speak. A voice she hadn't heard for many years. Pray.

A moment's hesitation, a moment only, and she spoke out loud, voice dry and raspy. "Father, please save me. I am doomed without you." She glanced at the alligator closing in, then at the cypress. "Mother said our family tree was rooted in Christ." A splash of water startled her. The alligator's snout was on ground to her right, powerful legs clamped to the muddy shore. Fleur clutched at the tree pendant around her neck and squinted her eyes shut, waiting for the inevitable.

But a shot sounded, followed by a loud splash and thrashing. She opened her eyes. A pirogue with two men in it called to her. One man, the barrel of a rifle still aimed in the direction of the alligator, the other--shouting something in French. Acadians.

Rescued. Heart slowed to an almost imperceptible beat, a sense of euphoria overwhelmed her. She looked down and clutched at the camera around her neck.

The loud noise of the shotgun had, for the time being, sent the creeping and crawling inhabitants of the tiny island to hide. The body of the alligator thrashed to rest, half on the land, half in the water. Red blood seeped from a single wound to the head.

She looked up. As if the world had slipped to a slower pace. Golden sun, filtered through mosses, birds soared through the still sky. But the two men paddled with furious intent until they reached the tiny patch of land, looks of concern on their tanned faces.

God had answered her desperate pleas for help. Or could her rescue be the product of pure chance? She'd called on him before to no avail. But the voice, the tiny voice was all-too familiar. Perhaps she would call upon him again sometime. For now, all she could think of was how good it felt to be in the land of the living.

Chapter Fifteen
A Wry Plan

Gerard plonked down in Bernard's office chair without being invited to do so.

"Well?"

Piper sat on the edge of the desk, crossed her legs and eyed him.

Bernard asked the man again, this time drawing the word out. "Wel-lllll?"

Gerard sighed. "I'm tired. I had to paddle back on my own." He stretched out his right arm and began rotating it. "Ahhh."

When he started on his left arm, Piper grabbed it. "What do you mean? You were supposed to woo her away from Louis, marry her and split the inheritance three ways once you got rid of her."

"The plan changed. I was making such progress. She's a hot little ticket, that's for sure. But she couldn't take her mind off her precious fiance'. Anyway, she's done for by now."

Piper tightened her grip on his arm. "What?"

The chair squeaked as Bernard bolted forward. "What do you mean, 'by now'?"

Gerard shrugged. "I left her there."

Bernard leapt to his feet. "You what? In the swamp?"

"By the tree with all the cottonmouths. The cypress tree is a hibernaculum, a snake den. . .a little something I studied at school. One of the professors told me about it. Snakes go there to winter. That's when they start to gather."

Bernard's features registered shock and distaste.

Gerard continued, his voice steady. "There are alligators too. I shoved her out the canoe and left her there. I predict one or the other will get to her before nightfall."

"Horrid." Piper turned away, clutching at her chest.

"I improvised. Take some initiative." He looked from one to the other. "Relax, you'll still get the inheritance and I'll get my money from you for doing the deed."

Bernard stretched out his hands and cracked his knuckles. Eyelids narrowing, he questioned Gerard further. "So you left her to die, did you? Are you trying to tell me you're not certain? There's no proof? You idiot!"

Bernard stood, pointing his finger. "If she's missing, there's no money in that. We'd have to file a missing persons report and wait years for the court to decide she's dead."

Piper gasped. "Years?"

He shook his head. "I tell you, she's dead. Of that I'm certain. No one could survive there for long, and certainly not overnight."

Gerard fumbled in his pocket. "D-did you know she was engaged?" He held the ring up in the air.

"Of course we did, you fool. And why would you take the ring off her finger? In case you hadn't thought of it, the ring is a most incriminating piece of evidence." He chewed off the end of a new cigar and spit it out. "For all your education, you're no better than Alcide. That's my fault for mating with a . . . "

"Father, stop!" Piper interrupted.

Gerard's face blanched, the air of cool confidence gone. "I'll get rid of the ring right away." His head sank low close to his knees, all signs of ego suddenly gone. He rubbed the back of his neck. "I-I thought I'd bring some kind of proof back with me."

He sat upright. "But I tell you, she's got to be dead by now. With all those snakes there this time of year, nobody sets foot on that little islet. Nobody."

"Don't do that. Please don't get rid of the ring." Piper held out her hand. "Give it to me. I'll take care of it."

Bernard's eyes darted to and fro, as if trying to decipher her thoughts.

After a moment's hesitation, Gerard dropped the glittering gem into her palm.

"Atta' boy." She smiled.

He looked to Bernard. "What's next? Should I go back and look for whatever's left of her? Blood? Maybe there's something . . ."

Nose turned up in distaste, Bernard waved him away. "Nothing--we do nothing except wait." Bernard puffed his cigar, eyes far away in thought.

Piper held up the ring to the light, admiring the fire of the stones. Though her eyes never left the ring, she addressed him. "That's right Gerard, save your breath to cool your soup."

Bernard smiled. "You heard her."

"All right then, as you say, I'll wait." Gerard nodded. "But I promise you, she's gone."

Bernard cleared his throat. "Boy, I think it best if you go away for a spell. You would do well to lay low for a while until all this blows over. The police might want to ask you a few questions since you were the last person to see her."

"But nobody saw us," he argued.

He reached in his drawer and pulled out a card. "Here, I have an old business acquaintance in Jennings who owes me a favor. Go stay with him a while."

Gerard took the card. "How long?"

"Until I send for you."

Eyes shifting, Gerard questioned. "Oh c'mon. No one knows I was even with her."

"Can you guarantee you weren't seen?"

Silent a moment, he answered. "Won't going into hiding make me look guilty?"

Piper interrupted. "But darling, you are guilty." She laughed. "Only we know that. As far as anyone else knows, there's nothing to connect the two of you. You didn't tell anyone else, did you?" She stood, straightening her navy blue skirt, and adjusted the fresh white carnation on her lapel.

"No one."

Bernard sat back in his chair, fingers entwined on his stomach. "Then pay a visit to my friend, Mr. Longfellow. And mind you, he doesn't have a telephone so you'll have to contact me every couple of days from the phone booth outside the general store. Got it?"

"Which one?"

Bernard scowled. "There's only one. I told you, it's a small town. Now go."

Gerard rose to his feet. "I-I don't like the idea of disappearing. How long will I have to stay there? There are things I need to take care of. What do I tell my family?" He shifted his eyes to Piper.

Piper sneered. "Don't be ridiculous. Do you want to go to jail? He'd look nice in prison garb, wouldn't he Father?"

She smiled at Gerard. "And as for your family," she blew on the ring and polished it on her sleeve, "I thought you and your father were on the outs. That is why you were staying with us, isn't it?"

Gerard looked down. "He's not pleased with the course of my life."

"In other words, he thinks you're a psychopath," Bernard laughed.

Gerald scowled. "It takes one to know one."

"That's enough." Piper interrupted. "Whatever your father thinks about you, he's taking steps to protect you. You should be grateful."

Her words did not elicit a response. Instead, Gerard smouldered, his anger palpable.

She tilted her head. "Weren't you on your way out?"

"Oh, and here." Bernard handed him a small wad of cash. "It's not much, but enough to tide you over. You don't get paid until we do. Got it?"

Silent, Gerard rose and pulled hard at the heavy double doors in his hurry to leave, perhaps intending to slam them shut. But hinged and well oiled, the doors closed sure and steady, an anticlimatic exit.

Bernard and Piper shared a look as the doors clicked shut.

"Why did you take possession of that ring? It's as incriminating for you as it is for him. I'm curious nonetheless. Gerard seems quite the fool, but you are his polar opposite."

She took her eyes off the ring for a moment, a wry smile on her face. "Father, is that any way to speak about your beloved business partner? Not to mention how you spoke about your devoted little henchman, Alcide."

"Hmmpf, that's what I get for taking that boy under my wing." He ran his hands through his hair. "It's just that I always wanted sons. I had high hopes."

"Your luck ran out with Alcide and Gerard. They're numskulls, both of them." She pursed her lips. "As for your crude remark earlier, I agree. That's what you get for consorting with the caliber of women you do. An adle-brained son who grows up to be one of your stooges and another son who fancies himself a cold-blooded killer."

Though she wished he hadn't, her father had been more than pleased to share how he had arranged for Gerard to be adopted by the Duplessis's who were childless. The baby, fathered by Bernard and a Storyville woman with whom he consorted, was to be brought to the Ursuline Orphanage to be raised by the nuns. But Bernard saw a business proposition in the process. Didn't he always?

He'd concocted a story about the mother, a young college student who'd found herself in a compromising situation with her boyfriend. So the child, soon named Gerard, Theodore Duplessis, was raised in an affluent household, the son of a prominent psychiatrist, and Bernard profited from the girl's "medical expenses," the new parents were more than happy to bankroll.

His brows lifted in mock innocence. "What else was I supposed to do?

After a moment's hesitation, she slipped the ring on her finger. "Pear-shaped, looks like a platinum setting." She held her hand up high. "See how it sparkles and catches the light! It's not a top of the line stone, but its well chosen. About as much as he could afford, but the very best quality for the price."

"Indeed." He reclined in his chair, scrutinizing her. "You want to be Mrs. Louis Russo, don't you?"

As if pained to pry her eyes from the sparkle, she cast a doleful expression his way. "Sometimes I think so. Not that he's the only choice I have. But I could do worse."

"He loves our little Fleur," he finished.

She nodded.

"But not if she's dead," he added.

She slipped the ring off her finger. "I doubt she is. She's got more lives than a cat."

"I don't think she's dead either, my dear. There is not a shred of doubt in my mind that Gerard botched it. But you-you wouldn't botch it. Not my Piper."

Surprised, her lips curled to the side. She pointed at herself. "You want me to handle things?"

He pulled out a lighter, flicked it, and relit his cigar. The smell of the butane lingered in the air. Sucking in air, puffing, sucking in air, puffing, Bernard got the cigar burning well before he spoke. "Why not you? You're smarter than most and you have the best possible motivation for wanting her out of the way."

Piper unfastened a long chain from her neck, inserted the ring, and slipped it over her head, hiding the pendant beneath her collar. She headed for the door.

"Well, what do you say to that proposition?"

Pivoting on her heels, to face him, she shrugged. "You're already working on an angle. I know you too well. What's your plan?"

"Plan?" He raised his brows in a profession of innocence.

"I'll think about it."

"Fair enough." He blew a trio of smoke rings into the air. "But don't think too long, my girl. As I said earlier, we're running out of time."

Chapter Sixteen
Je Reviens

Brothers Jacques and Labray Cheramie brought Fleur back to town. They shared dark hair, dark eyes and skin already well cured by the sun, though she judged them to be in their late twenties.

The men seated her in the middle of the pirogue, a small flat-bottomed boat of simple, yet efficient design. She noticed how much faster they glided through the waters, and that they used one-sided oars. The brothers moved forward with confidence. It was obvious they had no need of the blue ribbons to navigate their way through the swamp.

She scratched at her arms and legs, dotted with insect bites. Mud had collected under her nails but she didn't bother to try to clean them. Dark clay painted, smeared and dotted over her entire body. The pungence of rotten shrimp, fermentation, of rot, of soggy earth permeated the pirogue. Besides the filth on her clothing, she was drenched in perspiration. But Fleur cared little about the way she looked or smelled. A gladness to be alive enveloped her. The richness of each breath, of each new scene made her more aware, more thankful to be alive.

The waters low in the section ahead, but Jacques and Labray used long wooden poles to propel them ahead. The short time in the shallows gave rise to panic. Heart racing, she thought of what might have happened to her. She would have come to an unthinkable death, and no one would have ever found a trace of her body or what fate she'd have fallen upon.

Would Gerard attempt to take her life for refusing his attentions? The reality of her brush with death began to overtake her. She crumbled forward, eyes spilling over with tears. Over the past few months, she'd come closer to calamity more times than in her entire life. The loose railing at her flat, for instance . . .

Another time, she woke up early to the distinct odor of gas. Though dizzy, she shut off a burner on the stove and managed to open the windows. Mr. Clements had no idea how it could have happened. One time, on her way to meet Louis at his office, a car hopped the curb and came barreling towards her. A street vendor pulled her to safety an instant before the car sped off. Then there was the streetcar incident. How could all these things happen in

such a short time? She'd never had so many close calls in all her life.
I cannot think of it right now. I'll lose my mind.
Her heart began to race.
Passing through the shallow waters left her feeling clammy and hemmed in, trapped.
Longing for the whisper of a breeze to calm, to lift her hair and cool the nape of her neck, she looked around, heart pounding. Then, she spotted it, the final trail marker. Fleur gripped the coarse wood on both sides of the boat fearful she would lose consciousness. But the swamp began to increase in depth and within minutes they reached open waters. They pressed on and coasted smooth as silk into the slight coolness brought on by the late afternoon sun. A wash of liquid gold gleamed across the waters. Vine buds were beginning to unfold jeweled necklaces. Pin-sized insects skipped across the surface of the languid water. Gnats swarmed in clouds almost invisible from a distance.

Though troubled to keep her eyes open after her ordeal, she somehow felt refreshed. Her sense of direction in life had somehow gone awry before this day. But now, clarity had come to her, of life and death and purpose. The surety of her love for Louis filled her heart like a flame. Her doubts and ambivalence toward the supernatural had somehow changed as well.

She took in a deep breath and took her time letting it out. Like the trail of blue ribbons she had followed, she realized that God would always show her the way in life…whenever she asked…whenever she looked to Him. At that very moment, Fleur made up her mind to risk all and tell Louis the truth. Come what may. If their love was true and meant to be, Louis would accept her. If not . . .

The brothers arrived at a tiny store that sold bait, beer and hunting goods. Unaccustomed to the sight of a woman in the place, especially one in her state, she drew many inquisitive stares. But the brothers, protective instincts ignited, glared with sufficient threat to ward off any attempts from others to ask questions or seek to woo her favors.

Limbs soiled and caked in mud, hair astray, splatters of mud on her clothing—Fleur bowed her head, exhausted by her ordeal.

After calling the police, the owner showed her a place to sit. She asked him to call Louis as well, and recited his telephone number.

Fleur sank into a couple of large sacks of deerfeed, her body melding into it. The brothers kept a close watch nearby. In spite of her best efforts to stay awake however, she collapsed into a fitful sleep.

In her dreams she sometimes found herself flying, hovering over the landscape below, moving light as air, contrary to the laws of nature. She drifted, as a feather, through an open window, into a familiar room. Caught in an ethereal world, she found herself floating into her childhood bed. Snuggled between the covers, eyelids heavy, her breathing measured, she knew of a certainty, the ghost in the cedar chest would be along soon.

And soon enough, she heard the sound of footsteps clomping up the stairs to her bedroom. One, two, three…four, five, six. . . Her heart began to punch the inside of her chest. The ghost made the trip almost every night in her dreams. Seven, eight, nine. Eyes squeezed shut. Ten. I'm invisible. Eleven. Twelve. Thirteen. She held her breath. Fourteen stairs in all. The door creaked open. Her heart skipped.

"Fleur. Fleur." She bolted upright.

Louis held her by the shoulders, his face anguished. "You were screaming."

For a moment, the blur between dream and reality raked her emotions. Terror gripped her throat and she couldn't speak. But her breathing slowed as she took in the hospital room around her, finally settling on Louis's face. There were circles under his eyes, and she noticed his shirt collar was wrinkled.

"I was? I'm sorry. The dream . . ."

"Nurse." He called. "Nurse."

A middle-aged woman dressed in white ran into the room, took her arm at once and began taking her pulse. Then she checked her vitals and left to fetch the doctor.

"Darling, I can't tell you how relieved I am that you're awake." His stare bored into her eyes. "When I got the call, I could scarce believe what I was hearing on the other end of the line." His voice cracked. "Fleur, my Fleur, I don't know what I would do without you."

"Oh Louis. Where am I?" She brushed away beginning tears.

Hands curled around her shoulders, he held her close. "At the hospital. You had a nightmare."

Released from his embrace, she relaxed her head back on the pillow. "How did you get here so fast?"

"Fast? It's been twenty-four hours since you were rescued."

She turned her head away from him. A whole day?

"What about the dream?"

"It's—it's a nightmare that returns to me over and over. Each time I see more details--hear more--feel more." She brought her hands to her temples and rubbed. "I know it doesn't make sense."

"Fleur, its no wonder you're having nightmares. You've been through so much. And the police have only heard the story you told the two brothers who rescued you. A story that's quite frankly, hard to make sense of. The police will want to talk to you after the doctor's examination."

"Yes, of course. They need to catch him."

"Who?"

"Gerard Duplessis. The man who tried to kill me."

Chapter Seventeen
The Shadow Chasers

"Yes, that's correct," Fleur answered "Mr. Duplessis came to my door and, and invited me to accompany him for a canoe ride."

The police officer scribbled. "And you are acquainted with this man?"

"Not really."

He looked up. "You went on a canoe trip with a stranger?"

She lifted her chin higher. "I-I met him before, when I went to have lunch with my cousin, Piper D'Hemecourt at her, or rather at my house."

The other officer interrupted. "Which house? Yours or hers?"

She held her temples. "Both. It's rather complicated."

Louis intervened. "May I elaborate?"

"Please do," he said.

"The house Fleur is referring to is her family home. Her parents are deceased and her guardians moved into the home when she was very young to take care of her."

"So whose home is it?"

"The home belongs to Fleur, at least it will when she turns twenty-one."

"I see." He surveyed Louis with a shrewd eye. "And you are?"

"Louis Russo." He held out a hand.

The officers each took turns shaking his hand, though with deliberate slowness.

"What I meant is, 'and you are. . .in relation to Miss D'Hemecourt'?"

"Oh." He looked to Fleur. "I'm her fiancé."

The officers shared a look.

"Where's the ring?"

"Why, its on her . . ."

Louis came to a dead stop. "Fleur, where is it?"

She buried her face in her hands. "He stole it. Gerard slipped it off my finger right before he left me on the little island. Told me the snakes or the alligators would finish me off."

Brows in a furrow, he wrapped his arms around her. "What kind of fellow would do such a thing? A thief and murderer! Oh darling, I'm so sorry."

One of the officers coughed. "Miss D'Hemecourt, can you tell us more about this individual? Describe what he looks like, age, what you know about his background, things like that."

She untangled her arms from Louis and wiped her eyes on the sheet. "Of course." She shivered, pulling the sheets up higher. "I know that he's a friend of my uncle's and somehow involved in business with him. He knows my cousin Piper as well."

"Can you describe him?"

She reached for the glass of water on her food tray. Louis beat her to it and met her hand halfway. "Thank you." She swallowed. "He's t-tall and has blond hair."

Both officers scribbled and scratched what she said. "Eyes?"

"Hmmm?"

"The color of his eyes?"

"Blue I think. Yes, blue."

"Would you consider him attractive?"

"I suppose so." She looked from one to the other. "What are your names? I feel so awkward talking without knowing who I'm speaking to."

"Officer Tom Delaney."

"Officer Aubrey Clark."

"Pleased to meet you, gentlemen."

Louis was watching her, a puzzled look on his face. But he added, "Yes, I am as well."

"Now, if you don't mind, I would like to continue with the description of this individual whom you say kidnapped you and took you to the swamp and left you there to die."

She shook her head. "No, he didn't kidnap me at all. He invited me, said I should have a break from my painting and that I would be inspired to paint if I went to the swamp. That's why I took my c. . ."

Fleur gasped. "Louis."

His eyes grew wide. "Yes?"

"What happened to my Brownie? Did you see it?"

"I'm afraid not." He stood. "But I'll go and ask the nurse." He left the room.

Delaney pointed his pencil at her. "You were painting? I don't understand why you need inspiration to paint your walls."

She managed a slight smile. "I'm an artist. I was busy preparing for a gallery showing."

"Like Van Gogh or something?" Clark squinted.

"I am an artist, yes, but not to be equated with the talent of a Van Gogh."

"Never met an artist," he said.

"And the camera?" Delaney inquired.

"I took pictures of trees, birds, the water . . . and him."

"Say, that's good." Clark smiled. "Good.

Louis reentered the room followed by a young nurse. ". . .should be with her things in the cabinet." She opened the doors to a white locker.

From her bed she spotted it as soon as the doors opened, on top of her soiled clothing, a square brown object, the camera.

Officer Delaney stood. "Miss D'Hemecourt, we're going to put out an APB on the man and bring him in for questioning." He looked to Louis. "Until that time, I suggest you all take precautions for your personal safety. I'm going to call in a request to New Orleans, to have a squad car posted in front of your house, but I know they're short-handed right now. I can't promise anything."

"Thanks for your help. I'll make certain she's safe." Louis held Fleur's hand to his lips.

"Thanks to both of you." Fleur stared at the camera in Clark's hands. "I hope you catch him, soon."

***

The mood on St. Charles was somber. Informed of Fleur's misadventure and near brush with death, Bernard and Piper expressed shock and concern over the telephone, followed by anger at the man they thought they knew.

The film, taken from her faithful Brownie to be developed showed without a doubt that Gerard Duplessis had accompanied Fleur on the trip into the swamp. The pictures were of course, seized as evidence and the police were looking for him. So far though, Gerard had eluded them.

One of the pictures in particular, a perfect shot of Gerard, blond hair, shirt clinging to his chest as he paddled the canoe, left Louis strangely silent. Though Fleur longed to clear the air and ask forgiveness, the thought of broaching the subject left her panicked inside. A raw fear of losing him began to take hold.

Of course Uncle insisted that she move at once. The man knew where she lived. Not that the monster didn't know about the St. Charles address as well, but at least she would no longer be alone. Fleur consented. Servants were dispatched immediately to fetch her belongings and transfer her belongings to the Chinoiserie.

Her stay in the parish hospital had expanded. A fever shook her body, most likely contracted from mosquitoe bites.

Now safely home, ensconced in her beloved Chinoiserie, Philomene sat with her in the drawing room. Rain pattered on the picture window, but Fleur was nowhere near it. Philo insisted she sit in a wingback by the fire, a blanket draped across her lap. The howl of the storm whipped against the house and through trees. She closed the book she'd been trying to read. Picking at the same paragraph for over an hour.

"What you thinkin' of chile'?"

Reading glasses halfway down her nose, held around her neck by a chandelier of crystal beads, a birthday gift from Fleur. Philomene stared with purpose.

She swung her head toward the fireplace. "I feel so restless. I wish I could paint."

"Now you know what the docta said. He said you not s'posed to do nothing till tomorrow, an' I gave him my word, my word dat you wouldn't lift a finga to swat at a fly befor' dat day come."

Fleur turned her head toward her and smiled. "Philo you've always taken such good care of me."

"She sniffed and looked toward the window. "Don' say that. I always wish I'd done better by you, chile'."

Dismayed by the look of sadness on her face, Fleur continued. "Oh, but you did. You took good care of me all these years. And you took care of Tadpole too."

"An' Tadpole was chile' enough."

They shared a knowing silence.

"How is he?"

Philomene removed her glasses and put down her needlepoint. "Don' you worry for him chile'. You been tru 'nuf. He doing good staying wid the Russo's fo' now. Dey treat him nice." She sat back in her chair, resting her shoulder against one side. "Besides, I know who hurt him."

"Who? Tell me. Was it Alcide? I knew it."

"It waddn' Alcide who done it."

Fleur sucked in her breath, then gained it back. "Then who?"

"Gerard."

At the mention of his name, she buckled inside. Fear possessed her whenever she thought about him or about that day in the swamp. But shame also gripped her, shame and remorse that she'd kissed him, or that she'd entertained feelings of attraction.

"Gerard?"

"At first we all thought it was Alcide. He always mockin' my brother, speshly when he by da pond playin' with his fishes like he do. When I axe him who did dat to him, he tol' me the man what done it. Alcide always here and he a no 'count fella, so's I think he da one who dunnit."

"And?"

"I heard him talkin' to his fishes like he do an' he tol' dem, he say "it da tall brutha what done it'. She wagged her head from left to right. "Can you 'magine?"

"What did he mean?"

Philomene's mouth curled into a smile. "Dem two is da same. Deys chirren o' whoredom."

"Uncle's woman? But Alcide is Bernard's son, not Gerard."

"Dey bruthas from de same place."

"Storyville? My, my."

Philomene continued. "Tadpole hear a lot of things. He all over the house, sweeping up everybody's mess. People think theys no brain in his head so it don't matter what they say. Tadpole's head like a bucket o' nails, but he no fool. He kin hear an' I hear what he tells to the fishes and tadpoles. He heared Ber'nad an' Miz Florrie arguin' one night. He hear Bernard talk to Piper too. Tadpole know."

She struggled to take it all in, then thought of something. "Imagine that." Fleur bit her lip. "But Gerard is wealthy and educated."

Philomene held out both hands in an imaginary balance. "Your uncle got him 'dopted with a good fambly. Gerard growed to be a tall drink o' water. He handsome, but his heart wicked."

"What about Alcide?"

"Po' Alcide got to stay with his mama an' grow up in a baudello. He comely lookin', but short. Prolly remind Bernard o' hisself too much."

She went on. "His mama start hersef out in Storyville but when the army got it shut down, she went some place else. Dat Alcide no good, Gerard no good. 'An Piper no good neitha."

"What do you mean? I know she can be difficult, even devious at times, but. . ."

"Like I said, Piper no good. She jealous."

Memories flashed before her eyes, the look on Piper's face when she showed her the college acceptance letter, while she packed, as she waved goodbye at the train station.

"She didn't want to. I mean, I never thought she wanted to go away to school." Was the look she'd seen in her cousin's eyes a look of resentment?

"She want what you got."

Her heart sank. "Why couldn't she go too? She's just as intelligent, if not more." She wiped a tear.

"It ain' brains what kep her back. Your uncle don' have two coppa pennies to rub together. The only money he got is the bit he gets every month as your guardian, and whatever he squeeze out of his rich friends or wins playing the ponies."

She sprang to her feet as her thoughts added up to a disturbing conclusion. "They need the money." Voice quivering, she repeated. "My money." All at once, her legs, limp as cooked noodles gave out on her.

A white fog enveloped her consciousness and she was only a tiny bit aware of spiraling to the floor. But the floor became a vast swirl of darkness, and Fleur found herself again in her childhood bed. The attic room just as it always was. Her dolls, the art easel, chairs, chest of drawers. A gust of wind blew in through a window extinguishing a lone candle. With that, the door creaked open and a figure hovered in the doorway, illuminated by faint light below the stairs. She tried to breathe, but choked on each inhale.

***

She came back to awareness in her bed, Philomene at her side. Fleur pulled off a cold compress from her forehead and sat straight up. "What happened? How did I get here?"

"Hold on. You jus' keeled over chile'. She eased Fleur back down to her pillow. "I run to the kitchen an' Rueben help me bring you to your bed."

She shivered, lips quivering.

Philomene stroked her face. "What is it? The dream?"

She whispered a yes.

"Shhhh. It's jus' a dream. It'll pass."

After a few minutes, the unsettling thoughts passed as they always did and she recalled their conversation before her fainting spell.

"Is it true? What I thought I heard?"

Philomene nodded. "Yes."

Her chest heaved the next words. "They're trying to kill me. It all makes sense. The accidents, the near brushes."

They both looked up as a knock sounded on the door. "I'll go see who it is."

Fleur grabbed at her arm. "Don't leave me."

"Prolly Rueben checkin' up on us. I'll be back d'recly."

***

Philomene hurried to the door and opened it a crack. With the rain gone, she sniffed the air, fresh and clean and noticed patches of clear sky and shafts of brilliant golden sun. With sunlight, the fallen drops sparkled like little jewels on the ground. Any other day, Philomene might have given pause to enjoy the sight, but Alcide's belligerent face stared back at her from the side stoop. Hair soaked, pressed close to his head, he handed her a small package.

"From the docta." He cleared his throat and spit onto the tea roses. "Better let the boss man know."

She took it from him and closed the door. Leaning against it, she tore at the brown paper wrapping, then at the box underneath. Clutching the blue glass bottle in her hand, she held it to the light. Laudandum.

Her heart skipped a beat as memories flooded back. Heating sweet milk on the stove. A cup of milk, two teaspoons, shugga, a splash of banilla estrak, a pinch o' cinmon an' five drops, Laud'num. Carried on a small tray with a cookie, she made the journey two or three times a week, then every night. At first she thought it was for Fleur's benefit that Bernard ordered the concoction. With all the nightmares the child was having, a little something to help her sleep made sense. The concoction wasn't for the child however. He ordered her to take it to Florrie, who slept like the dead after she drank it. Philomene knew because she tiptoed in a half hour later at first. The next time she walked in fifteen minutes later, then ten, then five. If she'd dropped a bag of silverware on the floor, Florrie wouldn't have fluttered an eye. Such was the potency of the draught.

Before long however, Philomene began to suspect something else was going on. So one time she waited in the shadows and watched as he opened the front door. A woman bathed in the light of the full moon stood on the threshold.

Quiet as can be, she listened as they climbed the old wooden stair boards that betrayed their presence. Bernard arrayed in his fancy dressing robe--the scent of cologne overpowering. He entered an empty guest room with the woman and remained for a time.

She remembered the sick feeling in her stomach, a wildfire of chill bumps across her body. Hot tears fell down her face, rivulets ducking under her neck and down her bosom. Poor Florrie. In her own house! Dear Jesus. Oh Lord, help her.

Philomene held the bottle to the light. What would happen if she dropped it? She'd tried that tactic before. Both she and Tadpole had paid dearly for that rebellion. The ache she felt in her legs was of a surety related to that beating. Her bones were never the same after all the beatings. And Tadpole . . .

Heart aching, she thought of the implications of continuing to trifle with God's grace. She'd fallen on her knees seventy times seven to ask God's forgiveness. And there was no question in her mind of God's forgiveness and redemption, but no more. She'd resolved in her mind and in her heart to serve God and God alone.

"Philo? Are you coming? Where are you?" Fleur's sweet voice echoed down the stairs.

"Comin' chile'." She tucked the bottle into her pocket, launched away from the door and headed back upstairs to attend to the young woman. Mista Bernard would have to wait to hear about this delivery.

She found Fleur looking stronger, sitting up in bed, arms crossed. Anger seared her expression. "Philo, I've made up my mind to confront my uncle. I've had enough."

Philomene sat down in a nearby chair. "What's he gonna say? He's jus' gonna lie to your face, ain' he?" Or worse.

Eyes flashing to the right and left, she could see that her words had had an effect. Fleur was thinking about what she'd said. Good.

"Maybe him finding out you know ain' such a good idea. If the man want you dead--it because he want your money. You could skip town, go back to the big city."

"But this is my house."

"The finest house won't do you no good if you ain' alive to live in it."

"My gallery showing is so close. I can't leave before then. Everything I've worked for is in that collection."

"Then go after the show's done, chile'. Leave in the middle of the night. Tell no one."

She raised a hand to touch her mouth and gasped. "Uncle didn't want me to elope. He was quite specific when he commanded me not to. There can only be one reason for that. He doesn't want me to marry before my birthday, which is when I am to receive my inheritance."

Philomene's eyes lit up. "That's it. You and Mister Louis should go off and git married. Then you could ride your no 'count uncle and cousin out on the railcar and get rid of dem carpetbaggers. They won't have no claim to your money or your house, nuthin'"

"Louis is out of town for a series of business meetings he couldn't get out of. He'll be back for the show. I'll talk to him then." Her eyes sparkled. "I know he'll consent to marry me right away given the circumstances."

"The we have to keep dem from getting' to you for two mo' weeks."

She shook her head. "I doubt there will be another attempt on my life before the show. Uncle's invited all his colleagues and associates, and friends."

Philomene sat on the bed next to her and wrapped her arms about Fleur. "Then you best be married befor' the cock crows da at de end o' two weeks, or sure as the sun rise in da east, your uncle gonna be finish carvin' your headstone."

***

Piper let go of the crystal glass she had pressed against the wall of the Chinoiserie guest room. She'd stolen in earlier while the two sat by the fire and listened nearby for a while, and followed them upstairs after Fleur fainted. She'd settled into the guest room next door, quiet as a mouse.

Hand shaking, she placed the crystal glass on the decorative table next to the easy chair and eased down on it. Her instincts were right. Listening to those two had provided a world of useful information. Father would be interested to hear about their little conversation.

She glanced over at the other chair and chanced a whisper. "Were you able to hear any of that?'

He shook his head. "Tell me."

"They know more than we think." She'd been dismissive of her clueless cousin one too many times. The girl, now enlightened by their motivations, would be dangerous. And if the police were to catch up with Gerard, he'd spill the beans fast to save himself. Time for a new plan . . .

She explained it all to him, her voice low, and he listened to every word. While she spoke, she pulled the chain up from under her collar and held the ring dangling from it, swinging it back and forth.

He reached for it and held the ring between his fingers for a moment. Lips close to her ear, he whispered, "Darling, what if the danger to Fleur were all in her mind?'

"What do you mean?"

"If she were be declared mentally unstable, the family could have her committed to an institution and that would be that. The attempts on her life would simply be a product of her own fears and imaginings. All in the girl's pretty little head. With Fleur's propensity for strange behavior, declaring her mentally unstable shouldn't be hard to prove."

She clutched at his shoulders and kissed him. "Brilliant. You're brilliant."

He smiled.

    Truth be told, she'd never felt quite comfortable with the idea of taking her cousin's life. In fact, she was relieved to find out Fleur was still alive after Gerard's plan went awry. This idea would solve that dilemma and leave the way open for other possibilities. First things first, she'd have to put the kibosh on the elopement.
    She held the ring in her palm. "It's time for Louis to hear a few things about his precious Fleur."
    "Yes."
    "Then we'll see how anxious he is to marry her. What man wants damaged goods? Certainly not a rising young attorney from a good family!
    Piper let the ring freefall till the chain caught it."
    He lifted her chin and brought his lips to hers.
    The tenderness of his touch moved her to tears. "Dear heart."
    "I adore you, my love."
    She smiled and leaned back to admire him, eyes misty, a feeling of contentment warming her heart. The blue of his coat brought out his hazel eyes. *So handsome.*

Chapter Eighteen
Gallery On Rue Chartres

Almost eight in the morning, the humidity already insufferable, Fleur waited in front of the Camellia Grill. Planted on the neutral ground waiting for the next streetcar, she swatted at gnats or mosquitoes gnawing at her ankles off the damp grass and wondered how a fall day could be so miserable. She'd gone early for breakfast to try out the new place, and to celebrate.

Today would be her day to sink or swim. A cup of coffee and two eggs over easy with grits on the side was more than enough to quell the growl of an empty stomach, but she had no real appetite for it. Louis had readily agreed to elope, but could not leave his out-of-town commitment early. She held on to his promise to attend the gallery showing no matter what.

Since moving into the Chinoiserie, food had become the least of her concerns. Nightmares interrupted her sleep most nights. With Gerard still on the loose, she was glad to have Philo at her side, though she chided Fleur daily about her lack of a good night's sleep. Preparing for the exhibition occupied every waking moment for the past two days. Except of course, those moments she thought of Louis. She sighed at the thought of him, the dark waves of his hair, his smile, the way he looked at her.

Swat.

A glance down at the watch on one arm, she tightened her grip on the small valise, and clamped her shoulder snug over the portfolio. She had no intention of being late for the debut. Anxiety building with each passing second, she ran her free hand down her skirt to smooth fresh creases from sitting, then swiped at another gnat.

Clang. Clang. The bell announced its arrival. Finally.

Relieved, she spotted the streetcar ambling steady and sure along the tracks to her stop. The dark green paint on its body and the dusty red color framing the windows were equally faded by sun and the elements. Though picayune in size, she was surprised that there were still empty seats. She stepped on board the rear and handed the conductor a quarter. A short, sleight man, he made change for her from a metal money belt.

In contrast to the outside, the interior of the streetcar was deep and rich with wood tones, accented by shiny brass fittings. The polished wooden seats, worn to a smooth patina with constant use, seemed to glow like amber. Bright rows of light bulbs lined the ceiling and cardboard advertisements curved along the barrel-shaped edge of the wall and ceiling—Burma Shave: Romance never starts from scratch. Most others were advertisements for cigarettes: Lucky Strike, Chesterfields or Camels. Almost everyone she knew indulged in the habit. But she didn't. Neither did Louis, although he used to. But then, most men in the service did.

She glanced at her watch again. Ten after. Since moving into the guesthouse, she was trying hard to acclimate, to readjust, but she'd become accustomed to sleeping in cramped quarters. She thought about all the places she'd slept. As a child, her room was up a flight of stairs in the remodeled attic, then her college dorm room, the size of a closet, and more recently in the small French Quarter flat. The guest home in contrast, her home seemed like a palace, with three bedrooms, a sitting room, parlor, mosaic-tiled bathroom with a claw tub, and wrap-around porch, which mimicked the porch at the main house. And of course, with the whimsical pavilion right outside her door she enjoyed yet another living area.

The doors closed, and with the clang, clang of a bell, the motorman in the front of the car accelerated and they lurched forward. She sat down alone in a seat by a window and noticed, for the first time, that there were thirteen windows on either side of the streetcar--all open to take full advantage of the cooling wind.

A group of handsome young sailors in white caught her eye at the first street corner. Waving and calling after her, they beckoned, one even falling on his knees. She smiled and waved back, her face flushing at their antics.

The streetcar rumbled past columned antebellum and Louisiana homes edged in scalloped gingerbread; vast verandas with towering trellises of honeysuckle or jasmine and shaded tunnels of live oaks. In one yard, a cascade of wisteria poured fragrant violet blossoms from the top of the oak its tendrils had embraced. Thousands of flowers wafted perfumed air from two blocks away. Fleur closed her eyes and breathed in. Intoxicating.

Past the stone spires of Tulane and Loyola Universities, the lichen-sheathed stone gateposts of Audubon Park, the streetcar swayed in rhythmic fashion, side-to-side. The movement relaxed her troubled spirit. She rested the side of her head on the window and closed her eyes.

Ah, the breeze--glorious at first, until someone pulled the cord near the top of the bank of windows. A bell rang and they slowed to a full stop.

A man and woman stepped on. She recognized the man right away. He'd pulled her out of the way when she'd tripped into the path of the streetcar. Rivulets of perspiration driveled down his temples as he escorted the rotund woman accompanying him to a seat right in front of Fleur.

Fleur tapped on his shoulder. "Excuse me, but aren't you the one who pulled me to safety not long ago?" A blank expression answered her, but then the dawn of remembrance.

"I remember you. You're the dame, I mean, young woman who almost bought the farm. Say, I'll bet you have a new lease on life now."

"I certainly do." She smiled. "I just wanted to thank you again for your kind deed."

He looked to the woman who seemed preoccupied with something in her purse, then back to Fleur. "Mind you, I wanted to help, but I have a bad back. When I saw that young fella push you, I knew I had to do something, but another gent beat me to it. I don't know who it was and don't remember what he looked like either."

"Pushed me?" Fleur's jaw fell open.

"Someone pushed me?"

"Didn't you know? Oh yes, a hooligan. Young guy. Short but good looking, for a hooligan that is. At first I thought he might be your boyfriend an' maybe he had some kind of beef wit you."

"No." She stared ahead. "No way." If not for the height, she would have assumed Gerard to be the culprit, but the description fit Alcide to a tee.

A sharp jerk and the streetcar lurched forward.

After peeling off her gloves, the woman pulled a pack of cigarettes from her purse. When she offered one to the man, he pulled a lighter from his pocket and lit the flint with a swift pull of his thumb. She inhaled the acrid smell of smoke with butane.

The flash and smell of the lighter fluid ignited memories from her childhood. She stared at the man's back. Aunt Florrie and Uncle Bernard sharing a lighter on the veranda in the cool of the evening, smoking cigarettes, sharing thoughts over coffee and chicory. Fleur hid behind a large gardenia bush on the side of the house and listened.

Her dark hair, cut short and curled close to her face, Aunt Florrie spoke in a discrete tone from the wicker divan. "I don't understand why Babette can't take the girl. We have enough on our hands with our own child. How am I to manage with another?" She flicked ash into a pot of marigolds.

Fleur's uncle stared out at the expanse of green lawn and the street beyond. He didn't respond to Florrie at first, as if immersed in thought. He drew two full breaths of smoke and exhaled before answering. "Fleur is our responsibility. And as for my sister, she wouldn't know the first thing about caring for a child. Besides, Rene' would have wanted me to care for his only child. Why, he's barely in the grave and you're complaining. I'm rather disappointed with you."

"I-I'm sorry darling. Truly, I am. But I'm thinking of our family." Caution laced her voice.

He dropped the cigarette butt to the wood-planked floor and twisted it out with the sole of his shoe. "She is part of our family now. And you will manage just fine with another child. You have no choice." He stood, looming above her.

She looked up, her expression turned serious. "All right. I'll try." Florrie turned away with a pout, preferring instead to stare at the burning cigarette between her fingers.

"Besides, my dear," he added, "we are her legal guardians."

A glimmer of hope caused her to sit up straight. "And what does that mean for us?" she asked.

He blew on his nails and polished them on the tail of his shirt. "It means we have control over her estate, her life and her welfare. Of course there's a law firm involved and we are somewhat restricted, but I have a few friends who might be inclined to bend a few rules here and there."

"Oh," she answered, her red lips forming the sound.

He pulled something shiny from his pocket.

From the bushes, Fleur squinted for a better look at it. A coin. A silver dollar.

He drew close and whistled on the back of her aunt's neck. She shivered. "Darling…" he said.

"Y-yes?"

"You like your coffee sweet, don't you?"

Fleur noticed the coin dangled from a thin silver chain. In his hand, the coin swung to and fro. Her aunt seemed fascinated by it.

"You know I do," she answered breathless, her eyes now half closed.

"Then if you promise not to question me on this matter, I'll make sure you have plenty of sugar in your coffee. I know how you like to shop, to indulge in the finer things in life." Bernard, his face clean-shaven and smooth, brushed his cheek against hers. "And you deserve it, of course. I'll see that you get all that you need, and more."

She nodded, mesmerized.

"Do you trust me?" he asked, this time his mouth close to her ear.

"Y-yes."

"Good. Now it's time for a little nap. You'll wake up feeling refreshed and calm. You'll be happy about taking on Fleur."

"Yes." Her mouth seemed limp, voice void of emotion.

He plucked the cigarette from her fingers, extinguished it in the potted plant, and eased her head back onto the divan. Her eyes were already closed.

How could Aunt Florrie go to sleep so fast? Fleur considered what she had seen and decided that her uncle owned a magical coin. With it, Uncle Bernard could put anyone to sleep for a nap whenever he wanted to. Just like the Sandman.

Chapter Nineteen
Oil of Gladness

The streetcar slowed and she woke up, startled. Passing Lee Circle, she squinted the sleep from her eyes to get a better look. Brilliant even in the hazy light of morning, she admired the white doric column surrounded by four cast-iron urns dripping with pink bougainvilleas.

A bronze statue of General Lee standing atop the soaring column at least sixty feet up might as well have had his head in the clouds. The statue of Lee faced due north. Remembering her classes, the lesson on sculpting and statues came to mind. General Lee had vowed never to turn his back on the enemy. Good advice.

Though it hurt her eyes, she chanced a glance upward. Heat shimmered a gentle mirage around Lee's form. In a couple of hours, the blaze of hot sun would transform the gentle shimmer to a broil.

Nearing Canal Street, several people pulled the cable before she had an opportunity to, including the man and the woman sitting in front of her. As the streetcar swayed and ground to a halt, she rose and smoothed her cream beige skirt yet again--a perfect complement to the buff and black polka-dot blouse; her heels, neutral beige, trimmed in Dutch cream.

She decided to walk from Canal into the Vieux Carre'. The show would begin promptly at 9:30 and the walk there would only take about ten minutes. Plenty of time. Fleur decided to cut through Jackson Square. The azaleas, glorious in full bloom, had exploded into a burst of pinks and reds and whites. Wedding veil bushes rivaled them in proliferous splendor, cascading white Millie fleur blossoms. The low hum of honeybees droned lazily from one generous blossom to the next.

Fleur stopped to admire another statue--the equestrian form of Andrew Jackson on a prancing horse, two hooves in the air--a true monument to artistic skill and craftsmanship. Now this was a statue one didn't have to crane the neck to see. Three sweaty boys suddenly ran right out in front of her. She stumbled backward.

One of the boys, a street ruffian in a red and blue striped shirt scrambled up the statue and with a triumphant grin, pulled the iron sword from Andrew Jackson's sheath. His grin turned to a look of terror and the sound of a whistle alerted the other two boys. Sword in hand, he jumped down into an instant run, followed by the others. Two policemen approached. The younger one gave chase and the older, out of breath stopped near Fleur.

"Did you see them?" he asked between breaths.

"Why yes, I did." Fleur could not help but smile. "The boy wearing the striped shirt is the one who took the sword."

The policeman nodded, still gasping. "I know that one. He and his friends run the streets and think it a fine prank to make off with the general's sword." He waved a hand in the air. "No matter. I know where he lives—and the others. We always get it back."

The policeman took his hat off a moment and wiped a handkerchief over his balding head. "Thank you, ma'am. Sorry for all the ruckus."

"Officer," He stopped in his tracks. "Why doesn't the city just weld the sword in place?"

His eyes lit up. "Say, that's a fine idea. Instead of chasing these rapscallions all over the Quarters, we could have it welded in. Thank you, Miss, ah, I didn't get your name?"

"Fleur D'Hemecourt."

He tipped his hat. "Much obliged."

She continued walking, past the St. Louis Cathedral, over cobblestone and brick, parting a sea of bobbing belligerent pigeons, she walked the streets. Old smells, the smell of history— of oiled leather, tar and pitch, faded cedar, mule dung and the fragrance of Creole cookery. A sauté' of bell peppers, onions and garlic and a slowly-stirred roux, bricks and mortar, human sweat and toil.

Shaded from the sun, by second floor porches extended over the banquette bordered in curlicued wrought iron, the intricate designs shadowed into the street. Wooden storefronts offered an array of boutiques, charcuteries, restaurants and antiques. The fragrance of bubbling sugar and pecans wafted from a praline shop. When she inhaled, her mouth began to water. She stopped to buy a small bag. Louis, whom she'd discovered was quite fond of sweets, would appreciate sharing the treat with her. She hoped he'd be there. His schedule would be tight, but he swore, come Hades or high water, he'd be there.

Fleur stood before the shop on Rue Chartres. A large sign on a brass easel announced her show, complete with a smaller picture of her in a green silk dress and hat, paintbrush in hand. Trevor Brandt, the owner on the lookout for her from the window, came out and joined her.

"What do you think of it, Miss D'Hemecourt?" Tall and slim built, a snappy dresser, Trevor was a true connoisseur of art, fashion, design and the intricacies of society.

"I adore it." She flashed a smile and placed a hand on his arm. "You're such a dear." She turned to the two windows. "And I see you have some of my work featured in the windows as well."

"Yes indeed," he answered. "I'm expecting great things here today. Some of my favorite clients have confirmed they will be attending." He took her arm and placed it over his elbow. "Shall we?"

He led her into the gallery. She let out a sigh. With high ceilings and a row of three massive antique chandeliers, her paintings, done in oil were displayed along the bare brick wall. The old bricks, in ancient earth tones were the perfect backdrop to her work.

"Oh, Trevor. I-I'm overwhelmed."

"So am I." Louis stood in the doorway. Through the picture window beyond, Fleur noticed the young sword-swiper run past, followed a moment later by the policeman.

She smiled at the sight. But the sight of Louis gave her much more to smile about. He cut a handsome figure in a dark blue suit, crisp white shirt and maroon tie. Tanned, his wavy dark hair lent an adorable charm to his looks.

"Louis. I'm so glad you're here."

He kissed her hand. "I wouldn't miss it for the world, my dear."

Her eyes roving from one to the other, she announced, "I want to introduce you to Trevor Brandt. Trevor, this is Louis Russo; Louis, Trevor Brandt."

The men shook hands. "Pleased to meet you."

Trevor bowed his head, and seemed flustered, his voice cracking. "And I, you."

A shadow appeared at the door. Fleur peeked around the two men. Uncle Bernard stood, a dark silhouette, aimed in the direction of paintings on the wall. A shiver washed over her skin like a splash of well water.

"Uncle, how good of you to come."

At the sound of her voice, the familiar silhouette stepped out of the doorway and into the light of the room. Bernard turned his gaze from the wall and extended his hand, reaching for Fleur's hands. He clasped his around hers. "My dear, how extraordinary, indeed, how gorgeous you look today." He reached up to caress the side of her head, lingering on the soft curls.

She felt acid creep up the back of her throat.

"Now, Fleur, tell me about these pictures of yours."

"Her paintings," Trevor corrected, "are this way." He gestured. "Since you two gentlemen are early, let's have a private showing." The paintings were arranged to be viewed starting from the left.

Fleur and Trevor glanced at each other and shared a smile. Novices to the world of art often referred to paintings as pictures.

Bernard cleared his throat. "Yes, of course. Paintings."

"Well," she paused, "which one would you like to view first?"

"I take it we're not going to follow the viewing pattern. Oh well." Trevor smiled, tipped his glass and drained his champagne. "Shall we?"

Bernard scanned the wall and pointed toward the one in the middle. "That one."

Trevor walked toward it first. "Interesting that you should pick that particular one Mr. D'Hemecourt. This one is the masthead of our show. The one in particular is the masthead around which the entire work is showcased. Miss D'Hemecourt calls it The Room. Stunning, isn't it?"

The three of them moved forward to join Trevor. Done in rough layers of oil, the painting depicted a pale young girl, in a room without windows. Dressed in white, she wore a red bow in her long hair. Seated on the edge of a small wooden-framed bed, her attention fixed toward the door, a frame of brown wood with a beveled glass knob.

"What do you notice about it?" asked Trevor.

Bernard cleared his throat again, a nervous habit of his.

He's uncomfortable. She watched him.

He pointed. "The bottom of the door. There. Look, there's a gap at the bottom of the door that's bigger than most."

"And what do you see?" asked Trevor.

Bernard squinted. "I'm not sure."

Louis answered instead. "It looks as if there are two shadows. Shoes perhaps? Shadows of shoes beyond the door?"

"Bravo Louis." Trevor's thin lips curled up in approval. "Seems plausible."

Bernard shook his head, beads of perspiration on his forehead beginning to form.

"Don't you like it, Uncle?" Fleur's face glazed over. "It's the Sandman. Well, either the Sandman or the ghost."

She turned to the others. "There's a ghost in the house you know. As a girl, I was terrified of it."

Trevor shuddered. "I don't know how you slept at night. Did it come into your room? What did it look like? Gossamer mist?" He shivered as if terrified at the thought.

"Funny," she said, "I don't know how I ever managed to fall asleep, but I did." She continued, "Sometimes I'd hear the eerie sound of footsteps and I knew the phantom was there, right outside the door in the hallway, but that's all I can remember about it." She looked at her uncle. "Don't you like it?"

Face blank, eyes still on the painting, he didn't answer right away. He folded his hands across his chest and took an extended breath as if inhaling a cigarette. "Oh I do, Fleur. It's just, just a bit different. I'll be the first one to admit that I don't understand anything about modern art or art in general for that matter." He shook his head and moved on down the row, away from them.

Louis spoke. "Let me talk about this one." He looked closer. "This one's called 'Light and Shadow.' Sounds ominous." Without touching it, his fingers tracked across the length of the painting. "Spectacular detail."

"Why, it's the house." Bernard glanced back at her. "It's perfect. Looks just like the house at night. How much is it? I would love to have this one."

"Uncle I would be glad to paint one for you."

"Would you?" He ran a hand over one temple. "It's uncanny I tell you. Uncanny."

Trevor glanced at Fleur, blinking his approval of Louis, but noticed the arrival of several customers, early for the show as well--obviously eager to look. He clapped his hands and a butler came out from the inner courtyard with a tray of refreshments.

"Oh Fleur, he called, "There are some people I would like you to meet."

"I'm coming." Fleur turned to Louis. "Do you like the show so far?"

His eyes locked on the paintings. "I do, Fleur." He tapped her arm. "A masterful work, indeed. Compelling. And though I love the art, I love the artist all the more."

"Thank you for coming, my love. It means the world to me." She squeezed his hand.

Trevor called to her again and she walked over to him and the clients, as three more crossed the threshhold.

A few minutes passed. Louis found her at the center of a group of admirers, kissed her cheek and told her that he had to go back to work.

"But I . . ." Out of the corner of her eye she noticed Uncle Bernard listening. "I haven't seen you much."

He winked. "Rest assured my darling, you will. When your show is done, I'm taking you out for a celebration dinner. That is, if you're not too famous."

"I doubt that will be an issue."

"Don't underestimate your talents my pet." Bernard smiled. "Good day." Hat in hand, he strolled outside and placed it on his head. The door shut behind and he was gone.

Louis kissed her forehead. "Fleur, don't you know? Haven't you heard? You're the toast of the town."

Chapter Twenty
New Beginnings

Louis and Fleur walked the French Quarter banquette after dinner. Slick from an afternoon rain--steam rose from the pavers exposed to the heat of a brilliant sun. November was already upon them and temperature was still hot and humid.

Droplets of rain sparkled like diamonds in the street, on leaves and blossoms, and the sound of metal gutters whooshed down from rooftops.

"It's been difficult to keep the news to myself. I want to shout it from the rooftops. How does it feel to be almost married?"

She clutched the license in her hand and gave him a kiss. "Glorious. I still can't believe the lines at City Hall were so short."

He spread his arms. "God parted the red sea for Moses. Maybe he shortened the lines for us."

She stopped, leaned in and touched her lips to his. "I almost believe you."

Louis laughed and took her in his arms. "It seems everything is going right today—our wedding license, a smouldering kiss from my one true love and," he held up a bag, "pralines."

He took a praline from the wax bag. "I'm so proud of you Fleur. Your show was a stupendous success. Trevor was elated." He held out the bag to offer her one, but she declined.

Fleur felt a strange intoxication from within. "I still can't believe it. It's difficult to fathom. People actually liked my work."

"And bought every piece. Not one left. Not one," he finished.

"I know." She looked up for a moment.

Louis smiled and asked, "Did you just give thanks to God, Fleur?"

She stopped. "How did you know?"

He drew around to face her and cradled her face in his palms. "I can see it on your face, your whole demeanor."

Her brush with death had brought her closer to God. She found herself remembering little prayers and songs and sometimes little bits of scripture from her childhood. And she felt at peace. Somehow, in the midst of all the turmoil, there was an unfamiliar sense of peace.

He gave her a hug and said, "Now let's get going. I'm starving. And we have a lot to do to prepare. Are you sure you feel safe at home?"

"Philomene's been staying with me but I only feel safe when I'm with you."

He squeezed her arm. "Then I'll stay by your side forevermore."

They quickened their steps, but once on Royal Street, Fleur stopped in her tracks and backed up.

"What is it?" Louis asked, puzzled.

Inside the little shop window, surrounded by a sea of dark blue crushed velvet, was an intricately carved mahogany box inlaid with jewels and mother-of-pearl.

She caught her breath. "How extraordinary."

Drawn to it, she opened the door. He followed her inside.

"May I?" Fleur caught the eye of a man behind the counter. She pointed to the window.

The shop owner approached and carefully removed the music box from the window and set it on a round table. "An excellent choice, young lady. The dancing couple is hand-carved from ivory. The box itself is inlaid with amethyst and pale yellow topaz and mother of pearl."

When the elderly man opened the music box, a song tinkled out. Two tiny dancers, a man and a woman carved from ivory, began to waltz.

"If Ever I Cease To Love." His eyes traveled from her to him. "A carnival song, but some seem to think it is rather romantic. I have it on consignment." He paused, his beady eyes studying her face. "They say it belonged to a lady in town descended from French royalty."

The diminuitive dancers, he in a formal tuxedo and she in a delicate gown of sheer pink and lace, danced an endless loop before a sterling mirror on the inside of the lid.

"How much is it?" she asked, enthralled.

He approached them, hands clasped. "A king's ransom if you can afford it."

Eyes on the box, Louis answered. "Then I suppose I'll have to ask the firm for a royal raise."

The shopkeeper, sensing a possible sale, handed Louis a card.

"Don't be silly," Fleur laughed, "I was just admiring it, that's all."

They left the shop and continued walking. "Tonight then? Shall we leave tonight?" Louis asked.

"Philomene said we should, but I need more time. One more night."

Louis hugged her. "Then it's settled. You can stay at my sister's house. You'll be safe there. If you go back to St. Charles there'll be no one to protect you. And there's no gallery show to keep your uncle at bay. We'll marry tomorrow. I'll need to go in to the office in the morning and make the necessary arrangements."

She shook her head. "No, I'll stay at my Chinoiserie. Philomene will be with me. I need some time to get my things together. I've been so preoccupied with the show, I haven't done a lick of packing."

A furrow zigzagged across his brow. "It's not a good idea, my love. I don't trust them."

Fleur caressed his cheek. "If I survived being abandoned in the swamp I can survive one more night on St. Charles."

* * *

After a sleepless night
, Louis informed his colleagues at their morning meeting and received a rousing applause, numerous handshakes and pats on the back. Some of his co-workers had been introduced to Fleur at various dances, dinners and events. But even those who didn't know her seemed genuinely happy for the couple. The advent of a wedding seemed to inspire a kindred spirit. A jovial atmosphere filled the office.

Louis retreated to his desk to telephone a family friend, a judge who'd taken him under his wing when Louis's father died and encouraged him to attend law school. They would have to settle for a civil ceremony, though Louis would have preferred to marry Fleur in church. Circumstances dictated a different course of action.

He looked at his watch. Time enough to pick up the new ring he'd ordered. A plain band--he planned to replace it with a duplicate of the first ring when he'd managed to save enough. The inexpensive substitute would have to do for now.

He hadn't bargained on marrying in such haste. And though there was much to do, he didn't want to burden Fleur with any of the details.

From the business district, the French Quarter was just a stone's throw. Moving on pure adrenaline, he would rather have walked, but decided to cut the time and drive. He could leave straight from there to pick up Fleur and begin their new life together. His heart raced.

Everything was going as just as they'd planned. From the jeweler, he'd telephoned Fleur to tell her he'd be there soon. On the way back to his car however, Louis thought he heard familiar footsteps approaching from behind.

When he turned, his suspicians were confirmed. Piper greeted him.

"Why, hello Louis."

Dressed in a smart black suit and hat, the plume of a Red Indian feather angling slight to the side, she strode toward him. Red lipstick matched her shoes. A flawless, yet flawed beauty. When they dated, he thought her to be the perfect woman, until he became acquainted with her devious nature.

But Fleur had more than physical beauty. Besides her artistic talents and gifts, there was a genuine sweetness about her.

Do they suspect our plan?

Removing his hat, he greeted her. "Piper, how delightful to see you. I was just on my way back to the—er--office to tie up some things. You must be going somewhere important."

"Why, yes I am. A girl doesn't dress this way for a walk in the park."

He laughed. "No I don't suppose that's so." He glanced at his watch. "I don't want to appear rude, but I must get back to work."

She clasped a hand around his arm. "Louis, please, could you spare just ten minutes with me? I have a matter of some importance to discuss with you."

Piper drew close to him, her pulse points exuding an exotic perfume, intoxicating in it's nuance. He squinted. "Is it urgent?"

"Yes, I'm afraid it is." She pointed to a side street. "It's almost 11:00 o'clock. Let's go to Napoleon House and sit for a while."

"I don't have time, Piper."

"You have time for this conversation, believe me." She held onto his arm and pointed with the other hand. "It's on Chartres."

Perturbed, he tucked his car key into his pocket. "I know where it is. But we have to hurry."

She smiled. "Very well."

The walk to Napoleon House was excruciating and slow. He felt like a racehorse, ready to gallop out the gate. Whatever Piper planned to say would most likely be loathsome. Disturbed by that fact that Fleur stood in harm's way, he would have to hide his impatience from the woman. Every moment with Piper was a moment away from Fleur.

The two sat down at a small café table across from one another. A large painting of a young Napoleon Bonaparte hung on the wall, which over time had become a collage of medium brown and crème' tones—crème' where the plaster had peeled away. The ceiling and ancient bar gleamed of old wood, polished silver and brass fixtures.

Busts, bas-relief's and other historical items from the early 1800's decorated the interior. Piper placed her purse and gloves on a chair next to her. Louis placed his hat on the table.

A waiter approached. "Madame, Monsier, might I interest you in a beverage? May I suggest our Pimm's Cup?" Taking them for tourists, he began with an explanation of the house. "Famed not for the age of the home, once owned by Nicolas Girod, then mayor of New Orleans from 1812-1815, Girod offered his residence to Napoleon in 1821 as a refuge during his exile. But Napoleon never made it to New Orleans, dying instead on the island of Saint Helena. . ."

Louis interrupted. "I'll have café au lait, thank you."

"For me as well." Piper offered curtly.

The waiter nodded. "Very good, Monsier."

Piper placed her elbows on the table and rested her chin on top her hands. "You look well, Louis."

"Now please tell me what you want to discuss. As I said, there are pressing matters back at the office."

"Very well, I'll be concise." She leaned forward. "There's something you ought to know about Fleur before you run off and marry her."

"What? Why do you think? How did you?"

The waiter delivered two steaming cups and saucers to the table.

"Never mind how I know. The cat's out the bag. Tisk tisk. And father asked you not to."

"I still don't know how you found out."

Her eyes narrowed. "I'll bet Fleur is behind the hurry, isn't she?"

He didn't answer—nor did he have to. Louis knew the answer was written on his face.

Piper took a deep breath. "May I be frank with you?"

He coughed. A rising sense of dread sent shivers up his legs. "Of course."

"I'm worried about Fleur. Her state of mind is so delicate." She laid her hands on the table. "I need to ask you something." She took a breath. "Has she given you the impression?" She laughed. "It's almost too ridiculous to say. "That she is in perilous danger from her own family?"

His chest heaved.

"I can see it in your eyes. I'm afraid to tell you what I know I must." She fiddled in her purse and brought a handkerchief to her nose.

"Tell me what?"

Piper paused.

"Please."

"Fleur is not who you think she is. Poor girl."

"What do you mean by that?"

"It all started when she lost her parents. You remember how I told you about her tragic loss. She seemed to do well for a time. Dabbling in art seemed to help. But the truth is, Fleur has always been, well, different from most people." She accentuated by swirling her index finger near her temple. "Not quite right in the head."

She sat back against her chair. "Of course we, meaning her family, protected her. We kept her little secret from the rest of the world as best we could. But that's not all."

He took a long sip and slammed it down on the table. The only other couple in the room looked up. "You're saying she's crazy?"

She lowered her voice to a whisper. "Louis, I understand you're upset, but let's not make a scene."

He glanced over at the other couple. Anger seething, he tried to control the tone of his voice. "That's a very interesting accusation coming from you, Piper. Or have you forgotten that I am aquainted with your seemier side?"

Piper pressed her lips together. "I do not pretend to be perfect. But then again, I am not poised at the altar beside you, as Fleur is. Please hear me out. It's important that you gain control of yourself Louis, because I have something of extreme importance to tell you and—and it's not easy for me to do so."

He stared back at her. How much worse could it get? He'd just heard the woman accuse the love of his life of being mentally unstable. Could this be one of Piper's ploys? But if Bernard and Piper were plotting to do away with Fleur, how could the two believe they could get away with such a crime? The fact that Gerard tried to do away with Fleur cast a cloud of doubt on the veracity of both Bernard and Piper. Yet, there was a ring of truth in some of what she said. Certain things about Fleur were different. One might even say, odd. He'd overlooked a few of her peccadilloes. For instance--her inability to remember parts of her childhood.

"There's something else you need to know. She has . . . she's been involved before." Piper cleared her throat.

"I'd expect that from a woman as attractive and talented as she is. Wouldn't you?"

"In an intimate way."

Louis put the cup down and, throat tightening, gulped the coffee down. "What are you saying? Explain yourself, woman!"

Piper's brows wrinkled together. "Louis, my dear, it-it pains me to tell you this, so I'm just going to spill it all out. Fleur had a baby out of wedlock."

"What?" He froze.

"She was just a teenager. Father sent her away with the Ursuline nuns for the remainder of her term. It would have been a scandal to the family otherwise. You can certainly understand why we chose to be hushhush about the matter. Fortunately, he was able to get her into a good school a bit early. Her grades were impeccable.""

Stunned, Louis struggled to grasp what she'd said.

"You mean she--"

"I hate to be the bearer of this sort of news. I'd hoped Fleur would be forthcoming with you, but it's apparent she's decided not to be. Not that I can blame her. No one would want to expose such a sordid past, especially when there's so much at stake. I wouldn't want to risk losing someone like you either."

Distraught, Louis ran his fingers through his hair, fighting back hot tears. A dismal feeling came over him. Utter desolation.

Piper placed her hand over his. "Oh, but Fleur loves you so, Louis. Maybe the two of you can work things out. She's a lovely girl, through and through. We shouldn't judge her for an unfortunate indiscretion, a youthful lapse in good judgment."

Louis shook off her hands and stood. He could barely catch his breath. "I've got to go."

"Please don't leave. You're upset." Piper gestured toward the chair. "Sit here for a moment and compose yourself."

He reached for his hat. "One more thing if you please."

"Anything, anything at all."

He forced the words out. "Tell me, what happened to the child?"

She closed her eyes. "Stillborn. The child was stillborn."

Chapter Twenty-One
Seasons in Silhouette

Fleur gazed at her image in the dressing table mirror and applied a coat of Peony Eleanor lipstick purchased at Maison Blanche, her favorite department store on Canal Street. A blot of her lips on a tissue, followed by a slight smack, a final pucker, and she was done.

A delicate pink rose in the bud vase next to her silver brush set brought a shy blush to her cheeks. She lifted the tiny crystal vase, flower and all to her nose and inhaled. Like perfume. Their romance had begun, though she was ashamed to say, at Aunt Florrie's funeral, and since that day, Louis had made certain that her little vase was never without a fragrant reminder of his love.

Fleur leaned back in her chair and allowed her memory to float back to the day she fell in love with Louis. She placed the crystal vase back on her dressing table. Today she would marry her love, although not in the way she'd expected to. A church wedding would have suited them more. But these were unique circumstances. After all, the marriage, not the ceremony is what counts. Philomene had strummed the phrase into her spirit with constant tenacity. Dear Philo . . .

Still, a sigh escaped her lips. Most brides were happy on their wedding day, but then most brides were able to share their happiness with family and friends. Her wedding day would be like a chapter in a spy novel—rushed, and on the run.

A few tears began to well in the corners of her eyes. *If only I had my mother to share this day with, to give me advice. And I've no father to give me away, to walk me down the aisle.*

She held back a sob, stood and walked to the floor-length mirror tilted on its white-knobbed stand. The wedding dress was picture perfect. Irish lace inlaid with seed pearls, long-sleeved from shoulder to cameo'd neck and a flow of satin silk below. She lifted the dress to the side to reveal the white satin shoes, also inlaid with tiny pearls, crystals as well. The silk of her white stockings gleamed gossamer sheer against her skin. She lifted the dress still higher to make sure it was there. Yes, the blue garter on her thigh. A knock sounded against the door and she let go of the hem.

Without turning from her reflection, she asked, "Who is it?"

The voice behind the door answered, "It's me, Philomene. Can I come in?"

"Please do," she called out.

Eyes wide with surprise, Philomene sat on the bed. "What are you doing dressed in that? You know Mr. Louis is on his way."

"I know. It's just that I'll never have the chance to wear my wedding dress, and I wanted to try it on just one more time." Tears clouded her eyes.

Philomene came up behind her to gaze at their reflection in the mirror. She smiled. "You do look beautiful, chile' By all rights, it should be your mama standing behind you now, but I guess I'll have to do." She pulled a hankie from her pocket and wiped her eyes.

Fleur laughed. "Before we both break down into two pools, maybe you'd better help me out of this dress and into my sensible suit."

Philomene kissed her cheek. "All right, sweet one. Jus' you remember, it's de marriage, not the ceremony is what counts."

Fleur touched the woman's cheek and smiled.

With Philomene there to help her, Fleur was soon changed into a beige suit and heels, a small clutch purse and a small leaf-shaped hat with a fine veil to cover her face until she and Louis said their vows. She was about to tuck the tree of life necklace under her collar when Philomene stopped her.

"No chile', a bride needs a dimon' roun' her neck when she's fixin' ta jump over de broom." She pulled a small package from her pocket and handed it to Fleur.

"Mother's necklaces?"

The older woman nodded, grinning from ear to ear. As Fleur tore through the brown parcel paper, she pointed. "Dat one--the dimon heart would be nice."

Fleur looked over the pendants, remembering each and every one. The ruby with its passionate red, a veritable flame when held to the sunlight. The square-cut blue topaz bordered with tiny diamonds on a titanium chain. The pale yellow citron set in silver. A blue-green sapphire cut in a sunburst surrounded by tiny rubies. And last, the simple diamond heart cutout. Perfect.

"Oh Phil, thank you so much. I meant to ask you about them."

"Now that you leavin' I thought it'd be safe fo' you to take 'em."

Fleur stared at the jewels.

"What's wrong?"

"Phil." She gathered them in her hands. "Would you mind keeping them a little while longer? Until I return? I don't want to have to look after them on my honeymoon."

Philomene held out her hand. "Of course. I din' think of dat. Jus' a little while longa den. Awright."

Fleur stood, suddenly giddy. "Now where's my corsage, Philo?"

She pointed to two small packages on the bed. "Here, there were two packages delivered this morning. Dis ones the flowas. Leh me pin it on your lapel mon petit chou."

"Oh would you? Thanks so much."

Standing back to admire Fleur, she smiled. "You look like a movie star. Jus' like Greta Garbo." She smacked her lips. "Ummmm. Ummmm. That Mista Louis' gonna fall down in a heap when he gets a load of you."

"I hope so." She looked at her watch. "Five minutes past."

"Five minutes late ain' nuthin'." She held up the other package. "Dis came for you too."

Fleur sat on the bed and began fumbling with the brown string tied around the brown paper wrapper. "I wonder what it could be."

The string undone, she tore at the coarse paper wrapped around it and caught her breath. "It's the music box!"

"Woowee. Look at dat. I knew Mr. Louis was a top-drawer man. That box is 'spensive lookin'. Theys jewels an' mutha o'pearl all over."

Fleur opened the box, admiring the design. Inlaid with amethyst and pale yellow topaz and mother of pearl, it seemed to glow from within.

She opened it and, just as she'd heard in the little shop with Louis, the music box rendition of If Ever I Cease To Love tinkled out high notes. The tiny figures of the man and a woman danced an endless loop before a sterling mirror on the inside of the lid. Inside was a note card with her name in Louis's handwriting. She removed the note from the card and unfolded it.

"I-I fell in love with it at a little shop on Royal Street. Louis and I were passing by after the show, and happened to see it in the window."

"Why didn't he buy it for you then?" Philomene asked.

She held the box up. "I thought it was much too expensive. The shop owner said it belonged to royalty. I suppose Louis wanted to surprise me. What a romantic, extravagant gesture. He must have gone into debt to purchase it. Oh, but I adore it, and my Louis too."

Fleur handed the box to Philomene. "You'll have to look after this too if you don't mind."

"I'll put de jewls right inside, dats what I'll do."

At once, she began to read.

My Dearest Fleur,

How I love you. Since you came into my life, I've known such happiness and fulfillment. You are the embodiment of purity, grace and gentle kindness. I thank God that He, in His infinite wisdom, brought us together.

Now, before God, and the whole world, we will speak our vows, one to another and I will have you for my wife and you will have me for a husband. I pledge to thee, my love, my dearest heart, that I will forever love, protect and care for you all the days of my life, with all my heart.

My queen is surely worth a king's ransom…

Forever yours,

Your soon-to-be husband,

Louis

She sighed and held the note close to her heart.

"Dat was beyout'ful, jus' beyout'ful."

"Isn't it?"

"Mr. Louis sho' is a blessed man."

Fleur looked at her watch again. "Fifteen minutes? Louis is never late. I wonder where he is."

* * *

"Fleur. Fleur?"

Screaming, she bolted upright.

"Fleur." Philomene grabbed her by the shoulders. "You all right, chile'?"

Bathed in morning light, the room seemed strange, not at all familiar. The dotted Chintz curtains fluttered from a dewy swish of wind. She was aware of the a cool compress on her forehead, the rhythmic ticking of the bedside clock, the softness of cotton sheets dried in the sun, fragrant with grass and flowers. And Philo's concerned face hovering over hers.

She gripped Philomene's arms, Fleur's body tense with fear. Her voice choked out, "A nightmare…I think it was…a nightmare."

She held fleur close. "Darlin' shush now, Philo's here."

"I dreamt that Louis broke our engagement. That he said I was despicable. Not fit to marry." She began to twitch in sobbing spasms, crying like a child, like a little girl.

"There, there, chile'. There, there."

She cradled Fleur's face in her hands. Voice gentle and low, she spoke. "Now I want you to listen real careful to what I has to say. Jus' listen now."

She brushed a tear away. "Mista Louis—he did say them things."

"What-what do you mean?"

" He found out 'bout you stayin' wit da nuns an' all when you was young."

"No, no." Fleur turned away. "I should have told him. I wanted to, meant to tell him but I was frightened."

"It was Piper what tol' him. She a snake, that woman! Don't wish you no good a t'all. "

Fleur's body shook. "The baby."

A sad look in her eyes, Philomene replied. "Yes."

"Yesterday was supposed to be my w-wedding day. Louis . . . " She buried her head into the pillow.

"Shush, don't cry. You need to hear what I'm sayin'. I don' know what all else she tol' him, but he madder den a hornet when he come here an' he said some pow'ful bad things to you. Things he had no call to say." She stroked the young woman's forehead, staring deep into her eyes, rind-red and puffy. "An' it din happen yesterday. Happ'nd a week ago today."

"No, no, it couldn't be. A week?"

Philomene wiped her eyes. "Mista Louis, he don' know you like he should. He don' understand an' right now da man too mad an' too hurt to hear."

Fleur's body curled into deep, muscular sobs and groans.

She raised her head to shout toward the open door. " Cecelia, kin you bring some mo' cool water an' a cloth?" The maid came in at once, bearing what she asked for. Philomene rose and stepped aside, but stood like a sentinel, arms folded, staring down at her.

Cecelia sat on the edge of the bed, dipped a clean white cloth into a shiny copper bowl, eased her head down to the pillow, and folded the cloth on her fevered forehead.

"What's wrong Miz Fleur? You had yourself a bad dream, huh?" Only the edge of her dark hair, smoothed back from her face was visible. A white linen and lace headscarf covered her head, last year's Christmas gift from Fleur. Her eyes, dark as polished obsidian betrayed no emotion.

Between sobs, Fleur tried to remember. There was something important to say, but what? Something about the dream--the nightmare.

Cecelia glanced back at Philomene. "It all right. I'll take good care of Miz Fleur. Mista Bernard say he wanna see you right away in the parlor."

Philomene made a face. "In de parlor?"

"Yes'm, the parlor's what he tol' me."

Philomene's arms unfolded. A sigh escaped. "Dat da last thing I wanna do, but I s'ppose I have to."

"You go and do what you gotta do. Don' you worry. I take care of our sweet girl."

Philomene took Fleur's hand in her own. "If you need me baby, ask Cecelia to send fo' me. I promise to be back soon."

She noticed a look between Cecelia and Philomene. Fleur listened to her footsteps down the stairs, the sound slight, muffled by an Oriental runner. The front door creaked open and she was gone.

Cecelia got up and closed the door behind her, then walked to the dresser and poured a glass of water. Fleur watched as she pulled a blue bottle and an eyedropper from her pocket and added something to the water.

"Here you are, Miz Fleur. This'll help you feel better. Put you out too. Drink up."

"What is it?"

"Some good medicine. Now drink." She looked toward the door even as she urged Fleur.

Within a scant few minuste, the medicine and the cool cloth on her head worked wonders. She stopped crying and her head ceased its throbbing. But as for her heart, as for her heart. . .

"Is there anything else I kin do fo' you, Miz Fleur?" She smiled. "You can tell me."

She tried to answer but soon enough, her words came out a jumble and she felt herself drifting, floating farther and farther away. Cecelia's face faded in and out, then transformed into a red balloon and drifted upwards to the blue sky.

"Miz Fleur? Miz Fleur?" But the words melded into the squawking of birds in flight, patterning ribbons across the sky. She joined them at the tail. Like a roller coaster, up and down on the winds, ribbon shadows on the ground below.

Chapter Twenty-Two
Deadly Descent

Cecelia lifted the young woman's eyelids with her fingers. Satisfied, she sat back on the bed and called out. "You kin come in now."

Two muscular men in white coats entered the room. One had a crooked nose. The other had a more agreeable face, one she could fancy if the circumstances were different. She'd told them to wait quietly in the adjoining room. Luckily Philomene hadn't heard.

"Is she out?" The handsome one approached.

"She out." Cecelia could feel her heart beating faster.

The crooked nose man gestured to the other. "Okay, let's get her into the stretcher. Should be easy. She looks light."

As they transferred Fleur to the stretcher, the crooked nose man addressed Cecelia. "Mr. D'Hemecourt will have to sign the papers before we leave."

"Papers?"

"To commit her. She's crazy, ain't she?"

***

Fleur drifted into an ethereal light--somehow back in the attic room of her childhood again, this time, conversing with Philomene who sat on the edge of her bed.

"That' why they scere us. But dreams ain' real. Sometimes dat's a good thing and sometime it's not so good. Why, if I had a nickel fo' ever time I dreamt I was a movie star, I'd be as rich as one."

Grey hair and wrinkles somehow gone, a younger, spryer Philomene displayed her best pouty-lipped profile, limp wrist against her forehead.

Fleur laughed.

"Dat's my girl. "Philomene pushed the hair back behind Fleur's ears. "Look at dat beautiful face. You know baby, you could grow up ta be a movie star." She frowned. "But you're looking a bit thin and pale of late. I'm gonna go heat you a nice cup of sweet milk." She stood up and wagged her index finger. "You just rest here, and after you drink, I'll help you get washed up and dressed fo' bed. An' don' be impayshun neitha. I gotta drop off a tray of special sweet milk to your aunt's room first."

In a low voice, she answered, "I-I'm not thirsty."

"Now Miz Fleur, you need to relax and Mama Philomene won't take no for an answer."

"But I—"

From the doorway, Philomene turned around, "Now you jus' rest right dere." With that, she clomped off down the stairs.

Fleur laid back and stared at the ceiling, trying in vain to remember. The alarm clock ticked off seconds, then minutes as she sweated and shivered. The fear was still with her. She sat up and swung her legs over the side of the bed. Like a crushing weight on her chest, it pressed in.

And the sound, was it the sound of her heart beating, or the footsteps?

That's it. The footsteps in the dream--the nightmare.

But the footsteps she heard were real. The door creaked open. She held her breath and began to shake.

"Here I am." Philomene stepped in bearing a silver tray, moving slow and sure so as not to spill it. Without looking up from the tray she asked. "Did you get any rest, baby? It took me a little longer than I 'spected. Here's some warm milk with a lil' banilla an' cinmon too. It'll put you right to sleep so you won't have dos' bad dreams no 'mo."

She put the tray down and sighed, rubbing the small of her back. "I'm not as young as I used to be." Then she noticed Fleur, knees to her chest on the edge of the bed.

"Why Fleur, what wrong chile'?

Chapter Twenty-Three
The Best Laid Plans

Philomene shivered on the way to the office. But the shiver wasn't all due to the man behind the door. The weather had turned a trifle chilly in the past week. A damp cold, that nipped at her bones and set them to aching.

"You wanted to see me?"

Philomene stood at the parlor doorway. She slid the pocket doors shut behind her.

Bernard D'Hemecourt sat in an easy chair by the window tumbling a silver dollar from hand to hand.

When he didn't answer, she asked again "You wanted to. . ."

He barked back at her. "I heard you the first time." Turning his attention back to the view out the window, he asked, "Tell me, how's our favorite patient?"

"Miz Fleur, she comin' along. I 'spect she be all right in time. Her heart broke, dat's all."

"Is that all?" He threw the coin up in the air and caught it. "Did you get Piper in for the fitting?"

"Yessir, she been to two o' dem so far and deys jus' the dress rehearsal left."

"Good." He looked away from the window straight at her, a look that sent a chill down her spine. "Say, what about that draught?"

She didn't answer.

"Do you remember I told you to inform me when it arrived?"

The blood drained from her face. "Yessir."

"Yes Sir, I what?"

Her mouth moved to speak but she had no idea what he wanted her to say or if there was anything she could say to please him. Her legs trembled underneath her.

"Failed? Is that the word you're trying to say?" He bobbled his head up and down. "Yes you did fail." He stopped moving. "And that's why you're canned. Fired."

"What?"

"That's right. You've been replaced. Cecelia jumped at the chance to take over your job. She knows how to take orders. She doesn't ask questions. She does what I tell her to do." He pointed. "You don't."

"But Mista B . . ."

"You've fought and sabotaged my every move through the years. Don't think I haven't noticed."

She gasped.

"Your services are no longer needed here. Leave the premises at once--you, and your adle-brained brother. Get out. Oh, and don't ask for a recommendation either because I won't have anything nice to say about you." He smiled, "You're done in this town."

"Miz Fleur, I has to take care of her."

He stood. "She is no longer your concern. Besides, she's not living here anymore. At this very moment, she's being transferred to a mental hospital where she belongs. The girl's cuckoo—crazy—looney."

"No, it can't be!"

"If you don't believe me, go see for yourself."

Philomene, heart racing, ran to the front roothe window. She saw a white ambulance in the driveway and two men wheeling a stretcher to it.

"Fleur!"

Bernard lit a cigar and let his head fall backwards on a wingback chair, casually blowing smoke rings into the air above.

"Why would you do such a thing? Dere's nothing wrong with her." Philomene ran past him to the pocket doors and threw them open and stumbled out the front door. "Fleur. Fleur."

By then, the men had loaded her into the back of the ambulance and were closing the doors "No, what you doin'?" She threw herself at the men. "Let her go. Let her go now."

One of the men, the taller one deflected her to the cold ground. She rolled to her knees and tried to stand.

He pointed, eyes blazing with anger. "Stay away from the vehicle or I swear you won't get up the next time!"

The other man ran to the house, paper in hand. Philomene struggled to her feet, but fell backward, her heel caught in the grass. The one who pushed her was behind the wheel, with the engine running.

"Fleur." She called out, but Fleur didn't answer. Philomene beat the ground underneath her. Tears flowing, she called out her name again and again.

***

Bernard signed the papers and handed it back to the attendant. "There. All done."

The attendant gestured toward the window, a clear view of the scene. "Sir, what do I do with her?"

Bernard bit the end off a new cigar and spit it out. "Ignore the woman."

As the man exited, Cecelia entered the room and stood before him. He rose and stared her square in the face.

"Good job."

She bowed her head and smiled. "Yes suh. Thank you suh."

"You managed to find that Laudanum in Philomene's room and give it to the little bride-to-be. Bravo!"

"I feel sorry for Miz Fleur."

He wrapped an arm around her shoulder. "There, there Cecelia. Fleur isn't right in the head. She needs to be in a place where people can take care of her and keep her happy. People like that need to be happy. Don't you worry a day about the girl--she'll be getting the best possible treatment."

"Thank you, sir." She curtsied.

"Mista Bernard, befo' I go, I got some news to tell you."

"What is it?"

"Da boy took ill of a sudden, wit da chickenpox." She shook her head. "He got it bad all over."

"That's too bad. See that he's looked after."

"Yes suh." She paused at the pocket doors. Is there anything else, suh?"

Bernard turned from her and stood at the window, staring after the ambulance. The departure revealed Philomene on her knees, hands clawed into the turf, wailing. His lips curled in a smile.

"I'm so glad I have you Cecelia. It's so hard to get good help these days."

***

Fleur woke up, eyes reduced to slits, in a room without windows. No way to tell what day, what time, how long she'd slept. The walls and floor painted an institutional green. The rough linens on the bed were white, the smell of disinfectant emanating from them. She struggled to get up but her hands and feet were bound with leather straps to the bed.

Though she cried for help, calling for Louis, for Philomene, for anybody--no one answered. For hours, she screamed and wrestled against the tight leather straps until they drew blood. Why am I here? Where am I? God! Help me--please help me.

Finally, exhausted, she began to stroke her toes against the cold gunmetal of the bed, calming her enough to fall into a restless sleep.

Chapter Twenty-Four
Ties That Bind

Philomene approached the house a few days later in her Sunday best, a grey suit trimmed in black fur, black pumps and a glossy black straw hat accented with two shiny feathers that curved around one side of her face. As she stepped onto the veranda, the wind skidded dead leaves across her feet.

Ignoring the doorbell, she rapped on the door. A new maid answered, one that didn't recognize her.

Wide-eyed, the girl pointed to the side of the house, pleading. "What 'chu doin' at da front? Go round.

"I want to speak to Mista Bernard."

Panicked, the maid put a finger to her lips. "Shhhh."

"Go and tell Cecelia Miss Philomene is here and wants to speak to Mista Bernard right away."

She shut the door and within a minute Cecelia stood at the door, hands on her hips. "Whatchu doin' back here? Din' Mista D'Hemecourt tell you ta stay away outa here? An' what you mean coming to da fron' do actin' all haughty?"

"I mean to see Mista Bernard. I got some impotent news fo' him. News he wanna hear."

Cecelia narrowed her eyelids. "What kin' news?"

"I tol' you what kind. Now you go tell him."

"I'll tell him, but you goin' roun' to da back do' right now."

Philomene nodded to the compromise. After all, she'd made her point.

After a few minutes, Cecelia returned and led Philomene through the kitchen. The rest of the staff acknowledged her with their eyes, speaking volumes of support. Something was up in the house. Something bad.

She followed Cecelia on the path she'd taken many a time, down the long hall to the study and past the heavy wooden doors.

He stood behind his desk holding a book, reading glasses pushed halfway down his nose. His face, an unhealthy putty tone was splotchy and red in places. From here experience with the man, he was either angry or recovering from a bender. He gestured to a chair in front of the desk. Purse resting in her lap, cotton gloves holding the purse-straps, she sat down straight and tall.

"Have a seat."

The chair squeaked under his weight as he sat. "I trust you're doing well?" A smirk rippled across his face. To what do I owe this surprise visit, my dear?"

Ignoring the questions, she spoke up. "Hope I din' interrupt nothin' impotent."

"Nah, I was just reading."

Her eyes shifted to the book in his hands. She noticed it was upside down.

"Thank you. Tadpole an' I is doin' fine."

His voice deepened to a more serious note. "Let's cut to the chase. I hope this isn't a desperate attempt to get your job back."

She stared straight into his eyes. "I'm here to git a recommendation letter from you Mista Bernard. That's why I come here today."

His face flushed crimson before he broke out into a raucous round of laughter. Tears ran down his cheeks until he made himself stop. "Oh, do you?" The words just squeaked out before he began to cackle again.

"Yessir."

"And why, pray tell, do you think I might have changed my mind? I told you, you would never work in this town again."

She watched him in silence, waiting for him to realize what was going on. And soon enough, he did.

Bernard pointed. "What gives you the nerve to try and walk right through the front door and order a white man around? Eh? Just who do you think you are? Why, I could make one phone call and have you and your brother strung up on the highest oak."

She opened her purse.

"What's that?"

Philomene pulled out a letter. "This here's a letter o' reccomn'dayshun from Miz Florrie. You may 'member when I was goin' take dat job wit da Fauberg fambly when Miz Fleur went off to college, but I change mah mind? Miz Florrie said an awful lot o' nice things. It shore would be nice if you was to add sumpthin' nice at the end an' sign an' date it."

Leaning forward on his elbows, he sneered. "You're insane. I think you belong in the looney bin with Fleur. Why should I? Why would I do that for you?"

"Because I knows a lot more 'bout you den you think I knows. I worked here in dis house longa den anybody else."

"So you think you know something, eh? And you want to blackmail me into getting what you want. What? Go on. Tell me something about myself that you think you know." He batted his eyelashes, "I'm all ears."

Philomene paid no attention to his mockery. "Dere's a lot I could say, but only one thing that needs sayin'. You done a lot o' evil in your life and in dis house fo sho."

He swallowed hard, knuckles clenching and unclenching. "Now see here. I don't need to hear you preaching to me about right and wrong. You said what you had to say, but there's no proof to your accusations. I'm not guilty of any wrongdoing whatsoever."

She opened her purse again and handed him a slip of paper. As he read, the color drained from his face. He crumpled and tore it with savage fury, then gathered the remnants into an ashtray and set it on fire.

Philomene sat in calm repose throughout. "Dat ain' de original Mista Bernard."

His face blanched. The paper now reduced to grey ash, fell apart like a puzzle.

He stared at her--a sour expression on his face. A few moments passed, the silence of his thoughts heavy in the air. Finally, the man turned his back to her and stumbled to the window. "Give me the letter."

As soon as she handed it to him, he sat in the chair by the window and scratched some sentences. After signing, he held it high.

"Here."

She read it and smiled in spite of herself. "Thank you Mista Bernard. I knew you'd see things my way." Philomene slipped the paper into her purse and pulled the clasp together.

"I be leavin' now Mista Bernard. Thank you."

"Wait." He glared from his chair. "I'm curious about something. Why didn't you ask for money? Most people in your position would have jumped at the chance to blackmail me with the sort of information you have. Why?"

"Because I'm a chile' o' God."

He spoke through clenched lips. "I hope your God is watching over you, woman. You've made an enemy of me today."

She set her jaw like flint to answer. "Dat ain' nuthin' new Mista Bernard. Like Eve and de serpent, you and me always been at odds."

Chapter Twenty-Five
Maelstrom

Groggy. That's how she felt. Her mind, wound tight as a top, was spinning out of control.

Fleur looked around the room, although her head felt like an anvil. Without a window, it was difficult to tell what time of day it was. Or perhaps it was night. She tried to lift off the bed but found that she could not. It took a few minutes to focus. Ah, my hands, my feet are tied up. Leather straps attached to the metal bed, wrapped around her wrists and ankles. Her wrists were bruised blue around the straps and there were fresh cuts from the leather wearing against her skin. Though she couldn't see her feet, she knew there must be similar wounds on her ankles. The pain was confirmation enough.

She sniffed the air. The smell of medicine and disinfectant and stale urine rose. And the sound of footsteps indicated someone approaching. Light steps--one, two, three, four. The walk was one she recognized. Her heart beat faster and faster, as if it would leap from her chest. She caught a glimpse of a face at the small window in the door. She heard the jangle of keys in the lock. After what seemed an eternity, the door opened and a nurse stepped inside the room with a small tray.

Thin and as pale as her uniform, the woman in white put the tray down on a small table next to the bed. "I see you're up." She leaned down to turn a crank on the side of the bed. The top portion of the bed began to rise and Fleur's upper torso with it. She began to calm with her ascent and breath more assurance. Then she got a good look at the nurse.

The woman's face reminded her of a pony, long and lean with black beads for eyes. Her brows shaved bare and new, more dramatic parenthesis's penciled in an unattractive shade of brown replaced them--like a character in Japanese Kabuki theatre. Fleur's lips curled, an attempt at a smile.

"I'm so glad you're in a pleasant mood today Miss D'Hemecourt," she said. "Now it's time to take our medication." She changed her voice, as if speaking to a young child. "Are we ready to swallow our medicine now?"

Without waiting for an answer, she lifted Fleur's head off the pillow as she struggled, pinched her nose and when it opened in response, poured a small ruffled paper cup of pills into her mouth. She then shoved a larger cup of water to Fleur's mouth.

"Now swallow." she commanded stern-voiced.

Fleur choked the pills down as the woman dumped the cup of water down her throat. She coughed in violent response, her airway cut off. Everything went white. Fleur felt herself slipping away, losing consciousness.

The nurse whacked her hard on the chest and back a few times, ejected a few of the pills. Annoyed, she lifted her index finger in front of Fleur's face. "Next time, I expect you to cooperate with me. There will be no more of this behavior. I will not tolerate it."

The woman made her swallow the ejected pills and pushed her roughly to the pillow.

Spent by her fight for life, Fleur fought to catch her breath, exhausted. "How, how l-long?" she asked. Her tongue felt thick, dull.

"How long have you been here? Hmm. She leafed through the chart. As of today, you've been here for two weeks." She leaned forward, her face in Fleur's again. "But this is the first day, you weren't just a lump in the sheets. Now that you're awake, they can begin treatment."

"But you—you just gave me pills."

"Never you mind about that." She straightened and began writing on the chart. The doctor will be quite pleased. Oh, and you're supposed to have a guest come at 1:00 today. A man. He's such a dream. The other nurses are all jealous of my rotation. You're my only patient and I'm the only one who gets to talk to him." Her face lit up.

She pursed her lips. "He's come here before but you were too much of a "Dumb Dora" to notice." The nurse blew air out the side of her mouth. "I don't know why he even bothers. You're not much to look at."

The nurse closed the metal top on the chart. "Time to clean you up a bit. There's another visitor outside right now, your uncle."

The words struck terror into her heart for some reason. Fleur began to shiver. Bouncing her head side to side on the pillow, show mouthed. "N-no. No. No."

"Now don't start with me again you little brat. I told you, I will not tolerate bad behavior."

Fleur tried to turn her head away, but the nurse grabbed hold of her face and made her keep the back of her head to the pillow.

She held out her index finger to Fleur again as a warning, and turned her attention to the tray. She dipped a cloth into a white enamel bowl of cold water and squirted some liquid soap into the bowl. "You don't smell very fresh my dear. We can't have that, especially with visitors coming." The water and cloth became frothy with each squeeze. She bent over to sponge rough strokes across the tops of her legs and arms, then her face and neck. As she cleaned the woman dripped random water on Fleur's hair, careless as to her comfort or appearance. When she bent over her, Fleur noticed the name on her tag. Missy Moran, R.N.

"Your uncle seems like such a nice man. I saw him in church just last week." She wrung out the cloth in the bowl and laid it on the tray. "All done." She sniffed the air. "There, that will do for now, until I can give you a proper bath."

She lifted the tray with a smirk. "I'll send him in." Turning to leave, she spun on her heel, "You behave yourself, ya hear."

I don't want to see him. I don't want to see him. Somehow, Fleur was able to control the fear raging inside. *Why don't I want to see him?*

The footsteps again--he must have come to the door earlier with the nurse and then turned back to the waiting room. Bernard walked into the room, hat in his hands. Nurse Moran held the door open for him, a wide smile on his face.

Fleur's mind felt heavy, sluggish. A childhood memory surfaced without warning—one of fishing with her parents at their camp on the bayou. But quick as a photoflash, the memory disappeared. As if a sinker had attached, dragging it below still waters.

Short and squat, hair dyed a stark black her uncle wore a grey suit with suspenders and a red bow tie. He entered with an air of self-confidence, reeking of his signature cologne, beads of sweat visible on his forehead. When the door shut behind him, he pulled out a white handkerchief from his suit pocket and raked it across his forehead and neck.

"Hello my dear." He stood looking at her, his eyes roaming up and down her form. She stared back at him, trying to remember. Remember what? What? She watched as he looked back at the door, then at her again.

He put the hat down on the table, then walked to a sturdy metal chair in and dragged it across the floor close to her bed. The sound grated her nerves to the point of nausea.

From a closer distance, she noticed tiny white roots by his hairline. Fear pulled the hairs on her arm straight up. She watched as he grabbed at his jowly neck to loosen the shirt collar.

"It's hot today. You never know what the weather's going to be like here. Hot, cold, rainy, balmy . . ."

"Fleur, my dear dear girl! You can't know how it pains me to see you in this state. But I'm so glad you're finally awake so we can talk." He picked up a spare white pillow, placed it on his lap and leaned in close to the metal bar on the side of her bed. "Can you speak?"

Her eyes watched his every move. Her voice scratchy, she answered. "Yes."

"And, uh, how is your, memory these days?

She glanced away. "I'm not sure."

He smiled.

The medication dulled her tongue. But she mustered all her inner fortitude to ask two simple questions. "Why'm I here? W-when can I--go home?"

Bernard moistened his lips with his tongue. "I'll tell you girl. I promise. But first, don't you want to know how the rest of your loving family is doing?" Without waiting for her to answer, he continued. "I thought you would."

"Well, your dear cousin Piper is distraught over you. Of course, she's in a difficult position. Being your cousin and a friend to Louis. But she is trying to comfort and console you both."

The side of his lip twitched when he spoke. "Little Rusty's been sick with the chickenpox. He's suffered a bad case of it too, bad--bad case. In fact, the boy wound up in the hospital. We almost lost him. Did you know people can get chickenpox internally? But the young lad's recovering now. Doctors say he should be home in about a week and we can't wait to have him back with us. He's such a pleasant boy. I can't wait to get to know him better."

Fearful, she asked, "Is Philo at the hospital with him?"

She sensed some hesitation in his voice.

"No, I assume Collette is. Tough she hasn't been around a lot of late. Been leaving the boy in the care of the servants. I encouraged her to do so. The poor dear needs a break."

"But she. . ." Her voice trailed off, weak as a new kitten. "She. . ."

He looked back again to the door, as if suspicious. "Rest assured, somebody's taking care of him. Don't worry yourself." He pursed his lips. "Fleur, I don't mean to be rude by changing the subject, but there's something I have to chat with you about."

She noticed the darkness of his pupils as he looked back again in the direction of the door. "I came here to warn you."

The expression on her face must have been one of surprise for he leaned in closer.

"I know you were told some lies about me and your cousin Piper. It's almost laughable, something about us trying to do away with you. But I tell you, it's not true." As he shook his head, his jowls slobbered back and forth. "We're family for goodness sake. How could you think such a thing?"

Fleur could barely lift her head. "What?"

"I have reason to believe that Louis was the one with designs on you the whole time. He planned to marry and do away with you for your considerable fortune. Remember how I warned you about that? I did. Oh yes I did. I warned you about that very thing. That's what family does for family."

"I don't under . . ."

"Louis Russo is nothing more than a gold digger, a gigolo after your money and your life. His folks got into some financial trouble. His father made some bad investments. That's why they moved to Baton Rouge for a time. With his father gone, now it's up to Louis to win back the Russo fortune and I'm certain he saw you as an easy way to achieve that goal."

She blinked, trying to feel something, anything about what he said.

"And there's more my dear. I do hope you're up to hearing it."

She managed a faint nod.

"The reason I believe he was after your inheritance is because, and it pains me to be the one to tell you this, he dated Piper for a time."

"I-I know."

"Oh he told you, did he? And did he happen to tell you he was head over heels in love with her? Those two saw a lot of one another. But then when I vowed to disinherit her if she continued seeing him, he dropped her like a hot potato."

She strained to connect memory with thought. Disinherit? Piper has no…

He fiddled with the corner of her sheet, running in against his palm. "If you don't believe me, ask Piper the next time she visits you."

"She's visited?"

"Sweet lamb." He stroked her forehead. "Of course she has. We've all been to visit. In fact, I've been most attentive to you. I even hired a private nurse to look after you. She came highly recommended. Only the best for our Fleur--only the best."

"Even Louis. That's right, Louis, visits you as well, though I tried hard at first to keep him away. Granted, I don't allow him to get close to you, but the point is, you're free to come to your own conclusions about the man. Just remember what I told you about him. I warned you, girl."

He leaned back in his chair and stretched lazily. "Dear Fleur, do you finally understand what kind of man I am? A gentle soul--I wouldn't stomp an ant on the ground."

Her voice faded as the medication succeded.

"Louis . . ."

***

At five minutes to one, Louis Russo and Piper D'Hemecourt stood by the nurse's station signing in as visitors of the patient in room fifteen, Fleur D'Hemecourt. Piper had insisted they ride together in her new automobile.

He made note of Piper. Her mode of dress had none of its usual haute couture. Today she wore a simple beige cotton shift with minimal accessories save for gloves, hat and purse—the same with her makeup. Gone was the crimson lipstick and rouge as well as the red nail color. Most likely her new wholesome look was a vain attempt to win him back.

Tired and drawn, Louis held his emotions in check. Was it guilt that drove him to visit Fleur, remorse that his actions had caused her mental collapse, or a combination of guilt, remorse, and love? Though he despised himself for still loving the woman, there seemed to be no cure for his feelings. He put down the pen and sighed. Since that day, everything had changed, and nothing felt right.

After hearing about Fleur's indiscretion, he'd allowed vain imaginings to take over. Gerard came to mind again and again. He wondered why Fleur would go on such a trip with a man she'd just met. From what he'd seen in the pictures, Gerard was an attractive fellow, a man of persuasive abilities, no doubt. Based on what he'd discovered about her past, Louis couldn't help but wonder about the present. Was Fleur even capable of fidelity, or trust?

The walls, painted institutional green were supposed to evoke a calm and peaceful attitude to the patients, at least that's what Dr. Duplessis told him, but it did nothing for him. Instead, the color evoked imagery of needles, of medicinal smells, blood and bandages. He'd seen things in the war he wished he hadn't. Images imprinted on his brain that would never go away. No matter what pleasing sight he focused on, the images always managed to intrude.

The young nurse at the desk checked their names. "Miss D'Hemecourt, Mr. Russo, we'll just be a moment. Would you mind taking a seat?

"Is there any change, nurse? Is she any better at all? Please." He flashed her a smile, hoping that would do the trick.

She looked to the right and left, then picked up a chart. "I'm really not supposed to tell. There's a special nurse assigned to her. But. . ." She began to read. "According to Dr. Duplessis, there's been no change at all. She's delusional. Paranoid schizophrenic." Then lowered her voice to a whisper. "He's recommending electroconvulsive treatment." She offered a sorrowful face.

Thank you." Louis smiled, hoping to cancel the doleful expression. Does everyone believe Fleur is mad? He guided Piper to a nearby couch, allowing her to sit first. But instead of sitting down next to her, he began to pace.

She patted the couch. "Louis, please have a seat. You're driving me to distraction. It's like watching a caged animal, like one of the lions in Audubon Zoo."

He sank to the couch. "I'm sorry."

She examined his face and frowned. "You look awful. You're pale and your clothing is hanging off of you. Are you eating anything at all?"

"What's taking them so long?"

All of a sudden, the hallway and nurses station were alive with activity. A crash cart raced in one direction followed by all the nurses save one at the nurse's station calling for doctors.

Louis ran over to the station. "What's wrong?"

She yelled into the phone. "All physicians, report to Room L20 at once. We have a medical emergency."

"What's wrong?"

The nurse ran out from behind the desk. "Dr. Duplessis! His heart!" She sprinted down the hall.

Piper joined him at the desk. "How awful. What should we do?" She craned her neck for a better view.

Louis paced in front of the desk. "I tell you what I'm going to do. I'm going to visit Fleur while they're preoccupied with the emergency. I've got to make sure she's okay."

She squeezed his arm. "Oh no Louis. You'll get in trouble."

"Not if they don't catch me. All the excitement is on the other end of the hallway." He shook his arm from her grip. "You stay here and make excuses if need be."

"But Louis."

Before she could say another word, he grabbed the ring of keys strewn in haste on the desk, paused outside Fleur's door, turned the key into the knob and closed the door. He blinked in the low light, allowing his eyes to adjust, finally focusing on a crumbled form in the hospital bed.

Louis approached. Asleep, disheveled hair coiled against the pillow—Fleur. His heart ached at the sight of the leather straps binding her. He had only been allowed to see her from a distance in previous visits. This time he was determined to hold her hand.

Even hearing the news about her having a child out of wedlock had done little to dim his love. Fleur's face--so innocent, sweet. How could she have succumbed? But, he reasoned. Perhaps the woman she is now bears little resemblance to the indiscretions of youth.

She stirred in her sleep. Mumbling, she squirmed, perhaps bothered by a nightmare.

Louis too another step closer, fighting back tears.

Their wedding day was to be the happiest day of his life. But after Piper told him the truth, he'd had no choice but to call off the elopement. He'd sent a messenger, one they used at the office. That letter was in sharp contrast to the letter he'd written accompanying the music box. And far more difficult to write! Later, when he saw her face-to-face, the anger he'd bottled up inside spilled out. He'd said so many awful things—words he now regretted.

"Louis! Hurry." A sharp rap on the door alerted him. Piper.

***

Piper paced up and down the hall, keeping a close watch on Fleur's door. Why oh why did the man still care about her? She knew she'd triumphed the moment he called off the engagement, but now this? Absolute torture--having to dress like a nun to visit the stupid girl with him. Father insisted, demanded she pursue Louis. If Father only knew the recipient of her true affections . . .

That stupid nurse they'd hired kept Fleur knocked out for the visits. The lack of care the woman provided however could raise a flag of suspicion were it not for Dr. Duplessis. Fear sent prickle pears up her spine. If something happened to the doctor, the whole plan would have to be scrapped.

Piper drew closer to the door and put her ear to it. Nothing. A nurse stumbled back to the desk in tears, hand reaching clumsily for the telephone. Piper took long strides to reach her before she dialed. "What is it?"

Lips quivering, the nurse answered. "He's dead. Dr. Duplessis is dead."

Chapter Twenty-Six
Silent Witness

Philomene scrubbed her way down the hall. She'd traded her fine poplin skirts and polished chignon for a makeshift bandana tied round her head, long skirt and an old shirt, the sleeves rolled up to her elbows.

Her knees, and in fact her whole body ached from the physical labor of dragging herself across the floor all day, but she'd learned a great deal in only a couple of days on the job. Fleur was in Room Fifteen, which was usually kept locked except when the nurse with the skinny head was working. And the woman was sloppy about locking the door in between shifts.

The letter Bernard added to and signed did wonders to help her get a job as a cleaning woman at the mental hospital. Though she had far more experience and qualifications, she'd applied for the lowliest job. Besides, it was the only way she'd ever have been able to get to Fleur. She hoped and prayed that would be soon.

Four o'clock. The shift change was about to begin. Right on time, the nurse walked out the door swinging her boney hips. She raised her wrist to check her watch, and grabbed her purse from behind the desk. Instead of waiting for the other nurse to take her place, she strode off toward the door. Time to move. Philomene rose to her feet, stretching out her muscles as she did. Then quiet as can be, she kept to the shadowy parts of the hall, keeping an eye on the nurse's desk the whole time. She turned the knob slow and sure and slipped into the dark room.

The sleight figure on the bed didn't move. She pulled the light cord above the bed. Appalled at the sight, she felt sick inside, her beautiful baby--wasting away. Fleur's cheeks were drawn and gray, hair unwashed and greasy. There were red marks, bruises and circular marks on her wrists and ankles, wounds now oozing with signs of infection. She drew her face down to listen to her breath. Fleur's breaths came shallow and uneven. The child was drugged to within an inch of her life. If she didn't find a way to get her out of this place, she'd be dead for sure, exactly what Bernard and that creature wanted. She'd seen Piper accompany Louis for a visit the day before.

Good for her, nobody ever paid attention to cleaning ladies scrubbing on the floor.

Hired a week ago, she'd been there the day Dr. Duplessis died. In that short time, she'd seen a lot of things change. Patients loosened from straps, curtains opened to let in light, music playing in the halls, a happier atmosphere. The staff whispered about it, and Philomene listened. The new doctor, Dr. Peterson had taken over and was supposed to change things for the better. She hoped he'd get to Fleur soon. The first thing she wanted the new doctor would do? Get rid of the nurse assigned to Fleur's care.

"Fleur."

Philomene pulled the light cord and drew in a breath at the sight.

The young woman's eyes shifted like marbles underneath closed lids.

"Fleur, it's Philo. Wake up, honey. I'm here." She picked up both hands and raised them, with a gentle thump to her arms. "Wake up chile'."

Her eyes fluttered open but she stared straight up at first, as if she wasn't awake yet. Then she noticed Philomene.

"Baby, everthin's all right. Your Philo's here now."

Tears rolled down the outer corners of her eyes. "P-Philo."

"I'm goin' try an git you outa here jus' as soon as I kin manage it. You strong enough to walk?"

"I don't know."

'Lif' your arms for me, chile'."

With noticeable effort, Fleur strained to lift her arms but only managed a short distance.

"Da's what I thought. Dey had you here fo two weeks strapped in. You ain' moved much an' dey knock you out wit medicine. We got to git you stronga afore I kin git you out."

She noticed a tray of food untouched. The lazy nurse hadn't bothered to feed the girl though she was well aware Fleur was too weak to feed herself.

Spoonful, by spoonful, Philomene fed her, encouraging each bite. Limp as a noodle, Fleur took in half a bowlful of cold cream of wheat and part of a strawberry. Philo shook her head. But at least the chile' ate something. A bit of color had returned to her cheeks. Just a bit.

She loosened the straps on her legs and stretched out Fleur's knees, bending them forward and back, then did the same to her arms. Last, she lifted her up and forward, massaging her shoulders and back in an attempt to get the blood circulating again.

Philomene took her hand and examined it. "Look at dese nails. Dirt under dem. An your hair ain' been cleaned.

"I'm sorry."

"Awh chile'deys nuthin' fo you to be sorry fo. It ain' your fault. I'm the one who sorry."

She made up her mind to come back to clean and dress the wounds later with peroxide and bandages. It would be easy to get into the medical supply closet now that she knew where all the keys were.

Philomene stroked Fleur's forehead and planted a kiss. "Mama Philo gotta go fo now, but I'll be back ever day to check on you an' when I git you strong enough, I'm goin' take you outa dis place fo good."

She cracked the door open for a perfect view of the nurse's desk. The nurse, back to her, was searching the files for something. Philomene eased out the door and made her way down the hall to her bucket. She knelt down and began scrubbing. Somehow she had to make sure the child ate every meal. The girl had to get moving as well. She'd have to get her up and walking if they were to have a chance. It would be risky visiting her every day, but the girl was worth taking the risk for.

***

He slipped out the office, leaving a note with his secretary that he was out for a late lunch. Louis hadn't told anyone why he'd cancelled plans to elope with Fleur, only that the wedding was postponed for now.

Louis stood near and began to stroke Fleur's light brown ringlets, but noted the pallor of her skin. He pulled the light switch cord above the bed and gasped at the sight.

Her eyes opened with the light. Her lips moved. She whispered his name.

Louis ran to the door and called for the nurse. This time, a different nurse responded. Not the other one whom he'd developed a loathing. Fleur's nurse was dreadful, a woman devoid of compassion or even a work ethic.

"Yes, Mr. Russo?" A young dark-haired nurse arrived in answer to his call.

Fleur noted the kindness in her eyes. This one was different. Louis read her tag. "Nurse Robichaux?"

"Why, yes," she answered.

"Are you the one taking care of my Miss D'Hemecourt today?"

"I've just come on shift, Mr. Russo." She picked up the chart on the door and opened the metal cover. "Your wife was under the care of Nurse Moran, a private nurse, exclusively according to the chart. At the D'Hemecourt's request and Dr. Duplessis's order." She asked, "Is there some problem?"

"Well," he drew her aside to answer, index finger to his lip. "Please take a look at Miss D'Hemecourt. She's in a state of shameful neglect. Could you check on her?"

"Oh dear. Not at all Mr. Russo. Would you mind stepping out of the room for a short time then?

Ten minutes later, the nurse emerged, a look of frustration on her face. "Mr. Russo?"

"Yes?" he approached.

She glanced back at the room, then ahead at the nurse's station. "I must offer you an apology on Miss D'Hemecourt's physical condition and disheveled appearance. The patient clearly did not receive quality care for even the most basic hygiene. It doesn't appear she's been eating well, been released from her restraints much or for that matter been out of the room at all. I will remedy that situation right away, Mr. Russo and report this incident to my supervisor and the doctor at once. I can assure you, the nurse who was slack in her duties will be severely reprimanded or discharged."

"Why would the nurse be so slack in her care? Didn't the doctor notice her condition?"

She looked down. "The doctor assigned to her care was Dr. Duplessis, who, if you were not aware, passed away." She lowered her voice. "I know it's wrong to speak ill of the dead, but he did not come well-recommended. His replacement, Dr. Peterson is an excellent doctor and you can expect that Miss D'Hemecourt will receive all the attention she needs and deserves." She took a breath. "And you have my personal guarantee that I will do my very best to provide excellent care to this unfortunate young woman as well."

"Thank you Nurse Robichaux. I can't bear to see her suffer so." His voice trailed off.

She touched his arm. "Mr. Russo, would you mind waiting down the hall for about twenty minutes or so? I'm going to attend to her needs right away."

"Of course. Thanks again."

He sat on a drab couch in the hallway with a perfect view of Fleur's door and the nurse's station. Nurse Robichaux informed her supervisor, who took notes, then hurried off in one direction while she went in the other direction to attend to Fleur. He noticed nurses began to congregate at spots down the hall, speaking in whispered tones, their faces serious. That is, until the nurse supervisor returned, visibly annoyed and barking commands. She stormed down the hall to Fleur's room with three attendants to join Nurse Robichaux, and set the rest of the staff scrambling in different directions.

"Good." He leaned back, head against the wall, exhausted. Fleur deserves better than that.

Though he'd kept quiet about it, everyone at the firm, and at court seemed to know or suspect something about their breakup and Fleur's breakdown. Word spread fast. The shame of his fiance' being committed to a mental institution was humiliating. His family kept reasurring him that he'd made the right decision to call off the engagement. Louis knew most people expected him to do so given the situation. He sighed. Why did all this have to happen?

He began to pray in silence, mouthing the words. "Lord, please help me. If I marry Fleur, I'll be ostracized by society and frowned upon in my profession. But if I turn my back on her, I'll be miserable. And I'm afraid she'll die in this horrible place. I don't know what to do. I was the happiest man on earth and now I'm at the brink of despair."

Twenty minutes turned into thirty, then forty-five, then fifty. If the industrial clock on the green wall was correct, he had just ten minutes to return to work in time for an appointment. With reluctance, Louis informed one of the nurses at the desk that he had to leave, but promised to return after work.

Chapter Twenty-Seven
Red Sky

Bernard D'Hemecourt huffed and puffed behind his daughter as they walked across the broad expanse of lawn in Audubon Park. Most of the grass was still green, but with brownish splotches, caught in the throes of fickle February weather. However, on this day the temperature had climbed to seventy-eight degrees with the sun out.

Dressed in light jackets, the two ventured out for the sake of privacy, away from the prying ears of the house staff. Bernard had recently come to suspect them of disloyalty since the dismissal of their beloved Philomene.

"Rest assured, we had a good plan, an admirable one Piper. And if the good Dr. Duplessis hadn't ruined it by dying, it would have worked. She was getting weaker every day. It's unfortunate about the new psychiatrist. Dr. Peterson is a different breed, not the type to be bought. And he seems to be prying into her memories, trying to . . . "

A good ways ahead of her father, she called back to him, pointing to a tall oak. "Let's rest, okay?"

When they stepped under the shadow of the tree, the temperature cooled considerably and cast a shiver. Sheaths of grey moss ornamented the branches. Piper nearly walked into a tangle of it.

Leaning back against the expansive trunk, she lit a cigarette and exhaled, tilting her head back as she did. "I'm not fond of the plan. I hate seeing her waste away like that. It's disgusting. Don't you feel anything?"

"Not a jot or a tittle."

She rolled her eyes. "Sometimes I do."

Bernard pulled a silver coin from his pocket and began to throw it in the air. She watched him, intently.

He snapped his fingers. "Don't go getting sentimental on me, kid. That's the last thing I need to hear at this stage." He looked down at the coin, then at her. "Why think of her when should be thinking of Louis? Fleur is the roadblock between the two of you."

She sighed. "The roadblock? More like a chasm."

"Now, now. The girl's not as big a problem as you think."

Piper bounced back, eyes again animated. "I suppose you're right." She glanced over. "What should we do?"

"Hmmm?" He began to pace back and forth, tripping over the roadmap of roots protruding from the ground. "We have to get her out of there and get rid of her another way. Something fast. Nothing like Gerard envisioned."

"How? We've spent all this time trying to convince them she's got bats in the belfry. What now" Do we say we were mistaken? Or are we supposed to just turn around and say 'never mind'?"

Bernard punched at the air. "It should be so easy."

"We could spirit her out at night on the pretense we're saving her from a lifetime in the Looney Bin." She exhaled again and pointed her cigarette at him. "Your little nurse could help us."

He puckered his lips and spat on the ground. "She's gone, at least off my payroll. Fired for incompetence. I had to as soon as Dr. Peterson reported her."

She blinked. "How ironic."

"The woman's a little idiot, but a useful one." He wagged a finger. "I think you might be onto something though. We could find a way to sneak her out at night and take her some place. It would be easy to keep her in the guest house with Cecelia assigned to her. What about that?"

Piper blew out a final cloud of smoke. She threw the butt down and twisted it out with her shoe. "Okay, so we bring her home. How do you plan on getting rid of her there? And how do you propose to keep the police from putting two and two together?"

He grimaced. "Good point."

"There could be too many questions."

"We can't have that," he agreed.

She bit her bottom lip. "Remember, you no longer have a doctor in your back pocket, no one to rubber stamp a death certificate or write you all the prescriptions you need."

Bernard leaned an arm against a thick branch and put his head down against it. "I'm used to having all the answers, the spin on the situation, but there's just too much happening. Creditors breathing down my neck, gambling debts to be paid. And the carnival ball is just two weeks away. I tell you, I'm in a frenzy! February eighteenth is so close. Here I stand at the epitome of all

I've ever hoped for and I can't enjoy it. The lack of money's always been a damper on everything good in my life."

She stared up at a patch of blue sky between the branches. "I went for my final fitting. The gown is exquisite, breathtaking in fact." Piper pulled out another cigarette and lit it.

He looked over at her. "Since when did you take up tobacco?"

She shrugged. "I dunno."

"Well I don't like you smoking. It's not fit for a queen."

"I'm not really a queen." She attempted a tired laugh. "Only a pretender to the throne." A more serious tone entered her voice. "Besides, you're not a real king either." Eye to eye, she drew the cigarette to her lips and inhaled, then exhaled in his face.

He wet his lips. She could see anger boiling in his eyes.

Piper looked away. The park was deserted.

"Piper."

She returned her attention to her father's face, a scowl pulling every wrinkle toward the center.

"I hope you take my carnival ambitions with all seriousness. It's all I've ever wanted, to be part of this elite group. I've spent a lifetime pursuing this moment, and hoped, dreamed and maneuvered my way to achieve it. Don't view this goal of mine in a frivolous way, my girl."

She exhaled smoke through her nostrils. "All right." She threw the cigarette to the ground and stamped it out. "There, are you satisfied, Your Highness?"

"Thank you."

He wound his hand around a stick and waved it with a graceful sweep like a scepter. "Imagine the night of the 'bal masque'. I'll be in ermine of course with an elaborate crown. But when people get a load of your beauty, why, the sight will take their breath away. Your gown, it's elegant. Made of silver lame' and imported lace. Austrian rhinestones, silver bugle beads, crystals, a Medici collar, crown sparkling with jewels, a scepter." He reached to the ground and handed her a stick but she refused.

"And the night parade leading up to the meeting of the courts. You, of course won't get to see it because you'll be at the grande ballroom waiting for the court to arrive. Imagine the flambeau dancers. Measured steps, cakewalking, dancing revelry, spinning tiered torches." He went on. "The crowd, wild, frenzied, clamoring for trinkets."

Unfazed by his dramatics, Piper interrupted. "Time's ticking away. We have a court cotillion tonight."

He dropped both sticks to the ground and nodded. "Right." He cleared his throat. "How about this idea? You leave about eleven from the cotillion. I'll call that nurse and hire her short term to get the girl out the door and into your car. Then you drive and take a boat out to the camp."

"At night? I'll never find it in the dark. It's dangerous."

"You will if I send Alcide."

"Gerard knows the way better."

Bernard scowled. "Yes, my business partner would be your first choice, wouldn't he?" He grabbed her by the shoulders. "Do you think me a fool? I know what goes on between the two of you."

Her mouth fell open. "No, I'd never. . ."

"Your little clandestine meetings in the guest house. Did you think you were being discreet? I know more than you think I do."

"You are a fool if you think I'd let Gerard or Alcide touch me." She turned to go but he grabbed her forearm and squeezed it.

Face flushed, he raised his voice. "Stay away from Gerard. I mean it." He snorted.

"I don't know what you're talking about." Piper's eyes narrowed in defiance.

"Isn't it obvious? Gerard is a wanted man. And I don't need those two detectives coming round the house any more. I need that like I need a hole in the head. You need Louis!"

She remained silent, hoping he would believe she agreed.

"You see it's easy to be a little brat about things. But you and I will both get what we want if you play along. All I need is for you to do what I want when I want. Is that too much to ask? I told you, this is all I ever wanted and in order for that to happen, I need money." He ran a palm against his forehead, as if to cool the rising temperature inside.

Jaw set, she stared in the direction of the house. "I suppose you want me to figure out what to do."

His eyes widened. "You could put some knock-out drops in her drink. When she's out, you can dump her in the water."

"What about the body?"

"The gators'll take care of the body." He laughed. "Or—you could say the will-o-the-wisp took her."

"Gerard would find that amusing." She eyed him.

He met her gaze with an icy stare. "Indeed."

Piper toyed with the idea of telling him the truth. He'd really blow a gasket . . . if he knew if he only knew--about the baby.

Chapter Twenty-Eight
The Snare

Louis sat across from her in a hard metal chair. The abrupt cold of the surface kept him on edge.

"Why won't you at least tell me what happened?"

Exasperated, Fleur closed her eyes shut for a moment. "Louis, I've tried to explain to you time and again. I would if I could. I don't remember how I came to be in that condition, only that I was. The nuns took care of me. Oh Louis, don't you think I would tell you everything if I remembered?"

In silence, he fomented his next words. "I still don't understand how one could forget such a thing. It's not like misplacing a bobby pin or forgetting someone's name. It's not possible to forget something as momentous, as life-changing as that."

She gripped the chair arms till her knuckles turned white. "Louis, I understand why you feel that way. If I were in your shoes, I would be certain to want, even demand to know. But I tell you, I have no memory of it."

He interrupted. "I've spoken with Dr. Peterson. He told me that you suffered amnesia brought on by trauma of some sort. It's difficult for me to understand however, that your memories haven't returned by now."

"But they are coming back to me. Dr. Peterson says . . . "

"The good doctor seems to know more about you than I do. In fact, everyone else seems to know more about you than I."

A lump rose in her throat, an ache from her heart. "I wanted to tell you." She looked down. "In the swamp."

"With that man!" His brows crinkled. "Gerard."

"I knew it was wrong to go. I made up my mind to tell you. I know it sounds disingenuous to say so in light of the circumstances, but that's when I knew I truly loved you. He was behaving with inappropriate intent toward me. I refused his advances. All I could think of was you. All I could see was your face."

He rose and turned his face to the wall. "I knew it." Louis placed his palm against the wall and leaned forward, head down. "There was a feeling I had right here." He pounded on his heart.

"It's hard to describe but I knew in my heart you didn't tell me everything."

Louis swung around. "You were attracted to him."

Fleur leaned her head on the chair. "I'm ashamed to admit that I had a brief infatuation. But I'm glad I did, because after my ordeal, I had no doubt about my feelings for you."

Tears formed in the corners of his eyes. "Well I have doubts." He turned his face away to face the wall again. "Between the pregnancy and this, I feel as if you're not the same woman."

"If you feel that way, I don't understand why you keep coming back. You called off our wedding. Why are you here?"

His stiffened his back against the wall. "Isn't it obvious why I keep coming back? You must think me quite the fool."

She drew in a deep breath to quell the sob rising in her throat. "It seems our marriage plans have gone awry with little chance of restoration. Coming here to visit me must pain you. Why spin your wheels any more? I release you from all guilt at breaking our engagement. I'm letting you go. You're free, Louis."

There, she'd said it. Fleur felt as if all the life had drained from her. Weary, she tilted her head against the back of the seat.

Her words stung him. She could see it on his face, the face still so dear to her. Louis didn't understand. And why should he? No one could blame the man. How could she expect him to trust that she was telling the truth?

Better to let him go. As much as it hurt her heart to do so, she could see no possibility of a future with Louis. Without a solid explanation, he would always wonder about her past and worry about their future.

He inched toward the door, attempting to hide moist tears with his sleeve. "If that's how you feel I'll take my leave. But I pray one day . . . " His voice cracked.

Fleur spoke up with surprising ease. "Perhaps one day I'll see you with a wife and little children and you'll-you'll be happy. Maybe even wonder what you saw in me." Eyes too weary for tears, she brought together a weak smile. "Now please, go."

Louis, face forward, paused as his hand clasped the doorknob. "God go with you, Fleur."

"And with you, my . . ." He bolted through the open door.

". . .love." She stared straight ahead, fearful her heart might persuade her to call him back.

Philomene had given her a scripture only yesterday about a seed, something about allowing a seed to fall to the ground and die, so that it could bear fruit. Perhaps in letting Louis go, the love of her life, his soul would indeed prosper. She hoped it would be so.

A half an hour or more passed, at least she guessed so. There were no clocks in the room to aid in noting the passage of time. But the time felt like an eternity. As if her life had crumbled to ruins, down to the foundation.

A few minutes later, a familiar knock sounded on the door, a thoughtful consideration of her new doctor, who made a point of respecting his patients.

"Come in, Dr. Peterson."

He entered the room, his kind spirit reflected in a gentle smile and peaceful demeanor. Dr. Peterson had a heart of gold. How different from Dr. Duplessis. The new doctor had the straps removed from her bed. She was wheeled out into the courtyard garden daily to take in the sunshine. The nurses fed and bathed her each and every day, and made good on a promise to have a woman even came in twice a week to style her hair and do her nails. More important, Fleur had begun to walk again, though at first her legs crumbled underneath her.

"It's time for our session. Do you feel up to talking today?" His eyes, a vivid blue sparkled in such a way as to make him appear younger, but the receding hairline and grey around his temples spoke otherwise.

She nodded.

"All right then." He pulled the chair that only minutes ago had been occupied by Louis, back a bit further from her and sat in it.

"I noticed your fiancé was here for a visit." His eyes seemed to survey, to take in her physical condition.

"Yes."

"You seem a bit tired. Are you certain you feel up to conversing?"

She took a deep breath. "I released him--let him go."

He watched her, but said nothing. "Our engagement, though broken, was redeemable up until today. I know if I could have offered some explanation, no matter how sordid, he might have forgiven me."

"And?"

Thoughts and feeling swirled in her head. " I don't need his forgiveness."

Dr. Peterson sat back in his chair and folded his hands together. "How did you come to that conclusion?"

Perplexed, she held her temples. "I'm not certain. Sometimes I feel as if a river were about to rush through my mind."

"Have you every heard the story of Hans Brinker? The little Dutch boy who plugged a dike with his finger and saved his entire town from destruction?"

"Why yes," she smiled, "I have read it before. My mother used to read the story to me. It was one of my favorites."

"Well Fleur, I believe that situation is a very good illustration of the precarious situation you are now in. You seem to be holding back a wall of memories in the same manner."

She closed her eyes, as if to see the answer written on the insides of her lids. "I know the answer is there--inside that house."

His eyes registered a spark of interest. "That house? Isn't the home on St. Charles in fact, your house?"

"Well yes, of course but, what I mean is, the home stopped feeling like my home a long time ago."

"After the death of your parents?"

"Yes."

Fleur began to twirl sections of hair around her fingers. "Everything changed."

"I would imagine so." He shifted in his chair. "Do you think your aunt and uncle fulfilled their roles as guardians, or were they more akin to your parents?"

She burst out laughing. "Oh my, my, my, that's a good one." She pointed towards him. "Aunt Florrie and Uncle Bernard are, were, the farthest one can be from ideal parents."

"Why is that?"

"For one thing, they were never around much. Always off at some party or event and whenever they were around, they couldn't be bothered."

"Hmmm, and how did that make you feel."

She raised her shoulders and let them fall. "Sad, I suppose."

He was silent until she drew her eyes to his. "And Fleur, why do you think you're afraid of your uncle?"

She stared back at him. "I wish I knew."

He stood and walked across the room to stand in front of the green cinderblock wall painted green. He pointed to the cinder block and pulled a piece of white chalk from his pocket. "I visited the gallery on Royal Street."

"Did you?" Fleur asked, fascinated by his movements. Why?"

"I wanted to gain insight into who you are. I hope you don't mind."

"No, not at all. You're my physician."

He smiled. "You'll be pleased to know none of your paintings were available to purchase. The owner was quite pleased and most curious as to when you might begin work on another collection. That said, I was able to browse through the catalog." The doctor paused, "One painting in particular stood out to me."

His right arm began to move, wrist rotating as he drew--a bed, door and two dots at the bottom of the door. "The bed and the door, do those represent the bedroom you slept in as a child?"

Her heart fluttered out of control. "Yes, yes it is."

He used the chalk to point to the two dots under the door. "And what do these represent?"

"The . . ."

The doctor sighed. "Give me a try."

"There's a ghost in the house. And I know it sounds far-fetched, but it, the ghost, used to come to my room at night."

He tilted his head to the side. "Really? But ah, from what I've heard about ghosts and spirits, they're able to walk through walls and float, aren't they?

"I suppose you're right." She watched as his hand moved across the wall with the chalk and stopped at the two dots.

"What about these? Ghosts don't wear shoes, do they?"

She smiled. "Not as far as I know."

"So who do you think belongs to these shapes if they represent shoes, outside your bedroom door?"

A knock on the door interrupted. He looked from her to the source of the knock. "Yes?"

Nurse Robichaux cracked open the door enough to poke her head in. "Dr. Peterson, I'm sorry to bother you, but Room Nine, Mr. Rand . . ."

"Ah yes, I'll be right there." He walked forward to grasp Fleur's hand. "Fleur, will you please excuse me? Another patient is having some difficulties. I'll see you tomorrow. Please consider what we discussed today. Will you promise?"

Fleur could barely catch a breath. "I promise."

* * *

Philomene came to her room daily and today was no exception. She slipped in, as always, between shifts, bearing a small bouquet of pastel sweet peas. Pleased with the new level of care she was receiving, Philo no longer talked about breaking her out of the hospital. She wanted Fleur to be released on her own, the legal way. She had discovered that Fleur could sign herself out of the mental hospital any time had she signed herself in. However, her uncle had signed the papers. So to get out, she would have to be declared sane and competent by a doctor. Philo suggested Fleur begin by asking Dr. Peterson's help.

"Shouldn't I tell him about them trying to kill me?"

Philomene shook her head. "No chile'. They think you crazy iffn' you was to say dat."

"But it's true."

"You an' I knows dat. But it do sound crazy. You got to admit it. " She winked. "And dis no place to be crazy."

"To tell the truth Philo, I'm finding it hard to distinguish between what's true and what isn't. You're telling me one thing, Piper and Uncle Bernard are telling me another.

She slapped her knees. "Two o' dem don't have no acquaintence wit da trut an' I ain' got to tell you who dey is. Dem two is trifling wit God's good grace."

Fleur hugged her arms close. "And Louis, he just stares at me like I'm a big disappointment. I won't have to worry about that anymore."

Philo bit her lip. "I cain't hardly baleve I'm sayin' what I'm sayin' but dat boy still love you. I already tol' you how Piper poisoning his mind 'bout you so she kin git her claws into him, but she ain' havin' no luck in dat department. All he see is you. Dat man still lovesick wit you."

Fleur pounded her fist on her mattress. "I sent him away."

"What?"

"Don't you see? It's for the best. He can't marry trash."

Philomene cradled her face in her hands. "Now you listen to me Fleur D'Hemcort—you not trash. I don' eva wanna hear you describe yousef dat way agin, you hear?

"An' as for Louis, dat youn man got scered off. Dat's diff'nt. He got to thinkin' you was some kin o' floosy, hoppin' from bed to bed."

"But I did get pregnant, didn't I? Something like that can't just happen. Only in the Bible. But in real life, there had to be someone."

Tears welled in her eyes. "Yes chile' in da good book it happen like dat, but in real life, your life . . ." Her voice broke. "You was but a chile' y'self when it happened."

Fleur's chest heaved. "I should remember. But please, please, please, please, please tell me, who the father is. I need to know."

When she heard the question, Philomene found the nearest stool and sat down. "That I can't say for now. I'm still finding out fo' mysef'. You has to truss me, dat's all. It's dat plain."

"But I need to know."

"An' you will, I promise." She rose with some difficulty, counting the toll scrubbing floors had taken on her back. Fleur helped her straighten.

"Dere is one thing you kin do though." She pointed upward. "You kin invite de Lord Jesus into you heart."

"How?"

"Well, if you and me was in a chuch, we would make ouwa way up ta de alta and de preacha would pray you right into de kingdom. You'd confess de Lord wit you mout." She placed a hand on Fleur's cheek. "But since we here, jus' fall on you knees whenever you feels ready and axe Him into your heart."

Fleur blinked hard. "And what then Philo? Will I change? Will my life be perfect?"

Philomene laughed. "You change fo' shore but," she placed her hand over Fleur's heart, "in here. You become a new creacha in Christ. He forgives you your sins an' den you kin forgive others fo' what dey done ta you 'cause o' de love o' Christ in your heart. De love of God gonna ova flow like a fountain. You'll see."

She waved her head side to side. "Life shore ain' perfek though. Your spirit be perfek but your body goin' have some ketchin' up to do. Hard times still come, but you'll never walk alone through dem no mo' Jesus save, heal, protect and deliber. That jus' bout cover it all."

Philomene hugged her. "You think 'bout it. Betta yet, pray 'bout it." She pulled away. "Time fo' me to go'. Got to git back to work an earn me a living."

Fleur kissed her cheek. "Thank you for . . . for everything. You'll always have a job with me." She cracked a smile. "As soon as I get out of the Looney Bin."

***

An hour later she woke from a nap to find that her uncle had come to pay her a visit. But this time she viewed him with a shrewd eye. The man was not to be trusted, nor for that matter, was Piper. No matter what rationale he or she presented resting upon the ideal of family loyalty and trust, she came to the conclusion neither were worthy of trust. Both had the most to gain from her untimely demise and, truth be told, she'd come closer to her heavenly reward more times in the past few months than she had all the years of her life. Instead of trying to convince herself why her uncle and cousin would conspire to take her life, she decided to ask herself the opposite question. Why wouldn't they be involved?

He offered Fleur a glass of water, pouring liberally from the hospital pitcher at her bedside.

Knuckles wrapped around the metal bed rails, he stared intently at her. "Fleur, please listen carefully to what I'm about to say. Can you hear me? Are you listening?"

After a long draught, she passed the glass back to him. "Yes, I'm listening."

"There's a nurse who's going to come here tonight to help you. She's going to loosen your straps and help you leave this place."

Fleur responded, "I don't have straps anymore. Dr. Peterson . . ."

"Yes, yes I'm well aware you like Dr. Peterson." Sweat began to bead on his forehead again. He pulled a shiny coin from his pocket.

"Now there isn't much time, dear before the good doctor comes in to make his rounds. We have to hurry. Do you see the coin?" He grabbed her chin and pointed her face in the direction of his other hand swinging the coin on a chain. "Fleur? See how shiny it is? You remember the coin, don't you?" He started a movement with it, like a pendulum in front of her face. "I've had it for so many years. Watch the coin, Fleur. Keep your eye on the coin. You're weary. Tired. Getting sleepy."

Her eyes popped open.

"Uncle, w-what a surprise."

The shadow of a beard on his face, his expression was serious. "Fleur, listen to me very carefully. I've told you this before and I'm only telling you this again for your own welfare. You had a nervous breakdown because your fiance', Louis Russo, left you. Do you remember? The two of you were planning to elope when he found out about your little teenage indiscretion."

"I-I wish I could forget we ever met." She twisted her head from side to side in an agony of emotion.

Bernard grabbed her by the shoulders. "Listen to me. You can start over. Meet someone else. Do you want to stay here and rot? Why, these doctors will put you in a straight jacket, throw you into a padded cell, lock the door and forget about you. Is that what you want?"

Fleur began to sob.

He drew her to his chest. "There, there . . . "

She felt his hand stroking her hair. When he did, a flash of something came to her--a memory of him stroking her hair as a child.

"Now, there isn't much time. We're going to get you out of here tonight. When you leave this place there will be a car parked on the corner. You are to go with the nurse, get into the car and the person driving the car will take you to a safe place, a very safe place. You remember the camp, don't you? You know the one. Coeur de l'eau, the one on the bayou."

There were footsteps approaching, two sets. He dropped the coin into his pocket.

"When I snap my fingers, you will go back to sleep. Sweat in rivulets down his face, he swiped at them with his sleeve, "Fleur, you have get away from this place. You fear for your life." He hurried through the last sentence, and culminated by a curt snap of his fingers. He stood up as the door opened.

Chapter Twenty-Nine
Coeur de l'eau

The sound of thunder rumbled, dark and ominous through the building. Though there were no windows in her room, she could feel the building rattle. Fleur could smell the distinctive odor of rain. Of course, aside from the thunder, there were other clues, the squeaky swish of rubber-soled shoes, the sound of nurses hurrying inside from the wet wind, droplets shaken from drenched umbrellas. And the lights would sometimes dim for a few seconds, probably from lightening strikes.

Uncle Bernard said that tonight would be the night. With no wristwatch on her arm to consult, she would have to stay vigilant. The nurses came to check on her every hour. She counted as many visits as she could remember. By her figuring, it was probably ten or eleven o'clock in the evening. Soon, the nurse would be in to administer the medicine that would put her to sleep. *Do I even want to leave here tonight?* Her mind was beginning to clear, like walking in and out patches of dense grey fog.

The lights dimmed again, then came back to full shine. She thought of a story her college roommate told her about rabbits and lightening. Fran grew up on a farm where they kept hundreds of rabbits in a fenced-in yard with a hutch. One night there was a huge lightening storm. Rain and wind too. But the lightening was fierce. In the morning, when they went outside to check on their livestock, they found the entire pen of rabbits dead, except for one, the only rabbit that stayed in the hutch during the storm. Since there were no burns or scorch marks anywhere, the family had always wondered. Did a burst of electricity from the lightening kill the rabbits, or did they die of fright?

Right now, right this minute, Fleur felt as if she could die of fright. What would it be like? Though a prisoner in her room, she felt safe there. Her heart thumped, thumped against the inside of her chest as she heard a jangle of keys in the door. It was usual for the nurses to come in the evening with a smile and a tray of medicine in white paper cups. But when Fleur looked up, she was surprised to see the silhouette of the mean one, the bad nurse at the door. The woman, decked in nursing white had a short dark cape on, jeweled in raindrops. She looked behind for a moment to make sure no one saw her as she entered. The door swished shut.

The long, angular face, and the thin, greasy ponytail--Nurse Moron.

The woman feigned concern and approached the hospital bed. "Are you doing well, Fleur?" She ran her thin, dry fingers through her hair. "I see someone's come in to do your hair. It's all in such lovely curls. The color of honey." She laughed. "I'll bet your boyfriend sent a hairdresser in from one of those fancy salons just for you."

She walked to the chart at the end of the bed and opened it for a look. "I don't think I like him very much anymore." Nurse Moran looked up from the chart at her. "Did you know he had me fired?"

Fleur froze.

"Don't look so surprised, Little Missy." She pointed a finger and dabbed it against Fleur's chest. "I'm onto you. I know you put him up to it. You had a nice little talk with him, didn't you?" She paused to fondle her ringlets again. "So pretty. How I wish I had your hair, or at least a devoted boyfriend."

She laughed again. Not a pleasant laugh. "I wonder what he would think of you if I cut all those pretty curls off."

Fleur gasped.

The woman laughed. "Don't worry. I'm much too busy tonight to worry about making you look unattractive. I've got bigger fish to fry." She bent down and opened the drawers one by one in a chest of drawers next to the wall. The woman grabbed a mismatched outfit, Fleur's street clothes. "Here, put this on." Then she stuffed all the rest into a small satchel.

Fleur did not fail to see the irony of her situation, that she and the nurse should have switched places. The woman was mad.

"You smell different." She sniffed the air again. "Perfume too. Is it Chanel? Well, I can see your man spared no expense, eh?" She walked around to the other side of the bed. "Hurry up. I don't have all night."

"Okay." Fleur spoke, trying to stall. A part of her didn't want to go, but another part wanted to feel the rain on her face, to be free. Need time to think.

Nurse Moran moved her head in closer until her face hovered over Fleur's. "Maybe your guy wants to get his grimy little lawyer hands on your money. Did you ever think of that?" Her penciled brows rose, "You do have money, don't you?"

"I don't k-know any more."

The woman smiled, her teeth gleaming like cantelope seeds. Fleur shuddered.

"Sure you do. You're a poor little rich girl. A poor little looney rich girl."

Her face was so close to Fleur that she could feel the heat of her breath and smell its foulness.

"Your uncle told me that if I help you escape, there would be some money in it for me. Where is your money? Do you have some with you?"

Fleur turned her head to the side to avoid her eyes, her breath. "I don't know if I have any. My purse."

"I've already checked your purse. You had a few dollars in it, that's all."

"Get up," Nurse Moran commanded. "I'll help you." She helped her finish dressing. Fleur looked down at her outfit.

"But the blouse and skirt don't match."

Teeth clenched together, she spoke in a vicious whisper. "Shut up. Just shut up and do as I say."

Feet on the floor, her arm on the nurse, Fleur took a few steps and felt dizzy, her body still a bit weak and unsteady.

"We have to get out of here before the other nurse comes to check on you." The woman sat Fleur back on the bed. "I'll get your shoes and purse."

Tired so tired. By this time, Fleur would already have been asleep. But now it was time to go and she felt vaguely aware that she was supposed to go for some reason.

Solid sheets of rain still fell. Fleur could hear the rain pounding on the roof. The woman, skiddish as a cat, timed their escape while the lone nurse at the desk left to answer a patient's buzzer.

They slipped out to a freight door. Moran turned the key and the door squeaked open to an alleyway--walls of brick on either side. Drenched almost at once, Fleur's body woke from the urge to slumber. The chilled air sent trembles through her body. Excited by the prospect of freedom, she pressed forward with eagerness. And there, parked on the street, as she was told it would be, was the car. Even in the dark, the sporty red car stood out.

Nurse Moran pointed to it, and ran away in the night, tucking her jacket over her head. She soon disappeared down the street.

As Fleur reached the car, the door on the passenger side opened. Piper leaned over from the driver's seat.

"Get in."

Surprised, Fleur didn't move at first.

"C'mon, get in," Piper commanded.

Quick to obey this time, Fleur slid into the passenger seat and sneezed. Piper grabbed the door handle and slammed the door shut as the wind blew a fresh spray of rain inside.

"Here," Piper said, handing her an old quilt, "wrap this around or you'll catch your death. I mean--I don't want you to catch a cold or anything."

Dressed in a dark rain slicker, Piper seemed nervous, edgy. Fleur didn't recognize the car and wondered whom it belonged to. Shivering, she took the worn quilt and wrapped it around her waterlogged body.

Piper started the engine.

Fleur stared at her cousin's profile. "W-where are we going?"

"To the camp." Piper stared forward and turned the windshield wipers on, then the lights. "To Coeur de l'eau."

Her uncle had said as much.

Piper's knuckles, white with tension, sped through the city streets, almost empty at the late night hour. The rain continued to pour, a relentless, pelting rain.

Once outside the city lights, a velvet ribbon of road, dark and lonely seemed to stretch forever before them. Rain, frenzied and chaotic, tumbled across. Piper pressed her foot harder to the pedal.

Fleur stole a glance at the speedometer--almost 95 miles per hour. Her hand gripped the armrest on the door. She shivered, half from the cold and half out of fear. She glanced around at the interior. The smell of a new car--instruments polished to a high sheen, leather seats. Where did Piper get the money?

"Why are you doing this?"

"I'm saving you from life in a Funny Farm you little fool. Now settle down and try not to bother me while I drive."

Thoughts still a jumble she was beginning to see some things with more clarity in the absence of medication.

Strange little snippets, childhood memories were starting to return. For instance, Mrs. Brennan, the Grande Dame of them the Junior League, used to come over to visit Aunt Florrie. Decked in a sensible hat and outfit, she'd fold her white gloves on the table while Florrie poured a cup of Sassafras Tea. As expected, Mrs. Brennan would lean in, a conspiratorial tone to her voice. "Take tea, my dear. Sassafras is most effective in curing what ails the female form. Cleanses the blood. Mark my words. Sassafras." For years after that, she and Piper used the word to describe something untrue or ridiculous.

But now, even without Mrs. Brennan's bitter Sassafras, Fleur was beginning to feel more like her old self. Perhaps the cold rain had something to do with it.

She looked at Piper, mouth forming the word. "Sassafras."

Piper glanced, a surprised expression chiseling the hardness away. "I haven't heard you say that for a long time."

"Now, tell me the real reason you're doing this."

Piper tightened her knuckles on the wheel and eased them. "I am saving you from that place."

"You want my money."

Piper shrugged. "I won't pretend. Of course I want it. But I've decided I don't want you dead in order to get it."

"Why should I believe you?"

"There's no reason you should." She took her eyes off the road for a second and they smiled back at one another.

Two hours later, the rains stopped with as an abrupt finish as they had begun. The car veered off, onto a narrow-laned road along the bayou. The water, black as obsidian, paralleled the road in dangerous proximity. Nevertheless, Piper kept up the speed. One miscalculation and they'd be in the drink.

Of course, Fleur knew the way to the camp. The family made many trips there in earlier years, but with Aunt Florrie's extended ill health, the camp was seldom used. Fallen into disrepair from what she had heard.

About a quarter mile from the dock, the rains let up. Piper stopped the car outside a rustic cabin and honked. A porch light came on and a woman who appeared to be in her fifties ran out carrying a large bucket with a lid. She watched as Piper handed the woman some money and set out for the dock.

Steam rose from the bucket and the smell of savory seafood filled the car's interior. Fleur felt her stomach roll and growl in response.

They parked close to the dock. Beyond it was Bayou Lafourche, black as witch's water. They climbed from the car, stiff from travel; Fleur still wet and trembling. Piper brought out a flashlight.

Fleur was surprised to see an old man at the helm, wearing a rain slicker and hat. He helped them onto the boat without uttering a word and started the engine. Within a minute, they were skimming over the waters, into the heart of the night.

Cypresswood trees draped in mossy silhouettes, flying things--birds or bats. The sounds that might have identified them, drowned out by the noise of the motor. If they had taken a pirogue, the experience would have been quite different. Transcendent.

Fleur remembered childhood tales of Will o'the Wisps and swamp creatures, ghosts of Indians, Civil War soldiers and pirates all roaming the mists that crept along the edge of the water, eerie tales told in whispers by children far beyond their bedtime. And stories that rang more true, of people who wandered, lost in the swamps and marshes, never to be seen or heard from again. With not even a bone to bury, nor lock of hair for a grieving family member to braid and frame.

The boat slowed. The man at the helm eased it next to the dock and tied it off. He helped them onto the dock. And without a word, he revved the engine and sped off in the direction they had come.

"He's leaving?" Fleur asked, incredulous.

"He'll be back." Piper helped Fleur up the stairs. "Funny, I expected the woman's husband to ferry us."

"You don't know the man? How can you be sure he'll come back for us?"

"Don't be silly. He's probably a relative. Everybody's related around here. You know that."

They reached the deck. Fleur panted from the exertion. "I suppose."

With only a half moon, it was difficult to see, but the camp looked the same from the shape of it. A large structure on stilts to protect from flooding, animal intrusion and alligators coming in the door unannounced, the camp great house was still an impressive sight at first glance. They climbed the stairs and creaked open the main door to the great room. Piper struck a match on the bottom of her shoe and lit a large lantern on a wooden table.

High ceilings, with a second floor gallery of rooms surrounding the great room, it looked the same to Fleur. The same weathered furniture and armchairs in rustic pine and leather. Bookshelves lined with dusty volumes. A large candle chandelier hung from the middle of the ceiling, made from a jumble of antlers. Piper loosed the ropes holding it at the proper height and lowered it to begin lighting the beeswax candles, one by one.

"You don't want to die, do you?"

She found herself answering. "No, I don't."

Her voice, a monotone, Fleur answered in spite of contrary thoughts in her mind. Why am I answering this way? An internal struggle began, the fight to synchronize her thoughts and her words.

Piper, unaware of the struggle within Fleur, continued. "If you stayed in that institution, you would. How would you like to live in Paris and study art? Wouldn't that be better? You don't have any real connections here anymore."

She lit the last candle and blew out the match, releasing the pungent smell of sulfur in the air.

"You mean, since Louis . . ."

"That's right. And I'm not naïve enough to think you'd miss me or father for that matter."

"I want to go back to Dr. Peterson. He's helping me. "Why should I hide out here? Like I'm an escaped criminal?"

"You are, my dear. You're an escaped lunatic. I can see it across the front page of The Times-Picayune, the kind of headline that strikes fear into the population. Why, tomorrow, people will be barricading their doors and nailing their windows shut to keep the crazy lady away.

"That's not funny."

"It's not meant to be." Piper lit another match and held it to a camp lantern. Puzzled, Fleur touched her hand, pausing it in mid-air, the match still burning. The lantern lit, Piper blew out the match.

Fleur looked around at the room. "None of this makes much sense to me."

Piper touched her on the shoulder. Her green eyes seemed to glow in the light, like cat's eyes. "Dear, you're tired you know. After your time in the sanitarium, I wouldn't doubt your confused state of mind."

As she lit them, the room began to take on a brighter glow and Fleur began to see the disrepair, the torn leather chairs and frayed curtains, the cobwebs and hanging chains of dust. The greater light revealed more and more of the ugliness hidden in shadows.

Fleur sat down, shivering under the quilt as Piper fed tentative flames in the old fireplace. Perhaps Piper was right. She felt as if the clouds in her head were clearing. Now she needed time to think, to sort things out. Coeur de l'eau, a place of escape, rest, freedom, and warmth might be just what she needed for the time being.

"I'm going to get the bucket from the boat and set up the table on the porch. I heard your stomach growl, so I know you're hungry. I called ahead to arrange for our meal."

In a few minutes, Piper called Fleur away from the fireplace. They ate in a small screened-in section of the porch, a chill in the night air, but no wind or rain anymore. Neither missed the absence of conversation. They cracked open savory blue crabs, digging at the sweet meat inside, and bit into crisp corn and potatoes infused with spices. Fleur counted this her first decent meal.

Memories of past visits to the camp flooded her mind, a savory scent wafting through the air. Hands on a wooden boat paddle, Philomene stirring a large cast iron kettle over an open fire. Bay leaves, lemons, garlic, onions, pepper sauce, coriander, thyme, and oregano, the seasoned water boiling and ready. Into it, dropping ears of corn, small red potatoes, boudin and fresh artichoke. The seafood would be next, after the vegetables cooked. Fleur watched from the porch. In two baskets on the small camp table next to the fire, were blue crabs, fresh shrimp and oysters. Philomene would pause periodically to wipe her forehead with her apron.

A loud splash in the water below caught her attention. She left the screen porch to peer over the side. Piper joined her. But they could see nothing in the dark ink.

Fleur clasped the porch rail, shaking. A wind lifted beards of moss in the cypress trees and sent ripples through the dark water.

"We should go inside." Piper wiped her mouth. "You're cold."

Their appetites sated, Piper picked up what was left of their meal and threw it over the side. Then they each lifted the sides of the newsprint together, wrapped it all up and Piper brought it to the fireplace to burn.

They sat by the crackling flames in silence for a time. Frogs and crickets replaced the singsongs of cheerful birds during the day. An owl hooted in distant trees, and the sounds of other night creatures emerging from their dens or tree hollows.

"I have a proposition for you, Fleur." Piper eyed her.

"Go on."

"Leave it all behind. As I suggested earlier, go to Paris. Live and study abroad. Paint and be celebrated for your artistic skill to your heart's content."

"Give you and uncle my house, money—everything?"

"Not all your money. Of course you'd need some of it to live on. I'm not suggesting you abandon every last cent to us."

The nerve of them! Fleur raised her voice. "Now who's crazy? You must think me quite a fool."

Piper laughed. "It's not such a crazy idea. And I certainly don't believe you to be a fool. Consider this--you'd be free to pursue what you love. Free from the house and property—the memories." She whispered. "Free from your past."

Fleur held her breath at the last sentence. *Free from my past. Is that possible?*

"I'm merely asking you to consider my proposal. Believe me, mine is far better than what my father has in mind." Piper stood. "I'll be right back." She soon reappeared from the house with two small glasses of elderberry wine. "I thought we might have a small glass for old times sake. It's the last one mother made before she became ill."

"I shouldn't," Fleur backed away.

"Please." Piper cajoled. "Pretty please with cane sugar and a strawberry on top?"

Taking her silence for a yes, Piper handed her a glass, then held hers up in the air.

Fleur grasped it. "All right, then."

"To new beginnings."

Fleur lifted hers. "To new beginnings."

Chapter Thirty
Boiling Pot

The note came to his office by the hand of a scruffy messenger, a boy who, upon questioning, described the woman who gave it to him as "ugly." The woman, whatever she looked like, demanded money, lots of it with the threat that if he ever desired to see his "girlfriend" alive again, he ought to pay up and keep the police out of it. Fleur? Dr. Peterson had called earlier to inform him of Fleur's disappearance.

At 5:00 o'clock pm the next day, he was to drop off a briefcase filled with ten thousand dollars in hundred dollar bills to the doorman at the entrance of the Monteleone Hotel. Never mind that he didn't have that kind of money.

At the hotel, he was to ask for a note addressed to him at the front desk and leave right away. Instructions as to where his girlfriend was being held would be in said note.

Louis agonized over what to do at first, but picked up the phone to call Delaney and Clark, the two detectives already on Fleur's case. There was much too much at stake to risk losing her. Since her disappearance last night, police had begun to canvas the city, thus far to no avail.

They first theorized she might have wandered off, perhaps in a daze, forgetting her identity. But there were too many security measures in place for her to have wandered off on her own. The detectives suspected it was an inside job. The note confirmed something and someone more sinister behind her disappearance.

Louis suspected Bernard and Piper at once, but without proof, there was no way of implicating them. What made things even more suspicious was Piper's absence. Bernard told detectives his daughter had gone on a shopping trip by car to New York. In fact, she'd recently purchased a new car, a red Cadillac convertible coupe. But Louis knew that Piper had to be back in time for the carnival ball. She'd mentioned it. In fact, she'd invited him to escort her, but he'd declined.

***

A counterplot was set. The next day, detectives planted police officers in plain clothes, and stationed them at tables in the hotel restaurant, in the lobby and outside the door. Even a second doorman was a detective in disguise. The messenger boy was well known to the police, a French Quarter ragamuffin who got into mischief, but nothing more serious. The boy was found, cleaned up and brought to the hotel to sit in the lobby, a potted palm obstructing a clear view of him.

Louis stopped on the street to dab at his temples. He drew in a long breath. Per instruction, he walked through the entrance carrying a valise filled with phony bills, which he promptly handed to the regular doorman. The unsuspecting doorman had been handed a note earlier, instructing him to place the brown leather valise in a large mail nook for packages received by hotel guests.

Louis, following the next set of instructions, walked over to the reception desk and asked if there was a note for him. He received it from the clerk, tipped his hat and walked back out the main entrance. He climbed into the passenger door of an unmarked police car to watch and wait.

Within minutes, a stick-thin woman walked along the banquette, straight on to the nook. She looked both ways, then reached for the valise and began to walk toward the car. Louis recognized her as the negligent nurse assigned by Dr. Duplessis to take care of Fleur.

The surprised woman was soon surrounded by detectives and police and brought to the station for questioning.

Louis entered with the police to observe. The boy was nudged forward by one of the officers. He was hopeful the child would offer a positive identification.

He pointed. "That's her."

"You're sure?" Delaney asked.

"Yes Sir, I'm sure."

Louis flipped a couple of coins to the boy. "Thanks for your help, son." The boy's face lit up as he stuffed the two bits in his pocked and bolted out the door.

At the police station, Louis paced the halls, checking his watch constantly. He sighed. What seemed like hours of waiting had amounted to only one hour. He was relieved to see Detective Clark exit the interrogation room, though it was impossible to read the man's face for a clue to any progress in locating Fleur.

"Follow me, Louis." His detective friend walked him down the hall and handed him a cup of hot coffee. He reached in his pocket and pulled out a pack of cigarettes. "Smoke?"

"Yes to the coffee and no thanks to the smoke." Grateful for the hot beverage, he took a long sip and grimaced.

"Hey, easy there, buddy. That stuff is hot."

"Believe me, I know. It tastes like shoe leather."

The detective smiled. "We call it the Gumshoe Special." He continued, "You ready for this? The woman's ready to sing. Her full name is Missy Moran. You identified her as one of the nurses who cared for your fiance', ah, ex-fiance' at the sanitarium." He stuffed the package of cigarettes back in his pocket.

But the smell of stale cigarettes hung like a curtain in the hallway. They passed office doors, both open and closed, detectives questioning people, officers pecking out reports on typewriters and secretaries talking on the phone. Most had cigarettes either hanging out the side of their mouth or smoldering in dirty ashtrays.

"We checked her out at the hospital and found out she was fired for improper treatment of her patient, but here's the kicker. Fleur was the only patient she was assigned to. She's a private nurse hired by the family. None of the other nurses were allowed to care for Fleur."

Louis interrupted. "Care she wasn't receiving."

"An established fact," the detective continued. "She claims you're the one who had her fired." He touched Louis's arm. "She also claims the family said you wanted to marry Fleur so you could get your hands on her inheritance and then get rid of her."

"Tom," Louis looked him in the eye, "I love Fleur and want her back. I didn't plan to marry for money, though I could have married half a dozen girls in this town with a lot more money and a lot less problems."

The detective cocked his head to the side. "So you don't have any plans to knock her off after you're hitched?"

"No, but funny they should say that. I believe that's what her family is trying to do. Another week, or even a couple of more days of negligence and Fleur might have died. Bernard and Piper would have inherited her estate with no questions asked."

"Makes sense." The detective nodded.

The two resumed walking. The detective came to a stop in front of a metal door at the end of the hall. "One more thing Louis. Dr. Duplessis was Fleur's doctor in the-ah-hospital. Did it ever occur to you that he might be related to Gerard?"

Louis spun around. "No."

"For the record, he is Gerard's father, adoptive father to be exact."

Louis's hands clamped to his temples. "No! But it-it makes sense. Gerard's father would have an invested interest in keeping Fleur quiet, maybe for good. All to protect his son from prison." He shook his head. "Why didn't I make the connection? It's such a common name, the boy who shines my shoes, the grocer down the street from my house."

"Yeah, we figured that too." He motioned to an office down the hall. "That's Officer Morris Duplessis's office. The guy I buy shrimp from, his last name is Duplessis. My kid's teacher . . ."

"Right." Louis sighed.

Come on in." He opened the door to the interrogation room where two other detectives sat across from the woman.

Missy, hair askew, greasy strands plastered to one side of her face, smoked a cigarette, a look of defiance on her long face. "So, here you are, murderer." She pointed at him. "He's the one who should be sitting in my place."

"Hello again, Miss Moran." Detective Clark pulled up a chair and motioned for Louis to sit. "For the record, Mr. Russo is not accused of murder or any other crime."

He leaned forward on one elbow. "However, you stand accused of the crimes of kidnapping and extortion, so far. As far as we know, a murder hasn't been committed. Are we correct in that assumption or do you have knowledge contrary to that? Is Miss D'Hemecourt in danger? And from whom?"

She flicked her cigarette toward the ashtray, without bothering to aim. A bit of ash landed on the edge of the glass dish and the rest on the grey Formica table. The woman shrugged. "Maybe she is. Maybe she isn't."

"Once more, Miss Moran, who else is involved?" Detective Delaney sat on her right, asking the question without looking up from the stained brown clipboard he was scribbling notes on.

She blew a small cloud of smoke toward his face. "No one. It was my idea to get some money out of the man since," she looked at Louis square in the eye, "he took my single means of livelihood away."

"Miss Moran, are you aware that you stand to serve twenty years for the two crimes I just mentioned and if you turn out to be an accessory to murder, well, you won't see the outside of prison walls in your lifetime."

Her lips touched together and fell apart. Perhaps speechless for the first time, Nurse Moran gasped.

Detective Delaney, nose out of the clipboard continued. "However, if you were to give us some information we consider valuable, the judge might be inclined to go easier on you. Say, no more than ten years in prison."

"Ten years." She howled. Her hardened demeanor replaced by that of a fearful child. "No, I have my whole life ahead of me. I want to get married. I want a husband and some kids. Please, I don't wanna go to jail. I'll do anything to stay out. Anything."

"Than I suggest you cooperate. If you do, the judge just might go easier on you. Capiche?"

Her face paled and she stamped out her cigarette in the ashtray. Louis noticed a slight tremble in her wrist.

"Okay, but I want it on paper or no deal. Got it?"

The detectives looked at one another and agreed.

Clark clasped his hands together. "Now spill it, sister."

The woman squinted her eyes together, as if trying to rouse tears. "Mister D'Hemecourt paid me to take extra special care of his spoiled little rich girl niece. He told me I wouldn't have to do much of anything for her. Told me she was on the way out, and not to bother. Asked me to report anything she said too. That was at first." She took a sip of water.

"What about Dr. Duplessis?"

"He told me to strap her in bed and keep her sedated, that's all."

Louis broke in. "Did you bother to feed or bathe her?"

Her eyes shifted from the detective to Louis. "Why of course I did. What kind of a person do you think I am?"

"For your sake I'm not going to answer that question, Miss Moran." Louis folded his arms.

She sneered.

Detective Clark asked. "And did you feel that the doctor was treating Miss D'Hemecourt in what could be described as an effective or negligent manner?"

"I hate to speak ill of the dead, and God rest his soul, but negligent, of course. After all, Dr. Duplessis was the doctor. I'm just a nurse. We nurses have to take orders from those men all day every day even when we know they're wrong. Some times patients die because of it and we nurses have to live with that on our conscience. It's not easy--believe me. But what man wants to listen to what a woman has to say anyway?"

Louis had a sick feeling in the pit of his stomach. Listening to what this woman had to say about Fleur--about everything disgusted him. He could see the two detectives felt the same way by the looks they exchanged from time to time.

"Then, after I got fired because of him," she pointed at Louis, "Mr. D'Hemecourt hired me to do a special job. He gave me some money, a good chunk with the promise of more after the job was done, and told me to sneak in and help Fleur escape to a car that would be waiting outside. I heard him and a woman on the other end of the phone arguing about whether I should go in the car to a fishing camp, "Curdy Lurdy" something, somewhere in the bayou."

"What bayou?"

She shrugged. "It's in Thibodaux somewhere. I don't know. They probably decided my job was to get her out of there and that's that. Maybe I stood to get a bigger chunk of cash if they'd let me go too. But as it is, I'm still waiting for the rest of my payoff."

Missy shook her fist. "He can't treat me that way. I won't be cheated. I worked hard for that money and it's mine. That lummox won't answer my calls or give me the time of day. He owes me!"

"Tell me Miss Moran, do you believe Miss D'Hemecourt is in danger?"

"I dunno. And so what if she is? I say, good riddance. That's why I sent the note so fast. I had to be sure I got the money before anyone found out."

Louis felt sick inside. He excused himself and left the room.

Down the long hall and to the right he noticed a private phone booth and ducked in closing the door behind him. He buried his face in his hands. Fleur, what have I done?

He began to pray, asking the Lord to protect her, to bring her out of harm's way. He was so engrossed in prayer he failed to see Clark outside the door until he heard the taptaptapping against the glass.

He opened the booth door. A waft of cooler air filled the booth. "Sorry to bother you Louis, but we got a lead on that camp. It's called Coeur de l'eau and we've got to get moving. Thought you might want to come along."

Louis pulled a handkerchief out his pocket and wiped his face. "Coeur de l'eau?"

Eyes sparked with adrenalin, Clark placed his hand on Louis's shoulder. "Meet us out front. We'll bring the car around. Delaney's on the phone with someone with information about the case, a Dr. Peterson."

"Fleur's new doctor?"

On the way to the front entrance, Louis stopped at a water fountain to splash his face, and began walking at a fast place. Down a series of steep marble steps at the formal entrance, he noticed a man standing in front of a black Plymouth limousine, waving him to come over. The man took off his hat. Thinning hair, combed over the top of his head with hair tonic of some sort, eyes, small and black. Since the detective's car wasn't around yet, he walked over to the man.

"Yes? How can I help you?"

The man gestured toward the limousine. "Mrs. Elliott would like to have a word with you if possible."

Louis frowned trying to think of where he'd heard the name before. "Mrs. Elliott? I'm not sure I'm acquainted with anyone by that name. Are you certain you have the right person?"

He nodded, replacing his hat, grey with a tiny blue feather in the band. "Yes sir. Perhaps you might remember making her acquaintance at a funeral service?"

Of course, it was the day he'd seen Fleur, as if for the first time--the moment he'd fallen in love with her. He remembered her smile, the creamy glow of her skin, her laugh.

"Cemetery? Oh, now I remember. Why, I still have Mrs. Elliott's handkerchief. I forgot all about returning it to her."

"She would like to speak with you if you have a minute."

"Perhaps another time. I'm in a rush." The detective's car pulled to the curb in front of the limousine and a squad car parked behind. Clark got out.

"Is that you, Mouse?"

The man in the grey hat gave the detective's hand a hearty shake. "Sure is."

"Say, what are you doing here?"

He glanced toward the limousine. "Working a P.I. job."

"Mouse?" Louis stared.

Clark pointed. "Mouse is the nickname we gave him cause he hears what's going on. Sam Giuseppe is a private investigator—and friend. We work with him on a lot of cases."

"And we go back a few years, eh?" Mouse laughed.

Delaney joined them. "Got a call from a Dr. Peterson."

"I told him," said Clark.

"He claims Fleur's maid contacted him and told him Fleur's in danger. Says the uncle, cousin and two goons are out to get rid of her for the estate." Delaney moved his thumb towards the car. We've gotta go."

"Wait," Mouse implored. " There's a lady in that car over there who has some information that may have bearing on this case. I've done some investigating for her and can verify that as fact."

"Who is it?" he asked.

"Mrs. Adelaide Elliott."

Louis asked, "How did you know I was here?"

Mouse threw his hands in the air. "Please. It's what I do for a living, Mr. Russo."

"Tell you what," Clark glanced at Delaney. "Mouse is working for the dame in that car. Got some information about this investigation. How about they follow us? Mouse and me'll switch places. I'll drive the car with Louis and the woman. She can explain along the way. Mouse rides with you, Delaney and tells you what he knows."

He nodded his agreement.

Louis opened the back seat door while Clark climbed into the driver's seat.

"What's this?" Adelaide asked. Garbed in a sage green dress trimmed in beige with a matching hat, her eyes sparkled at the sight of Louis. "So, we meet again. Please do come in and have a seat." She rapped on the seat in front of her. "I'm not acquainted with you, young man."

"Mrs. Elliott . . ."

She smiled. "Adelaide, please."

"Adelaide," Louis corrected, "this is Detective Clark and he will be driving the car.

Clark tipped his hat. "Pleased to meet you ma'am."

Louis continued. "Mou . . . I mean, your private investigator is in the other car with Detective Delaney and he'll be explaining what's going on to him."

"Oh, and where are we going?" she asked, a look of surprise on her face.

"To Coeur de l'eau," Louis answered. "It's their camp in Thibodaux. We think that's where they took Fleur and we've got to get there as soon as possible. It'll take about one and a half to two hours at least."

"Adelaide placed a gloved hand over his. "Then we must go at once, Louis. And I'm glad we will have the opportunity to talk along the way. There is a lot I have to say, so much I must tell you."

With the squad car leading the way out of town, the three cars formed a train and were soon heading through the city. But the limo took the lead after that.

Louis gave the detective directions. "Bayou Lafourche runs down Hwy 1 to the southeastern tip. I'll tell you where to get off and park. Then we've got to find a boat."

"Sounds good, Louis." Hands gripping the wheel, the detective answered without taking his eyes off the road.

Adelaide spoke up. "I'm so glad you've both met Sam. He's the private investigator I hired to look after Fleur. He began shadowing her the day after Florrie died, God rest her soul."

"Why?" Louis asked.

Clark glanced from the driver's seat.

Adelaide pulled a dainty handkerchief from her purse. "A promise."

"What kind of promise?"

"Why, to protect her, of course."

She dabbed at the corners of her eyes. "If I am to tell the story, I must tell the whole story. We might just have enough time between here and there." She smiled.

"Are you boys ready?"

Louis rapped on the driver's seat. "I'm ready, how about you?"

Clark nodded.

"Florrie and I were best friends growing up. But when she married Bernard D'Hemecourt, everything changed. She changed. But we remained friends in spite of that. She was most like her true self when we were together. Sweet and caring."

She brought the handkerchief up to her eyes again. "That's how I remember her."

Clark's voice carried from up front. "Ma'am, what does that have to do with Fleur's disappearance?"

She rapped on his seat with her cane. "Everything, young man."

Louis noticed him smile.

"Now where were we? Oh, that's right. Florrie. She married a man who knew very little about how to make money, only spend it. Bernard went to university of course, but didn't do well. Graduated with a general studies degree by the very skin of his teeth. But he made acquaintance with quite a few influential people and made connections." She tilted her head. "Oh he was and is, very good at social nuances."

"I can attest to that." Louis lamented.

"And," she continued, "He learned some interesting skills from the eclectic group he consorted with--hypnotism for one. Bernard learned it as a hobby at first, but he practiced his newfound skill with none of the respect and good manners most in that profession practice. He would hypnotize people for his own amusement, for parlor tricks at parties and I'm certain for other reasons and occasions."

A question came from Clark in the driver's seat. "Who?"

"I suppose by that you want to know if he hypnotized his wife or the children. The answer is yes. I was more aware of its effect on Florrie. She drew away from me for a time. Adelaide sniffled into the handkerchief. "Those were difficult years."

"Then, pardon my forwardness, but in light of the situation, may I ask what you're point is concerning our present circumstances?"

She paused to cough. "My point is that I think Bernard used hypnosis on Florrie and on the girls, though to what degree or purpose or for how long, I cannot say. He would pull a coin from out his pocket, an old Roman coin he acquired at an antique shop. All I know is that Florrie was not the same person for many years. And those girls, they didn't behave in a normal manner either. He seemed to have an uncanny control over them all. The plucky girl I grew up with, my dearest friend was gone, for a time at least."

Louis started to say something, but she continued. "When Florrie became ill and bedridden, he didn't seem to bother with her much anymore. We became close again during those years. She would ring me on the telephone most often. On the occasions when we did visit in person however, we had to resort to subterfuge. Bernard didn't want her talking to anyone. Florrie's servant, Philomene was instrumental in spiriting me in the house without Bernard's knowledge.

She brought the handkerchief to her mouth again, took a deep, raspy breath and coughed.

"Bernard's brother Rene' was a natural businessman." She pointed at Louis. "Rene' knew how to multiply a dollar and he made quite a lot of money. It was such a terrible tragedy when he and Eleanor died."

"Yes," Louis said. "It was."

"If Fleur hadn't gotten sick right before they left, she would have been with them on that trip as well. There but for the grace of God. But the accident may not have been an accident at all, not according to Florrie.

Louis could hardly believe his ears. "Are you telling us that Florrie believed her husband to be responsible for the accident that killed his brother and sister-in-law?"

"Oh yes. Indeed yes."

She began to cough.

"Maybe you need some water." He pointed out the window. "I noticed a gas station. Maybe they have a water fountain. We could stop."

She shook her head. "No I'm fine young man. Thank you." After a lengthy pause, she spoke again. "Florrie told me she'd discovered something questionable about her husband. Bernard hired a man, a mechanic to service the vehicle before Rene' and Eleanor's trip. The man was an ex-convict. She found out he'd served time in prison, but before that he worked as a mechanic."

"So Fleur's parents? His own brother?"

"As I said, Florrie believed her husband was responsible for their deaths."

Clark asked. "Do you know the name of the man? Why didn't she say something? And why didn't you go to the police with this information?"

"They came to an understanding. Fleur's life for Florrie's silence."

She let out a sigh. Adelaide pressed her face against the window and looked out, soaking up tears in her handkerchief. "Knowing that about him, that her husband was such a monster took all the fight out of her. Florrie stayed bedridden the entire time Fleur was away in college."

"I did as my friend asked. My goal in this matter is twofold, protection and evidence gathering. My late husband was an attorney, much like you Louis."

"Sam not only did a wonderful job of protecting Fleur, with the exception of the swamp debacle. Fleur's escape from the clutches of that horrid man could only be ascribed to divine intervention. But he did manage to collect a great deal of evidence to make a formidable case against Bernard D'Hemecourt." She turned to Louis. "Now I can go to the police and provide them with everything they need to convict the man."

But would it be too late? Louis uttered a prayer with his heart. Please God, I ask You to save her life. Give me another chance with her. I love Fleur so.

Louis bent over in his seat, hands clasped together. All I ask is one more chance.

Chapter Thirty-One
Bal Masque

Philomene slipped into the main house early in the morning with Rueben's help. She hid out in Florrie's old room, now closed off and cold, the furniture draped in white bedsheets, looking like a wintry haunt for ghosts and spooks. Perfect. The other servants would avoid it like the plague.

She stood near the door to listen to Bernard get ready in the adjoining bedroom. Whistling, then singing, "Shoo-Fly Pie and Apple Pan Dowdy, I never get enough of that wonderful stuff."

Rueben had informed her that Bernard had an appointment today, a practice for the carnival ball. It was to be an all-day affair, a dress rehearsal. With Alcide as his driver, the house would be free, with the exception of Cecelia. But they'd made careful plans for her. A phony note from Piper, detailing a list of items Cecelia needed to pick up for her from half a dozen different stores on Canal Street, all related to the upcoming bal masque and her role as queen. Collette was out on a bender somewhere. No one knew where. And the boy, poor little Rusty was still in the hospital recovering from a bad case of chickenpox.

She heard Bernard's feet tap down the staircase. A servant opened the front door, probably the new girl. Philomene eased a slice of sheer curtain at the window and looked out. Alcide held the car door open for Bernard, and took his place at the wheel.

Philomene sank in Florrie's rocking chair. Many nights' she'd spent in this chair, talking to the lonely woman she used to despise. But a curious thing happened when Florrie got sick. She changed. Started listening to the Bible verses Philomene read to her, wanting to know more.

She paused in mid-rock to the sound of something large scraping against the floor, the vibration of a low thud and the closing of a door. She resumed rocking.

Bernard didn't care about his wife at all. In fact, her being bedridden made her a liability. Even though he slept in the next room, the man hardly ever paid her a visit, and he didn't want other people visiting either. Discouraged them in fact. Told folks Florrie was too tired to receive visitors. That didn't stop Piper from visiting each day. The only time she ever saw any type of emotion in the girl was during these visits with her mama. The rest of the time, Piper was cold as an icehouse in January.

Bernard's edict didn't stop Florrie's friend Miz Adelaide from visiting neither. She always found a way to see her.

Her thoughts turned back to Fleur. She hadn't wandered off from the hospital as some suggested. Philomene knew in her heart of hearts the girl had been taken somewhere by someone. Frantic, Philomene had confessed her motive for working as a cleaning lady at the hospital to Dr. Peterson and told him everything she knew regarding Fleur, everything. To her surprise however, the seemed to know and understand Fleur as well, if not better than she knew her.

The answer to Fleur's whereabouts was somewhere in the house, more than likely in Bernard's private office, and Philomene aimed to find it. Piper was missing. So was Gerard, and now Fleur. Piper and Gerard must have taken her.

The signal, a tiny knock on the door, sounded. She turned the knob. Rueben smiled. "They gone fine'lee."

She whispered. "Did you move it?"

"Yes ma'am."

"Good." The "it" was the box, the harbinger of death. When she first started working at the house on St. Charles, she thought it was a tall tale, a ghost story folks whispered about. But the box was real enough. She'd seen it in Florrie's room right before she died. But Rueben couldn't keep secrets from her. When she'd found out that Bernard used him as the muscle to move it from its secret hiding place to terrify weak-hearted Florrie, a plan started to form in her head.

The two made their way down the servant's stairway, avoiding the creaking parts of each stair, fleet-footed the both of them, from years of sidestepping the D'Hemecourts. Rueben pulled a skeleton key from his pocket and opened the door to Bernard's office. They entered in and he shut the door slow but sure behind them.

"What we lookin' for Phil?" Rueban glanced around the room. Besides the desk with its infamous Oxblood leather chair and the two formal chairs in front of it for visitors, there was a wall of bookcases, a plaid easy chair by the window and next to that, an ornate globe of the world on a carved stand.

She pushed the chair out of the way and pulled at the main drawer. "Locked." Philomene sighed. "Dis is were he keep all his secret thangs. It's got to be here."

Rueban smiled. "Step aside girl. Papa got dis." He pulled a miniature Swiss Army Knife from his pocket and selected the smallest utensil, then went to work on the drawer. Within thirty seconds, he had the drawer open and Philomene wagging her head in disbelief.

She pulled the drawer open to the limit. Her throat almost closed up at the sight of the gun, remembering Bernard's threat so many years ago. There was a box of bullets next to it, and a harmless box of metal staples for the stapler. She found a packet of Black Jack chewing gum. Under a stack of speeding tickets were two faded birth certificates, one for Piper and one for Alcide, with Bernard listed as the father.

A brown paper bag caught her interest. She pulled it out and opened it. Inside were two short stacks of bills. Cash money. But she shuddered at what she found under the money inside the brown paper bag. Pictures. Dozens of photographs of men, some in situations with women or what looked like illegal activities. She thumbed through them, swallowing back the bile that rose in the back of her throat. She reached out for Rueben and grasped his arm. "You see dis? I recognize some of dese men. Know'd e'm fo' years. Look like dis how he making his money on the side. He blackmailin' folks. Long as nobody know he behind the blackmailin', he safe."

Eyes wide, his breath came slow. "I done seen a lot in my years. I know what dis man kin do." His voice cracked. "We got to leave, got to get outta here."

He grasped her shoulders. "Why don' you and me leave dis town and go and git married? We been sweet on one 'nutha fo a long time. Mebbe its time we do sumthin' bout it, git away from dese crazy folk."

With gentle force, she pushed his hands from her shoulders. "Rueben, you know how I feels concerning you, but I ain't leavin' til dat man is dealt wit. You know its de right thin' to do. We got to do right."

The shiny black telephone on the desk rang. They both jumped. Ring.

"Should we answer?"

"You do it." Rueban said. Ring. "Go on."

Philomene picked up the receiver and answered the telephone as she had for so many years before. "D'Hemecourt Residence." A man on the other end began speaking. Voice smooth and oily, she knew at once he was a salesman.

"I would like to speak with Piper D'Hemecourt please."

"Miz Piper is out of town."

"Oh that's right, she mentioned she'd be taking it for a spin."

Philomene swallowed hard, improvising in her mind. "Yes, ah, she was takin' it on a drive, Suh."

"To the family camp, that's it. Said she'd take it for a drive and we'd finalize the paperwork today.

Coeur de l'eau! Philomene held the phone out so Rueben could hear better. They both mouthed the name.

"Suh, may I pass her on a message from you when she returns?"

"Yes, if you could mention that Mr. Galliano, Roger Galliano called. I'm the man she purchased the automobile from. Is there a Mister D'Hemecourt?"

"Dere's her father."

"And his name?"

"Be'nard De'Hemecourt."

"Is he available?"

"No, he not here."

"Could you ask him to contact me as soon as possible? I'm sure there's a misunderstanding."

"A misunderstandin'?" Philomene looked to Reuben.

"Well--I'm embarrassed to say this over the telephone, but there's been a slight problem with the check she left with us." He coughed. "It seems the check has been declined."

Philomene took the man's number down and hung up the phone. "Dat's where dey took her. We got to tell da poll-ease."

He shook his head. "Not me. I ain' setting foot in no poll-ease station. Dey not gonna believe you an' me. Dey'll put de blame on us some kinna way. You mark my words."

Philomene considered his words. Reuben was right. But she had to try. An idea came to her. "What if I tells Docta Peterson? De pole-ease is gonna believe him."

He looked to the door, a bead of perspiration on his temple. "He gonna tell you ta put a egg on ya shoe an beat it."

She shook her head. "Naw, Docta Peterson a good man. He listen to folks."

"He gonna listen to us?" His eyes widened.

She put a hand on her hip and stared back. "Yeah, he listen to folk like us."

"Okay den. I truss wut you say." He shifted from foot to foot. "Now lets git outta here. I'm getting' the hebbie jebbies." Rueben walked to the door and put his ear against it.

"You won' hear nuthin' through dat doe, it's too thick. Hol' on a minute.'" She pushed the drawer fast, but stopped halfway when she spotted something. A picture of Rusty? She picked it up and turned it for Rueben to see.

He reeled backwards at the sight.

Red hair combed back neat as a pin, gaps in his teeth, freckles—a recent photograph.

"Sweet Jesus." She covered put her hands over her mouth. "It's God's good grace de chile' got sick when he did, or sure as the debbil carry a pitchfork, Ber'naud woulda laid his hands on him already."

"Why?"

"He want him dead too."

"Why he wanna kill a baby?"

"I'll tell you in a little bit. We gotta git out here first."

"You right, we gotta go." Rueben shook his head. "Dat car salesman ain' never gonna see that car agin."

An impulse overtook her good sense. Before she closed the drawer, she reached in and took the pistol and box of bullets and stuffed her pockets.

Chapter Thirty-Two
All The Comforts Of Home

Late in the afternoon, Fleur awoke, venturing down the stairs in her bare feet. She stood at the bottom of the stairs taking in the smell of coffee and chicory percolating on the stove. She caught a glimpse of and bacon and eggs sizzling in a black cast iron skillet.

Piper, apron tied at an awkward angle, hair askew, tended to whatever else she was cooking at the stove.

Fleur stood in the doorway. "You? Cooking?"

Piper turned around. Pale and drawn, she seemed quiet, without her usual spark. "I have many untapped, and hithertofore, unknown talents."

She gestured to the table and chairs in the kitchen. "Have a seat. I'll get your plate." Piper looked her up and down. "Nice outfit."

Last night Fleur had searched a dusty chest of drawers and found a pair of old pajamas to wear to bed. Though they hung on her like a tent with all the weight she'd dropped, at least she felt somewhat normal. A pair of ill-fitting pajamas was better than a hospital gown.

"Umm, smells delightful." Fleur sat down, yawning all the while figuring different ways of escape.

Dressed in dungarees and a plaid shirt, her hair pulled away from her face in a triangular scarf, Piper looked up from the stove. "I hope you're hungry. There's something about the bayou air that always invigorates me. I sleep like a log and eat like a horse."

"Why am I here?"

Piper stared out the window. "Coffee?"

"Why did you bring me here?"

Piper didn't answer. Instead she lifted the white metal drip pot with a thick dishtowel and brought it to the table, pouring her a hot, steaming cup.

"I told you last night. To protect you, to give you an option."

"Since when are you interested in protecting me?"

"Now Fleur, don't get yourself all upset."

Fleur stood eye to eye with her cousin. "Stop talking to me like I'm crazy. You and I both know I'm not."

"How did you sleep?"

"You and uncle had me committed to get your hands on my estate. Last night you effectively issued an ultimatum—leave or die. Am I correct?"

Piper continued unfazed. "You talked quite a lot. In fact, I could hear you from the next room. As if you were afraid--something about the ghost. Are you still afraid?"

Two could play that game. "Breakfast smells good. What is it?"

Piper's face tensed up. She returned to the stove and came back with an old scratched plate, two eggs over easy, two slices of bacon, sausage and toast, with a small bowl of grits.

Fleur stared at her food, her stomach deciding she was hungry. She also decided to answer. "I had that dream again, the same one I've had for years. I was back in my old room. Except this time, it was different. Instead of a ghost, it was a man, and he kept trying to come into my room at night. I couldn't see his face, though I tried."

Piper turned to stare out the window again. "Aren't you having any breakfast?"

"No."

Fleur broke the yolk with her fork. "Since I returned to New Orleans the dream is different. I see new details every time.. Dr. Peterson thinks I'm close to a breakthrough. That's why I need to get back."

Piper rested her elbows on the table. "What did you see this time?"

Fleur swirled the yellow yolk, chopped the egg in pieces and mixed it into her grits. She grinned, "I like to mix my egg with my grits."

"I know." Piper crinkled her nose in distaste. "Tell me what you saw."

Fleur stopped her fork in mid-air on the way to her mouth. She rested the fork in her plate. "This time, he took a step towards me and I could almost see his face. There was a fog over it, but the vapor started to draw away as if some unseen force were blowing on it."

Piper tended the stove. She lifted the round cover with a black metal rod and dropped a small block of wood into the flames below.

"I want to go back to New Orleans. It's not unusual for you to lie to me Piper, but this time you've gone too far. You've taken me here against my will. I have no intention of staying. Even if I have to swim back, I'm going home."

Piper laughed. "You know better than to swim in these waters."

Fleur pushed the plate away.

"All right. Do you want to hear the truth?" Piper sat down in a chair next to her, a companion to the rickety wooden chair Fleur sat in. She reached for a kitchen towel, threading it between her fingers.

"I was part of father's plan."

"How could you?"

"You know how persuasive he can be. He knew I what I wanted, needed. The money for a proper dowry and Louis."

"Louis?" Fleur held her breath for a moment.

"Father wants me to marry him. The reason I told him about your past was to get him to call off the elopement, not because I want him for myself."

Fleur knew Piper's guilt, but hearing it from her own lips was devastating. "He broke my heart!"

Piper brought the hankie to her eyes. Fleur watched in wonder.

"He didn't marry you, but he didn't stop loving you either. Why do you think he comes to see you?"

She shrugged. "Guilt."

"You little fool. Can't you read his eyes? He loves you and you can't even recognize it. When he and I were dating, he never looked at me that way."

Confused, Fleur tried to sort out what Piper told her. What a shock to see her cousin cry, and even more so, to tell the truth! She wondered about Louis, remembered the hurt in his eyes when they'd said goodbye. He had lost weight and there were circles under his eyes. She'd noticed all that, but her mind, so foggy at the time failed to see the significance. Philomene had tried to tell her as well. A slow, steady, warmth began to creep into her heart. After all this, could he still care?

"Piper, thank you for telling me the truth. I know in my heart you're telling me the truth. But I want to know why all of a sudden decided to do something decent. Why are you helping me now?"

Piper raised her head and closed her eyes. A tear escaped out one side and rolled down her cheekbone. "I hate my life. I want to leave the house and go and live somewhere, anywhere--with my husband."

Fleur pushed her hair back. "What husband? You're married?"

Piper brought her hands to her face, the balled up hankie nestled in between. "And I'm pregnant with his child."

"Pregnant? Who is he?"

Piper jumped up and ran to the dish bowl. Her body heaved in an arc. She vomited.

Fleur came up behind her. She ran a kitchen towel under the faucet and gave it to her. Piper sank to the floor, wet towel against her face. Fleur sat beside her.

"Jack."

Shocked, Fleur found her voice. "Louis mentioned him. Said you told him about someone you'd been dating in secret because your father didn't approve."

Piper nodded, the towel falling away from her mouth. "Yes, that's right. And now I've found myself in a family way. What am I going to do?"

She brought her knees to her chest and began to tremble. Fleur drew close and wrapped her arms around her.

"This is such a shock. But if you're married, why worry? Tell your father the truth."

She shook her head. "We can't yet. He's in the service."

"Still?"

"He's a career officer."

"But I thought—well—Louis led me to believe your fellow was in sales."

Piper dabbed her eyes. "He's mistaken. Jack is career military."

Fleur studied her. "But can't you join him wherever he's stationed?"

"No, I can't."

"Why not?"

"I can't tell you. Stop asking."

Piper grabbed her hand. "Listen to me, Fleur. I've wanted to tell you this for a long time."

"Tell me what?"

"When it happened to you, you fell apart. Didn't know who you were for a time. After the stillbirth, you were traumatized. At first, you didn't even remember you were there with the nuns or that you'd been pregnant."

"I know that."

She grasped both of Fleur's hands in her own. "It was Fleming."

"Collette's husband? How could that be?" Fleur covered her mouth.

"Back when you were a teenager, he used to do work for father. He was at the house quite a bit. He used to look at you all the time, but Philomene kept a close eye on you. She kept him away."

Fleur took a scant breath. "Why did I go with the man? I don't remember any of it."

Piper swallowed hard. "

Dizzy, Fleur tried to stand. The room began to spin. A bright light covered her eyes and she felt herself melting to the floor. She heard her name being called.

"Fleur, Fleur!"

She realized it was Piper calling. But she was already gone. Floating again. Drifting slow, lazy. As always, she drifted in through her bedroom window, the dormer on the east side. White curtains fluttering like ship sails, a pink and white storm lantern glowing on the bureau. She came to rest in her bed. Soft linens that smelt of the sun, she nuzzled into her pillow.

She heard the door creak open and almost at once, a heaviness pervaded, overwhelmed. Smothering under the weight of it, she tried to scream. But Fleur could barely breathe under the crush.

She strained to open her eyes. Soon enough, the gentle breeze from the fluttering of her lashes blew the fog away and the face over hers came into focus. Fleming LaSalle.

"Fleur?"

Piper tapped Fleur's face. She felt a cold compress on her forehead. Moving, by sheer force of will, she struggled to sit up, leaning against a small bank of kitchen drawers.

"Fleur!"

She opened her eyes and stared into Piper's. "I remember."

Eyes puffy, outlined in red, Fleur gushed out the words. "It all makes sense now. The dreams! Dr. Peterson was right. The breakthrough he told me about. That man, he . . ."

Fleur hung her head at her knees, her breathing labored.

Piper continued. "People always thought you were strange. They whispered. Said you were crazy. She threw the towel away from her. "But I knew the truth all along."

"You lived in blissful ignorance. How often I wished I were you. And how often I wished my memory would disappear as yours did. Do you know why mother slept so well? She was drugged. Father used to bring his women to the house late at night. Whenever father needed her out of the way, he had your sweet little Philomene bring her warm milk with knock out drops in it. How do you like that?"

"But Philo brought me milk at night."

"Yes your precious Philo brought you milk, but there was a different ingredient in mothers. With the exception of one night . . ."

"What do you mean? What are you saying?"

Piper stood and walked to the window. "One night I waited in the kitchen on the pretense of conversation as she was heating the milk on the stove. When Philomene was distracted, I switched the cups."

"What? Why would you?"

Piper wrapped her arms around her shoulders. "Because I owed Fleming money. Like father, I had to beg, borrow or steal to keep up appearances. Mother was useless. Father only cared about himself. Fleming wanted something in return, something I was unwilling to give. So I gave him you instead."

Fleur drew a hand to her mouth and began to weep. "Why would you do that? Did you hate me that much?"

Piper wiped her eyes, as if to stop the flow.

"I didn't, don't hate you." She leaned forward on the table and buried her face in her hands. "I was sorry afterward, truly sorry. However, I began to reason with myself. No one would ever know. You wouldn't remember any of it."

"Months later, the family discovered you were pregnant and everything changed."

Fleur cried. "Your parents accused me of horrible things, and-and I couldn't deny any of it. I couldn't remember."

Piper fell to her knees. "Please forgive me. I've lived with the secret, with the guilt all these years. And now that I'm in the same condition, I understand."

Fleur turned her face away. "I don't know if I can right now. It's too much at once. Overwhelming." The two sat in silence, the solace of tears between them. After a time, Fleur rose to her feet. Resolve in her voice, she commanded, "I need to go back."

Piper nodded. "All right. The boatman is supposed to return this afternoon. You'll need to put on something decent."

"The nurse made we wear . . ."

"I know, look in my room, there should be some in the top drawer." Piper stood as well and reached for some wood and a match. "I'll put the kettle on. I could use a cup of tea. We've been bawling so much, I feel shaky."

Fleur wiped her face with her hands. "Very well. I'll be back in a minute." Fleur walked the short flight to Piper's room and found a pair of beige pants and a white square-shouldered blouse in dotted Swiss. She found a light jacket in the closet and put it on.

Since she and Piper were almost the same size, everything fit well. Eager to get going, she bounded down the steps and found Piper out on the porch overlooking the water.

"Tea?"

She drew the collar up on the jacket. "Yes, please."

Piper, wearing a white oversized cableknit sweater, seemed warm enough in the damp air. She poured Fleur a cup from a worn teapot.

The camp played host to every worn dish, utensil or piece of furniture from the household. That used to be part of its charm. Now in the state of disrepair the camp was in, the worn and cracked tea service only added to the sorrowful mood.

Fleur sat next to Piper in an Adirondack chair and sipped.

"No one's going to believe I'm married. They'll say I have a child out of wedlock too. Funny how our sins come back to haunt us, but I guess I deserve it."

"But you'll be living far away. Perhaps somewhere exotic, depending on where he's stationed. What branch of the service is Jack in?"

Piper shifted to her side. Facing Fleur, she answered. "The Air Force." She tipped her cup and drained it. "I think I feel well enough now to eat."

"Good, remember, you're eating for two." Fleur smiled.

Piper got up and started off. "Stay and soak up the sun. You're pale. You've been cooped up in that hospital room for too long."

"Okay, thanks."

"He should be here by then."

The winter sun glistening off the bayou was warm, pleasant. Later in the year, and the heat might be intolerable. She closed her eyes and thought of her days as a child soaking in the sunshine, light filtering through her lids like a Chinese lantern, a soft orange glow--warm and full of promise. With her eyes closed she could hear the sound of the water lapping up against the dock, birds chirping in the trees above, the creak of wet wood, and the clipped buzz of mosquito hawks flying around. Dozens of them, iridescent wings, delicate bodies like butterflies, circling.

She thought of her predicament and Philomene's words came to mind, "you kin invite the Lord Jesus into you heart an' become a new creacha in Christ. He forgives you your sins an' den you kin forgive others fo' what dey done ta you 'cause o' de love o' Christ in your heart. De love of God gonna ova flow like a fountain. You'll see."

Exactly what she needed--a fresh start. God had proven Himself to her time and again. Louis seemed to set a high store by God and Philomene was most certainly a woman of faith. Her parents served Him as well. Perhaps the time had come.

Fleur rose from the chair and sank to her knees on the deck of the rough wooden porch. "It's hard for me to forgive a man who could do the things that he did, but your book says we are to forgive and Philo told me too. In the swamp, you answered my prayers when I called out for help." She took a deep breath and forced out the words. "I forgive Fleming. What he did to me was monstrous! But I know I must."

And Piper, I forgive her too and I ask you to forgive me of all my sins and come and live in my heart. I want to be the new creature in Christ Philomene told me about. I want to start fresh in life. You are the Lord of my life and the true love of my life dear Jesus."

Tears rolled down her face, this time, tears of joy. Fleur felt light as a feather, as if a load of rocks had been removed from her back." She hopped to her feet, looking skyward to smile. I must tell Piper. She started toward the kitchen and heard a muffled shout. She ran through the door and stopped short. Piper, tied and gagged sat at the kitchen table in the same chair she'd sat in earlier--her eyes wide, terrified, imploring.

"Who?"

Before she could finish asking, strong arms grabbed her from behind and dragged her to the other chair. She was no match to his strength. Gerard worked with speed and efficiency. Before she could move or run, her hands and shoulders were strapped with rough hemp ropes to the chair. He gagged her mouth and coiled ropes around her ankles as well.

With both women tied, Gerard straightened up and smoothed his hair back. He removed their gags and leaned back against the kitchen wall, a smile on his face.

Piper spoke first. "Untie us!"

"Why should I do that?" He lifted her chin with his index finger. "Think of the fun I could have." He grabbed her neck with one hand and tightened his grip, pressing his lips hard on hers until she struggled to breathe. In an instant he released her and took a step back. "See what I mean?"

Piper, her face pale, strained to catch her breath. She spat, contempt spiking from her eyes.

He lifted a hand as if to strike her.

"Leave her alone. She's with child." Fleur shouted.

He squinted in disbelief. "With child? You mean her little tete'a tete with the mystery man produced a child? How touching, although I can't imagine her as a mother. A 'gator'd be a better mother than her."

Fleur watched as he circled a peculiar swagger around the table, enjoying their confinement and the power he had over them. He paused in front of her chair, resting his hands on the chair arms, "Little lady, you and I have unfinished business." His eyes traveled down to her form-fitting pants. "What a sweet little ensemble you have on. I can't wait to see what's underneath." With that, he grabbed her head in his hands and brought his mouth close to hers, his breath foul.

Fleur screamed. "Get away from me. Stop it. You're insane."

His face flushed red. Gerard ran his index finger down her neck to her décolletage and settled at the first shirt button. "C'mon now. Those are harsh words from such a pretty mouth. Besides, ain't you the one who spent time at the funny farm?"

He swiped the sweat off his upper lip with the back of his hand. Gerard loosened the first button, a grin on his face.

Suddenly, a heavy rap and vibration sounded against the house.

Gerard lowered his hand and took a breath between clenched teeth. "Girls, it looks like we've run out of time." As he spoke he began unraveling the ropes binding them to the chairs, but kept their hands and feet bound separately.

Piper sneered. "When my father finds out what you've done, you'll wish you were dead."

"Oh I doubt he'll find out. You see Mr. Longfellow has a long-standing grudge against Bernard D'Hemecourt. He's not quite the ally your father thinks he is."

"Who is he?" Fleur asked.

"You've already met him, Sugar. He's the one who took you here."

Piper drew in a breath. "The man in the boat?"

"That's right."

"Why would you do this?" Fleur asked.

"Why not? Your father shipped me off to the boondocks so I'd be out of his hair. And my father died in the meantime. Not that I cared about going to the funeral but I would certainly like to return and collect my inheritance. If I get rid of all the witnesses, I won't have a thing to worry about. Mr. Longfellow has proved to be a very encouraging fellow. I believe I'll get rid of him last."

"How can you possibly get rid of everyone and believe you won't be caught?"

Gerard held his arm high, in dramatic pose. "It was a fire--a terrible fire. The entire family was trapped in the house." He sighed and let his head fall. "A tragedy."

"You'd—you'd set the house on fire?" Fleur asked.

"Not me. It was the gas stove. You see, there was a leak. Merciful in that they all died in their sleep first. But then the gas ignited."

Monster! Fleur thought of Collette, of Rusty, of Philomene and the servants. Even Bernard and Alcide didn't deserve to die that way.

He wiped his nose on his shirt. "No more fun and games." Gerard looked them over. "It's a shame, you know." He ran his palm down Fleur's leg.

Her body stiffened in response. To her surprise, he withdrew it.

"As I said, Mr. Longfellow is here and the man is all business. That was his paddle no doubt against the piling under the house. I've learned a lot from him." He repositioned and tightened the bandanas around their mouths, and stood at the door. "I'll be back to get you soon. Gotta load you girls onto the rowboat one at a time. Then we'll all shove off together and scout out the perfect spot." He held onto the doorframe with both hands and angled his head in her direction. "And this time Fleur, I'll stick around to make sure those gators get their fill of you."

Fleur and Piper looked to one another for comfort but there was no comfort to be had, save for the expressions in their eyes. Fleur did the only think she knew to do. She looked up and prayed with all her heart.

Father, help us!

Chapter Thirty-Three
Alligator Pear

A view of the light blue sky above, pink clouds swelling with new rain, made the trip seem almost normal--serene. Long shadows crept across the water, carrying the stillness that comes before the change in shifts. Before the creatures of the sun find rest in the dark night and the nocturnal creatures stir to begin their wanderings. The sound of the oars was rhythmic, calming but for the fact of the two men behind them and their intentions.

Longfellow was indeed an old man, with a hardboiled face, tanned to leather by the sun and a hooked nose. Piper nudged her at the sight of the man, the very man who ferried them to the camp. He sat in the middle with his back to them as he rowed--bony shoulders protruding like a gargoyle. Longfellow stared back at them once, lingering for a moment, as if to savor the silent revenge he would have on Bernard D'Hemecourt.

In the center of the boat, the stench of tin buckets bloodied with fish gore nauseated her. Gerard had set Piper next to her on the floor of the boat at the stern. Their hands bound in front and feet coiled tight made it impossible to find a comfortable position. Her hands were beginning to go numb but she felt something touch her wrist. At first she thought Piper reached out or comfort, but she began to work on the ropes that bound Fleur's hands. Pulling, loosening.

The men maneuvered the boat down a narrow channel--their destination, the swamp.

Fleur wondered at the sounds of strange birds, the howls of animals in the tangle of vines, tropical undergrowth and thicket along the banks on either side of them. Curious creatures in the black water leapt up in arcs and down again before they could be seen. Splishes, and ever-widening circles in the obsidian flow--the squeaks of baby alligators amid lotus blossoms floating on the surface.

The rowboat passed under a wild alligator pear tree. Green fruits hung from its branches in abundance, the outside of the fruit rough as a gator's hide. She remembered something Philomene told her about alligator pears. What was it? She strained to remember.

"Fleur, you is like de alligator pear,
". . . tough on de outside an' soft on de inside."
In the mirror of water ahead, she began to make out dark shapes, something in the murk like moss-covered rocks that moved. Alligators, a half dozen of them at least, some their eyes cresting the water, others lounging on the muddy bank. Unusual to see so many concentrated in one small area unless they'd been feeding. Then to her horror, she realized what the tin buckets were for. What they'd planned was unimaginable. Most likely, Longfellow had chummed the water.

Fleur closed her eyes and began to pray. There's got to be a way out of this. Lord, you showed me the way out of the swamp before and you sent help. Please send help right now. We're in desperate need.

When she opened her eyes, she felt a minute vibration underneath the boat. It seemed to come from the water below. She looked to Piper. The low hum of a motor!

The two men paddled faster at first, casting fearful looks behind. Fleur was unable to turn her head to look behind, but Piper, in a more favorable position could see. Unable to speak for the gags covering their mouths, Fleur trained her eyes on Piper's as her cousin gazed out behind the boat. She had to blink the water from them to focus. Fleur watched Piper's eyes as a slow light crept, then sparkled through the green of her iris, dancing the golden flecks. Fleur could see it in her eyes. Like a smile. A leap for joy.

As the low hum grew louder, Longfellow motioned to Gerard and the boat slowed, still gliding from the forward motion. Gerard, who sat at the bow, jammed a paddle into the water to slow the motion and bring the boat to a full stop but the waves created by the approaching boats had begun to rock the rowboat and propel it ever farther. The two men looked at one another.

A horn from the closest boat sounded. Longfellow and Gerard sprang into action, the old man stepping with surprising agility across the boat towards the women, and Gerard staying at the bow to keep the balance. The old man grabbed Fleur by the ropes on her feet and hands and lifted. Longfellow seemed determined to have his revenge.

Terror surged through her body. She squirmed and twisted. Heard shouts. The horn. She knew her only chance was to wriggle from his grasp. Fleur felt the tremble of his muscles. Though strong, he couldn't handle her contortions for long. She arched her back and twisted hard to the right and she fell from his arms back into the boat.

The force of her fall rocked the boat and the old man tottered for a brief second. A look of utter horror on his face, he lost his footing and plunged overboard. His fall attracted the alligators and though he bobbed to the surface screaming for help, the tan of his face was replaced by the blanche of raw fear. A second later a violent jerk pulled him down by the legs, down under the water. A feeding frenzy followed, of blood and flesh and unspeakable gore.

But Fleur didn't look at the scene for long. When she dropped from his arms, her leg hit the slat of the wooden seat. The impact snapped a bone in her leg. She writhed in pain, trying hard to keep from vomiting. If she did, she would surely choke to death.

Gerard had managed to steady the boat. He stood arms raised and began to move toward the center.

A command sounded. "Stop where you are."

But Gerard kept moving. One hand reached into his boot. She knew his intentions. At this point he had nothing to lose. Due to the fall, Fleur was closest to him. He grabbed her by the hair and pulled her to him. She moaned, waves of intense pain causing her agony. He held a knife to her throat. From this new vantage she could see two motorboats behind them. The police and Louis at bow. The sight of his face brought her instant comfort. Louis's hands clutched at the rim of the boat.

"Let me go and nobody gets hurt. You keep me here and this little lady goes overboard to feed the gators." He smiled. "I still have her." He glanced at Piper. "You know I'll have this one over the side before you can get to her."

"Raise your hands or we'll shoot."

"I doubt that. You might hit the little lady."

To show how earnest he was, he set his arms underneath and lifted Fleur. He looked from Fleur to Louis, their gaze intent on one another. "Awh, how touching." He pouted at Piper. "Darling, isn't it nice to see these two lovebirds?"

Louis gave Fleur a look that said everything that needed saying. Forgiveness. Love. She wondered if Louis could see the difference in her, if he recognized the new creature in Christ. Or would she die without anyone else on earth knowing?

"Cease what you are doing and give yourself up," the police ordered.

Unlike the old man's, Gerard's arms were steady, but she felt a surge of energy in them before it happened. All of a sudden he hoisted her up and over the side.

She hardly had time to take a breath before hitting the water. The cold of it shocked her at first. She thrashed to the surface but couldn't stay up. The gag held water in her mouth.

***

They'd left Adelaide at the dock with Sam, instructing him to call for an ambulance just in case. Whether serendipity or divine appointment, the group happened upon two men with motorboats who'd just arrived for a weekend of fishing. Louis was grateful to God. The anxious trip to the camp would have been even more so if they had arrived to find no one there. But he'd spotted the rowboat in the distance and with the help of binoculars recognized Gerard at the helm.

The second he saw him hoist Fleur into the air, Louis had his coat and shoes off and jumped overboard. *Father, help me. You shut the mouths of the lions for Daniel. Please shut the mouths of these reptiles for us in Jesus' name.*

In a matter of seconds, he reached in and grabbed her from behind. He pushed the gag down but she wasn't breathing. He kept swimming, making his way back sure and steady to the motorboat. The policemen began firing shots into the water around him. The power of the reptiles surged through the water. He could feel their strength in the currents when they changed direction.

They made it to the boat. Delaney and Clark hauled up Fleur first and began administering mouth-to-mouth resuscitation as they released her bonds. Halfway over the side of the boat, Louis looked back.

But the alligators were busy feeding on their latest victim, Gerard.

The officers helped Louis over the side difficult with wet clothing. "The girl in the boat pushed him over with her feet."

But Louis barely heard what they said. Fleur was coughing up water.

Chapter Thirty-Four
Bete' Noire'

Bernard's roadster was parked at a haphazard angle outside the structure. In addition, a side door to the warehouse was open. A small windowpane broken nearest to the doorknob, indicated he might have gone inside and that something might be awry with his frame of mind.

Hot on his trail, they'd followed him as he fled the house, still in costume, leaving his distraught driver behind. From home, he'd lost them briefly on a wild chase, buying mere minutes before they caught up. Now, the carnival king would answer for his crimes.

Louis looked around. Curious choice the man had stopped here of all places, a warehouse for Mardi Gras floats in Algiers, where a local artist named Blaine Kern created most of the fanciful creations.

He'd left Fleur's side in the hospital, answering the invitation from Delaney and Clark to join them in Bernard's arrest. Adelaide and Piper stayed with her, though Fleur had been administered strong pain medication after her bone was set.

Louis wondered if anyone else could hear his heart thumping.

They entered from a side door. One of the officers found the board and threw on the master switch. The entire warehouse lit ablaze. A cavernous room occupied by no less than ten Carnival floats, the sight of mythical creatures, beasts of prey, magical trees and many other fanciful designs in bright colors drew the eye to a hundred places at once. Nonetheless, all eyes were soon drawn to one area in particular.

In the center of the warehouse, atop the King's float, Bernard, the "Mystick" ruler sat in a drunken sprawl upon his royal throne. His kingly skirt rode high on one side, legs squeezed into white tights hanging over one chair arm.

Bleary-eyed, Bernard lifted his head and watched from a sideways stance enter the warehouse. Garish swathes of rouge splotched over his jowls. Blue eye powder smeared above his eyes, dark liner over his lids as well. As they approached, he lifted a whiskey bottle in a mock toast, then to his mouth and took a long swig.

"Sooo," he slurred. "You fown me a lassst."

The detective gestured with his hand to the officers to circle round the float. An officer moved to secure the exit.

Louis stood before the float, Bernard staring down at him.

"Don look a' me 'at waay. Comus'is dah god of revelry, ya kno'. An' drinkin' an' dally-yance." Bernard hiccoughed in succession, then straightened up in the throne and broke out in song.

"Shoosh fly pies an' able pan dowdee. I can't get 'nuf..." His eyes closed and he sank back against the chair.

"Mr. D'Hemecourt?" The detective called him again. "Mr. D'Hemecourt?"

He jolted forward, head jerking. "Whaa" He smacked his lips together. "Oh, iz you again."

The throne seemed to tremble under his weight. Louis guessed the throne had a wooden frame covered with paper mache and gold foil or leaf, strong enough for carnival day, but perhaps not for the abuse Bernard was inflicting on it. Some of the decorative papers and embellishments had come off on the wall behind the throne, no doubt from his drunken antics.

"Schpeaking of dally yance, Mister Rue-so, whaddya think of my daughter, eh?" He tried to point at Louis, but his index finger moved up, down and to the side as he spoke. "If you marry Pip-Pip-Piper, you'll get a good—hiccough—woman." He continued. "A good wife."

Louis looked over at the detective.

The detective stepped forward. "Mr. D'Hemecourt, I'm afraid I have some news to convey to you."

Bernard jerked his head in the direction of the detective and tried to rouse himself off the chair, but missed the chair arm with his hand and fell forward on his knees. "What?"

Angry at the paper he found himself mired in, he began to lash and tear out at it with his arms. He threw off the crown, then pulled and yanked off the beard and brows held in place by spirit gum.

"Mr. D'Hemecourt, are you all right?"

He didn't answer at first. After a drunken delay, he responded, eyes wide like an animal caught by car headlights. "Whadya say?"

"Mr. D'Hemecourt, I'm afraid I have some rather bad news to convey to you. Your business partner, we believe he passed away today."

"What?"

Part of the beard hair stuck to his right hand. He tried to shake it off until he heard what was said. "P-passed a-way? Did you say what I think you said?"

"Yes, Mr. D'Hemecourt." The detective stole a glance toward Louis, who nodded. "He fell into the bayou and, ugh, drowned today. He attempted to murder both your niece, Fleur and your daughter Piper. "

Upon hearing the news, he stumbled to his feet, gesturing with his scepter. "Piper's not s'posed ta die. Dat's pure nonsensh."

"Supposed to be Fleur, you say? What about your niece?" The detective took a notepad and pencil out his pocket.

Bernard swayed his head to the right and to the left. "Fleurs the one whose s'ppos'd to die, not my girl. You're mistaken. Dat's right."

He took a few steps and without warning, slipped, falling forward onto a large paper mache rose, smashing through the wire mesh underneath. Blood gushed from a wound on his hand.

"Let me help you." Louis and an officer ran to retrieve a rolling stepladder nearby. But before they could climb it to mount the float, Bernard jolted to his feet and back to the throne. Blood leaked from the wound on his hand. He settled down on the chair.

"Stop. Don' come near." He held up his scepter and waved it in a slow, shaky demi-circle. "The King," he paused to form the words, "has spoke." He struggled to hold up his head. "Hecsh really dead, eh? An' Fleur lives. Well. Well. Well." He belched.

Tremors shook him. "Do you know what aye found in mah rome?" He held his arms out wide. "A biiiiiig box. So big." His mouth curled inward. "Ats nawt good." His head waved forward and back. "Means I'm a dead man." He laughed. "That's what it's s'posed to mean, anyway."

The detective signaled to the officers behind the float. But all at once, Bernard pulled a shotgun from the side of the throne. "I said don' come nany closer." The officers stopped in their tracks. The detective motioned for Louis and the officer beside him to back away.

Bernard's head swayed and he swallowed hard. "All my life, I always had second bessst. Never enough of what I needed." He rolled his tongue out as if peanut butter were sticking to the roof of his mouth." The scepter fell by his feet as he balled his hand into a fist. "Dats why I learned to take what I wanted." Tears began to roll down his face, cutting new swathes through the thick stage makeup. He reached upward with both hands, a shotgun high in the air and began to cry out loud. Crisscrossing his arms over his head, he wiped his sleeves over his face. "All I wanted, eva wanthed wasch to be king." He pointed the shotgun into the air and fired at the ceiling. A loud bang sounded as the weapon discharged.

The reflex from the shot propelled him over the side of the float, his body a crumpled heap. Louis watched as a policeman checked for a pulse. Bernard head had made contact with the bare concrete below. A flower of blood bloomed beneath his head.

Chapter Thirty-Five
Signs Of Life

Fleur woke up in the hospital again--grateful to be alive and breathing. The minute her eyes fluttered open to Louis, she said a silent prayer of thanks to God.

Pain ached up and down her leg where she'd broken the bone. She moaned in the process of trying to sit up.

"Maybe you shouldn't try to move. Let me call the nurse."

She looked him over, noticing how different he looked. Leaner, sorrowful, and there was something in his eyes. Confidence? Faith.

"No please. Not yet." She tried to smile through the pain as he helped her sit up. Fleur noticed a pitcher of ice water on the bedside table. "Would you mind? I'm so very thirsty."

He moved to pour her a glass. She drained it in one swallow then handed it back to him. He placed it on the tray table.

"Ah, thank you, I feel much better." She took his hands in hers, noticing he wore a workman's shirt, and a pair of scruffy pants. "Louis, something happened to me when I was at the camp."

He froze at her words. "I know what happened. Piper told us everything."

"No, not that. It's something else." She paused, her concern for Piper overtaking her desire to tell Louis her news.

"Before you tell me your news, I must tell you some other sad news."

"What is it?" Her eyes searched his.

"Your uncle ..."

He explained the chase and encounter at the float warehouse, and how her uncle sustained a fatal wound to his head when he fell.

"Piper? How is she? The last time I saw her was in the boat right before I went over." Fleur looked at the empty bed next to her.

"The detectives are with her now.

She closed her eys. "How awful for her! I can scarce believe it myself. She's in a delicate way, you know."

"What do you mean?" Louis had a perplexed look on his face.

"She's with child."

"What?"

"She confided in me that she and Jack were married, in secret and that she's with child."

A look of shook registered on his face. "The doctor didn't mention anything about that. Some cuts and bruises, but otherwise, fine. That's what he said."

"Can I see her?"

Adelaide thought it best to take her back to New Orleans with her. Piper needs someone to care for her, to help her through this, and you're in no state to do so."

"I don't know what state she'll be in after hearing the news about her father."

"Could you ask Piper to come to me? I'd like to talk to her."

"Certainly."

He left the room to retrieve Piper. A few minutes later, she entered, surveying the room with a quick glance. Hair pulled away from her face in a severe knot, she wore a simple brown skirt and white blouse. She sank to a small metal chair next to the bed. "You have enough flowers in here to open a florist shop."

"It appears so." Her heart took a tumble at the sight of her cousin. Dark circles eclipsed her eyes. She reached for Piper's hand. "How are you?"

Piper allowed her to hold her hand for a moment but withdrew it. "I'm not sure." She fiddled with a gold chain about her neck, running it through her fingers round and round. "I'm rather numb about Father's passing. Part of me is grieving, the other part is glad. Isn't that awful to say?"

"Under the circumstances, it's quite understandable."

"Aside from that shocking news, Adelaide and I have had some interesting discussions."

"Really?"

"She seems to think that father had some sort of control over us through hypnosis. Fleur reached for another pillow and tucked it behind her so she could sit up straighter. She winced at pain the movement caused. "I'm all right. There are some interesting thoughts on hypnosis and control."

"Oh . . ." Piper leaned forward, resting her palm on the bed."

"Dr. Peterson was planning on sessions of therapeutic hypnosis in my treatment, but we never got to that point. He told me hypnosis would aid in unlocking the lapses in memory. He told me that a hypnotist can utilize hypnosis and persuasion for both good and bad purposes. A person might become more willing to do what the hypnotist says and accept their suggestions, but the person retains his or her own free will. A hypnotist cannot force anyone to go against morals or values."

"You mean, like commit murder or rob a bank or something on that order?"

"Yes, that's right."

"Then maybe Miz Adelaide mistook our behavior as evidence that we were under his hypnotic control. But maybe father did make suggestions to us. You know how he likes to get his way with things. I know he used it on mother."

Fleur winced. "I saw him hypnotize her once, though I didn't realize that's what it was."

Piper leaned forward and stared at Fleur, face-to-face, searching her eyes. She pulled a mirror out of her purse and held it up for Fleur to see herself. "There's joy on your face. You don't look as if you've suffered at all." She turned the mirror on herself. "I look like a wreck and I feel like one too." She held up her hand "See how my hand is trembling. Can you believe it?"

But Fleur noticed how shaky the smile was. Something about Piper wasn't right.

Louis stepped into the room. "Piper, Miss Adelaide is waiting in the car. One of the police officers volunteered to drive you both back and see you get home safe."

"Oh yes, of course." She stood but Fleur reached out to clasp her arm.

"Piper, I love you."

She lingered, eyes on her cousin. "How can you tell me that? I've done appalling things to you. I did everything I could to ruin you."

"I forgive you."

Piper shook her head and ran past Louis through the door.

"Louis?" Fleur implored.

He ran into the hall. Fleur heard him call after her. Louis walked back in shaking his head. "Let her go. Perhaps Adelaide will be able to help her through her grief."

Louis sat on the edge of the bed. "I think I know what you were about to tell me earlier." He kissed her hand and held it close to his lips. "Now our joy is complete."

"And now you need to tell me what I can't recall. I'm quite keen on finding out what happened after the old man dropped me and broke my leg. All I can remember from that point is when Gerard threw me overboard. How did I survive the alligators?"

He leaned close to her and rested his cheek against hers. "I didn't think about the danger. I jumped in. I had to save you."

"But you could have. . ." Tears welled in her eyes.

"You too."

"I couldn't bear it if you'd died trying to help me." Fleur stroked his hair.

He turned his lips to her cheek. "But I didn't. God protected us."

"Louis, I love you. I've never loved anyone else and I never let anyone else love me."

"And you are my dear heart," he whispered in her ear.

"Ah ahm." Somebody cleared their throat in order to make their presence known.

"You seem to be recovering."

Louis sat up. "Tom. Thanks for coming.

Dressed in the uniform of a plainclothes detective, a dark suit, tie and hat, he removed it before he leaned over to kiss Fleur's cheek. "Thanks for being alive young lady." He clapped his hands. "You two deserve a standing ovation." He pointed at Fleur. "The damsel in distress and," he pointed at Louis, "the hero."

He rubbed his hands together. "I tell you, I wouldn't have had the guts to jump into that water with all those reptiles. Frankly, I thought you were a goner. But here you are." He waved his hat.

Delaney winked at Fleur. "If you ever have a doubt that this man loves you, think back to that day and you'll never second guess him."

"Oh, I'll never doubt him again." She put her arms around his shoulder and drew Louis close"

"Say Louis, I wanted to tell you earlier. That's some getup you're wearing. The boots are what top it off though." He laughed.

"I had to buy some at a general store since my suit was ruined. Are you telling me I don't look like a promising young attorney in this?"

"I could tell you that, but I'd be lying through my teeth."

Delaney and Louis broke out laughing. Fleur smiled. "I'd laugh too boys, but it'd hurt too much."

When the laughter subsided, Delaney fell silent. Hat in his hands, Delaney held the flat side against his stomach and circled the band with fingers. "I hate to have to tell you all this, but Alcide is still on the loose. Clark is following a couple of good leads, but until then you two need to look over your shoulder. With carnival season in full swing, the department is pretty busy."

Louis sighed. "Understood."

"And there's something else, probably nothing, but—well—we couldn't find any remains. Though he couldn't have survived. Nobody could have."

"Oh Louis." Fleur buried her face in his sleeve.

Louis stared back at the detective. "But we did."

Chapter Thirty-Six
Little White Houses

A week later, they gathered in the Saint Louis Cemetery to lay Bernard to rest in the family tomb. Fleur sat in a wheelchair, her leg in a white plaster cast, handkerchief in her hand, Louis at her side.

"*Domine Iesu, dimitte nobis debita nostra, salva nos ab igne inferiori . . .*"

Piper and Adelaide sat together in the first of two rows of wooden folding chairs set up at the tomb. Collette sat behind them, in an uncharacteristic state of quiet. She'd left Rusty at home in the care of the servants. The child had come home from the hospital less than a week ago and his doctors deemed it too risky to have him exposed to the outdoor air during his recovery.

"*. . .perduc in caelum omnes animas, praesertim eas, quae misericordiae tuae maxime indigent.*"

Fleur glanced around noticing that Dr. Peterson kept a respectful distance from the immediate family. So did other acquaintances of Bernard who either needed the peace of mind seeing his body put in a grave or thought it proper to pay their respects.

She felt sorry for the young priest who'd struggled to find good things to say about her uncle during the church service. Fleur noticed he resorted to saying a lot of prayers instead. Now at the conclusion of the graveside service, he sighed and closed his prayer book, sprinkling the last of the holy water from a crystal vial.

She watched as Babette surged forward and leaned her body against the tomb, sobbing, her grief palpable. Piper moved to comfort her, but her movements seemed mechanical, forced.

Louis leaned down and whispered, "Darling, are you ready to go back to the house now?"

"Yes, we should return before everyone arrives for the reception."

Louis lifted the brakes and began to push her forward, but stopped the wheelchair as she called out to the doctor. Thin and tall, he wore a dark navy suit, white shirt and tie.

"Dr. Peterson, thank you for coming."

He drew near and shook Louis's hand, then grasped one of hers, placing a kiss on her glove. "And how are you feeling these days Miss D'Hemecourt?"

"Much better, thank you."

"I'm very pleased to hear that."

"You will come to the house now, won't you?"

"Yes, of course. I'd be honored to attend."

Louis shook his hand. "We'll see you there."

***

Louis pulled the sedan up the long, familiar drive of the house on St. Charles, and Fleur began to see the home with new eyes. She remembered how the house and the grounds looked in the days of her childhood.

In subsequent years, the house had become a place of sorrow and foreboding. The home suffered neglect. It was hard to tell where the flowerbeds began and the weeds ended. Hibiscus bushes, long ignored, had grown leggy and out of bounds. Dead branches on all of the trees needed to be cut. The massive oak, whose branches once held her swing, now shaded a dumping ground of pottery shards and other garden waste.

The home had shingles missing, paint peeling near the top dormers. She also noticed a couple of shutters askew on the upper windows and a section of gutter hanging on the side. Only the Chinoiserie seemed to have fared well, a fresh coat of paint, and the pavilion kept in immaculate order. Wisteria trimmed. Tea roses tended to. Fleur supposed that her uncle wanted her to move into the guesthouse and had taken measures to make the move attractive.

An array of cars were already parked across the lawn, though the guests who attended Florrie's funeral reception were far more numerous. Though deceased, Bernard had become a social pariah in a relatively short time.

Louis parked the car and turned to her. "I'll get the wheelchair out."

"Wait." She took his hand. "I'm not looking forward to this, having to be pleasant to people with all their questions and snide comments. "What happened with Bernard is quite a scandal, but that's only the tip of the iceberg."

"I'll be by your side. Don't worry. Just because someone asks you a question doesn't mean they deserve an answer. Let me give you a tip from an attorney I know." He winked. "Answer a question with another one."

"A question for a question. Darling, I believe you're a genius. Why didn't I recognize that before?"

"I don't know, why didn't you?"

She smiled. "Well, what do you know? It works."

A couple drove past them and parked their car smack dab in the hydrangea bed.

In disbelief, she followed them with her eyes. "Louis, when we're married, we're going to make some changes around here."

He saluted her. "Yes ma'am."

She sighed. "We might as well go ahead inside."

"Wait," He wrapped his arms about her waist and kissed her. "I love you Fleur D'Hemecourt."

She touched her index finger to his lip and leaned in. "And I love you Louis Russo."

Foreheads touching, she wiped the stain of her red lipstick off his face with her hankie. "You didn't solve the problem, but you sure boosted my morale."

"Glad I could help, Mrs. 'Almost' Russo."

"Say, I like the sound of that."

"Good, you'd better get used to it." He opened the door. "Now if you don't mind, I have a wheelchair to remove from the sedan."

***

In spite of her concern, Fleur managed to sidestep many a question with Louis's clever trick. Soon surrounded by women pouting pity, offering droll condolences, the inquisition began.

She spotted Mrs. Brennan, the Grande Dame of the Junior League, sitting in a wingback chair. Fleur decided to wheel over to her, though doing so was quite difficult. The wheelchair was a cumbersome affair, of metal and leather and rubber wheels. No one offered to push her. As Fleur came closer to the woman, she noticed the passage of years had not been kind. Stooped and grey, older, her face fallen as if her skin weighed too much. The most noticeable difference however was the addition of loose skin under her chin. She beckoned Fleur.

"Oh my dear girl, how terrible for your family, for you to lose your uncle and Piper to lose her father."

As always, decked in a sensible hat and dress, she'd crossed her white-gloved hands on her lap. Fleur called for a cup of Sassafras Tea, and when it arrived, she poured a cup for the woman.

"How nice of you to remember my favorite tea. My, my, the times we live in. You know I lost my son, my only son in the war."

"No, no I didn't. My condolences to you."

Mrs. Brennan cleared her throat and resumed talking. "We lost many brave young men. But," she pointed, "Louis returned unscathed. You must be very grateful for that."

She glanced over at him, and he returned her gaze, dark eyes sparkling. "Why, yes."

"And you two are—are to be married I hear? You make a fine couple." When she spoke, the turkey waddle under her chin vibrated with a life of its own.

"Such a good match for him given the state of his family's finances bequeathed by his late father. Mind you, his father was a good man, but not very clever with investing. He lost almost everything in the crash of '29 and never quite recovered. Was your uncle in favor of the match?"

She continued without waiting for a reply. "Such a tragedy with Bernard. I grew up with him. Oh he was quite the Romeo in those days and a true raconteur. So entertaining. However, he was not a skilled businessman. His brother, your father had a brilliant head for business." She stopped to take a sip from a china teacup. Fleur noted the tea service, her mother's favorite. The same service Florrie had snuffed many a cigarette in through the years. She noticed Philomene draw close.

"And what will become of Piper? I've heard she's penniless. Her father left this earth, owing a great deal of money to quite a few people you know, including my own beloved husband. What's to become of her?"

A sinking feeling in her stomach made her realize that Mrs. Brennan had a mission in common with the rest of the women, to gather information. In fact, she noticed a group of women had inched closer, well within earshot. Gossipmongers.

Fleur took a sip of tea. "What do you think will become of her?"

Mrs. Brennan's mouth fell open, her blubbery lips trying to form words. "Why I-- how could I?"

"Miz Fleur, I hate to interrup' but theys a telephone call for you."

Sweet Philo! Rescued at last! "Thank you, Philomene. If you'll excuse me Mrs. Brennan, I have a matter to attend to." She smiled sweetly and signaled to Philo. Fleur found her wheelchair rolling to the office, the infamous office Bernard had commandeered so many years ago.

She opened the door and shut it behind, wheeling Fleur opposite the easy chair by the window.

"I so glad to git you away from dem vultchas Miz Fleur. But you handle it good. Miz Brennan, dat high'n mighty woman, huh mout still hangin' wide open. In all mah years I neva seen nobody shut her up dat quick." She slapped her knees. "Dat tickle mah funny bone fo' shor."

Fleur put her hand over her mouth and giggled. "It is funny."

But Philo stopped laughing all of a sudden and looked her over.

"Ain' nuthin' but skin 'n bones. Time ta put some meat on you chile'." She raised her index finger. "I be back wit a plate o' food."

"Oh Philo, I'm really not hun. . ."

"No backtalk now ya, hear? Mama Philo know what's good fo' you." With that she left the room.

As the door closed, Fleur turned her attention to the window. A dazzling day welcomed her eyes. Sunshine lit every leaf and blade of grass. With Mardi Gras a week only a week away, signs of an early spring were already in the air. A cache of sparrows lit from a Bradford Pear tree, fanning apart, then closing together as they flew.

Within minutes she heard a rap on the door. Philomene didn't wait for a reply, but entered with a steaming plate of food.

"Now eat up.'"

Fleur sighed. "I suppose if I refused, you would feed it to me."

Philo's eyes flashed. "You know me. You be eatin' one way or nuther."

She laughed. "All right, but while I eat, tell me what's going on in the house."

Fleur took up a silver fork and began on a mound of jambalaya. Sliced Andouille sausage, tender chicken, shrimp and bits of ham sautéed with onions, garlic, celery, tomatoes and the flavor of savory bay leaf.

"Delicious."

Hands on her hips, Philomene demanded. "I know. Jus' eat. I'ma do de talkin'."

Fleur motioned to the easy chair. "Sit."

Philo looked from the chair to her and smiled as she sat down. "Tadpole happy to be home. He speshly happy now dat Bernard n' Gerard an' Alcide ain' roun' no mo."

Fleur nodded.

"I let go Cecelia mysef'. I knew I would feel good to let go someone like huh, but I din feel good. I knows she got lil' chirren to feed. I had a good talk wit huh and she sorry, real sorry. So I was wondrin if you would give huh a recmendayshun."

"My, that's very generous of you Philo after the way she treated you." She sighed. "I'll consider it. But I'll have to talk to her myself."

Philo clapped her hands together. "Be kind to one nuther, tendahawted, fo'givin' on nutha, as God in Christ fo'gave you. Ah men."

"I like that one. Where is it in the Bible?"

Philo held her hands high. "Epheeshuns fo'thirty-two." She pulled something from her pocket. "And speakin' o' forgiveness, I got a few things to talk to you 'bout."

Fleur felt her heart quicken.

As if her head had suddenly become too heavy for her neck, Philo's head fell forward. Philomene sank to the floor and held onto Fleur's knees. She looked up, tearful. "Fleur, you know I love you wit all mah hawt."

She nodded, too surprised to speak.

"I-I has to confess sumthin' to you." She turned her head to the side.

Fleur rested her hand on Philo's head and began to stroke it.

"I done wrong by you. You uncle had me unda his thum early on. He use Tadpole to scere me to doin' things fo' him."

"Like what?"

"You memba de sweet milk I used ta make?"

"I do."

"Well, some nights your uncle had me made me put a speshul milk for Miz Florrie, wid Laudanum in it."

"I know. Piper told me." Philomene looked up at her, surprised.

"He tol' me at first it was to hep huh sleep. Miz Florrie had her pains." Her voice broke. "But it make her weak over time. Got so she couldn' sleep without her milk at night."

Fleur's lower lip trembled.

Philomene went on. "He want her sleeping so she don' know what's goin' on in the house. Bernard bringing his hawty women true de door. I couldn' bear him hurtin' her no mo, so I try to stop him. I say I ain't givin' Miz Florrie dat to drink no more."

She drew away and lifted herself onto the easy chair. "Ber'naud git mad. But he din hurt me at first.

The muscle over her left eyelid began to twitch. She opened her mouth to speak and closed it, as if the words tangled into a knot on the way out. Finally, her struggles produced the words. "He lay his hands on Tadpole. Beat him to a pulp wit a board."

As if the imprint of the sight were emblazoned on her eyes, she stopped and stared, sucking in frenzied breaths. "An den took to me."

She lifted the hem of her dress and rolled down her cotton stockings. "I healed up an' so did Tadpole, but I din' walk de same. Now I'm olda, it pains me a lil' mo'."

Fleur caught her breath. A map of scars covered the older woman's legs, her knees, even her ankles. "Philo." She traced her fingers across the path of pain and burst into tears, reaching for her. They held onto one another, the ebb and flow of sobs unlocking years of pent up hurt and emotion.

Finally, Philomene pulled herself away to her chair. "Philo, thank you for telling me. You're a very brave woman. I admire you all the more. I'm so sorry, and ashamed of my uncle--ashamed to be related to such a monster."

Philomene closed her eyes, wincing. "You shouln' be thankin' me. I should be beggin' you forgivness."

Fleur leaned back in the wheelchair. "You suffered for Tadpole and Florrie's sake and mine over the years—even at the risk of your own brother's life. God will hold my uncle accountable for everything he did in his life. But as for you Philo, consider yourself forgiven. I will be forever grateful to you dear one, and you and Tadpole will never have to worry about money. I'll see to it."

Philomene covered her mouth for a moment, rocking back and forth. "They's sumthin mo fo' you to see, chile'. It's almos too hard now to bring dis up but I got to. Lord knows I got to." She reached in her pocket and handed her a fold of paper.

Fleur unfolded it, a document of some sort, with caution. Her heart was boombooming inside her chest.

A Birth Certificate?

Philo drew her lower lip up next to her teeth. "Sumthin' I had mah suspishuns 'bout. I foun' it in de corthouse records."

Fleur read it, eyes widening with interest. "A certificate of live birth." She smiled. "Oh, it's Rusty's birth certificate."

She read on. "Hotel Dieu Hospital. Mother." Her hands trembled. M-mother—mother. She stopped. Looking to Philo, the paper almost slipped from her hands. "How can that be?"

Philo reached out to steady her hands. "Keep readin' chile'"

Through sheer force of will, she held the paper in front of her and spoke the name her eyes had already seen. "Fleur D'Hemecourt. And the father?" The paper slipped from her hands.

Fleur screamed. "But my baby died. The nuns told me the baby was dead. That it was God's judgment on me for my sins. That He took the baby's life because of me, of what I did."

"I cried for him. They told me he was dead. . ." Fleur wrapped her arms around her chest and rocked back and forth. "But there was no on to turn to. No one to hear me."

Philomene threw her arms around her. "Chile' I came as soon as your uncle let me come. Ber'naud keep everone away from you. He din' want no one to know. He made up a plan to lie, to tell you da baby dead."

Tears. Tears. Tears, clawing jagged lines down the length of her face. Her body trembled and shook. Philomene tore off her apron and gave it to Fleur to sop them up.

"He musta give de baby to Collette an arranged for huh an' Fleming to git married. That way he keep de chile close in de fambly I s'ppose."

Philomene sniffed. "Collette a bad muther. When dat woman drink she don' care bout nuthin' else. She careless as can be."

"Rusty. Rusty's my child. My baby. Born alive."

"Yes, Fleur. When I foun' out I wanted to tell you when you was in de hospital, but couln' till you was stronga. An' den you wen' missin' an' all." She took her hands. "Nows your chance to take propa care o' de boy. Collette ain' no kind o' muther fo' him. She din' even visit him in de hospital when he sick. What kind o' mama do dat to dey chile'?"

Fleur held her head up. "I'm his mother--I'm his mother."

She looked out the window again. The sun still shining bright and beautiful, birds chirping singsongs to one another, but once again, life had taken a strange turn, a twist into the unknown. Though her thoughts were in a muddle her heart knew what to do and she followed it--a small voice among so many louder ones, yet commanding in a way like no other.

"Philo, please bring Louis to me, then Piper. Could you do that for me, please?"

She smiled. "I be right back Miz Fleur."

***

Louis entered the room. Dark eyes, dark hair, shiny waves of it tamed back from his face. "Here you are. I wondered where you'd gone off to."

She held out her arms. "Oh Louis," and began to sob. Fleur explained everything, handing him the birth certificate. "Piper told me the whole thing, how she switched the cups of milk. She arranged for Fleming to. . ."

Philomene let out a loud gasp. "Dats how? Piper done it?" She shook her head. "Dat girl ain't right. Lord knows she neva been right."

"What do you mean?"

"I wondered how you got wit chile'. Dat's how Fleming got to Fleur, wit huh help. She was knocked out on Laudanum."

"You mean to tell me the man took advantage of a—a mere child--of Fleur that way?" Face red, Louis covered his face with his hands.

"Dat's it. Dat's wut he done."

He paced back and forth in front of the desk and glanced over at Fleur. "Your uncle sent you away to protect the family's reputation and then lied to you? He led you to believe the child was stillborn or miscarried?"

The world seemed to be moving at a different pace. His words, drawn-out, slow. The shock of hearing the truth made her blood run cold. The man had forced himself on her.

An acid rose in her throat. "I-I'm going to be. I think I'm going to be sick."

Philo picked up the trashcan by the desk and Fleur vomited.

Louis left the room and returned right away with a wet cloth for her face.

"Darling, I'm so sorry to upset you. You've been through so much. I wasn't thinking."

Though weak, she felt better in a way, as if purged from the lies she'd been forced to carry inside all these years. "It all makes sense now, why I couldn't remember anything."

Arms folded, he stared out the window.

Philomene stood at the open door. "Mr. Louis, you got to see sumthin' else. Dis only de tip o' de iceberg wid dat man."

He turned to face her.

She walked over to the desk, and pulled open the unlocked drawer. He followed.

"Me and Rueben fount dese."

He looked at the pictures and clenched his fist. "I'm sick at heart. Bernard no doubt used these photographs to blackmail people."

Philomene squinted her eyes shut. "I hates to speak ill o' de dead, but dat man was rotten to de core."

"I have to agree with you."

"Louis?" Fleur took a deep breath. "Louis, I want to raise Rusty."

"What did you say?"

"I want to take back my son."

He walked to the easy chair and sat. "I'm listening."

"I can't do anything to change my past, but I can do something now. Rusty is my child and he was taken from me." She trembled.

Louis reasoned. "He is your child, but I implore you to remember who his father is." Tension lines formed between his brows.

Philomene spoke from behind the desk. "Mr. Louis, I know you a man o' God but you can't go getting hard of heart. Dis child in'cent. The way he was bawn not o' his choosin'. God gave him life an' he got choices on how to live it."

"Fleur, you're asking me to accept a child that is not my own." Louis clasped his hands together, head forward. "I know you were traumatized by what happened, but . . . ."

Philomene spoke up. Romans 8:14-16 "All who led by the Spirit of God are chirren of God. So you have not received a spirit of slavery to fall back into fear, you received the Spirit of adoption as sons, by whom we cry, 'Abba Father.' The Spirit Himself bear witness wit our spirit that we are chirren of God."

Philomene held a hand up in the air and as she prayed, her face took on a pained expression. "Lawd, we know dat all things work tagetha fo' good to dem dat love God, to dem who are de called accordin' to his purpose."

His eyes, dewy with tears followed each word.

"Louis," sobs chopping Fleur's speech, "I understand if you don't want to go through with-with the wedding. It's asking a lot of you."

"No, Fleur." Louis fell on his knees before her. "I don't want to lose you again."

"Please pray about it, Louis."

He rose and kissed her. "I will, my love."

Philomene cleared her throat. "Miz Fleur, Mr. Louis, I don' like to interrupt, speshly now, but I looked all over for Piper an couldn' fin huh, so I set some o' the other help out to look. Theys s'pposed to let me know when de do."

***

They decided to rejoin the reception since Philomene informed Fleur some of the guests were ready to leave. The crowd had thinned much since Fleur retreated into the study. She felt as if history had rewritten itself in so short a time.

Louis pushed Fleur around the house and veranda. The view through the windows calmed her--a perfect view of her beloved Chinoiserie. She sighed.

He walked to the front of the wheelchair and bent down. "Fleur, I don't mind carrying you to the Chinoiserie if you want to sit there."

Fleur heard the snap and billow of the long white curtains in a balm of a late afternoon breeze and was about to call Philomene to have someone shut them when she heard a scream.

She turned her head toward the sound. Alcide stepped out from the curtains, grey gunmetal in his hand. He pointed the gun straight at her. "You killed my father."

A stampede of people screaming and running out every exit, knocking down chairs, vases filled with flower arrangements and dishes of food. Soon there were only a handful of people left in the room.

"Don't do this." Louis stood in front of Fleur, protecting her with his own body.

"Louis, no." The grey muzzle of the pistol held Louis, rock steady in Alcide's hands.

"Move out da way. I got a bone ta pick wit dis woman." He shook the gun. "Move or I'll shoot."

Voice calm, Louis continued to speak. "Why do you want to take her life? She's done nothing to harm anyone."

"She kilt him."

"Your father was intoxicated. I saw him fall off the float in the warehouse."

"You seen him do it an you din' try to help him?" Alcide face wet, he wiped it with his free sleeve. "He's all I had." With new resolve, he held the gun high and called out. "Quit hiding behind him woman. You—you put dat box in his room and scared 'em plenty. Dat waddun' right to do."

"Put dat gun down Alcide. or as God is my witness, I'll shoot ya daid."

Alcide spun around. Philomene held Bernard's pistol in her own two hands, tracking him.

"You an' Piper treated me like I was nuthin'" He waved the gun in a circle. "Well you wanna know sumthin'? Her mama din' die in bed like she thought! Florrie was drugged an' buried while she was still alive. He couldn't wait for her to die, so he had to help her along. Said it'd be painless. But Gerard went by her tomb with a stethoscope later an heard her callin' out."

Babette let out a high-pitched scream and collapsed to the floor near the doorway.

Confused, he turned it back to Louis, then to Philomene. Sweat formed on his brow and face. "You put that gun away or I'll shoot 'em right now" he shouted. He took a step towards her.

Fleur heard a low moan and saw Adelaide, in a chair by the fireplace, clutching at her chest.

Eyes narrowed, Philomene clicked the cylinder. Voice smooth as oil, she told him, "You takes a 'nother step to and you gonna get what you deserve."

Perspiration beaded on top his lips. He spun round to shoot, but Philomene's bullet got to him first. Alcide collapsed to the ground, a bullet wound to his shoulder. Fleur heard herself screaming. The smell of gunpowder filled the air. There were screams from people still on the grounds, and the whine of police sirens. Louis wrestled the gun from Alcide's hand and stood back against the wall. Fleur locked eyes with Philomene, still holding the pistol, gray smoke rising.

* * *

In the hours that followed, confusion reigned. Police officers, ambulances, throngs of guests and onlookers filled the house. In addition to Alcide's wound, the medics were concerned that Adelaide might have had a heart attack. Both were taken by ambulance to a nearby hospital. In the chaos, Fleur had forgotten all about the search for Piper.

Philomene, though shaken by her heroic act, was able to give a statement to police. Witnesses vouched for her. Bernard's gun was taken as evidence. Now Philo sat on a small chair next to Fleur, her head on Fleur's shoulder. Louis stood talking to a couple of policemen.

From the corner of her eye, Fleur saw Rueben approach, a strange expression on his face. "What is it?"

Philo raised her head and sat up straight when she saw him.

Reuben took a step closer, his voice low. "Miz Fleur, we found Miz Piper." He held a key in his hand.

"What's that?"

Philo interrupted. "Dat's a skeleton key. Why you need dat?"

Reuben looked from her to Fleur. "Like I said, we fount Miz Piper."

"Where is she?"

"She in the Chinoiserie. In a upstairs room."

"Why? What's she doing there?"

He paused. "Miz Fleur, I knows you cant walk up dem stairs by yousef but I could carry you on up."

"What's wrong? Is she all right? She's not . . . " What if Alcide had found Piper first?

"She alive." His chest rose and fell, as if he could scarce get another word out.

"All right. You can carry me up." She motioned to Philomene. "Please tell Louis."

He wheeled her across the lawn to the Chinoiserie. Dark clouds had begun to gather reflecting beams of storm-filtered light An eerie sheen cast on the house gave it an unearthly glow.

Once inside, he stood beside her chair at the foot of the stairwell, staring upwards.

Rueben was a strong man. She remembered the way he was when she was a child, but now, in such close proximity, she realized how he'd aged. Grey hair at his temples notwithstanding, he moved slower. Or could it have something to do with their destination?

He strained a bit as he carried her up the last few steps, stood holding her in front of the door, and tried to reach for the knob. But she extended her hand to save him the trouble. At the same moment, they heard a creaking sound, like a rocking chair coming from behind the door.

Fleur looked up at Reuben, a peculiar terror in his eyes. She turned back to the door and turned the key in the knob. Whatever was behind that door, she would soon find out.

The door creaked open as old doors do. But this time, the sound of it sent a wave of shivers down her back. An open window billowed diaphanous curtains in ghostly coils, silhouetted in the surreal light of the approaching storm. The smell of rain in the air, Fleur's heart beat faster at the scene before her.

Piper sat in a rocking chair holding a bundle in her arms. When they entered, she seemed unaware of their presence. Reuben set Fleur down in a wingback chair across from her cousin.

"You are my sunshine, my only sunshine." Piper hummed the rest, patting the bundle as she rocked, a smile on her face.

Fleur swallowed hard when she noticed the glint of a diamond on her cousin's finger. The diamond engagement ring Gerard had slipped off her finger in the swamp! Her voice came out in a mere whisper. "Piper?"

She looked up. "Fleur, why I'm so glad you're here. Her head turned towards a chair beside her. "Darling, I don't think you've met my cousin, Fleur D'Hemecourt."

Fleur heard something and saw that Louis and Philomene had quietly entered the room. Louis stood behind her chair, hands on her shoulders. Philo stood behind Reuben and watched.

Puzzled, Fleur looked at the empty chair. "What do you mean?"

"Fleur, I'd like you to meet my husband, Jack Holcombe."

"Jack Holcombe?" Philo backed into the wall, knocking a picture frame to the ground.

"Who are you talking to, Piper? What's that you're holding?"

She smiled. "Silly, this is my baby."

"B-baby?" Fleur looked up at Louis. Philomene whimpered into Reuben's back.

"Yes, of course. Do you want to see her?"

"I-I do. But my leg is broken and I can't get up."

Piper glanced over at her cast. "That's right. How thoughtless of me. I'll bring her to you." She stood, bearing the bundle in the crook of her arm and leaned down to show her.

Fleur held her breath. The "baby" was one of Fleur's childhood dolls, a porcelain doll named Lucinda, one of her favorites. The doll's complexion now yellowed, tiny cracks like veins ran through her youthful face. The doll's eyes, a transluscent blue, opened and shut with every movement, clumps of missing lashes furthering the macabre appearance.

Philo mumbled something, head shaking. Though the mumblings grew louder, Piper seemed oblivious.

Fleur listened closely and finally made out what Philo was saying over and over again. Her body slid down the wall to the ground as she spoke. "Jack Holcombe be dead. His plane shot down. He dead. He dead."

Piper began to hum again, rocking the bundle with her arms. "Fleur, isn't she beautiful?

Before Fleur could reply, Piper answered.

"But of course she is. She has her father's eyes."

Chapter Thirty-Seven
The Last Waltz

"We're fine. And I'm so pleased to hear that you are as well, Aunt Babette." Fleur smiled at Philomene. She raised the pitch of her voice in deference to the woman's hearing difficulties.

"No more crutches." She held the phone away as her aunt babbled on. Fleur made googly eyes at Philo. "All right dear, we'll see you soon. We don't mind that you'll be late. I'm so sorry your bursitis is troubling you. Oh, I am on cloud nine, thank you."

Philomene moved across the sitting room to stand facing her. She took Fleur's hands and backed up to get a better look. "Lemme get a gander at you, chile'." She smiled. "You a beautiful bride."

Fleur kissed her cheek and gave her a hug. "Philo, if it wasn't for you, I wouldn't be here in my wedding gown."

Philomene looked down. "I wish . . . "

"What is it? What do you wish?"

"I wish I coulda known what to do to save your parents. God rest they souls."

She nodded. "If only they could be here today. But I think they would approve of you representing them."

Philomene glanced toward the window overlooking the garden. "I'm not sure folks out dere is gonna approve."

Fleur took her hand. "I don't care what anyone thinks."

A smile creased Philomene's face. "Still de same lil' Fleur. I wouldn' have it no other way."

Fleur straightened the carnation on Philo's dress. "I guess it's almost time."

"One thing, chile'."

"What is it?"

"I-I was thinking 'bout how yo daddy used to untangle all dem necklaces fo you all de time. How you went to him to help you do dat 'cause you couldn."

"Yes," she laughed, "I was always going to him for help."

"Well, I was thinking 'bout how dis time, your Heavenly Father's de one who done de untangling fo' you. He untangled all de mess of your life, separatin' de trut from de lies and makin' all tings work fo good."

Fleur took a step to the full-length mirror and stared at her reflection. "It's true." She wiped a tear away. "I feel as if I have a whole new life."

Philo peeked from behind her. "You do."

A knock sounded.

"I best go git in place now." They embraced. "See you out dere."

Piper opened the door. Philo stopped to hug her, then continued out.

Dressed in lilac, her light green eyes glimmered in jeweled contrast. Her long hair was styled in an attractive wave, adorned on one side with a fresh gardenia blossom.

"Well Fleur, do I look like a proper matron of honor?"

Fleur stepped towards her and embraced her. "Yes, you do my dear. In fact, I'm rather fearful that you've outdone the bride." She stepped back to look at Piper face to face. "I'm going to fret about this now." She took a playful bite of her index finger. "No one's even going to look at me as long as you're around."

"Don't be silly. You're a vision of loveliness, Fleur."

She put her arm around Piper's shoulder. "I'm so glad you could be here today. It-it means quite a lot to me."

Lower lip trembling, Piper leaned in closer, her head on Fleur's shoulder.

This new vulnerable side of her cousin would take some getting used to. Perhaps in time.

Fleur eased her away and adjusted the gardenia in Piper's hair. "Tell me, are you doing all right in your new home?"

"Oh yes we are. It's quite nice there."

She heard a small commotion outside and stole a glance out the window.

A lady harpist in an elegant beige gown entered the pavilion. She sat down and began to play, the strums of Bach soon filling the air. But Fleur looked forward to hearing the other selections she'd chosen from Beethoven, Rachmaninoff and Vivaldi as well.

"It's time." Fleur touched her shoulder. "Guess we ought to move into place."

"Best of wishes, Fleur." Piper flashed a wide smile. "I hope your marriage will be as happy as mine."

"I hope so." Fleur rested her hand on Piper's cheek a moment. Then she turned to take her place at the open door of the parlor. The Chinoiserie was arrayed in a backdrop of fragrant wisteria. Honeysuckle dripped from the soaring pinnacle. The pavilion, surrounded by a circle of tea rose bushes in full bloom set the stage for their ceremony. White satin ribbons adorned the trellises and columns. A pure white carpet runner stretched from the house to the Chinoiserie and stopped where the couple would soon stand.

Family and friends gathered in rows of wooden folding chairs, Dr. Peterson and Adelaide among them. Though doctors at first thought the elderly woman had suffered a heart thrombosis, upon examination, her heart had been deemed sound.

Chairs along the aisle were adorned and decked out in a winding flow of ribbons and fresh-cut flowers—tiger lilies, white roses and gardenias set off by foxtail ferns.

The harpist ran her fingers across the strings in a sweeping glissindo, the agreed upon signal to begin the processional, Pachelbel Canon in D.

Louis took Philomene by the arm and walked her down the aisle. Resplendent in a grey silk gown, and a French straw hat cascading with lilac sprigs, her wide smile warmed Fleur's heart.

She'd insisted Philo sit in the place of honor usually ascribed to the bride's parents. Once Philo was seated, Louis took his place at the altar, a bower of wisteria surrounding him. She watched him smile at his mother, sister and other family members, then focus on the aisle.

Piper walked with measured steps down the long row of pristine white carpet alone, and took her place on the left. Louis, who chose not to have a best man, stood to her right dressed in a crème tuxedo dinner jacket, the pastor in between. Hands clasped in front, Louis stood, eyes where all eyes were staring—towards the parlor door of the main house, where the bride would emerge.

Heart pounding, Fleur took a breath and stepped forward. Since meeting Louis, she'd dreamed of this moment. At times, she thought she would never live to see it. But now, the time had come. The man she loved with her whole heart stood near the place she wholeheartedly loved, her Chinoiserie. And all that separated them now was a simple walk down the aisle.

Arms entwined on both sides with Officers Delaney and Clark, she smiled at each.

Clark leaned in and whispered. "Don't be nervous. You'll do fine."

Delaney winked, "Amen to that."

She whispered her thanks and took a first step. Clothed in her white wedding dress, Fleur felt as if she was floating down the aisle, her steps graceful and measured--calm. The gown, of rich Irish lace inlaid with seed pearls, was long-sleeved from shoulder to cameo'd neck with a charming flow of satin silk below. She wore the matching white satin shoes, inlaid with seed pearls and crystals. Miz Adelaide had offered two diamond combs for the "borrowed" part of her ensemble, to wear in her hair. For something blue, Philomene provided the blue silk garter on her thigh.

And as before, Philo had insisted the bride wear a diamond. From the music box given her by Louis, Fleur had selected a pear-shaped pendant from her mother's jewelry collection. The pendant matched her engagement ring to perfection. Dr. Peterson had managed to switch the original pear-shaped diamond ring, appropriated by Piper via Gerard with the similar replacement ring Louis had purchased instead.

When she and Louis stood facing one another in front of the pastor, Rusty began his trek down the aisle. He wore a miniature version of Louis's dinner jacket, red hair brilliant against the crème color of the suit. Carrying a white satin pillow, the ring in the center, Rusty grinned from ear to ear.

She couldn't help smiling at the sight of the boy. Odd to think of herself as a mother and yet, Rusty had awakened a motherly instinct in her, regardless of the circumstances of his conception.

A tear trickled down her cheek as she and Louis exchanged vows. She felt as if her heart would burst with love for him. Louis slipped the ring on her finger.

". . . I now pronounce you man and wife. Louis, you may kiss your bride."

She watched his lips form the silent words. "I love you." Her husband's arms circled her waist, drawing her close. When her lips met his, all care and concern melted away. She felt safe, content in his presence, peaceful.

After the ceremony, the reception was to continue throughout the afternoon. Tables were set up across the neatly tended grounds. Guests lingered in the golden light of the afternoon. Soft winds from the Gulf of Mexico cooled the air. Louis and Fleur relaxed after the meal with a walk around the grounds. Fleur spotted the doctor walking as well. The two caught up with him.

"Dr. Peterson."

He was talking to a woman she recognized from the hospital, Nurse Robichaux. This time however, she wore a fashionable dress, appropriate for the ceremony.

As they approached, Fleur heard him speak.

"Could you please check on on Miss D'Hemecourt?"

She nodded. "Yes, doctor." She strode off towards Piper, who sat at a table conversing with Adelaide.

"Doctor, I want to thank you for bringing Piper here today. It means so much to us."

"I was only too glad to bring your cousin so she could attend the ceremony. I believe it means a lot to her too."

Louis asked, "Is she--the same?"

The doctor glanced in her direction, then back to Louis. "If by that you mean she thinks she's married and has a baby, then yes, she is the same."

"Oh." Louis bowed his head.

"The man she imagines she's married to, well, Philomene told me he was real."

The doctor nodded his affirmation. "Yes, Jack Holcombe was an officer in the Air Force. Piper dated him for a short time. But I checked his name, and according to military records, he died about six months before the war ended."

"Oh," Fleur blinked back tears. "Were they, I mean, do you think they were serious about one another or was it . . . "

"All in her mind?" He sighed. "I suppose we may never know. But with proper care and therapy, perhaps we'll find out more."

Fleur finished, "I do hope so."

"Yes, we're quite hopeful. There are new drugs and techniques. This is a very exciting time in the field of psychotherapy."

"So there's hope?"

"Of course there is." He added, "And Mrs. Russo."

"Yes?"

"Speaking of that, may I suggest a final therapy for my 'star' patient?"

She smiled. "Go on."

"I suggest you put down your thoughts in a journal. I've found the practice to be quite theraputic."

Fleur looked to Louis. "What do you think, Mr. Russo?"

He touched his nose to hers. "If it makes you happy, Mrs. Russo, then I'm for it."

"An excellent answer, my love."

"If you two lovebirds are quite finished," Dr. Peterson grinned, "it's about time to make our exit. We have to get back." He looked at his watch. "Again, congratulations to both of you."

Louis answered, "Thank you for coming."

"An honor and pleasure."

After saying their goodbyes, Louis and Fleur continued to walk. Strolling over the clipped green grass of the estate, a cup of tea in one hand, Louis's clasped in the other, Fleur flirted with her memories, both good and bad.

Louis had advised Fleur to avoid further scandal and stay out of the courts to get Rusty back. But Collette was nowhere to be found. Weeks later the coroner's office called. A woman's body, fished from the Mississippi river was positively identified. Police surmised the woman had been murdered, but the body was too decomposed to determine if that was true.

Although there were no leads or clues as to who might have murdered Collette, Fleur was certain her uncle had something to do with it. Collette knew his secret. But so did her husband, and Fleming hadn't been heard from in months.

Delaney and Clark promised if Fleming were found alive, to bring the man to answer for his crimes, among them, conspiring with Bernard to disable the engine of the car carrying Fleur's parents, resulting in their deaths.

Alcide was in jail awaiting trial for attempted murder and more. Though, if the extent of his crimes were known, he would likely be given the electric chair. Still--a part of her grieved for him. Alcide was as much victim as he was aggressor. Mentored by his own father whom he loved and longed to please, Bernard had lured his son to a life of crime.

Gerard on the other hand, seemed genetically predispositioned to deviant behavior. His body was never found, but the police were not concerned. It was unlikely Gerard had escaped the same fate he'd planned for Fleur and Piper.

Though there were loose ends still to be tied, Fleur felt a sense of relief. Now she knew, now everyone knew the truth. And that truth had set them free.

When Louis lifted her hand to his lips, Fleur decided the present time warranted her attention more than any past events.

"Fleur," his eyes sparkled, "what are you thinking about?"

She sighed, content. "Nothing--everything." As they drew near the pavilion, she heard the familiar tune of the music box.

Louis and Fleur looked at each other and said his name together. "Rusty."

Fleur grinned. "I suppose Rusty is as fascinated with that music box as I was with my mother's jewelry.

The waltz tinkled out like a wind chime. They put down their teacups and began to dance. And as they waltzed past the trellis, Louis reached for a handful of wisteria and sprinkled the blossoms over their heads.

Chapter Thirty-Eight
Bouquet Garni

New Orleans, Louisiana
1949

Pencil in hand, Rusty Russo sat at a wooden artist's easel on a levee overlooking the Mississippi River. Fleur sat beside him, alternately penning her thoughts in a diary and in between, offering instruction to the budding artist.

Wildflowers poked between slender green grasses at their feet. Honeybees hovered over patches of clover, zeroing in on the white pompom flowers. A breeze lifted her hair and filled her heart with inspiration as she began to write.

The alabaster doors of the past are now sealed shut, filled with darkness, old bones and dim memories. But sometimes the dip of an oar into shadowy decay, or the silt of murky thought, bubbles up the blue of an eye or a strand of blond hair. And memories in green mist take the form of phantoms. But those who dwell in the land of the living, the fertile delta between birth and death, between things past and things to come, between good and evil . . .

"When will the cal-o-pea play again?"
"Hmmm? What?"
Rusty's faced smiled back at her. His cheeks glowed with good health and he'd grown tall as a bean sprout in the past year.

She put her fountain pen in the spine of the leather-bound journal and closed it. Hand on his small shoulder, she answered, "Soon, mon chou. Soon. Did you like the song I taught you?"

"Yes." He bobbed his head up and down. "I wanna sing it." His pounded his feet on the ground.

"You have a great deal of energy. Perhaps we should go for a stroll after this."

"Uh-uh." He shook his head. "Not till I hear the cal-o-pea play."

"Calliope, dear." She pointed to the Steamboat Natchez docked at the Toulouse Street Wharf nearby. It's a steam pipe organ. The ship has plenty of hot air to play the music."

She nudged him with her elbow to regain his attention, and pointed. "The steam plumes from the—the giant whistles and plays wonderful music. You'll hear soon enough."

"Goody gumdrops." He grinned wide. "Can I play a song on it too?"

"Perhaps we can persuade the captain to allow you." A smile bloomed on her cheeks, blushed pink with the sun—or so Louis had told her. She'd removed her hat at the easel. Hats tended to get in the way of good art.

Fleur pointed to the drawing. "It's very good, Rusty. Don't you think so too?" Her hand hovered over the paper. "I would suggest a little more shading on the side. That would do the trick-- and the smokestacks need a bit more detail."

Rusty stopped, turning his head to the side. "Yes, I see that. Thank you, Mother."

Eyes misty, Fleur ruffled his hair with her hand. "Thank you, son."

She waved as Louis approached, bearing Roman candy he'd purchased from a cart.

He called out. "I couldn't decide which one to buy, so I bought a variety."

She smiled and shook her head at her husband. Having a child seemed to bring out the child in him.

Rusty leapt from his seat and ran to him. "Father, may I have some?"

"Yes, you may. Which flavor would you like?" Louis displayed the long sticks of taffy candy wrapped in wax paper and pointed to each. This one's chocolate, and this ones vanilla, and this one's straw . ." Before he could finish, Rusty plucked the chocolate one from his hand and was in the process of unwrapping it.

Louis smiled at the boy. "I suppose chocolate's your favorite."

"Yes sir, it is." He took a bite of the taffy and jumped up and down. "It tastes good. Thank you."

He tipped his hat "You are most welcome, son." With that, Louis joined Fleur at the easel.

She let out a mock sigh. "If only he felt that way about spinach."

But Louis was already engrossed in the drawing. He took a step back from the easel and pouted his lower lip in approval. "The details on his rendition of the steamboat are truly remarkable." He made a wide circle with his hands. "And the clouds in the background. The sky. The water. This painting shows a great deal of talent in the one who painted it."

He held out his hand to her. When she took it, he pulled her to him, her other hand resting on her belly, plump with child. "Do you know what I think?

Their faces close together, she asked, "What do you think, Mr. Russo?"

"Well, Mrs. Russo, I think Rusty gets his talent from his mother."

She touched his lips with her finger, the diamond ring catching the sun as she did. "I do believe you're right. And because you are, I believe I'll reward you with a kiss."

As her lips touched his, the calliope on the Riverboat began to play and all at once Rusty began to sing at the top of his lungs. Arms entwined, they listened as he sang out the words Fleur had taught him.

"If ever I cease to love, if ever I cease to love, may the fish get legs and the cows lay eggs. If ever I cease to love. If ever I cease to love, if ever I cease to love, may the Grand Duke Alexis ride a buffalo to Texas. If ever I cease to love . . ."

The End

Thank you for reading Alligator Pear. If you enjoyed the story, please do me a favor and leave a review. You might even encourage me to write a sequel!

If you'd like to find out more about me, and my books, visit my web page at:
http://www.lindakozar.com

You can also follow me on:

Facebook:
https://www.facebook.com/linda.kozar

Twitter:
https://twitter.com/LindaKozar

Pinterest:
http://pinterest.com/lindakozar/boards/

Visit my blogs:

Bookish Desires:
http://bookishdesires.blogspot.com

Babes With A Beatitude:
http://www.babeswithabeatitude.blogspot.com

Cozy Mystery Magazine:
http://cozymysterymagazine.blogspot.com

Radio:

Gate Beautiful Radio Show:
http://www.blogtalkradio.com/search?q=gate-beautiful

Biographical Information:

Linda Kozar is the co-author of Babes With A Beatitude—Devotions For Smart, Savvy Women of Faith (Hardcover/Ebook, Howard/Simon & Schuster 2009) and author of Misfortune Cookies (Print, Barbour Publishing 2008), Misfortune Cookies, A Tisket, A Casket, and Dead As A Doornail, ("When The Fat Ladies Sing Series," eBooks, Spyglass Lane Mysteries, 2012). Strands of Fate released October 2012 (Hardcover/Ebook, Creative Woman Mysteries), and her nonfiction title Moving Tales, Adventures in Relocation, released in 2013 (Indie-Published). She received the ACFW Mentor of the Year Award in 2007, founded and served as president of *Writers On The Storm*, The Woodlands, Texas ACFW chapter for three years. In 2003, she co-founded, co-directed and later served as Southwest Texas Director of *Words For The Journey Christian Writers Guild*.

In addition to writing Linda is Lead Host of the Gate Beautiful Radio Show, part of the Red River Network on Blog Talk Radio—interviewing Christian authors from Debut to Bestselling, airing the 3rd Thursday of every month. She and her husband Michael, married 24 years, have two lovely daughters, Katie and Lauren and a Rat Terrier princess named Patches.

Represented by: Wendy Lawton, Books & Such Literary Agency

Member of: CAN (Christian Authors Network), RWA (Romance Writers of American), WHRWA (West Houston Romance Writers of America), ACFW (American Christian Fiction Writers), Writers On The Storm, The Woodlands, Texas Chapter of ACFW, Toastmasters (Area 56) The Woodlands, Texas, The Woodlands Church, The Woodlands, TX.

Made in the USA
Charleston, SC
02 November 2013